LOVE WITH
A STRANGER

*Also by Janelle Taylor
in Large Print:*

Anything for Love
Destiny Mine
By Candlelight
Defiant Hearts
Promise Me Forever
Wild Winds

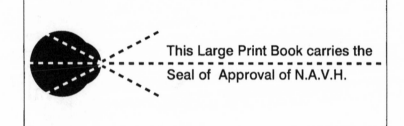

This Large Print Book carries the
Seal of Approval of N.A.V.H.

LOVE WITH A STRANGER

Janelle Taylor

G.K. Hall & Co. • Thorndike, Maine

Published in 2000 by arrangement with Zebra Books, an imprint of Kensington Publishing Corporation.

G.K. Hall Large Print Romance Series.

The text of this Large Print edition is unabridged.
Other aspects of the book may vary from the original edition.

Set in 16 pt. Plantin.

Printed in the United States on permanent paper.

Library of Congress Cataloging-in-Publication Data

Taylor, Janelle.
    Love with a stranger / Janelle Taylor.
      p. cm.
    ISBN 0-7838-8973-9 (lg. print : hc : alk. paper)
    1. Divorced women — Georgia — Saint Simons Island —
Fiction. 2. Saint Simons Island (Ga. : Island) — Fiction.
3. Large type books. I. Title.
PS3570.A934 L68 2000
  813´.54—dc21
                                          00-021598

Dedicated to:

My camping buddies and in-laws, Joe and Sheila Taylor, who made this research trip and others in the past so much fun.

My good and longtime friends in Evans and St. Simons Island, Bud and Peggy Carter and their son, Keenan, a marvelous entertainer with "Ziggy Mahoney" at Bennie's Red Barn on St. Simons Island.

My dear and longtime friend, Becky Weyrich, who's also a talented writer and St. Simons resident.

Chapter One

A black Chanel purse slipped unnoticeably from her fingers to the carpet as Cassandra Redfern Grantham sat down on a Victorian bench at the foot of the bed and clasped her cold hands in her lap. Even after five days of grieving, she still found it difficult to believe Tom was gone forever, killed in an automobile accident at midnight on Sunday. She felt numb and alone, her friends having been pushed aside long ago by Tom after she married the multi-millionaire two and a half years ago and was sucked into his busy and unfamiliar world. Following a hectic schedule and four plane flights over the last five days, her head throbbed, as if it refused to allow the aspirins she had taken earlier to work their magic. Even the wine she had drunk at her stepson's insistence during their flight home tonight failed to relax her tension and weariness, though she was feeling limp and a little dazed. She attributed those odd sensations to what she had endured this week rather than to effects of the Chablis and little to eat.

As she stared at the ten-karat diamond ring and fifteen-stone matching wedding band on her finger, Cass thought about the man who had put them there. He'd been only fifty — vital, energetic, so youthful in appearance, despite silvery streaks at his temples. She glanced over her shoulder at a picture of him on the nightstand, one taken in Kenya during their first year of marriage while they were on safari there.

The five-by-seven photograph revealed that Thomas Grantham — clad in a khaki outfit and outback hat, holding a hunting rifle and leaning against an acacia tree — was handsome and happy. There was a near-tangible charisma about him. His green eyes appeared to dance with the sheer joy of being alive and being who he was, and his broad grin enhanced that impression. He had a commanding presence, which explained, along with his business acumen, why he was so successful, so admired and respected by people in all social classes. She didn't know what he was worth; he had never said and she had never asked, but she knew he was an extremely wealthy man. Tom had loved the good life and had been fortunate he could afford it. He had said to her often: "Life is to be enjoyed to the hilt, my beautiful Cass, every minute, every hour, every week, every month, every year. Take all it has to offer and never look back in regret." Why he had chosen her — a working girl from a poor country background — to marry when he could have had his choice of wealthy socialites with blueblooded heritages a mile long could only be explained by his love for her, and Tom had made her feel special and cherished, more than she deserved.

Cass knew she had married him in part because she was lonely and unfulfilled and, at thirty-three, had heard her biological clock ticking loudly for a mate and a child. All of her friends and co-workers had married and had children, which made her and her life so different from theirs, giving them less and less in common as the years passed. They had left work each day to head for cozy homes and happy families while she was greeted by a small condo and solitude. She had yearned for a home and family, and realized too late it had been a mistake not to discuss those needs with Tom before their marriage, as he, she soon discovered, didn't want another child. Cass had tried to accept Tom's decision. In the beginning, she had found his world to be stimulating and fun; she had traveled all over the world, seen and done many things, and been given more gifts than she could count. But the shine on his golden but exhausting existence had dulled after two years. Those old yearnings for a home and family had resurfaced, though she kept those desires a secret from Tom. She doubted that Tom ever realized he wasn't the great love of her life and all the fulfillment she needed, but she still often felt twinges of guilt that his love wasn't enough to make her whole.

9

Cass remembered how she had done her best to learn and to do everything she could to please him, to make him happy, and to help her fit into his world of big money and enormous power. Tom had been patient, instructive, considerate, and — at last she could admit — at times, controlling and demanding. He had lavished her with expensive clothes, jewels, and cars. She had felt pampered, and treasured. Surely it was only natural for a lonely woman to be overwhelmed by him and his enticing world.

Cass's gaze shifted to the brass statue of a kneeling Atlas holding the world — a grapefruit-size crystal ball — on his shoulders. When Tom had given her that gift shortly after their marriage, he had joked it reminded him of her: a worrier who feared she would disappoint him or embarrass him. He had always insisted she had never done so, that he was proud to have her on his arm, to have her as his wife. She had no doubt she would have done just about anything to hold her second marriage together, to learn to love him more, to strengthen their bond. Now he was gone, and she was alone and facing the enormous challenge of creating a new life without him.

She had no family to comfort and distract her and she knew very few people nearby. Tom hadn't wanted her to get involved in local activities or even with charity work until he decided which ones, and he'd lacked the time to make those choices. She had stopped going to the historical society meetings when he disapproved, though she had sneaked to several plays at the Ritz Theater in Brunswick. She had taken tennis lessons at the Sea Palms Club, but Tom had asked her to only play when he was there in case she got injured. She had some local aquaintances, but no one she could call or visit and to whom she could pour out her heart. Those people she *had* met were Tom's friends and business associates, not anyone she would turn to in her hour of need. Her old friends in Augusta, to her shame, had been left by the wayside after her whirlwind marriage, so she was too embarrassed to phone one of them — even Kristy — at least for a while. She recalled her mother saying "You have to be a friend to have a friend" and she hadn't been a friend in much too long.

For two and a half years, she had lived solely for Thomas Grantham and been cut off completely from her past. Where, when, and how her self-confidence and independence vanished she didn't know; it had been a gradual and unnoticed process. Now her freedom had been returned to her, and she wasn't certain how to deal with it.

Until tonight, she had not been given time to think about her future after the tragic news was delivered by a local policeman just after midnight on Sunday. She and Thomas's son Peter had selected Tom's casket on Monday and

11

chosen a mortuary in Brunswick to embalm his body and send it to another one in Los Angeles. Tom's friends, distant relatives, and business associates had been notified of his sudden death. On Tuesday, she and Peter, who was being suspiciously nice for a change, flew to LA where they met with friends and acquaintances from seven to nine at a mortuary there. On Wednesday, Thomas Ethan Grantham was laid to rest during a large funeral service, which was also attended by a cold drizzling rain, gray clouds, and several grieving strangers. While she rested afterward, Peter had taken care of pressing business at a local import-export company owned by his father.

Today, she and Peter had flown home to Sea Island. The time zone changes and connection at the Atlanta airport where they took Tom's private jet to the nearby McKinnon Airport on St. Simons Island had created a long and tiring day. It was during the long flight between Los Angeles and Atlanta that certain realities and buried memories began to haunt her. By the time they landed, she was mentally, emotionally, and physically drained. She knew the worst repercussions of this tragedy loomed ahead for her.

It was ten o'clock Thursday night. She was home alone, a wealthy widow at thirty-five. She was bracing herself for the war with Peter over Tom's money which she was certain was sure to come soon.

As if that dreaded thought summoned him, her twenty-six-year-old stepson knocked on her bedroom door. Cass took a deep breath, ordered her head to stop spinning and pounding, and replied, "It's open, Peter; come in."

Cass's brown gaze watched Peter walk across the room and sit down beside her on the long bench. She saw his hazel eyes drift over her face before he gave her one of his disarming half-smiles. A section of midnight-black hair dangled over his forehead in a mischievous and sexy manner. She admitted he was handsome and virile, like his father. Also like his father the six-foot-tall bachelor with a playboy reputation was well groomed, well educated, and intelligent. But there the similarities stopped. Peter Grantham was a clever, skilled, and deceitful charmer. He was also selfish, greedy, arrogant, and spiteful. He was being very good during this horrible episode, but she didn't trust him. No matter, she reasoned, it was best to respond in like kind, for now.

"You look exhausted, Cass," he murmured sympathetically. "You haven't even changed clothes or taken off your shoes. I saw the light on and knew you were still up, so I thought I should come check on you. Are you all right?"

Cass focused her gaze on the carpet as she answered. "I'm as well as can be expected under the circumstances. I know what's happened is real, but it's so hard to believe he's gone. If he had been sick for a long time . . . but this just came out of nowhere."

"At least he didn't suffer; the doctor said he went out instantly. Knowing my father, he would rather be dead than crippled or disfigured."

She wasn't convinced that last statement was true, but she agreed to keep the peace. "Tom was a proud and active man, you could be right."

"I know I am. Now, why don't I fetch you a brandy while you get undressed and hop into bed before you keel over?"

Cass perceived that Peter was watching her intently, furtively, probably searching for any signs of weaknesses he could exploit. She knew he had even less affection for her than she had for him, but they were pretending otherwise in an undeclared truce. "I've already had those two glasses of wine and the aspirins you gave me earlier. I'll be fine after I get some sleep."

"You have something stronger if you need it. Remember you've only taken a couple of those sedatives Doctor Hines brought over on Monday morning."

"Thanks, but I don't think I should take Valium atop wine."

Peter withdrew a brown plastic bottle from his pocket and pressed it into her hand. "I saw them on the kitchen counter and grabbed them because I thought you might need one tonight. There's no harm or shame in admitting you need something to help you get through a ter-

14

rible time like this."

"Thanks, and you're right. I really appreciate how kind and thoughtful you've been since . . . this difficult week started."

"Dad's loss has been hard on both of us. We've had our problems since you and he married, and it's probably my fault, but that's over, Cass. We need to stick together now. There will be a lot of personal and business matters to handle next week. I'll be going to work tomorrow to take care of any problems that might have arisen while we were gone. Employees tend to get a little nervous and crazy when they don't know what's going to happen to their jobs and the company. Inez will be here at seven, so let her know if there's anything you need. But *I* think what you need is rest and quiet."

"Again, you're right. I am exhausted, so I'll get ready for bed. Thanks for coming over to check on me. Would you lock up and turn on the alarm system as you leave?" *I wish your father had never given those two keys to you. Well, this is my home, and I'll ask you to return them soon.*

Peter walked to the door. "Good night, Cass," he said. "Sleep well, and call me if you need anything."

"I will, Peter. Thanks and good night."

"I'll check on you tomorrow after work."

Cass forced out a smile and nodded, already dreading Saturday evening. She watched Peter until he was out of sight and remained sitting

15

until she heard the door close in the quiet house. His covert stares and unusual behavior worried her. *A lull before the storm, Cass. Be prepared for trouble.*

Since his father died, Cass had not seen Peter shed a single tear; nor were there any telltale signs of private grieving exposed in his gaze or in his voice. The only thing that seemed to gleam in his hazel eyes were dollar signs from his imminent inheritance. She was glad he didn't live in the enormous house with her, though his residence — a large and luxurious guesthouse — was only a few steps beyond the back door. His bachelor pad overlooked the olympic-size pool and cabana and was within view of her bedroom veranda, which was how he had seen her lights.

Peter was nine years her junior, making her age closer to his than it had been to his father's. From the first moment she met him two days before she married Thomas, her stepson had found subtle — and on occasion when they were alone, overt — ways to let her know he did not trust her or approve of the marriage. But Peter made certain he never revealed his true opinion of her to others, as his father detested being challenged in any way. She had mentioned Peter's ill feelings to Tom several times, but soon realized there was no point in pursuing the issue since Tom either insisted it was her imagination or reasoned that his son's reaction was natural, considering the differences in their ages and backgrounds. For now, Peter was being nice even in private, which surprised and intrigued her. She had expected him to behave in public, since both Grantham men were staunch believers in public images and in keeping "dirty linen" hidden.

Cass took another deep breath, forced her weary body to rise, and placed the Valium bottle on the nightstand. She entered a huge walk-in closet. Built-in dressers with jewelry drawers, shoe racks, shelves, cubbyholes, and hanging bars at various heights held garments and shoes from the best designers and stores across the country. She had clothes and footwear for any occasion, most of them selected by Tom or picked by in-store advisers. Tom had spared no expense to adorn her in the finest items, and she had been most appreciative of every purchase.

While donning a sapphire satin nightgown — Tom had loved her to wear satin to bed — and performing her nightly ritual by rote, she realized how happy she was that Tom had purchased this sprawling two-million-dollar house five months ago. It was beautiful and elegantly decorated, with perfectly manicured grounds that boasted of several gigantic live oaks draped in spanish moss and surrounded by beds of ivy. For the two previous years, she and Tom had traveled through the US and foreign countries for business and pleasure. They stayed in expensive hotels and plush resorts or in the four other residences Tom owned in New York City, San Antonio, Los Angeles, and Aspen. Tom had a restless and adventurous streak, with energy that was sometimes difficult for her to match. He had loved to stay on the move and to sample treats from every table fate placed before him. He had told her often he was going to slow down and settle down soon, but she knew he couldn't or didn't want to do either. "Soon" would never come now.

She had been astonished when he purchased the Mediterranean-style home, moved her in, and suggested she remain there during the last five months while he traveled alone seventy-five percent of that time to take care of business. When he got lonely, he would arrange for her to join him for a few days.

She hadn't minded that change in their life-style, and loved the easygoing and tranquil existence on the island, though neighbors were rarely present in their hugely expensive "winter homes" and "vacation cottages." She knew she hadn't done anything to cause Tom disappointment or to diminish his love for her. She was convinced he had sensed her travel weariness and settled her here out of love and concern. He had called almost daily and sent flowers or gifts at least once a week during his absences. When he was home, they were together constantly, in bed or out of it.

For many reasons, she hadn't slept with Tom while dating him, and he had never pressured her to do so. Thomas Grantham had known how to romance and to pleasure a woman with skill, generosity, and stamina. She was going to miss those splendid bouts of lovemaking.

It hadn't been that way with her first husband, though Brad's lovemaking had been pleasant. She had been forced to admit she wasn't enough for Brad; he also needed other women. But she wouldn't allow Bradley Stillman to steal into her thoughts tonight. She'd divorced him at twenty-four and had never looked back in regret because Brad had destroyed all of her love and respect for him. She was glad they'd had no children to keep a tie between them, though she had remained friends with his sister, Kristy, after the divorce.

Cass grasped the edge of the counter to steady herself when a wave of dizziness suddenly assailed her. She felt weak, as if her body were turning to warm honey which could spread across the rose-colored Florida tiled floor at any moment if she didn't lie down. She glanced at the mirror above the floral sink and noticed her cheeks were flushed though the rest of her face was pale and her pupils seemed dilated and strange. She concluded she was more fatigued than she had realized or the wine was having a delayed reaction on her depleted system. She spread the washcloth over the edge of the sink, flipped off the bathroom light, and walked in a near wobble to the king-size Rice bed. She yanked the covers aside, absently wondering why Inez had not prepared the bed as usual before leaving tonight, and climbed between cool and colorful sheets. She turned off the Tiffany lamp, her fingers trailing down the Goddess Diana base and knocking the Valium bottle to the floor. She heard it fall, but made no attempt to retrieve it. She rolled to her right side and stretched out a hand to the empty spot beside her. Despite his tiny flaws, she thought, Thomas Grantham had been a good man, and a wonderful husband; fate had been cruel to snuff out his life so prematurely and in such a horrible manner. She closed her eyes and wept until she was released from her anguish by merciful slumber.

Cass opened her eyes, stretched, and yawned. She glanced at the clock on the nightstand to discover it was nine in the morning. Since she normally arose around seven, she was surprised she had slept so late. She heard the faint cries of seagulls and waves lapping at the beach beyond their property. Sunlight streamed through the windows and doors to the veranda, as she'd forgotten to close the drapes last night. It was going to be a beautiful spring day, she decided with a smile as her stomach announced its hunger with several growls. The moment she wondered what she was going to do after breakfast, the grim reality of her husband's death crashed in on her. She grimaced and tears blurred her vision.

Someone knocked on the bedroom door and Cass realized Inez was there and must have closed the door after her arrival. "Come in," she responded, but the door was already opening.

"I'm sorry to disturb you, Mrs. Grantham, but the police are here and insist on speaking with you."

Cass sat up and stared at Inez, wondering if the doorbell might have been what had awakened her. "The police?"

"Yes, ma'am. I told them you were still in bed and in mourning and to return later, but they refused. They're waiting in the living room."

A mystified Cass looked at Inez but the older woman kept her face blank. The fact that she wore her dyed black hair pulled back in a bun so tight it stretched her skin over her cheekbones added to her upleasant expression. Cass didn't like the unfriendly woman, but she was an excellent housekeeper and cook. After moving to Sea Island, Cass and Tom had been told that good domestic help was hard to find, so he had insisted they keep the disagreeable creature. Her husband had been adamant that she would not become a maid or cook in her own home.

"What do they want, Inez? Is it about Tom's . . . accident?"

"I don't know, ma'am. Do you want me to ask them again to leave? Or do you want to call

Mr. Peter home to deal with them?"

Cass tossed aside the covers and put on her slippers as she replied, "Neither, Inez. Tell them I'll be down as soon as I'm dressed."

"As you wish, ma'am."

Before Inez could leave, Cass ordered in a pleasant tone, "Would you please offer the gentlemen some coffee?"

"As you wish, ma'am; it's ready in the kitchen. I'll bring you a cup to help you wake up."

"Thanks, and I'll have my breakfast on the veranda after they leave."

"As you wish, ma'am."

While observing the woman's departure, Cass retorted silently, *If I did as I wished, you would have been gone long ago, you irritating — Watch it, Cass*, she warned herself, *don't get yourself all worked up; and Inez is being nice today.* For Inez, an offer to bring her coffee was a huge and unexpected kindness.

Cass headed for the bathroom to freshen up, dress in a casual outfit, and put on at least a smidgen of makeup. The coffee was waiting for her when she emerged and she took a few sips. She couldn't imagine why the police officers had come, but the last thing she wanted to talk about was Tom's automobile accident and death. If it was only a courtesy or general inquiry call, she reasoned as she hurried, why had they insisted that a grieving widow leave her bed to speak with them?

She finished the coffee, used a refreshing blue mouthwash, checked her appearance, and left the room.

Cass entered the large and formal living room, paused just inside the archway, and asked, "What can I do for you gentlemen this morning? This has been a long and trying week and I wasn't expecting company so early."

"I'm Detective Adam Beals and this is my partner, Detective Carl Killian," one of the men announced. "Have a seat, Mrs. Grantham; this might take a while. We have a lot of questions to ask before we can clear up this matter."

Beals seemed short and stocky; Killian looked lanky. She couldn't tell how tall either actually was since neither man rose from his seat when she entered the room, nor apologized about intruding on her privacy. It was apparent — since no coffee cups were visible — that they had refused Inez's offer. Neither man smiled, and Beals's voice sounded as gruff as his expression appeared. Inexplicable panic shot through her. "What kinds of questions, sir? The only things I know about the accident are what the officer who delivered the news told me."

"Was it an accident, Mrs. Grantham?"

"I beg your pardon?" she asked in confusion, noting how Beals stressed the word "accident" and sent her a skeptical look before he continued.

"We've already spoken to his pilot and the woman who flew in with him that night. He's the only one who drove that particular car, right?"

Cass nodded. "What woman? Tom didn't say anything about bringing a business associate or guest home with him, and I wasn't told someone was in the car with him. Was she injured? Is she in the hospital?"

"No. He dropped her at the Embassy Suites on Golden Isles Parkway, a Miss Gretchen Lowery, a model, twenty-three, blue eyes, blond hair."

"Her name isn't familiar to me and Tom didn't mention her when he phoned Sunday morning. Perhaps he gave her a lift home as a favor."

"That isn't the case; she said they were . . . close friends. Was there any trouble between you and your husband? Did he have any enemies?"

"Why were you in bed when you were expecting his return?" Detective Killian added.

Cass's gaze shifted to Carl Killian. "Why would you ask about our personal relationship? What does that have to do with Tom's accident?"

"Mr. Grantham's wreck hasn't been ruled an accident," Beals said.

Cass eyed Adam Beals closely. "I don't understand . . . The other officer told me Sunday night —"

"He spoke prematurely. We aren't sure it was just an accident; the car's still being examined.

24

Would you answer my other questions?" Killian interrupted.

Cass gaped at Killian. "If you haven't finished inspecting the car, what makes you think it wasn't an accident?"

"Gut feeling and experience with crimes."

"Crimes?" She echoed Killian's alarming word as she felt her legs go weak and her head spin.

"Murder is a mighty serious crime, don't you think?"

Cass focused her gaze on Beals. "Are you trying to tell me my husband was . . . murdered?" She saw Beals shrug. "That's impossible."

"Is it? From what I hear, he was a very wealthy and powerful man."

"Yes, but Tom didn't have any enemies. Perhaps a few people didn't like him, but no one *hated* him. Gentlemen, I'm not feeling well this morning, so I think you should leave now and return on Monday."

"This is just preliminary questioning to help us clear up this case, Mrs. Grantham, but we can talk downtown if you prefer."

Cass repeated Killian's word. "Downtown?"

"At the station. We just thought it would be nicer to do it here."

Who, Cass wondered, was this Gretchen and why had she been with Tom earlier on that ill-fated night? And why were these detectives being so insensitive? "Should I call my lawyer?"

Cass heard herself ask him, though she didn't know why she did. She'd read too many mystery novels and watched too many dramatic movies while having little to do during Tom's many absences. That would account for it.

"Do you need one?"

"You make it sound as if it would be a good idea."

Killian suggested, "Perhaps I should Mirandize you, Mrs. Grantham, just so there won't be any misunderstandings later."

"Neither a lawyer nor my Miranda rights are necessary, sir. I just don't like having my privacy invaded, so just ask your questions and let's get this over with so I can rest," Cass told them as she took a seat in an armless turquoise chair, compelling her to clasp her hands in her lap. She ordered her wits to clear in order to deal with the astounding situation. She had the oddest feeling that Beals and Killian had tried to catch her off guard with their sudden appearance and bold queries. Perhaps she should summon Peter before she continued to speak with —

"Do you remember my other questions? Will you answer them?" Beals demanded.

Cass almost glared at the flush-faced detective with his challenging gaze and stern expression. Both these heartless men were causing her to feel irascible and edgy. Suddenly she didn't care if she were polite or cooperative or if her behavior made her look suspicious. All she wanted to do was finish this horrendous episode and get rid of "Mutt & Jeff" so she could take a long bath in the Jacuzzi garden tub and have breakfast on the veranda overlooking the ocean where fresh air and bright sunshine could clear her mind and warm her icy soul. She was tired and hungry. She felt weak and assailed. She was angry. Her nerves were raw, and it was a struggle not to squirm in her seat or scream at the detectives, tell them to go to hell and get out of her home.

Cass fought to retain her poise and wits. She couldn't imagine what was wrong with her. Perhaps she was suffering from delayed shock, total exhaustion, and/or depression. Despite her best intentions, she almost gritted out her words, "First, I would like to say this isn't a kind way to treat a recent widow. My husband has been dead for less than a week when you invade my home and demand I be awakened the morning after I return late from his funeral. You ask ridiculous questions and make crude insinuations without explaining to me why you're here. I find you both rude and inconsiderate. Now, shall we continue with the business at hand so you can leave as soon as possible?"

"Calm down, Mrs. Grantham, and we'll —"

"Calm down!" Cass almost shrieked at Killian. "Right in the midst of a terrible ordeal, you come here and treat me with gross disrespect and cruel insensitivity and expect me not to be upset! Rest assured I will report your

27

behavior to your superior and to my lawyer and stepson. You have no right to mistreat me in this manner." She rushed to answer their intrusive questions. "My husband and I were happily married; ask anyone who knows us. As to Miss Lowrey, I have no idea who she is or why she flew here with Tom. As to why I was in bed at midnight, Tom said if he wasn't home by nine it was because he was being delayed and he would return on Monday morning, so I wasn't expecting him back that night. As to why he didn't phone me from McKinnon Airport after he landed, I assume it was because it was late and he knew I would be in bed."

Cass's chest rose and fell as she spilled forth the information in a near breathless rush. "In the past, if Tom flew in late, he slept in one of the guestrooms to keep from disturbing me. As far as I know, he has no enemies, but I've never been involved in his business dealings and know nothing about his companies or associates. As to the Volante, yes, only Tom drove that car; it was his favorite and he didn't allow anyone to touch it besides his mechanic. As to his tragic accident, I only know what the policeman told me Sunday night. As to Tom's wealth, yes, he was a very rich man. I have no idea what he's worth, because I didn't handle his money or even our household expenses; you'll have to question his bankers and accountant for those answers. I can't even tell you if I'm in his will or am his life insurance beneficiary, but I presume, as his wife, I am. Did I leave anything out, gentlemen? If so, ask your questions fast and leave." She saw Killian glance at Beals and nod.

Killian responded, "That should cover everything for now, ma'am. If we have any more questions, we'll see you next week. And if we've upset you, I apologize, and please accept my condolences for your loss. I did bring along Mr. Grantham's briefcase and other belongings which we salvaged from the car. I put them over there."

Cass's mind shouted, *It's too late to pretend to be nice, you bastard!* "Before you return and harass me again, be sure you have a written report on the reason for Tom's accident which justifies another visit. And if you do return, make certain you don't leave your manners outside my front door." She watched Beals frown, but the shorter man held silent, wisely, she decided, as she might verbally rip off his auburn head if he dared her to do so. Killian nodded and sent her a forced smile.

Cass walked the two men to the front door and closed it behind them without biding them good-bye. She retrieved the sack filled with Tom's possessions and his briefcase and went upstairs to place them in her closet until she was in a mood to look at them.

Minutes later when Inez entered the spacious master bedroom suite, she found Cass pacing

29

the carpeted floor, muttering curses about the detectives, and seeming to tremble in anger. She noticed that the younger woman's cheeks were rosy but her face was pale, and her eyes looked strange to her, almost wild. She had never seen the brunette in this agitated state.

"Are you all right, ma'am?"

"I will be as soon as I calm down, Inez. I've met few people as rude and cold-hearted as those two snakes."

"Would you like your breakfast now?"

"No, I'm too upset to eat. I'm so tense that it probably wouldn't stay down. What I need is a long soak in the tub and a nap. I feel drained."

"Why don't you take one of those pills Doctor Hines brought over to relax you? Maybe you should lie down and nap before your bath."

Cass stopped pacing like a caged animal and looked at the housekeeper who was acting in a pleasant manner for a change. "Perhaps you're right, Inez; I feel totally out of sorts and exhausted."

"Would you like some fresh orange juice to take the pill with?"

"Thanks, but I'll get some water from the bathroom. I'll turn off the ringer on my phone, so don't disturb me unless it's an emergency."

"Yes, ma'am. You rest and get to feeling better."

"Thank you, Inez, and I'll let you know when I'm up again."

As Inez left the room, she concluded that the medicine Mr. Peter had told her to slip into his stepmother's coffee or food this morning hadn't worked. The near-crazed woman surely needed calming down and shouldn't be so stubborn about taking the doctor's advice. Perhaps the potent sedative she had suggested — as Mr. Peter had asked her to do — would do the trick. She certainly stood a better chance of keeping her job if she helped Mr. Peter and she got Mrs. Grantham out of an irrational and agitated mood.

Chapter Two

From far away, Cass heard someone calling her name and felt someone shaking her left shoulder; it was a familiar voice, but it was so faint that she could not place it. She struggled to surface in the murky depths that held her captive. Her lids were so heavy and she felt so weak that she couldn't seem to open her eyes. She kept wriggling her forehead and brows to help her part those stubborn lids. She needed water to soothe her dry throat and mouth. She wanted to turn over and go back to —

"Cass . . . Cass, wake up! Inez said you've been asleep since this morning. It's almost seven at night!"

At those shouts and a rougher shaking, she finally managed to open her eyes and look up into Peter's handsome face. The concerned expression in his hazel gaze registered, and, even with a foggy brain, she wondered if it was an honest show of worry or just an excellent pretense. "What did you say? What do you want?"

Peter sat down beside her. "I just got home from work and Inez told me you've been asleep all day. She didn't want to leave you alone until I got here. Are you all right or do I need to have Doctor Hines come over and take a look at you?"

Still in a groggy state, Cass struggled to sit up and prop herself against the headboard, unmindful of her touseled brown hair, puffy eyes, and sensual sapphire nightgown.

After Peter pulled the top sheet to her shoulders and pushed a stray strand of hair from her face, she took a deep breath to finish clearing her head. "I must look a wreck. I feel as if I've been run over by a fast train that reversed and took a second strike at me."

Peter chuckled and jested, "You've looked better on past occasions, but I don't see any real damage. How do you feel?"

Cass took another deep breath. "Like a lump of melting butter but at the same time as heavy as a rock. That Valium knocked me out cold; maybe I shouldn't have taken two on an empty stomach. But, I'm awake and fine now. Or I will be as soon as I take a shower and drink some coffee."

"Inez said you haven't eaten all day. She tried to wake you up for lunch and again late this afternoon, but you were out to the world. She figured you needed sleep more than food. Now, why don't you take that shower and slip on some clothes while I prepare us some coffee and something to eat?"

"You know how to cook?"

"Rather well, I must say, so don't look so skeptical. A bachelor can't eat out all of the time and I have been on my own for years. What about one of my special omelettes and some toast?"

"It sounds wonderful to me; I'm starved, and I need a cup of coffee desperately. Thanks."

Peter nodded and said, "I'll see you downstairs in . . . say about twenty minutes?"

"Perfect. Make the coffee strong; I need the caffeine."

"You best go easy on it or you'll be awake all night."

"Were there any problems at the seafood company or the electronics firm?" she queried him about two of Tom's eight businesses, as the remaining six were in other towns and states.

"Just minor ones and I handled them. We'll talk more while we eat. I'm starved, too; I skipped lunch and just ate a pack of crackers."

After Peter left the room, Cass noticed her luggage sitting on the floor, still waiting to be unpacked from her trip to Los Angeles. She recalled why that chore wasn't done and why she had been so upset and taken the tranquilizer. She wondered if the police had gone to see Peter today after speaking with her; if so, it seemed odd that he didn't phone her or rush home afterward to see what they had asked and what she had answered. Even if the detectives hadn't seen Peter today, surely, Inez would have told him about their visit and her reaction, one that she was embarrassed and baffled to recall. No doubt Peter was planning to discuss the matter tonight and that was his reason for awakening her.

As Cass showered and dressed, the shocking episode was replayed in her head like a videotape. True, the men had been rude and insensitive and their timing was lousy, but she couldn't imagine why she had behaved so rudely, almost as if she had freaked out. But wasn't that natural under those circumstances? After all, they had implied Gretchen Lowrey was Tom's . . . There was no way that could be true. And they had speculated that Tom had been . . . murdered. Surely that wasn't true, either; it couldn't be. What was worse was they sounded as if she were a suspect; that was absurd and frightening. She didn't want their private lives invaded by those two slugs, based on . . . On what?

Cass hurriedly brushed her long brown tresses and went downstairs to the breakfast room, dismissing the troubling thoughts.

Peter glanced up from his cooking and smiled. "Now you look like yourself. For a minute there, you had me worried, Cass."

"I'm sorry; it wasn't intentional. Now, what can I do to help?"

"Pour your coffee; I already have a cup. And you can start the toast. It should be ready when this second omelette is done."

After she finished those tasks, she asked, "What's next?"

"See if I've missed putting out anything. If

35

not, take a seat and get prepared to have your tummy filled with a real treat."

She passed her gaze over the table to find that it was completely set with dishes, silverwear, placemats, and napkins. All of the needed condiments were there, too: salt, pepper, sweetener, butter, and jelly. Peter had positioned them across from each other at the beveled glass ring that was supported by a large square ivory pedestal with floral gold-leaf accents on all sides. Four Louis XVI-style chairs with golden tortoise finishes on Italian beechwood surrounded it; their seats, rounded backs, and a section of the armrests were covered in an ivory fabric with gold pinstripes and self-welting. It was lovely, but too formal, she felt, for a breakfast room; she would have preferred something more casual, but an interior decorator whom Tom had hired had chosen it, just as the man had selected everything else in the house, including most of the accessories and artwork. When Tom had brought her "home" for the first time, the house was ready for immediate occupancy, down to perfectly landscaped and manicured grounds. Even the walk-in pantry, freezer, and refrigerator were stocked; and Inez already was employed.

Cass wished she could have had a say in decorating the house, but Tom had wanted to surprise her by having it finished and ready to enjoy. It wasn't that she didn't like the decorator's excellent taste, but making those selections herself would have made it seem more like her home. She hadn't even known about its purchase until Tom flew them over to take possession early last October. They had stayed at the nearby Mobile 5-Star Cloister resort on two occasions, so he had known how much she liked this location. Yet, it would have been nice to have been consulted.

"What are you thinking about so intensely?" Peter asked as he put a plate with an omelette and two slices of toast before her.

"About the day your father surprised me with this house. All I had to do was walk in and unpack a few suitcases. Everything was finished. He'd even had my clothes and belongings sent here from the other residences. He was a unique and wonderful man, so thoughtful and generous. I can't imagine him being gone and never seeing him again."

"Life goes on, Cass. You have to accept reality, just as I have, no matter how difficult it is," Peter said kindly.

"I know. I learned that bitter truth after my parents died."

Peter didn't remark on her statement because he knew from his father that Cass's parents had been killed in a train crash while taking a vacation she had suggested and paid for years ago, an anniversary gift from a child the couple had borne in mid-life. "Taste your omelette before it gets cold," he said to distract her thoughts.

"Thank you, Peter, for doing this," she said

before she cut into the omelette prepared with, two kinds of cheese, sauteed onions, diced ham, and assorted herbs. She took a bite, then swallowed it, looked at him and smiled. "It's delicious," she proclaimed. "A master chef couldn't have done better."

"From somebody who's eaten in the best restaurants in the world, that's an enormous compliment. Thanks."

It felt strange for Cass to be eating and genially talking with Peter. The only times they had dined together in the past Tom was always present. They had done as little talking as possible in private and with polite pretense in public. Now, here they were in a cozy setting, alone, and being astonishingly cordial to each other. Even so, she didn't know what to talk about. She decided to follow Peter's lead and waited for his next move, which didn't come until he finished eating most of his food and leaned back in his chair.

"I've ordered audits on all of Dad's businesses and full reports on his holdings. As soon as they're completed, we'll meet with his lawyer and go over them and his will. I've already contacted his insurance company, so they have the paperwork in progress. Since you and I are co-beneficiaries, I'll let you know what happens in that area. There is one important matter we need to discuss tonight, if you don't mind."

Cass nodded for him to continue, anxiety nibbling at her.

"I know we haven't gotten along well, but I hope we can put that behind us now. During this past week, I had a chance to study you closely and I realized I had misjudged you and never given you a fair chance. It's clear to me that you loved my father and he loved you, and you two had a happy marriage. I hope we can become friends, Cass; if not, at least we can have a truce because we'll have a lot to take care of together in the coming months. Think about what I've said before you answer while I pour us some more coffee."

Cass watched Peter rise, collect their cups, and walk to the counter. He poured hers, then pushed his cup aside.

He turned and said, "I think I'll have Kahlua instead. Do you want any?"

"No, thanks, coffee is fine with me."

Cass waited in silence for his return with their drinks, wondering if she could trust his unexpected turnabout. If he was angry about her inheriting Grantham money and holdings after less than three years of marriage and if he was planning to fight her tooth-and-nail for every dollar she received, those feelings and intention were well concealed. She couldn't help but question his motive for suddenly being so nice! She told herself to watch him with eagle eyes for signs of deceit, but to pretend to accept his offer and hope it was sincere. After he sat down and she thanked him, she said, "Little would please me more than for us to become

39

friends, Peter. I'm sure that would have delighted Tom."

Peter smiled and said, "You're a special woman, Cass. My father was lucky. As somebody who's still caught up in the dating game, it can be miserable and frustrating at times. I realize I've gotten quite a reputation as a playboy for dating so many women while looking for Miss Right. You and Dad were lucky you found each other and had several good years together; that's more than a lot of couples share."

Peter chuckled before he added, "But my misbegotten love life isn't what we need to be talking about tonight. I have the enclosure cards from the flowers sent to Dad's funeral and a few notifications of donations made to several charities in his name; I expect there'll be more of those coming in later. The printing company I use at work is doing up thank-you cards with special messages on them."

"I agree, Peter, and that was thoughtful of you. Those details hadn't even entered my mind, and I realize I haven't been much help to you in this matter."

"I didn't think about it, either. We have my secretary to thank for the reminder when she offered to help with the project. The printer told me he would put a rush job on the order and they should be ready Monday afternoon, at least a good portion of them. I've decided to hire a temp next week to address the envelopes for us so we can get them in the mail as soon as possible. You might want to look over the names on the enclosure cards and read the sympathy notes this weekend; they're in that box on the counter."

Cass glanced in the direction he pointed.

Peter took a sip of his drink. "If there are any messages or people you want to respond to personally, pull out their cards and I'll bring you some of ours as soon as they're ready; I'll do the same. The temp can address them for us, so just clip their notes to yours. Is that all right with you?"

"I would prefer to address and seal my own notes, if you don't mind. I don't want a stranger reading special messages I've written to Tom's friends."

"That's no problem. When they're finished, I'll collect them and mail them for you."

"Thank you, Peter, I really appreciate your help."

"Let me know if you think of anything I haven't done. This sort of thing is new to me."

"I wish it were new to me. My parents' deaths were a long time ago and I had forgotten there was so much to do afterward. I'm glad I had you there to help me with the arrangements this week."

"I'm sure that was a tough job to handle alone."

"Yes, it was."

"Being an only child, too, I'm glad you were

here to help me."

"Thanks." They were both quiet for a long moment, then Cass said, "Since you cooked and served dinner, I'll clear the table and clean up the kitchen."

"We'll be done faster if I help. I'll collect the dishes and rinse them while you load the dishwasher."

Cass wished he had just left. She was beginning to feel edgy again, and assumed it was because of the stressful nature of their topics and spending time with this man she wasn't sure could be trusted. She didn't want to think or plan tonight. She was tired of talking about grim matters and only wanted to be alone, relax, and not think about her troubles and anxieties.

As Cass was putting things in the refrigerator, Peter asked, "Do you want any more coffee before I empty the pot and wash it?"

"No, thanks. I'm sure I've had more than I need. After staying in bed most of the day and having two cups, I'll probably be awake half the night."

"If you get tired but you're too jittery to sleep, take one of those Valiums. But just one, Cass."

"I'll remember, and thanks for your concern."

As she loaded the dishwasher, Cass reasoned she should get their last topic out of the way so he could leave when they finished their chores.

"Did Inez tell you I had a visit from two police detectives this morning?"

"So did I," Peter revealed, "but I didn't want to spoil our dinner talking about it. I was running around part of the day taking care of errands, so it took them until late this afternoon to catch up with me. I didn't phone you afterward because we needed time and privacy to discuss the matter."

It sounded to Cass as if he answered the questions forming in her mind before she could ask them. "They were rude and insensitive, Peter, and downright intimidating." She related the episode to him. "How did they behave with you?"

"They were smart-ass all the way and covered that same ground with me. They're stupid if they think somebody killed my father. Nobody tampered with his car; it was kept in a fenced area when not in use. The only other person with keys is the mechanic who services it, and he's totally trustworthy. It was an insult to Dad and to me to even hint that anybody could hate him that much. I told them not to bother me again unless they had evidence of foulplay, which they don't."

Cass loaded the two plates as she pointed out, "Either there has to be something strange that caught their eye or they're just snooping out of curiosity. They certainly could use lessons in manners. I should tell you, Peter, they annoyed me to the level of being rude in return."

"I know; Inez told me; she could hear you yelling at them from the kitchen. She said you were a nervous wreck after they left and that's why you took those tranquilizers."

Cass felt her cheeks flush. "I'm really embarrassed about how I behaved. My parents taught me good manners and respect for elders and authority. I've never been hot-tempered like that before, but they made me so angry with their crude insinuations and near accusations. Maybe it was a result of delayed shock or something. Whatever happened to me after they dropped their bombshells, I know I made a terrible impression on them. If they come back again, I guess I owe them an apology."

"You're wrong, Cass; they owe *you* the apology. Don't talk to them alone again; insist on me or Simon Johnson being present."

She dried and put away the skillet as she asked, "Why do I need a lawyer? I don't have anything to hide, and I want this matter resolved fast."

Peter draped the dishcloth over the double-sink partition and leaned his left hip against the counter. "Don't be naive, Cass. Men like that can have a cunning way of twisting innocent answers and causing you trouble. We don't want them digging into our lives and exposing family dirt."

Cass finished her work and faced him to

query, "What kind of dirt, Peter?"

"I didn't say we have any, but everybody has things in their past or private lives they don't want the world to learn. Things can leak out during investigations, innocent things that might be twisted and become harmful to our family reputation. My father was a rich and well-known man, those scandal rags would delight in finding some innocent or forgotten angle they can exploit for money. I insist. If Beals and Killian call you or come around again, refuse to see them until you phone me and I get hold of Simon Johnson."

Cass was becoming more fidgety by the minute but tried to conceal her tension. "Won't it look suspicious if I refuse to answer their questions and demand our lawyer be present? And the same applies to you."

Peter knew he had to rush their conversation before she got too antsy to finish their talk. It was obvious to him that the drug he had slipped into her coffee was working properly for him to carry out his plans. "What does that matter when neither of us has anything to hide?" he asked. "We just want to protect ourselves and our interests, and Dad's reputation. For them to imply he was murdered and to start probing us for suspects before they finish examining his car for the cause of his accident tells me they're looking for trouble and hoping to find it. At this early stage, they have no right or reason to be exploring that absurd possibility. Don't you agree?"

Cass nodded before she asked, "Tell me, Peter, do you know who Gretchen Lowrey is and why she came to Sea Island with Tom?"

Peter knew those answers from keeping tabs on Tom, but he wasn't going to reveal any of his father's carefully concealed flaws and weaknesses to Cass. Learning the truth could cause her to become furious and quickly spiteful. He needed to get her under his control before his father's will was read. Thomas Grantham, he knew from experience, was an unpredictable man, so Peter couldn't imagine what that will would contain. For certain, he didn't want Cass to walk away with things that rightfully belonged to him. He was glad Inez had phoned him and given him a report on the detectives' visit, so he had been prepared for his confrontation with them. He repeated to Cass the same lies he had told Beals and Killian, "She's a model, but I've never met her. Dad was planning an advertising campaign for Smooth Rider, Texas-G Beef, and Grantham Seafoods; maybe he wanted to see how she acted around crabs and lobsters before he hired her to do the ads and commercials. He might have been planning to shoot a test video or photos with her at the company or on one of the shrimp boats. She certainly couldn't be a prospect for the job if she was scared around sea creatures or cattle," he said with a grin. "I know Dad wanted to use a fresh approach. Since she's a 'new face', she would be a good choice for those campaigns, if she had acting skills to match her good looks. When we spoke on Saturday, he said he was bringing home a surprise for me to check out, so I assume Gretchen was it."

Cass decided that Peter's conclusions were credible about using a beautiful model to advertise beef products from his San Antonio ranch and company, or his seafood company in nearby Brunswick, or his golf cart company in Augusta, Georgia. Tom also had an electronics firm in Brunswick, Big-G Real Estate in New York City, A Taste Of Heaven restaurant, and A View Of Heaven art galley in Aspen, an import/export company in Los Angeles, and small investments in other men's companies. She had seen ads and commercials for those businesses in the past, and always with beautiful half-clad women in them. "Is that what she said to the detectives?"

"They didn't say, but I told them what I just told you."

"How did they know Miss Lowrey had flown in with Tom?"

"Dad's pilot told them when he was questioned Tuesday morning before we left for LA. From what I gathered from those detectives, they went to see Miss Lowrey that evening. Obviously they didn't find anything suspicious about her because they let her leave town on Wednesday."

Cass wondered why Peter hadn't mentioned the woman to her, as the pilot must have told Peter about her on Tuesday. "Taking her to the Embassy Suites explains what he was doing on the highway so late at night and in the opposite direction from the airport to home, but Beals thought it was odd I was in bed when Tom was on his way home."

"Don't worry about it, Cass; you told them the truth. I suppose he got busy and forgot to phone you about his change in plans."

Cass took a deep breath before she asked Peter, "You don't think Tom was . . . murdered, do you?"

"If he was, it'll be one of the biggest shocks I've ever gotten." *It'll rank right up there with my discovery of his dark secret and his news about marrying you. Soon, Cass, I'll have you right where I want you, out of your skull and under my thumb.*

Cass felt as if bugs were crawling around under her skin and were taking tiny bites of tissue inside her head. She felt excessively warm, though the early March temperatures were comfortably cool. "I hope and pray you're right, Peter. Now, is there anything else we need to discuss?"

"No, and you're looking exhausted, so I'll leave you alone to relax."

Cass observed his departure. She locked the door and pressed the code to set the burglar alarm system, picked up the box of cards,

48

flipped off the light switch, and headed to her bedroom.

She made certain her drapes were drawn so Peter couldn't see her pacing the floor as she attempted to walk off her mounting tension. Perhaps she wouldn't feel so keyed up if she hadn't drunk two cups of strong coffee. She glanced at the brown bottle on her nightstand, but decided she wouldn't take a Valium until she was sure she needed one. She had never taken tranquilizers until this tragedy struck, but Tom and Peter's local physician had recommended them after she became so upset by her husband's sudden and violent death. The medication had calmed her Monday and helped her sleep that night, but she feared becoming dependent upon it. Yet, she felt as if she wanted to jump out of her skin and scream at the top of her lungs for relief from whatever was attacking her mind and body.

Cass decided to unpack her luggage instead of going through the sympathy cards, which might only increase her anxiety. As she worked, she sipped water to quench her unbearable thirst. When the cases were finally emptied, she put them in a large closet in another room and returned to hers to prepare for bed.

Sitting on her closet floor, Cass noticed the brown paper grocery sack and Tom's briefcase. She had forgotten to tell Peter that Killian had brought them over this morning, as Tom had left his luggage aboard his private jet to collect the next day. She decided she should pull out anything personal to her and turn the rest over to the officer tomorrow. She retrieved the sack and emptied its contents on her bed: keys, wallet, two tattered gift-wrapped boxes, a current novel, a demolished video camera, and other small possessions. It was amazing to her that the intelligent Peter hadn't missed his father's belongings and asked about them before now. She couldn't help but wonder if Beals and Killian had studied the items.

The wallet held credit cards, three pictures of her, one of the two of them, and over seven hundred dollars in cash. The novel, an unusual choice for him, was a historical romance by one of America's best-selling authors; perhaps, Cass concluded, Miss Lowrey had left it behind by accident. She knew that Tom often had carried a video camera with him in case he saw something he wanted to record or to tape meetings when a secretary wouldn't be there.

Cass unwrapped the two boxes with their mangled paper and ribbons. She was astonished by the sexy garments within. One box contained a fiery red silk teddy with black lace trim and a crotch slit; the other, an ebony nightgown in a see-through sheer material; both had lacy cut-outs so the woman's nipples would protrude. They were hardly the type of garment that Tom normally purchased for her and she couldn't imagine why he had done so. Then Cass noticed they were not her size. That observation baffled her even more, because Tom chose most of her clothes and shoes and knew her sizes by heart. Obviously the store clerk had picked up the wrong sizes or, more likely, she reasoned, the wrong items to gift wrap for him. She tossed the naughty lingerie aside.

She looked at the remaining items in the sack, but found nothing more of interest to her. Her fingers toyed with the keys on Tom's ring as she eyed his briefcase and wondered if she should open it. Since there might be something for her inside and he was her husband, there was no reason why she shouldn't open it and check its contents.

Cass sat on the bed, placed the case between her spread legs, and unlocked the catches. After lifting the lid, she saw papers, pens, a current business magazine, a calendar with a spiral binder, an address book, note pad, a jewelry and a cigar box, and two videotapes. She opened the oblong black velvet box first to find a gold bracelet of hearts with a diamond in the center of each. Her eyes misted and she winced in painful sadness as she touched the parting gift she assumed was for her.

Cass opened his calendar and read notations about appointments. She gazed at the large "G" penned in on Friday, Saturday, and Sunday, March first through third. Oddly, "Home" was written in on Monday, the day after he flew in and the one following his death.

51

Obviously Tom had meetings with Gretchen Lowrey for three days and wasn't expecting to come home until after the weekend. "Pick up packages at Marie's" also was recorded on last Friday's square. She glanced at the boxes nearby and saw gold stickers with that boutique's name on them.

An unbidden thought came to mind, *If he bought them for Gretchen, they wouldn't have been in the car when he was killed after dropping her off at a hotel, unless he forgot to give them to her.* If they were for another woman and if not for the accident, she would never have seen them, since only Tom used the Aston Martin DB7 Volante convertible.

Cass scolded herself for such wicked thoughts and kept reading the March, February, and January entries. She saw other meetings listed and unknown names penned in here and there, sometimes only a woman's or a man's first name. No less than every other day it said: "Call C." Sometimes "Send flowers" or "Send gift" was included. It almost sounded as if he required a reminder for his "thoughtful" gestures.

Her fingers flipped through the pages of his address book and her gaze found the same names featured on his calendar, but only first names and phone numbers, no addresses. It bewildered and intrigued Cass that she didn't recognize those names.

Most of the papers her eyes scanned pertained to business. Those she would pass along to Peter. She looked through a collection of receipts held together by a gem clip, as Tom was a stickler for matching them to monthly bills. There was a receipt for the naughty lingerie in the wrong size, more costly than she had imagined, so it should be returned for a credit. Another was for the gold-and-diamond bracelet, an expensive item from an exclusive jeweler in New York City. There were restaurant bills and two for hotels: one for the local Embassy Suites where he had paid in advance for Gretchen Lowrey to stay there for four days; the second was for a hotel in New York, which didn't make sense to her because Tom had an apartment there. He could have paid the bill for a business associate or consultant, but she was still puzzled because the registration was in his name, not in the person's who had used it and run up an expensive room service tab in the process.

Her fingers checked the lid pockets of the case and withdrew several coin-shaped items. She gaped in horror at the condoms in her palm. Tom had no need for contraceptives since she was on the pill and he never used them with her.

Slowly, yet rapidly, horrible suspicions entered her aching head. It was as if a sadistic puzzle had been tossed into her lap and she was putting it together, and watching it form an ugly picture of betrayal. She did not want to believe what she was thinking. It couldn't be possible, she told herself. Tom had loved her, only her!

Cass's darting gaze touched on the two video tapes. Something told her to watch them carefully, for answers. She snatched them up, leapt off the bed, and walked to the entertainment unit in the sitting area of the master suite. She slid the first tape into the narrow slot, and sat down on the edge of the small sofa. She pointed the remote control at the TV and turned it on, then did the same with the VCR before pressing the Play button. As colorful images filled her vision and voices flooded her ears, Cass instantly knew she was not prepared for what she was discovering about the man she had loved and married.

Chapter Three

At first, Cass was too shocked and numbed by what she viewed to cry or become furious or to even press Stop. The tape began with her husband and a beautiful blonde she assumed was Gretchen Lowrey having sex in various positions and ways. During one episode, Gretchen held a camera — probably the demolished one lying on her bed nearby — and filmed the steamy action while Tom performed oral sex on her, with the model laughing in amusement, or moaning in ecstasy, or giving instructions as to what felt best or for him to do next. Anguish knifed Cass's ravaged heart every time Tom lifted his head to smile or speak or to run his tongue over his lips before he returned to feasting on Gretchen's willing body.

Eventually it was Tom's turn to film and be pleasured, and the blue-eyed female appeared to do her task with skill and enjoyment. Cass heard him moaning and saw his hips writhing in delight. She heard him saying crude words in a strained voice as he gave his orders or praised her actions. As Gretchen's mouth and tongue and hand lavished his engorged member with near feverish attention, Tom cautioned her to slow down and then told her to halt before he climaxed too soon. "You can finish later, you little witch," he chuckled. "Right now, I want to fuck your brains out; mine, too. Just let me set this thing up over there. Where's the Off button? I found —"

Cass knew there was a time lapse when the camera was turned on again, positioned on a chair at the foot of the bed. She assumed they were in a hotel room because she didn't recognize the setting. The camera was angled perfectly to capture a close-up view of their ensuing intercourse.

Cass squirmed in rising agitation. Her mouth was dry, and her body was warm and itchy. She needed relief from whatever ailed her, but some dark force was coercing her to discover the extent of Tom's sins.

Cass pressed the Fast Forward button and discovered other sexual episodes on other dates. It was evident there was nothing Tom wouldn't do for, to, or with that blond bitch; and Gretchen did the same for him. She cursed and damned the passionate couple who were razoring her very soul.

As Cass was about to halt the tormenting tape, another shocking tryst appeared on the thirty-five-inch screen: Tom having sex with two women, a brunette and a redhead. The television — bought for watching from the bed that was twenty feet away, not this close up — sent out a picture large enough for her to catch every detail.

As Tom directed and filmed, the women cavorted on the bed for a while, stimulating and satisfying each other, either one at a time or simultaneously. After joining them, he continued to record as the brunette and redhead used their hands and mouths to work on his erect penis as a team, sometimes playfully fighting and arguing over not getting a fair share of him.

A change in the action and positions indicated a time lapse during the rendezvous. She saw Tom put on a condom before he took turns driving his rock-hard erection into first one woman and then the other as the females lay side by side. The positioning of the camera gave Cass an excellent view of Tom's face as he betrayed her and their marriage vows with vivid enthusiasm.

Cass had been struggling to ignore the jitters she had been enduring since dinner with Peter, but the weird sensations were mounting. Those imaginary bugs were chewing at her mind and body as they had this morning before she took two Valium and crashed in bed. She pressed the Fast Forward button and allowed the remainder of the tape to go by swiftly.

Ugly, accusing thoughts whirled uncontrollably through her mind. *You kept those videos locked in your briefcase so you could watch them over and over during our separations and probably masturbate to them, didn't you, you sorry sex fiend? You selfish bastard! You filthy traitor!*

When the first tape finished, she leapt up and ejected it, then shoved the second one into the VCR so roughly that the unit was moved backward a few inches. It was as if she had to punish herself for trusting him, for loving him, for allowing herself to be so despicably fooled by him. She had to know if there were more sordid accounts on the second tape or if it was blank. She didn't think she could hear or see anything worse on it, but what she learned was even more devastating.

Cass's brown gaze enlarged and her mouth went agape as she sucked in a gasp of sheer disbelief. She was too astounded to press the Stop button to halt the shocking images and sounds that invaded her brain and her once-happy home as she saw Tom having sex in various ways with a man, a young and handsome and virile male. She could hardly believe the things her husband was saying — those endearments and vulgar words — and what he was doing with another man; yet, she could not deny what she saw. The fact that Tom used a condom with his handsome lover provided little comfort. He was probably only interested in protecting himself — not in protecting her.

Cass could not watch any more. She couldn't bear to learn if other men or multiple male partners were on that second tape. As she thought about Tom kissing her with that same mouth, touching her with those same hands, and entering her with that same penis with which he'd pleasured so many others during their marriage, a wave of nausea wafted over her. She turned off the TV and VCR, then the bedroom lights. She locked her door to make certain Peter didn't come in to check on her and see the tapes. Stripping off her clothes she jumped into the shower. She scrubbed herself from head to feet and took a douche, feeling dirty inside and out and urgently needing to cleanse herself thoroughly.

As she dried off, Cass recalled seeing the name Zak on Tom's calendar and in his address book. He'd been one of those few strangers at Tom's funeral. She also remembered seeing those two women's names in both places, so Tom, she deduced, had been cavorting with all of them on a regular basis. She had no doubt that his secret life was the reason why he had secluded her on Sea Island! She had been fooled, misused, and betrayed in the worst way possible. Humiliation and rage gnawed at her.

After she yanked on a nightgown she found Tom's keys and went to his office downstairs. She unlocked his desk drawers and located the item she needed: his calendar for the previous year. She flipped through the pages for last January through December. Her gaze narrowed. She clenched her teeth in fury.

You sorry bastard, she cursed silently, *if you weren't already dead, I would be tempted to kill you myself! How dare you do this to me! You've been screwing around the whole time! You were even meeting your lovers while I was traveling with you! So these were your "important business" meetings! You bastard, Tom Grantham! You're worse than Brad was. Haven't you ever heard of STDs and AIDS? You could have caught something and brought it home to —*

Sheer terror engulfed her as that reality stormed her angry mind and she turned her thoughts to a practical bent. *Oh, my God . . . I must get myself tested immediately. Whatever will I do if he's given me some awful or lethal disease? How did I ever love a treacherous snake like him? How could he fool me so completely and for so long? I never even suspected anything was wrong. I wonder what Peter will think when he learns about — No, no, I can't tell Peter anything about this; I can't tell anyone. Think of the horrible scandal! I have to destroy those tapes before anybody finds them . . .*

The images of Beals and Killian shot into her head like bullets. If the detectives had used Tom's keys to get inside his briefcase and they saw those tapes . . . "That would give me a motive for murdering the sorry bastard!" she muttered. "So will that prenuptial agreement if or when they learn about it. Damn you, Tom, damn you!"

She copied the names and phone numbers of Tom's lovers and listed the dates of the probable assignations and any information she knew. She straightened the papers in his desk, relocked it, and went to her bedroom, where she put the notes, the two tapes, and condoms in the safe Tom had installed in her closet for her jewels.

Afterward and as best as she could, she rewrapped the lingerie she now knew had been purchased for another woman, perhaps the one on the first tape. She tossed those gifts into the grocery sack, then scowled as she dropped in the offensive camera that had filmed those sordid trysts, along with other items taken from it earlier. As she was tossing things back into Tom's briefcase, the cigar box missed her target and its lid fell open on the bed, revealing a black leather object.

Cass picked up the five-by-seven-inch book, noting its closure strap and lock. She was certain it was a diary, containing private material she couldn't handle reading tonight. She found the key and removed it from Tom's ring. She placed the sack and briefcase in her closet to wait until she was ready to give them to Peter. The diary and key she added to the collection in her closet safe.

As she worked, memories of how she had met Tom and his pursuit of her came tumbling through her distressed mind. Tom had said she was the only woman he had ever met who liked him for himself, not for his wealth and power. He had been amazed when she returned expensive gifts because she insisted she did not know him well enough to accept them. When she refused to have sex with him, he thought it was because of her high moral standards, but her true motive had been to avoid being just another trinket on a rich man's string of affairs. They had gotten close when he came to Augusta to consider buying the golf cart company where she worked and she had been assigned to show him around town and to take notes at their business meetings. Not once had she imagined she was being stalked like innocent prey.

She had loved him, though not wholeheartedly, so maybe she was partly to blame for what happened to her. His money was an attractive bonus, she confessed, though she had not married him for it. He had given her a generous checking account and several credit cards with high limits, but an accountant/manager handled finances, including all household bills, so she didn't know how wealthy he was.

She now realized that Tom cunningly had slowly gained control over every facet of her life, down to selecting her clothes and friends and planning her schedule. He had insisted on no children and no career for her. She had been unaccustomed to a life of enormous wealth and constant travel, yet she had tried to please Tom and fit into his unfamiliar world. Knowing now what that world included, she grimaced and chastised herself for being so blind and foolish, so trusting, so stupid!

Cass noticed the box of sympathy notes nearby and her tormented mind shouted, *Let*

Peter's secretary do them! You'll pay for this evil, Tom, somehow, you'll pay for what you've done to me!

She cursed him again, then took a Valium. She didn't want to think anymore tonight; she didn't want to hurt anymore tonight; she only wanted sleep to give her relief from her mental agony.

As Inez swept the front porch early the next morning, an Orient Blue BMW pulled into the driveway and a casually dressed man joined her.

"My name is Doctor Jason Burkman," he announced. "I'm an acquaintance of Mrs. Grantham and I wanted to stop by to extend my condolences and to see if she's all right and if there's anything she needs."

"She's doing as good as can be expected. I'm taking care of her and seeing to all of her needs. So is the young Mr. Grantham and Doctor Hines."

Jason had met both men and didn't like or respect either one. He hated to think of the lovely and gentle woman who, he had played tennis with twice and treated as a physician three times, being in the care of either man. He had been drawn to Cassandra immediately, but had held his feelings in check for months since she was a married woman. It had been quite a while since he'd seen her last, but she'd often been on his mind. "I've phoned several times to inquire about her, but she hasn't returned any of my calls. If she's home, I'd like to see her."

The housekeeper knew the handsome doctor hadn't gotten through to the house because Peter had changed the telephone number to an unlisted one while they were in Los Angeles and had the old number assigned to his residence out back where either he or his answering machine took the calls. Peter had told her it was to spare his stepmother from receiving unwanted or business calls, but she wasn't sure if that was his sole motive. "I'm sorry, Doctor Burkman, but Mrs. Grantham isn't feeling well and she isn't seeing visitors yet."

"Perhaps I should examine her and see if she needs any medication; I have treated her several times in the past."

Inez recalled Peter's orders about not letting anybody in to see his stepmother. "As I told you, she's under the care of Doctor Hines. Maybe you should phone Mr. Grantham at work to check on her."

Peter Grantham is the last man on earth I would call for any reason after what he did to me! There was something about the woman's tone that intrigued Jason. "Would you mind asking her if I can speak with her for a few minutes?" He saw the housekeeper look at him oddly and hesitate before she nodded and told him to wait on the porch.

She went inside and checked to make certain

her employer was still asleep. So, as Peter had ordered yesterday morning, she told the blond physician, "As I tried to tell you, sir, Mrs. Grantham isn't seeing visitors at this time. When she's ready to have company, she'll phone you. Until she does, it's best if you don't trouble her again. She's grief-stricken over her husband's death."

That wasn't the response Jason had hoped for, and he wasn't sure if he believed it came from Cassandra herself. "Would you tell her I came by?"

"Yes, sir," Inez said, knowing she would not. She watched the man drive away and reminded herself to report the visit to Peter.

Jason glanced at the front of the sprawling Mediterranean house as he turned onto Sea Island Drive. Something wasn't right here. He had the impression the housekeeper hadn't even spoken to Cassandra about him. Strange, he mused, very strange.

At eleven o'clock, Cass sat at a glass-topped verdigris table on the downstairs patio while she had a late breakfast of black coffee with sweetner, mixed fruit juice, and a toasted bagel with no-fat cream cheese. She hadn't risen until thirty minutes ago, but still felt tired and depressed; her brown eyes, dry and scratchy, her body as limp as a wet dishcloth. Her life was a wreck, her marriage had been a sham, and she didn't know what her future held, or even her present. She couldn't get those sordid images and sounds out of her head and wished she hadn't found the tapes or viewed them. She recalled her mother saying, "Never let your mind become a trash heap by allowing people to dump garbage there."

In her wildest dreams she could not have imagined that Thomas Ethan Grantham could be so evil or that she could be so blind and stupid. She had let that handsome and charismatic vampire suck the life from her and pull her into his dark world and change her forever. She was as cut off from her past and her old self as if they had never existed. Somehow she had to find her way out of this gloomy maze with her soul intact. She didn't know what she would do if news of his affairs leaked out. People might think she was like her husband and ostracize her. Perhaps they already knew about Tom's dirty secrets and maybe that explained why no one had phoned or come to visit his recent widow. True, she had no close friends here, or permanent neighbors. But didn't, she reasoned as she fidgeted, good manners and breeding dictate that at least a few of Tom's acquaintances would contact her? What had happened to common courtesy, compassion, southern hospitality?

Maybe they never liked or accepted me in their social circle, she mused. *Now that Tom's gone, they don't have to pretend anymore. I wasn't born or reared as one of them. I sneaked in by marrying up. I'm nothing more than a country girl from a poor family. I couldn't even hold on to my first husband; he screwed around, too.* She sighed in dismay. *For heaven's sake, what's wrong with me? Going off the deep end? I'm as edgy and prickly as a cactus! Get a grip on yourself before you wind up in a —*

Cass jumped and squealed when Inez spoke from behind her. She bumped the table leg with her knee when she twisted in her seat. She just managed to halt herself before — so unlike her — cursing the woman.

"I'm sorry, ma'am, I didn't mean to startle you. More coffee?"

Cass rested one hand on her chest as if to help slow her racing heart. "No, thank you, Inez; I'm stimulated enough today. Have you checked the phones to be sure they're working?"

"They're working fine, ma'am. Why do you ask?"

"I guess I'm just disappointed that nobody's called me."

"Maybe folks don't know what to say to a new widow or they don't want to disturb you this soon after his funeral. You and Mr. Peter have gotten plenty of pretty sympathy cards. Do you want me to bring out the box so you can read them?"

"No! I mean, no thanks; I'm not in the mood for more sadness today." She thought that sounded like a flimsy excuse following her out-

67

burst. "I think I'll walk out to the mailbox and check it."

Knowing she was supposed to intercept any mail that didn't get forwarded to Peter's new post office box, Inez set down the coffeepot as she offered, "I'll go for you. Maybe he hasn't come by yet, so no need for you to waste your energy when you look so tired."

Cass's troubled mind scoffed, *Being nice again today, are we?* "That's kind of you, Inez, but I need the exercise and diversion."

Cass headed for the brick walkway that separated the main house from Peter's residence and garage. She walked along the curved driveway that edged the ivory stucco and glanced at the enormous live oak with its spreading limbs draped in silvery Spanish moss, its leaves as evergreen as the thick and lush bed of ivy surrounding its huge base. She reached the mailbox and peered inside: nothing there.

Her vexation increased at being ignored by the many people that Tom had known. Then again, she reasoned as she grit her teeth and frowned, maybe they knew Tom too well. Perhaps they had associated with him only because of his wealth and status and they hadn't truly liked or respected him and felt the same way about her.

Cass looked up the tree-shaded street of expensive homes. She loved the beauty and tranquility of the long and narrow island and its semi-tropical climate and verdant landscape.

Even so, she couldn't decide if this was where she wanted to spend her life, as so much of this small island and others nearby was geared toward tourists and vacationing residents. The rear of her home bordered the glistening Atlantic with its lovely beach of soft white sand. The other side of the island provided sweeping marsh views and wetlands, a buffer between the ocean and mainland. From previous excursions and visits, she knew the islands were steeped in history and they offered numerous diversions.

Diversions, her mind echoed, that was what she needed to chase away her sadness, torment, and strange moods. She could do volunteer work and get involved with the arts, as there were numerous social and service organizations available in Brunswick and the Golden Isles. Perhaps she could take continuing education classes at Brunswick College or begin a new hobby. She could get back into church activities, even take up tennis once more, perhaps play with Dr. Jason Burkman again. No, that might not be a good idea since he's a handsome bachelor. People might gossip. She *was* tempted to visit him professionally for a check-up to see what could be done about her crazy mood swings, but that might give him a bad impression of her. Until she got a grip on herself and her life and she waited a proper mourning period, she should avoid Dr. Burkman's discerning blue eyes.

As she started to head back to the house, Cass heard a feminine voice calling out to her from down the long and winding street. She turned in that direction.

"Mrs. Grantham! Mrs. Grantham! Wait up for a minute!"

Two middle-aged women, dressed in fashionable casual outfits and coiffed perfectly, hurried toward her. Cass assumed with a warm relief they were distant neighbors coming to offer their condolences and to extend offers of friendship.

The first woman said in a near breathless voice, "We heard about your husband's accident and we were wondering what happened to him."

Cass was taken aback. She had expected them to express their sympathies and to offer help. "I beg your pardon?"

The second woman said, "We read about Mr. Grantham's accident in the newspapers and saw a report on the television, but it didn't tell us much. What happened? Why are the police investigating it?"

Cass was outraged by the audacious women who were only interested in obtaining gossip they could share with their friends. "I haven't the slightest idea; you'll have to phone the police for answers to your . . . curious questions. If you'll excuse me, I'm rather busy this morning."

The presumptuous women looked as if she

70

had insulted them by refusing to feed their greedy appetites. Cass half-turned to depart, but was halted when one touched her arm.

"Wait, Mrs. Grantham! Surely you have some idea why they're —"

Her nerves raw, Cass interrupted. "I just lost my husband and my thoughts are elsewhere, so I haven't read the newspapers or watched TV. I don't have any inkling what those foolish reporters have said. Tom had a tragic accident and he's dead; that's all I know, so I can't appease your curiosity. Good-bye."

As she walked away, Cass heard the women whispering but could not make out what they said. She glanced up at a noise and saw a vehicle slow down while its occupants stared and pointed at her and her home as they chatted among themselves. She increased her pace to get out of their sight behind her house. She found Inez waiting for her on the stone patio.

"What's wrong, ma'am? You look upset and pale. You're shaking."

Cass told the housekeeper about the two incidents.

"Just busybodies, ma'am; pay no attention to them."

"Where are this week's newspapers?"

"In the pantry in grocery sacks; I always save and recycle them."

"Please bring them to me so I can learn what everybody else knows."

"Are you sure you want to see them? There's

pictures of Mr. Grantham and his car in them. It's an awful sight. Don't hurt yourself that way."

Cass prayed that no reporter had gotten hold of dirty facts about Tom and printed them. Had their private life been opened up to scrutiny, and did a scandal loom before her? "I have to know what's being said about him and the accident," she told the woman. "If we've become a subject of gossip, I need to know about it."

"As you wish, ma'am. But before you start on them, do you want some herbal tea to settle your nerves or one of those pills from Doctor Hines?"

Merciful heavens, please don't let the news be that bad! "Herbal tea is fine for now, Inez." *And I hope I don't need anything stronger after I read them.*

Before Inez reached the double French doors, Cass changed her mind. "On second thought, bring the newspapers to my bedroom. The sun is too bright for reading out here." *If I freak out, I don't want a witness to report my crazy behavior to Peter.*

After the housekeeper brought the tea and stack of newspapers to her room, Cass thanked her and said, "When you finish your chores, Inez, you can leave, and it was kind of you to come in on Saturday."

"After what you've been through this week, ma'am, I thought you could use the extra help and company. I'm willing to stay until evening."

"That isn't necessary, Inez, but thank you."

"I'll come in tomorrow for a few hours."

Damn it, woman, just shut up and leave! You don't have to cater to me to keep your crummy job! Just get out of here and stop annoying me before I lose my patience and temper! She halted her ugly thoughts. *Be nice, Cass; she might be the only person on the island speaking to you!* "There's no need for you to do that, but thank you for the kind offer. You need your rest, Inez, and I'm sure you have things to do at home. I'll be fine, and I really need some time alone."

"If you change your mind, ma'am, just call me and I'll come over."

"I will, and thank you again for being so kind and helpful."

As Inez left the room, she reminded herself to tell Peter that the medicine she was putting into Cass's food was not working, because the woman was acting as jumpy as a cat with its tail near a rocking chair and her eyes had a strange wild glaze. Perhaps Dr. Hines needed to prescribe something stronger to pacify the agitated woman. Knowing Cass didn't like her and might fire her when her head cleared, Inez felt a power in putting something over on her boss. It would be to her own advantage, Inez thought, if the medicine mellowed and calmed the woman as it was supposed to do. And, as long as Cass was off balance, she needed her

73

help. Yes, the gleeful Inez planned, she must tell Peter that Cass needed more medication, enough to keep the woman too relaxed to think clearly or to cause trouble.

Chapter Four

Cass decided to take a long walk on the beach to calm her tension before subjecting herself to what she might discover in the newspapers. As she waited and watched from her front bedroom window for Inez's departure before leaving on her stroll, she saw several vehicles slow down before her house and stare at it. An occupant in one actually pulled over, leaned out of his window with a camera, and took a picture of it! Whatever the media was saying, it must certainly be titillating.

Cass scanned every newspaper printed since Tom's accident late Sunday night, and she read every detail that concerned her. Monday's paper showed a picture of Tom's crushed convertible, the first time she had seen the mangled red Volante. The driver's side had taken the brunt of the hit before the car rolled over several times and landed upright. The article said he hadn't survived the "high speed crash" after his "brakes failed for an unknown reason" and he'd lost control of the vehicle while not wearing a seat belt. Tuesday's paper featured Tom's picture and a lengthy obituary about the "prominent local resident, businessman, and multi-millionaire." Wednesday's had an article about a police investigation into the cause of the mechanical failure and reason for a missing air bag that possibly could have saved his life.

Faulty brakes . . . Missing airbag . . . Cass reasoned that even if someone had tampered with Tom's car, she wasn't responsible and there was no way she could have disabled his brakes and safety device. She didn't know anything about cars, and she was never allowed near his vehicle; no one was except the serviceman. At least she now knew why the police were suspicious of foul play.

If you were killed, my adulterous husband, I wonder if one of your discarded lovers or one of their sweethearts or spouses did it. I don't dare reveal such filth to "Mutt & Jeff!" If they are good detectives, let them uncover the facts!

Cass returned to her reading. Wednesday's paper also mentioned that Tom was driving home after returning from a trip and dropping off model Gretchen Lowrey at a hotel on the Golden Isles Parkway. It said that after giving a statement to the police about their relationship, Miss Lowrey left town to return home to New York City.

I bet a million dollars you didn't tell them the truth, did you, you sorry piece of trash? I wonder what they would think if they learned you lied and they got a look at that sordid videotape. Would you roll over in your grave, dear Tom, if I tarnished your memory and good name by selling that second video to some sleazy tabloid?

Cass pushed aside thoughts and emotions that were deliciously vindictive, though totally out of character for her. Friday's newspaper had an interview with Peter, but it mostly told about him taking over his father's companies and elaborated on the two local ones where the new boss and owner planned no changes. She was curious about why he hadn't mentioned that article.

Cass wished she knew what this evening's paper contained, but it had not come yet. She was surprised the media hadn't pestered her for interviews, but was glad they hadn't. With luck, Beals and Killian would release a statement soon that the wreck was only a terrible accident and there was a credible explanation for why his airbag was missing. She had suffered more than enough torment since Tom's death and she didn't need to be drawn into a murder investigation, or to become a suspect, which was ridiculous.

Is it, Cassandra? Tom's countless affairs, and that prenuptial agreement, and a hefty inheritance give you plenty of motives. You're a wealthy woman, so you could have hired a hit man. Good grief, Cass, are you nuts? — She stopped her imagination from running hog wild!

She glanced at the statue of Atlas bearing the weight of the world and scoffed that his burden was nothing compared to those on her shoulders. She glared at the Kenya picture of Tom beside the bed until she leapt up and tossed it into the nightstand drawer. Her troubled mind told her to get rid of all reminders of him in *her* home! *But not too soon,* she warned herself, *or I'll antagonize Peter before everything's settled.*

She paced the floor as she imagined ways to evict Tom totally from her mind, as he had expelled himself from her heart with his betrayals. She sipped the herbal tea, though it was cold and flat. So many jumbled thoughts attacked her brain that she wanted to scream at them to give her just a short respite. She couldn't understand why she was so antsy, as she'd never been a high-strung or neurotic person, not even during her worst moments in the past dealing with her parents' deaths and the unfaithful Brad. She turned on classical music and tried to read a magazine to distract herself, but that didn't work.

Finally, Cass carried the Valium bottle into the bathroom. After opening a capsule and dumping half its contents and reclosing it, she took a partial dose of the tranquilizer to take the edge off her anxieties. Perhaps, she reasoned, a nap would help calm her edginess.

When Cass awoke at five o'clock, she was a little sluggish but her tension was almost gone. She freshened up and straightened the bed, then gathered the newspapers, and put them in the pantry downstairs for Inez's recycling collection. She prepared a cup of French Vanilla coffee, this time using decaffeinated. Just as she reached out her hand to turn on a small-screen television to catch the evening news, someone knocked at the back door. She found Peter standing there with a smile on his face and two plastic carrying bags in his hands.

"I hope you haven't eaten; I stopped at Mullet Bay and picked us up shrimp platters with coleslaw and french fries and shrimp fritters."

Cass noticed that he hadn't used his key to let himself inside, and she resisted the temptation to request its return. She smiled and said, "I was just deciding what I was in the mood for, so your timing is perfect. Come in. What can I pour you to drink?"

"A Coke will be fine for me, thanks."

"Did you just get off from work?" she asked. "Is everything okay at the company?"

Peter chuckled. "Yes and yes, thank goodness. The staff and employees appear to be accepting me as boss. Of course, they're used to me running the two local companies for Dad."

When they were both seated at the breakfast-room table, Peter said, "You look and sound better this evening, Cass. How was your day?"

Cass finished chewing the fritter before she answered, "To be honest, Peter, good and bad." *The longer I'm friendly and polite,* Cass reasoned, *the longer I can ward off any problems with him.*

"How so?" he inquired before biting into a

large golden-fried shrimp.

Cass told him about the snoopy ladies and inquisitive drive-bys.

"That's to be expected, Cass, considering who my father was."

"Perhaps, but it's rude and insensitive. I also read all of this week's newspapers. I'm glad reporters haven't been pestering me."

"I was hoping they wouldn't; that's why I granted them an interview yesterday. Did you see it? Did I do all right with it?"

"Yes and yes," she said, using his previous response style, then devouring several french fries and a forkful of coleslaw.

Peter chuckled again as he worked on his meal, then he said, "With luck, this intrusion will be over soon."

"I hope so."

They ate and drank for a few minutes in silence.

"Peter, do you think it's possible that someone murdered Tom?"

"No, Cass. Since my father was a rich man, they have to make sure no foul play was involved. I just wish they would keep their mouths shut to the media until the evidence proves it was only an accident. As soon as that automobile serviceman returns from his trip and he's questioned, they'll get their answers. We just have to ignore the fuss until everything is settled."

"Maybe I should get away for a while. I feel

trapped in my own home. If I go out, I'm sure to confront more pushy people. I don't want to be gawked at, or whispered about, or interrogated by strangers or reporters. I feel alone. No one has called or sent letters to check on me, on us. It's as if we've been stricken off their lists. If the phone didn't have a dial tone, I would think it was out of order or disconnected."

"That's probably because I've been getting calls and mail at the office. I have more sympathy cards to add to the box I left with you. I suppose they know me better and perhaps didn't want to disturb you."

That explanation lifted her spirits a little, but she was still disappointed at being snubbed or overlooked by Tom's friends. "I guess I'm just feeling out of sorts. Maybe a trip would do me good."

"Please, not yet, Cass; we have to take care of business and personal matters first; and I really don't think you should be going away alone in your state of mind. You've suffered a terrible shock and loss, so how you feel is normal, I should think. What you need is rest and quiet to get yourself back together. Relax by the pool, get some sun and fresh air, eat good food, take naps, exercise in Dad's gym, let Inez wait on you hand and foot. I also advise staying out of the public eye to avoid subjecting yourself to snoopy people and reporters; Inez and I can run your errands. And take those Valium if you need them. I'm sure using them for a short time won't harm you. In a few weeks, you'll be your old self again. By then, we'll have all our matters settled. Then, take a vacation. I need you here, Cass."

"You're right, Peter. What good would it do me if I leave before everything's settled? I'd just be taking my problems with me, I wouldn't be able to relax and enjoy myself."

"I know what might relax you tonight; let's take a walk on the beach; it should be deserted by now."

"That's an excellent idea."

"You'd better grab a windbreaker; it's cool and windy out there. I'll clean up the table while you fetch your things."

"Thank you, Peter, for everything you're doing for me," she told him before leaving the room and thinking how odd it sounded and felt to be thanking Tom's son time and time again for being nice.

Cass put on walking shoes and selected a thin jacket to keep her arms warm. She noticed the briefcase and grocery sack, collected them, and returned to the kitchen to initiate her pretense about them.

"I almost forgot about these, Peter; those two detectives brought them over yesterday. They were in Tom's car when . . . he wrecked it."

Peter placed the briefcase on the counter and tried to open it, but it was locked. He dumped out the contents in the sack, then pushed aside the two gifts and said, "These must be for you."

"Probably, but I'll open them later. I don't want to get sad and weepy on you. The novel isn't mine; perhaps Miss Lowrey left it in his car that night," she added when he tried to hand the book to her. From the corner of her eyes, she watched for any revealing reaction to that fact and the model's name, but detected none. She decided that either Peter masked his feelings well or he was in the dark about his father's secrets.

"This camera is totally smashed, so I'll toss it in the trash." He checked the wallet, handed her the cash and pictures, and said he would destroy the credit cards since she had her own. He used the keys to unlock the briefcase and, with it facing him, checked its contents. "Mostly business papers and Dad's calendar. I'll take them with me and go over them later." He removed the house and burglar alarm keys from his father's ring and laid them on the counter, pocketing the others to take to the business offices.

Cass watched Peter lift the lid on the black velvet box and tell her it was another gift for her. She accepted it and closed the box. "Tom was always bringing me things; he was a generous person," she murmured, hating to compliment her betrayer.

"Unless you want it for sentimental reasons, I'll keep the wallet."

"Please do so, Peter."

"You still want me to keep Dad's Rolex and his ruby ring?"

"Yes, they should be passed along to his only son, and there was no need to bury such expensive items with him."

"They'll be special to me. Now, let's get off this sad memory lane and take our walk. Grab your margarita and let's go."

"That's my favorite drink. I'm sure it's been long enough since I took half a Valium this afternoon for it to be safe. Somehow I don't think I'll be needing another one tonight."

"You took half? I don't understand."

Cass explained how she had lowered the dosage. "I just needed a little to calm me so I could take a nap. I got upset by those meddlesome women."

"That was clever, and it obviously worked. Ready to go?"

"More than ready. Which drink is mine?"

"Either one, I mixed them the same."

Cass picked up the plastic cup with a handle nearest to her and tasted it. "Um-m-m, delicious. Thanks."

After locking the door, Cassandra and Peter Grantham strolled side by side down a stone walkway to the end of the lawn and stepped onto sand as soft and white as sifted flour. They passed through an opening in the picket-like privacy fence and skirted low dunes with tall grasses and sea oats wafting in a breeze.

The tide was out, so the water, as clear and blue as the heaven overhead, moved in and out with leisure, and created a wide spanse for walking. The sun had set recently, so the western sky was still ablaze with vibrant colors on the horizon. To their left and right, portions of other nearby islands were in view. Expensive homes lined the beach in both directions. It was a peaceful and lovely setting, a serene time of day.

As they walked halfway between the low dunes and water's edge and sipped their drinks, Cass asked Peter, "Are you planning to stay on Sea Island?"

"I imagine so, at least for a while. Dad's other companies have good managers, so I'll probably run everything from here because the two local companies are the only ones that need me around most of the time. Of course, I'll have to check on them personally from time to time."

Cass swallowed the tart liquid before she surmised aloud, "That means you'll be traveling on occasion like Tom did?"

"Not as much. My way of thinking is, if you hire good men, let them do the work and stay out of their hair. After being married to Dad for almost three years, you know he had a restless spirit. He had to keep busy and moving and have plenty of challenges. Not me; I prefer to stay put as much as possible. I guess you could say, I prefer living and working in a near paradise to battling excessive traffic, smog, and noise in those rat-race towns. What about you, Cass? What are your plans?"

Cass lowered her cup from her lips and clasped it between her hands. "I haven't made any, but I should give it some serious thought within the next few weeks. I love this area and the house, but one might be too large for a woman alone and the other might drive me away if things don't settle down soon. I suppose it's obvious I haven't made any friends here and this might not be the best time to start looking, not with everybody so intrigued by Tom's accident. The way things are now, I wouldn't know who was seeking me out for myself or only as a source for obtaining gossip for their little cliques."

"As soon as the investigation's closed and we become old news, things will change. I had no-ticed you kept to yourself most of the time, even when Dad was away. Strange, but you've never struck me as being a shy person."

"Most of the time I'm not. I tried to get into several activities to help me get to know people, but Tom wanted me to stay home until he had time to check out who and what I had in mind."

"You're a beautiful woman, Cass, he was probably afraid you might meet somebody and he'd lose you before he settled down. He told me he was planning on doing that at the end of this year; it was to be a surprise."

"It certainly is, he never mentioned anything like that to me."

They strolled in silence for a time as dusk slowly crept across the secluded location. Finally, Peter suggested they turn and head back.

As they strolled homeward, Peter talked about the protected species — dolphins and Right whales — that seasonally roamed the coastal waters, and about shrimping. Several times he made jokes, to which Cass laughed in genuine amusement.

"We're making progress, Cass, and I like this relationship better. It's a shame we both stayed so stubborn for so long."

"You're right, Peter, and I'm grateful we've both changed."

Cass suddenly noticed somebody — a telltale light behind the person — watching them from a window. No doubt the snoop wondered why the young widow and her handsome adult stepson were ambling along a romantic beach in approaching moonlight, sipping cocktails, laughing, and chatting less than a week after Tom's death. She certainly did not need that kind of gossip added to the supposed rumors already circulating about her and Tom and the accident. "Let's pick up our pace," she suggested to Peter. "I'm feeling very relaxed, even drowsy."

"Am I so boring I'm putting you to sleep on your feet?" he teased, but knew it was what he had slipped into her drink that was doing the trick. He noted how her pace had slowed, her body had loosened, and her lids were drooping.

"No, the person to our right has binoculars trained on us, but I am feeling most relaxed, thanks to you, this walk, and a delicious drink. I think, after a warm bath, I'll be ready to snooze like a baby tonight."

"Good, because I'm sure you need it." *So do I, to go through Dad's desk in privacy.* "How would you like to go to Sunday brunch at the King and Prince tomorrow about eleven?"

Cass loved the resort restaurant on neighboring St. Simons Island. "Do you think we should?"

"Why not?"

"People might talk, Peter, if they see us out having fun this soon."

"They're going to talk whether we go out or not. We don't have anything to hide about Dad's accident, and we are family, friends."

"You're right again. Eleven o'clock it is."

"A splendid decision, Cass. Here we are, so I'll say good night."

Cass took the cup from his hand, smiled, and told him good night before she entered her home to shower and get to bed while she was still calm.

Following what Cass considered to be a pleasant evening and an improvement in her mood and behavior, things changed the next day, or rather returned to their previous state before deteriorating rapidly.

By Sunday evening, Cass was a bundle of raw nerves. At brunch, either people had actually stared and whispered at the two of them or Cass had imagined they did. Her mood had darkened and her tension had increased by the minute as she tried to force herself to relax and eat and to ignore those around them. Peter had cautioned her to stop frowning and clenching her teeth several times, and she had snapped at him once to leave her alone. Finally, he had suggested they leave before she embarrassed herself.

At home, she had apologized to him and told him she didn't know what had gotten into her, though she was still struggling to gain control of herself, then taken his advice about a Valium and a nap.

Monday was much the same for her, due in part to another visit from the two offensive detectives who came by to see if she had thought of anything helpful. Cass had told them again she didn't know of anyone who had wanted Thomas Grantham dead, but she wasn't sure if she was convincing in view of what she had learned about her deceitful husband following their last visit. If the men had pried into Tom's briefcase and knew she was lying, it wasn't apparent to her. The men probed for information about Tom's net worth and will and beneficiaries, but she told them to ask Tom's lawyer or son about those matters since they had not yet been discussed with her. She told them she would not speak with them again without Simon Johnson being present, and in parting, she demanded they finalize the investigation as soon as possible and stop tormenting her.

Cass was appeased a little when Killian apologized and told her they would comply just as soon as the serviceman was questioned about the missing air bag and faulty brakes.

After their departure, Cass told Inez not to allow the men in the house again, not without Tom's lawyer being present to guide and protect her. Then she took a Tylenol to ease her pounding head.

On Tuesday, Cass awoke with the determination to stay calm and busy that day. After breakfast and against Inez's cautions, she went to a nearby spa with hopes a shampoo and blow dry, facial, manicure, pedicure, and body massage would help her drab appearance and turbulent emotions.

Instead of relaxing her, Cass realized she was getting more and more agitated with each ensuing procedure. The masseuse's fingers seemed to dig into her flesh, pinch her muscles; the facial seemed to irritate her skin; and the beautician seemed to claw her scalp during the shampoo and pull her hair during the light teasing and comb-out. During the manicure and pedicure, it was as if the girl was shoving her pleading cuticles back with a screwdriver and as painfully as she could manage.

Cass knew she was grimacing, moaning, and complaining at each stage of discomfort. At first, each woman tried to chat with her, but she made it very clear she wasn't in a mood to talk. Cass saw each woman frown and try to hurry their specialty, no doubt to get rid of her. She wondered if they were being intentionally rough or if it was all in her wild imagination or her body and nerves were exceptionally sensitive today.

Cass's head throbbed; her face was pale; her cheeks were rosy; her eyes looked strange. She just wanted to escape the torture chamber. She knew her condition was noticeable because three of the women asked if she was all right. Despite her annoyance with them, she thanked them and told them she was fine, just getting over a twenty-four-hour virus that had weakened her.

She paid her bill, noticed she wasn't asked if she wanted to make another appointment, and rushed to her cashmere-beige BMW. She rested her sweaty forehead on the steering wheel for a few minutes and tried to wish away her trembling. She was certain those women at the spa were gossiping about her and concluding she was having a nervous breakdown. *Perhaps I am,* Cass silently accepted the possibility. *I'm cer-*

tainly feeling and acting crazy these days! All she wanted to do was lock herself in her bedroom, take a Valium, and go to sleep until she felt better.

Cass took her own advice about the tranquilizer and rest, but they worked only until the next morning.

On Wednesday, Dr. David Hines was called over by Peter during his lunch break. Cass's stepson had been summoned home by a worried Inez.

Following an examination and blood withdrawal with the housekeeper present, Peter joined them to hear the doctor's report.

Cass listened to the stocky middle-aged physician as he diagnosed her condition as a major depression, delayed shock, severe exhaustion, and either a panic or anxiety disorder. He prescribed several medications, a well-balanced diet, and ample bed rest. "I really don't want to take drugs day and night," she told Doctor Hines. "Won't bed rest be sufficient? Or a vacation?" She saw the gray-haired man shake his head.

"If you want to get well, Mrs. Grantham, you'll have to follow my advice. This isn't just a simple case of sadness and fatigue we're talking about; you have physical and emotional problems causing your symptoms. Your blood pressure is elevated, your pulse is rapid, and your heartbeat's a little irregular. By your own admission, you're having headaches, dizziness, weakness, flushing, mood swings, low energy, trouble sleeping, and panic attacks. If you go away, you'll only be taking your medical problems with you, and they'll get worse. I would suggest hospitalization, if I weren't sure you would resist going. If you take your medications, remain in bed as much as possible, and let Miss Doughtery take care of you and the house, you'll be well by . . . at the latest, mid-April. If you refuse to follow my orders, you can wind up with severe complications that won't leave you any choice except an extended hospital stay."

"I feel ridiculous, Doctor Hines. I'm not the first woman to lose her husband, and I've never become a nervous wreck in the past when dealing with adversity."

"People have different ways of dealing with grief, Mrs. Grantham, and it's obvious your body is telling you something is amiss. If I'm wrong, which I can assure you I'm not, the results of this blood test will tell me."

"What will you be testing for, Doctor Hines?" she asked, worried that Tom might have given her a sexually transmitted disease, or worse . . .

"I'll run a wide-screen check so I won't miss anything. Sometimes chemicals or hormones run amuck at stressful times like this. I also want to make sure your potassium, glucose, hemoglobin, and iron levels are okay. It wouldn't hurt for you to take a multi-vitamin and drink extra fruit juice. I want you off of stimulants: no coffee, tea, colas, or chocolate."

"Listen to him, Cass, and do as he says," Peter advised. "David Hines is one of the best doctors in town."

"But he wants me to take a lot of medication, Peter."

"If you had the flu or some other illness, you'd take medicine. Right?"

"Yes, but this is different," she protested. "It's partially emotional and that scares me," she admitted to Peter. Yet, she didn't want to get worse, which appeared to be the direction in which she was heading. Even so, she hated for potent drugs to be her salvation.

"You aren't the first person to need help in that area Cass. Before you know it, you'll be your old self again."

Cass pulled her gaze from Peter to focus it on Hines. "Are you positive this is the only line of treatment for my problem?"

The physician cupped his chin with one hand and tapped his lips with his forefinger as he pretended to think. He knew he had to do as Peter demanded or the younger man could destroy his reputation, career, and life. Besides, he told himself, he wouldn't be drugging the woman for long and wouldn't be doing any permanent damage to her, as Peter only wanted her incapacitated for a few weeks, not killed or made into an addict. But what worried him as much as Peter carrying out his blackmail threat was the fact he had to provide extra drugs from samples he received from pharmaceutical companies to go along with store-bought prescriptions, which would tie him more tightly to this illegal deed if it were exposed. He didn't know how Peter had learned about his sexual practices and preferences because he had guarded that secret well over the years; so had Tom.

Hines took a deep breath and said, "Yes, Mrs. Grantham, this is what you need. If you don't do as I say, things will only get worse for you. I promise you, none of the drugs I've prescribed are addictive in these dosages or for short-term use, if that's what's worrying you. Besides, I'm going to keep a close watch on you. I'll check on you at least once or twice a week. However, I would advise against having other visitors; we don't want anybody annoying and upsetting you and interfering with your treatment. In my opinion, you should confine yourself to the house and let Mrs. Doughtery and Peter tell everyone you're away on a trip. Besides, the medication will relax you to the point you shouldn't be driving, shopping, or going out alone; and you don't want people seeing you — shall we say? — not at your best."

Cass saw him smile as if he thought that statement was amusing, which it wasn't to her. She didn't like this creepy man, but he was Peter's physician and had been Tom's, and he did have plenty of so-called upper-class people as patients. She wished Dr. Burkman was treating her, but she didn't want Jason to learn she had a mental disorder or to see her in this awful state. With reluctance, she nodded concurrence.

Hines continued, "You'll also want to be careful you don't take a fall while you're dizzy and weak because that's how you'll feel for a while from the medication, and I advise you to take extra caution in the bathtub. Oh, yes, if those detectives come here again, Mrs. Doughtery will refer them to me and I'll tell them you can't be harassed because you're under medical treatment. Besides, that nonsense should be cleared up this week. Just lie around and nap, watch television, read, and let Mrs. Doughtery wait on you. I'll give her my instructions before I leave; she'll be in charge of giving you your medicine and keeping a schedule chart. You may be forgetful and might take too much or skip doses."

"I promise to take good care of you, ma'am," the housekeeper said.

"We both will," Peter added.

Cass realized that Hines must have questioned Inez and Peter about mood swings and other strange symptoms. "Thank you," she told them and forced out a smile for each person.

"Now, before I leave, I want to give you a shot to get the medication into you as quickly as possible. Very soon, Mrs. Grantham, you'll be fine again."

Cass extended her arm and allowed the injection. Getting well was what she wanted more than anything so she could pick up the pieces of her life and make a fresh start. Within minutes, she felt her head spin and her lids get heavy, and she surrendered to the mellow sensations tugging at her like gentle waves at low tide.

Peter looked at Inez. "Would you please brew some coffee so we can talk at the breakfast table? Doctor Hines and I will be down soon."

Inez nodded and left the two men standing near the woman's bed.

Hines glanced at the closed bedroom door, then at Peter. "I've done what you said, so don't forget your promise of silence."

"As long as you keep your part of our bargain, my lips are sealed."

"Don't worry, she'll be under your control as long as she's given the medication. Just make sure nothing happens to her."

Peter caught the man's meaning and smiled. "I certainly don't want another suspicious death on my hands, so we'll all be careful with those drugs. All I need is for her to stay out of my hair for a few weeks, a month at most. Then I don't care where she goes or what she does."

After the men left and spoke with Inez downstairs, Hines departed.

Peter told the housekeeper, "Mrs. Grantham needs watching and tending day and night and that will be a lot of extra work for you, so you'll get that large raise and bonus that I mentioned for taking care of her. Cass should sleep most of the time, but I can sit with her while you grocery shop or run personal errands. Are you sure you don't mind moving into one of the guest rooms for a while? If so, I can hire a nurse."

"It's no bother, Mr. Grantham, and your payment is most generous."

"Excellent. If there's an emergency or you need me to sit with her, just page me; you have my number. Remember, Inez, don't let those detectives in to see her, and tell anyone else she's out of town until the end of April. I'll do the same thing. We can't let anybody or anything upset Cass or she could have a complete nervous breakdown."

"I understand and I'll follow your orders."

Over two weeks passed in a hazy blur for Cass. At times, she was vaguely aware of eating, bathing, sitting in a nearby chair for sheets to be changed, hearing the television or music or the vacuum cleaner running, and taking her medication. A few times, she knew Peter was in the room with her and was talking about Tom's will and various businesses, but she was too dazed to grasp much of what he said or to care whether she did or didn't understand and agree. With his help, she managed to sign papers he needed, including a power of attorney for him to handle joint business matters, with Dr. Hines and Inez witnessing her signatures. If anyone phoned or came by to visit her, she was unaware of it.

She did hear Peter say that the mechanic had returned to town and had told the two detectives that Tom had hired someone to illegally remove the air bag because he didn't want it popping out accidentally during a fender-bender and injuring him as he'd heard had happened to others. Even so, the investigation had not been closed to that date.

She also heard Inez tell her that inquisitive people were still riding by, and staring at the house, and a few were taking pictures. She also heard the woman say something that sounded like, "Thank goodness Mr. Grantham's not in the newspapers or being talked about on TV anymore. Folks will forget about this mess soon. You just take it easy, ma'am, and get well."

On Thursday afternoon, March twenty-eighth, Peter Grantham left for Los Angeles on business, confident all matters were under his control.

On Friday morning while Cass was sleeping, Inez went to Peter's residence behind the main house to do a thorough cleaning.

Jason Burkman saw the housekeeper, carrying cleaning supplies in a handled container, enter the large guesthouse and assumed she would be occupied for a while. From his vantage point at the edge of the sprawling home and concealed from a neighbor's view by dense bushes, he had been watching and waiting for a chance to sneak inside to see if Cassandra was there and if she was all right. He had noticed David Hines's automobile in the driveway several times during the past few weeks, and he had been in a local drugstore yesterday morning when the housekeeper stopped in to pick up prescriptions for Cassandra. If she was out of town as he'd been told when he tried to visit her again, that incident didn't make sense to him. Nor could he understand why Cassandra would still be refusing to see or speak with him. Besides, if there was anybody he mistrusted and disliked almost as much as he did Peter Grantham, it was David Hines. Suspecting what he did about the snooty physician, he couldn't bear the thought of David's hands being on her. Somehow he had a gut feeling something was wrong and he felt compelled to check out his hunch.

Chapter Five

Jason had intended to peer in windows to see if he could catch a glimpse of Cassandra Grantham and convince her to see him, but the housekeeper's departure gave him the perfect opportunity to make contact without any interference. He crept toward the back door, but it was locked. He checked the French doors to the patio to find one partially opened, perhaps to let in fresh air. The woman must have forgotten about it.

Jason sneaked inside the house and listened for a minute, but heard nothing. He made his way to the kitchen and glanced inside; no one was there, but he noticed the medicine bottles and a tablet and pencil on the counter. He went upstairs and checked each room he passed until he located the master bedroom, where he saw Cass sleeping.

Jason didn't know how much time he had, so he rushed to her side and tried to awaken her. "Cass . . . Cassandra, it's Jason Burkman. Can you hear me? Can you open your eyes? Cass, wake up."

He waited for a minute, then tried again, shaking her shoulders this time.

Cass heard the masculine voice calling to her from far away and Jason's image filled her dreamy mind. She struggled to rouse herself and look at him, but she was too tired and weak.

"Cass, can you hear me?" Jason asked, shaking her again, that time more firmly.

Cass moaned and moved, but couldn't obey his summonings.

"Open your eyes! I have to talk to you."

Cass sighed, grasped his hand, and snuggled it to her cheek as she rolled to her side.

Jason eyed the beautiful woman. Her long hair was mussed and she wasn't wearing makeup, but she was captivating nonetheless. He sat down and gazed at her. His fingers pushed aside strayed locks of dark-brown with hints of a lighter shade. He let them stroke her cheek, fulfilling a long-denied desire to touch her. Her skin was as smooth as glass and as soft as cotton. He allowed them to wander over her full lips and wished he could steal a kiss. He drifted them down the entreating column of her neck and over a creamy-colored bare shoulder. He was warmed by the way she nestled his other hand against her flesh. He wanted to pull her into his arms and embrace her. He wanted to hold her and comfort her. He hated seeing the once-vibrant woman in this sorry condition.

Cassandra Grantham had made him feel again, desire again, after his bitter divorce which came less than fours years after losing his first and beloved wife to breast cancer. She had made him smile and made him realize he could love again. The perfect woman for him had entered his lonely world last October, but she had been taken; now, here she lay in a terrible state, though freed from the marital obstacle that had separated them.

Maybe, Jason admitted, it was selfish and greedy of him to pursue Cass, so soon after her husband's death; yet, he justified his actions because he didn't want to risk losing her before he had a chance to win her. Despite his desire for her, he would behave as nothing more than a friend until a proper mourning period passed and she was ready to love again. Until that day arrived, he didn't want her to shut herself away from the world and suffer alone, or to move out of his reach before she had healed enough to be approachable. He —

Jason pulled away his hands and straightened to listen. Yes, he had heard something; the housekeeper was coming. He knew Peter was gone because he had been at the airport picking up a package when the bastard left in his company's private jet. He quickly rolled under the bed and out of sight. From beneath the almost floor-length coverlet, he watched the woman's feet approach the bed, stay there for a minute, then leave. It was obvious she had returned to check on Cass and probably would do so again soon. After he heard the back door close, he left his hiding place and peered out-side, watching Inez until she reentered Peter's residence.

He rushed downstairs and checked the pre-scriptions and schedule which he had noticed earlier. She was on heavy doses of tranquilizers and antidepressants, enough to keep her dazed at most times to near unconsciousness. It hadn't been long since her last dose, which meant she was too affected by it for him to get through to her, but he would give it another try. He didn't have any proof she was being drugged against her will or overdrugged with-out her knowledge, but a gut feeling told him to pursue the matter, especially since she was being secluded and Peter Grantham was in-volved. He took a pill from each container and stuffed them into his pants pocket, noting that two bottles were simply marked with an *A* and a *B*. He would check them out later in his *Physician's Desk Reference*.

Jason hurried to Cass's room and failed again to awaken her. If only he could speak with her and find out if she was being treated willingly, but that was impossible. He knew he couldn't hang around much longer and risk being dis-covered before he had proof of wrongdoing, which an analysis of the pills should tell him. If nothing was wrong, he could get into a lot of trouble for being there on the sly.

Jason withdrew a small pad and pen from his pocket and wrote a message to Cass. He went into the bathroom and opened several drawers until he located the object he needed and placed his note there, praying she would find it soon and with a clear enough head to grasp his warning. Somehow he knew, even if he was mistaken about her being mistreated, she would not tell anyone about his secret visit.

He returned to the bed and gazed down at Cass, longing for her to open those beautiful chocolate-brown eyes and look at him, smile at him, speak with him. He leaned over and kissed her soft lips, then sneaked from the house to where he had left his BMW down the street. He headed for his office to see what he could discover.

At six o'clock, Inez helped Cass take a quick bath and slip into a fresh satin nightgown. Afterward, she took a seat in a moiré-covered vanity chair while the woman continued her grooming.

"Before your next medicine is due at seven, let's get you fed," Inez suggested. "I fixed a nice chicken pot pie from scratch, and cut it up in small pieces to make it easier for you to eat. Would you like some milk or juice with it?"

"Either is fine, Inez. Thank you."

"Now, let me brush your hair for you. That should feel — There's the phone. Are you strong enough to sit here while I go answer it?"

"I'll be fine. I won't move a muscle. I doubt I could."

After Inez left to go down the hall to answer the phone in another room, since Cass's bedside one had been removed to prevent disturbing her, Cass opened the drawer to fetch her brush. Mercy, she hated being so weak and helpless. She couldn't even bathe herself! And sometimes, she even required help eating! Darn it, she wasn't a baby or an invalid! Today she was going to brush her own hair for a change.

Cass's gaze widened as she extracted a small note from the bristles of the brush, and read a shocking message. Her mind was still fuzzy, but not enough for her to realize she had to keep it a secret. She was glad she had found it at the time of day her mind was at its clearest. Quickly, she concealed the paper beneath a box of perfumed powder. She returned the brush and closed the drawer. It hadn't been a dream, she told herself; Jason Burkman had been in her —

"I'm back. Are you all right, ma'am?"

"Doing the best I can, Inez. Who was on the phone?"

"It was Mr. Peter, calling to check on you. I told him not to worry."

"Thank you. Have any visitors come by to see me?"

"No, ma'am. Remember, everybody thinks you're away on a trip?"

"Oh, yes. It's just that my mind gets so cloudy on those pills."

"I know, ma'am, but you won't have to take them much longer. Now, let's get your hair done and get you back into bed so you can eat."

After Inez left the room with her tray, Cass removed the pills from her mouth, slipped from the bed, and almost staggered into the bathroom. She couldn't flush them, as Inez would hear the toilet running, so she dropped them down the shower drain. She withdrew Jason's note and read it again, then concealed it in the pocket of a pair of pants in her closet.

Back in bed, Cass thought about the physician who somehow had sneaked into her house and hidden a note for her that told her not to take any more medication, to get her head cleared, and to call him when it was.

Cass wondered how he had carried out his stealthy visit and why. No matter, she was ready and eager to return to the land of the living. This was the clearest her mind had been since she began treatment. Other than feeling weak, she experienced no other symptoms. It was obvious that Dr. Hines's diagnosis was right and his suggested treatment had worked. She hoped she wouldn't have a relapse of her condition after she got all of the medication out of her system.

She closed her eyes, summoned Jason's image, smiled, and drifted off to sleep thinking about him and his daring behavior.

When Inez entered her room at eleven and roused her, once more Cass pretended to take the medication in a drowsy state. As soon as the woman left, she disposed of the capsule in the same manner as earlier.

She curled to her side, took a deep breath, and closed her eyes. She didn't want to think about any disturbing issues tonight and risk upsetting herself. She wanted to remain calm and relaxed while she waited for her head to clear before she pondered serious matters. Besides, she couldn't recall the details Peter had mentioned recently about Tom's will and businesses. Despite her reluctance, persistent thoughts invaded her troubled mind.

Thomas Grantham. . . . He had hurt, humiliated, embittered, angered, and betrayed her, just as Brad had done years ago. She didn't know why her husbands had cheated on her or why she hadn't been enough for them or why her spouses had turned out to be such terrible choices.

Nor did she have any idea at this point what she was going to do with any troubles with Peter. She didn't want to think about firing Inez, which would seem heartless of her after the woman had taken such good care of her during her . . . Had it been a mild nervous breakdown? Had the grim truth about Tom almost driven her over the brink of madness? Surely not. Surely it was only a mild case of depression and delayed shock whose symptoms had been intensified by anxieties, exhaustion, and anger. She had given herself time to calm down and become strong again so she should be fine very soon.

She didn't want to think about moving from this house and Sea Island to get rid of all reminders of Tom and their life of deception. She didn't want to think about seeing a gynecologist soon to make certain she was disease-free. The sorry bastard had done more than risk giving her a STD; with AIDS running loose, he had endangered her life! Years ago, he had charmed and deluded her, had married her to supply him with a facade of respectability while he went on his merry way and did as he pleased on the sly. She never should have allowed him to manipulate and dominate her. She never should have sacrificed her hard-won independence and friends to please him; she had to recover both and her self-respect. She admitted she was partly to blame for what happened to her; without her permission Tom couldn't have taken over her life or betrayed her for so long and so wickedly.

Life was filled with choices; and she had made some sorry and costly ones in the last sixteen years. Now, another man was knocking at her emotion's door. And she didn't know this one well enough to judge his character and motives. It seemed as if she was always falling in love with a stranger.

Dr. Jason Burkman . . . They had never dated or kissed or touched. Yes, he was irresistibly virile and attractive. Yes, he had many superb traits. Yes, he stirred her emotions, her passions, but she had held them in check. Why, she mused, was he trying to . . . sneak into her life and confuse her? What did he want from her?

They had met last October at the Ritz Theater while she was attending a play during one of Tom's many absences. They had sat next to each other that night and chatted genially. She had subsequently seen and spoken to Jason at the club. Jason had been her tennis partner twice, before Tom asked her to stop practicing so she wouldn't get hurt while he was away. Then she had encountered Jason at the local historical society meeting she had attended several times in hopes of joining and learning more about the area into which they had moved; Tom also had squashed that activity.

She had seen Jason professionally on three occasions: when she sprained her wrist, contracted an ear infection after swimming, and when she dropped hot grease on her foot. After that last incident, Tom almost had ordered her to stay out of the kitchen before she was injured again. Why she allowed Tom to rule her life so much, she couldn't say now.

Cass shoved Tom from her mind and resummoned Jason. He had told her his first wife had died years ago from breast cancer. She also knew he had divorced his second wife a little over a year ago; the club's tennis pro had told her that. She knew he had grown children — twins, a boy and a girl — both living elsewhere, and that the daughter had twin sons.

Cass longed to have at least one child of her own, but there were reasons during both of her past marriages why she didn't. Now, the only way she could bear a child was to find another man who wanted children and marry him. At thirty-five, had she, Cass fretted, waited too late for that blessing? She would be even older before she could find another man, the right man, and make a new beginning. Could Jason —

Don't even think about him in that way! She chastised herself. *Men with grown children rarely want to start new families. Besides, I hardly know him. He seems wonderful; he's handsome; he's desirable; he's enjoyable company; he seems to like me. But he could have a hidden dark side like Brad and Tom possessed. Leave me alone, you two snakes in the grass!* her mind shouted.

Cass realized she was getting tense and almost wished she had taken the tranquilizer or sedative. *You don't need drugs, Cass; you have to get off of them completely and deal with your problems in the right way. Go to sleep,* she told herself, and soon obeyed that order.

As Cass was having breakfast, Inez smiled

and told her, "Doctor Hines phoned earlier and said not to give you your medication this morning because he's coming over to examine you and he wants you clear-headed."

Cass was surprised and pleased to hear that news.

After Hines arrived, he checked Cass's pulse, listened to her heart with his stethoscope, took her blood pressure, looked into her eyes, asked her and Inez questions, and then smiled and nodded.

"You're doing much better, Mrs. Grantham; all of your readings are almost normal. In fact, you're doing so well I'm going to reduce your medication to a minimum. It's time for you to start getting up and around a few times every day; by that, I mean doing a little exercise like walking around in the house to get back your strength. I still want you to take it easy for another week or two; no going out or overexerting yourself. And don't talk to anybody who might upset you. If you continue to progress, I'll keep increasing your activities and lowering your dosages until we can stop them completely and you can return to a normal life."

"That sounds wonderful, Doctor Hines, thank you. I was getting tired of being confined to bed and staying dopey all the time."

"I'm sure this has been difficult and scary for you, but the treatments have worked, am I not right?"

"I can't argue with how I feel, which is much better."

"Let me know if you experience any headaches, nervousness, panic attacks, loss of energy or appetite, mood swings, or depression."

"I will."

"Don't worry, sir, I'll keep taking good care of her," Inez said.

"You have a good woman working for you, Mrs. Grantham; she's done better than any private nurse could have."

Inez smiled and thanked him, though she greatly disliked him.

"He's right, Inez, and I'm most grateful for all you've done for me."

"Thank you, ma'am. Is there anything else I need to do, sir?"

"We'll go downstairs and I'll set up a new treatment schedule. Just keep feeding her well and giving her vitamins and her medication and don't let her do too much when she's out of bed. She'll still be weak and wobbly for a while and we don't want her falling and injuring herself. Good-bye, Mrs. Grantham; I'll check on you again Tuesday."

After the two left her room, Cass snuggled into the bed and smiled, pleased with her progress and steady recovery. The change in her treatment was just what she needed to carry out her plan.

Before he left the house, Hines collected the

old charts and the two unmarked bottles. He told Inez to begin a new chart with the changes he had made, then departed, leaving only the store-bought prescriptions in Inez's possession. If Peter got angry with him for allowing the woman to regain her senses, Hines mused, he would explain that she couldn't stay on those medications for more than a few weeks without them becoming addictive and noticeable to others and to Cassandra. He had already stuck his neck out far enough, too far, for that despicable blackmailer!

When Inez went to the mailbox later, Cass phoned Jason Burkman. She asked him to come by to see her at two o'clock while Inez was out running errands for her, then she quickly returned to her room and leapt into bed.

She could hardly believe the date on the newspaper, yesterday's, that Inez had brought her to read: Saturday, March twenty-ninth! She had lost almost eighteen days of her life! Despite what Hines had told her about lowering her dosages, she pretended to take the anti-depressant and the tranquilizer when Inez brought them to her. The two capsules had joined the others down the shower drain.

Her head was unfogging more by the hour, and she needed it clear for what she had in mind to do this afternoon. Of course, she had to get Inez to agree to her request and without arousing the woman's suspicions. Most importantly, it depended upon Jason arriving at their pre-planned time.

At one-forty-five, Cass summoned Inez and told her, "I want you to go to the grocery store and pick me up some new magazines and some sherbet and ginger ale. I'm in the mood to read and to have a float."

"But I shouldn't leave you alone, ma'am."

"I'm doing fine today, Inez, and I'll rest while you're gone. I won't answer the phone or the door. I'll stay in bed and watch TV or nap."

"But, ma'am, you might need me."

"Please, Inez, magazines and a float are what I need. Do you have any money left in the household cash box?"

"Yes, ma'am, plenty. I'll go, but I'll return as soon as I can."

With obvious reluctance, the housekeeper left to run the errand.

Cass watched from the window until Inez's car was out of sight. Her gaze widened as she saw Jason arrive from the other direction and pull into her driveway; since she lived on the main road and the only entrance to the small island was in the direction Inez had taken, Cass assumed he had been waiting down the street for the housekeeper to leave.

She felt an odd surge of excitement as she checked her satin robe to be sure it was fastened and went to greet Jason at the front door.

She smiled and said, "Hello, Doctor Burkman; it's good to see you again. Please come in."

Jason was surprised by her sunny smile and genial greeting, but mostly by her clear eyes and poise. Today, she was the vital woman he had seen on many past occasions, who had stirred his passions and warmed his heart, not the sedated female he had viewed yesterday. "I'm glad you called because I've been worried about you since your husband's death. I've tried to reach you several times and stopped by once to see you to extend my condolences. I hope you got my messages."

Cass stared at him for a minute in confusion. "I'm afraid I didn't, but I'll check into the curious matter. I haven't been well since Tom died, so Inez and Peter have been protecting me from outside annoyances. I don't mean you're one," she hurriedly added. "Actually, I'm glad to see you; I was beginning to wonder if everyone had forgotten I was alive because I've received close to no calls, mail, or visitors since Tom's accident. I suppose most people just don't know what to say or do. Also, I don't know many people here on the island."

"Why is that?" Jason asked as he followed her into the house.

"Since we moved here, Tom was away on business much of the time, and our closest neighbors aren't permanent residents. It's hard to socialize as a single woman in a couple's world. Also, Tom preferred to be around when

I met people or took on new activities."

In other words, he liked to keep you secluded and all to himself. Since you're so beautiful and desirable, I can understand his fear of losing you. "As a single man and a local, I know what you mean; it's hard to make friends in an area like this. We're neighbors, because I live toward the end of this street, so perhaps we can help each other out in the future when one of us needs a companion for dinner, a play, or tennis."

"That would be a nice arrangement at the proper time." Cass noticed how appealing he looked in his casual pants and golf shirt whose blue shade enhanced the color of his sapphire eyes and tan. His hair was a mingling of light and dark blond, straight, full, and combed back from his arresting face. When he smiled, he revealed snowy white teeth and engaging laugh lines around a full mouth. She realized she was almost staring at him. She laughed away her embarrassment and said, "Where are my manners today? Have a seat. Would you like a cup of coffee or a cold drink?"

Jason could hardly take his eyes from her lovely face. Her voice and laughter were like tantalizing treats to his hungry ears; the sight of her, like delicious food to his starving senses. As he followed her into the living room, he tried to ignore how the floral satin robe flowed over her shapely figure or how her brown hair tumbled down her back or how she was wearing a smidgen of flattering cosmetics and a fragrant scent. "No, thanks. I'm relieved to see you looking and sounding so much better; you had me worried."

Cass wanted to use their remaining privacy to solve a mystery. "Why did you sneak in to see me?" she asked.

"As your doctor and friend, I was concerned about you when I couldn't get through to you to check on you. Besides, I thought it was a little odd for Inez to be picking up prescriptions for you at the drugstore on Thursday if you were out of town. I was at the store when she came in that day. And, since I live down the street, I've seen Doctor Hines visit you several times. I assumed you were having a hard time dealing with your recent tragedy and might need a friend. If I'm wrong and being intrusive, please tell me."

"You aren't, and I'm glad you came. I was just surprised by your way of contacting me."

Jason grinned. "It was extreme, but it was the only way to reach you."

"Inez and Peter have been screening my calls and visitors to protect me. Since the police have been investigating Tom's accident, people are curious and nosy." She told Jason about those meddlesome episodes. "It made me nervous and leery of people and provoked me to seclude myself for a while. It's obvious you couldn't awaken me, so I guess that alarmed you."

Jason nodded, then explained how he got

inside without being seen. "I saw the medication on the kitchen counter and I couldn't arouse you to talk with me, so I knew you were out cold. Frankly, I was afraid someone else might find my note, but I took the risk."

"I'm glad you did. After I found your message in my brush, I followed your suggestions. Besides, I was tired of being confined to bed and staying doped up all the time. I just had to get my head clear enough to do something about my condition."

"I can see you did and I'm glad. That's some heavy medication you're on, Cass. I have to say I don't agree with how he's treating you, unless there's something I don't know or understand about your medical problem."

Cass told him about the reduction in her medication and revealed all that Hines had told her. "I guess you could say I sort of fell apart under the stress and from exhaustion and shock. Those busybodies and detectives also took a toll on me. If you keep up with local news, you know the police are investigating Tom's accident; they find a few things about it suspicious and they've questioned me twice, being rude and insensitive both times. They made distressing insinuations about him and his death, and they upset me terribly. I didn't have any family to turn to and I haven't seen my old friends in years and I'm a near stranger here, so I felt alone and scared. But I'm better now."

Jason had heard insinuations about the accident, but he was astonished to learn the police were interrogating Cass as if she were a suspect in Tom's possible . . . murder. That explained to him why she had gotten into such a nervous state. "I'm sorry you've been having such a tough time, Cass, and I hope I can be of help in some way."

"You are helping, just by being here and being concerned about me. Most of the people I've known and socialized with during the last two and a half years since I married Tom were his friends and associates, and they've dropped by the wayside. I suppose that's normal since they didn't really know me except as his wife and I wasn't a part of their social circle before we married. I was just a small-town country girl."

"So was I, so we have that in common." He chuckled. "I mean, I was from the country near a small town. What about . . . your stepson? How are things with him, if I'm not being too nosy?"

"Peter has been kind, considerate, helpful." *For a change.*

Jason noticed an odd tone to her voice, as if she weren't being totally forthright. "If you don't mind, Cass, I'd like to see your prescriptions and examine you."

"The medicines are in the kitchen, so follow me."

Jason was annoyed with himself for losing the

120

pills and capsules he had taken from those bottles; they had fallen through a hole in his pants pocket! Then, after leaving her yesterday he'd been called in on an emergency and had gone to bed late and exhausted. He hadn't discovered the pills were missing until this morning. He had planned to force his way past the housekeeper this afternoon if he hadn't heard from Cass by then. He hadn't been able to save his first wife during her battle with cancer but he was resolved to save Cassandra.

While Cass observed him, Jason lifted each bottle and read the label, then the dispensing schedule. He not only found the changes she had mentioned, but also noticed the unmarked bottles and old chart were gone, which told him Hines had removed them this morning. If something had been wrong, he had no proof; it would be his word against those of Hines, Peter, and the housekeeper. If he questioned them or made a fuss about the strange matter, it would seem as if he had a reason to lie to obtain revenge on Peter. Also, if he asked about the other pills and chart, they would know he had sneaked into the house; and Peter might cause him trouble. At least Hines had lowered her dosages and stopped giving her those mystery pills. He would hold silent about his suspicions for now, but he would still keep a close eye on Cass and her progress.

There was something about Jason's expressions and mood that Cass found intriguing. "Well?"

Jason locked his gaze with hers. "I'd like to take over your case, unless you prefer to remain as Hines's patient."

Chapter Six

Cass studied him for a moment, then asked, "Why? What's wrong?"

"You've been a patient of mine — and I hope, a friend — since your move here, so I think I know you and your medical history better than Hines does. I realize he's decreased your medication and you were suffering from depression and anxiety, but I don't feel it was bad enough to be giving you those high dosages. When I came over yesterday, Cass, you were almost out cold; I don't think you needed to be sedated to that extreme point or ordered to complete bedrest for weeks. A milder dose and with more time between pills should have been sufficient to calm your nerves while you adjusted to your loss."

"Are you saying Doctor Hines is incompetent?"

"It's just that I don't believe your temporary condition warranted so many pills. You needed to be aware enough of reality to grieve, to cry, to be angry at fate, and to think about the past and future. Otherwise, when the drugs are withdrawn and your head clears, you still have the same problems and your feelings are bottled up. Medication should *assist* emotional recovery, not halt or delay it or put you in the same situation when you stop taking it. Or worse, make you dependent upon drugs for relief."

"Doctor Hines told me none of them were addictive. Did he lie?"

"Some of them can be abused if they're taken too long or without proper supervision. In my opinion, a housekeeper isn't qualified to judge that for him. If he was going to treat you with maximum doses, he should have brought in a nurse to dispense the medication and watch you for any adverse reactions. I know Tofranil, the antidepressant he gave you, shouldn't be given for more than a few days to a couple of weeks and Librium, the tranquilizer, should be limited to three weeks. Were you experiencing panic attacks and anxiety?"

"I suppose so; I did act a little crazy on a few occasions." She related the alarming episodes and her symptoms to him. "Maybe what you're telling me about those drugs is why he reduced them today."

"If you agree, I'd like to wean you off of everything this week and see how you respond. In fact, I'd like to call in a private nurse to take care of you for a week or so. I want her to handle your medication, keep a check on your vital signs and reactions, prepare your meals and oversee your diet, and get you to exercising daily to regain your strength. I can see you're weak. Isn't that right?"

"You're very perceptive, Doctor. I am feeling weak and shaky, but not nervous or irritable. That's a good sign I'm not having a relapse, right?"

Jason smiled at her. "Don't worry about a relapse, Cass, I won't allow that to happen to you. How many pills have you skipped taking?"

"Three doses; sometimes I'm given one capsule or tablet and other times, several. I skipped the seven and eleven doses last night, and Hines phoned and delayed this morning's schedule until he examined me. But I didn't take anything after he left because I was planning to sneak you in this afternoon. If he suspected I wasn't taking them, he didn't let on to me. The first thing he gave me on the thirteenth was an injection; I remember little after it until last night. I've had short periods of mild alertness at bath and feeding times; other than that, I've stayed pretty crocked."

"We need to get you back on a small dosage because sudden withdrawal isn't good for you. I just told you to stop long enough to clear your head so we could talk. I promise, you won't be crocked on the amount I'll prescribe, just relaxed. Now let's get you into bed so I can examine you and then you can rest."

"Follow me," she told him once more, then led him upstairs.

Cass removed her robe and got into bed. She watched him set his black leather bag on the foot of it, open the satchel, and remove several instruments. He took her temperature, pulse rate, and blood pressure, then recorded those numbers on a pad. She wondered if the heat she was experiencing from his contact and close proximity registered on the thermometer. When he looked at the color of her finger and toenails to check her circulation, she liked the feel of his strong hands on her own hands and her feet. He checked her elbow and knee reflexes with a rubber-headed mallet, his light grasp on her wrist and ankle arousing. He looked into her eyes and ears and mouth with a slender silver object which brought his face close to her, close enough that she could smell his heady cologne and feel his spearmint-scented breath on her skin. He listened to her heart, then he listened from behind her, asking her to take occasional deep breaths. As he did his tasks, his touch was gentle, his behavior, professional, and his gaze, comforting. Yet, being close to him, in only a nightgown and panties, and feeling his hands on her flesh, was stimulating.

Cass jumped suddenly from the provocative pose as a grating voice shouted at him from the doorway.

"What are you doing to Mrs. Grantham? How did you get in here? Get out this minute and leave her alone or I'll call the police!"

"Calm down, Inez. This is Jason Burkman, my personal physician. I asked him to check me over, and I let him inside."

"You told me you wouldn't answer the phone or door!"

Cass was shocked by the woman's rude and bold behavior. "Calm down, Inez," she ordered in a stern voice, narrowing her gaze in warning. "This is my home and you work for me. I have every right to do as I please. Doctor Burkman is here at my request."

"I'm sorry, ma'am, I was just surprised to see him with you. I wasn't sure your head was clear enough to know what you're doing. And what about Doctor Hines? He's been treating you for weeks."

"When Doctor Burkman came to visit, I decided I wanted a second opinion, so I let him examine me. I'm going to switch to him."

"You shouldn't do that, ma'am; Doctor Hines is helping you. Look how much better you are."

"I prefer Doctor Burkman, Inez. He's seen me several times in the past, but I've been too dopey to request him after Doctor Hines gave me the shot and all those pills. Now that I can think clearly, I'm changing physicians."

Inez realized she was irritating her employer and decided she shouldn't point out that Hines and Peter would be upset with the change. "If that's how you want it, ma'am, it's fine with me. Do you want her medicine and schedule to stay the same?" she asked Jason.

"You won't have to worry about that anymore. I'm having a nurse come in later today and take over Mrs. Grantham's care."

"A nurse? Why? I've been doing a good job for her."

"Yes, you have, but she needs a nurse, not a housekeeper, tending her."

"I see. If you need me for anything, ma'am, I'll be in the kitchen."

"You can do something for me," Jason said. "You can bring me all of Mrs. Grantham's prescriptions and the charts you've kept on her."

"Yes, sir, right away."

When Inez returned shortly with the bottles and pad, Jason asked, "Is this all of them? Where are the other recordings?"

"Doctor Hines was here this morning and collected my charts, and this is all he has. Except for vitamins, and aspirin for a headache."

Jason knew what he had seen in the two mystery bottles were not vitamins or aspirin, but he couldn't press the matter now. He reasoned that either Hines was rotating her between different drugs or the older man was giving her too many combinations simultaneously. He suspected the missing capsule was the antidepressant Prozac and the missing tablet was one of two antianxiety agents, Ativan or Xanax; he wished he had committed their sizes and colors to memory, but he had been in a distracted rush yesterday. "Thank you, and that's all for today."

"Do you want me to stay while you check Mrs. Grantham?"

"Thank you, but I've already finished my examination; a thorough physical isn't necessary at this time; I'll do that at my office on a later date. Don't worry, I'll settle this with Doctor Hines."

"As you wish, sir. Call me if you need me. Shall I close the door?"

"That isn't necessary, Inez, and thank you for running those errands." Cass didn't want her to close the door because she suspected the woman might eavesdrop. By leaving it open, in full view of her employer, Inez had to go downstairs.

Cass glanced at Jason and whispered, "She can be a royal pain in the rear. I didn't hire her and never liked her, but Tom insisted she stay on. I was planning to let her go soon, but now I feel obligated to her for taking such good care of me."

"Don't be, Cass," he whispered in return. "If she gets on your nerves again, just let me know and I'll help you find another housekeeper. I have a wonderful lady working for me and she just mentioned she has an opening coming up."

Cass thought about how wonderful it would be to get the sourpuss out of her life and hair, but she didn't want to act on the situation too fast. Considering what Inez had done for her during her illness, she would give the woman one more chance to correct her ways. "Thanks, and I'll keep your offer in mind. Now, what's the verdict on me?"

Jason related his plan of treatment. Cass listened as he spoke with a nurse who agreed to take charge of her case.

After he hung up the receiver, Jason smiled and said, "You'll like Linda Carnes and we're fortunate she's available; she's an excellent nurse and a nice person. She has a wonderful personality and all of her past patients adored her. I hope it was all right to ask her to move into one of your guest rooms for a week or so; that should be long enough to get you back on your feet."

"It was fine, Jason, and I'll enjoy having another woman around for company. As you can see, Inez and I are nothing alike."

"I don't want to offend your housekeeper, but Linda is to be in charge of your diet and meals. She'll have you up to par very soon."

"Is that the promise of a superior golfer?" she teased him, then asked, "Are you sure I need to keep taking those pills?"

"For a while. Going cold turkey might make you jittery. Linda is a good listener and honors her patient's confidence, so talking to her about certain things might help you. You've suffered a terrible tragedy and your life's been turned upside down, so it's normal to be angry and to cry. And remember, just because you're venting your feelings doesn't mean you're having a relapse, so let those emotions out when they work on you."

"Thanks for the advice," *but I can't talk to anybody about my fears and doubts; I can't reveal what I've learned about Tom and our marriage and about how scared I am that he might have given me some horrible disease. Still, it would be nice to make a friend and talk about other things.*

"Well, I'd better get going," Jason said, rising. "I have another patient to check on at the hospital. Linda will be over at noon tomorrow, so I'll stop by to introduce you two and get your new treatments underway. You'll have to do your part, Cass, by trying to stay calm and obeying Linda's instructions."

"I promise, because I want to get well. Thank you, Jason; you're a good friend and doctor. You'll call Hines and tell him about the change, right?"

"I'll take care of him this afternoon. I doubt he'll give you a hard time, but if he does, I'll handle him. I've made a chart for your prescriptions. I only want you to take Librium, five milligrams, three times a day, and ten milligrams at night to help you sleep; those are mild doses compared to what you were on. I won't use the Tofranil — it's a strong antidepressant — unless it's necessary. The dispensing schedule is listed. Just check off each dosage today and in the morning before you take the pill; that way, you won't forget and take another one. Tomorrow, Linda will take over giving them to you. I've written down the names of several herbal teas that'll help keep you calm using nature for assistance. If you have a headache, just take Tylenol. Record any symptom you experience: time, duration, type, and what seemed to bring it on. And call me if you need anything. Anything, Cass, even just to talk. My home, office, and pager numbers are on the card on your nightstand by the phone."

What I need most is total freedom from my past, which I'll achieve somehow, with your help. "I will, Jason, and thank you."

"You don't have to keep thanking me, Cass."

"Why, because you're going to send me a fat bill for your services?" she jested. "House calls must be expensive."

"I'm doing this more as a friend than as your physician." *Forgive me, Cass, for wanting to get you healed swiftly for selfish reasons, but I can't help myself; I'm totally in love with you, woman. I have been since that night we met at the Ritz Theater. I'd give just about anything to be the next man you give your heart to.*

"You aren't fooling me, Doctor; you just need your tennis partner back because you can lick me with one hand tied behind your back."

Jason almost sighed aloud in relief, fearing she had read his thoughts; he knew it was wrong to think about romancing a new widow in a vulnerable state. "Great day, I've been busted and exposed! How did you guess?"

"I remember how much you enjoyed whipping me on the court. I can recognize that old cat-who-ate-the-canary look."

And what a beautiful and delicious canary you are, Cassandra Grantham. "Maybe I'll take over your lessons and teach you how to beat me."

"That would be fun, after I regain my strength," *and the willpower to be around you without having these feelings of sheer lust. Tom's body is barely cold and you're craving another man! Shame on you,* she admonished herself. *Jason is too wonderful to use to get over Tom's betrayal.* "I've enjoyed our visit today. Since the funeral, you're the only person I've really talked with besides Peter. I'm glad you were a persistent sneak."

"That's a nice compliment. After you're fully recovered, you need to get out and meet people, make friends, get into some interesting activities and sports. I'll be more than happy to introduce you around and be your escort. I can certainly use a charming dinner companion. Single life can be tough and lonely, so can trying to get back into the swing of things; I know from personal experience."

"It's too soon to be thinking in that direction but I'll keep your invitation in mind when I'm ready to venture out again."

"I'll make sure you do . . . I'll say goodbye now, Cass; you rest and take care of yourself."

"See you tomorrow, Jason, and . . ." She paused and laughed before adding, "Thank you for everything."

133

Jason chuckled. "You're welcome, Cass. Good-bye."

After he stopped in the kitchen to go over the changes with Inez, Jason left the Grantham home in a good mood. As he got into his BMW, his grimace came swiftly as he realized that a vengeful Peter could destroy his bond with Cass by revealing the truth about the past to her.

Inez watched the handsome physician drive away and frowned, suspecting this development was going to irritate Peter to no end. She hoped he didn't hold her responsible because she had done the best she could to follow his orders. She didn't know how to reach him, since he was between destinations. He had phoned early this morning to check on his stepmother and wasn't due to call again until Sunday afternoon. With that nurse moving in tomorrow, perhaps Mrs. Grantham wouldn't want her to come in on Sunday or stay there at night any longer, which meant she would miss Peter's call and the means to give him a detailed report. No doubt he would call her at home after he spoke with the woman and made his shocking discoveries. She hoped he wouldn't fire her because she needed this lucrative job.

As Cass relaxed in bed, she sipped on the sherbet-and-diet-ginger-ale float and glanced through the magazines that Inez had brought to her after Jason's departure. With the aid of the mild tranquilizer and knowing somebody really cared about her, she was calmer than she had been in weeks. She liked having a clear mind and realized she could not escape reality in a drugged daze. She had to get well and take control of her life and make plans for her future. She didn't know what she wanted to do with herself yet, but she knew she shouldn't make any hasty decisions. There were business matters to settle so she would know where she stood financially. Since Tom might only have been using her as a cover for his secret activities and never really loved her, it was possible that he hadn't included her in his will and might have left everything — or almost everything — to his only son.

Cass lowered the magazine and stared into space. She could not understand how love could be slain so fast and completely. It was as if Thomas Ethan Grantham had murdered every genuine emotion she had ever experienced toward him. She felt nothing good for her deceased husband. She could not forgive him for his repugnant betrayals, or understand why he had committed them. Perhaps if Tom's weakness had been only one brief affair, she might have been able to forgive him, but that was not the case.

She recalled how she had forgiven Bradley Stillman for his first offense because she had been naive and trusting and believed his seemingly valid excuses, even taking on part of the blame for his straying. She hadn't given him a third chance to strike out; she had left him upon the discovery of affair number two. She had loved Brad, had adored him with that pure innocence of first love.

With Tom, it had been a mature love, a settling in a way for the best thing to come along in the ten years since her divorce and one soured romance. With two strikes against her for terrible choices, could she ever risk making strike number three. She wouldn't worry about that matter any time soon.

As sordid images from those two videotapes tried to sneak into her head, Cass dismissed them swiftly. She didn't want those ugly feelings to torment and destroy her. She had to accept that dark reality and, if she could not forget the past, ignore it.

On Sunday at noon, Jason Burkman and Linda Carnes arrived within minutes of each other. Cass took an instant liking to the vivacious, pretty, and genial nurse in her late twenties with her very short but thick and fluffy blond hair and green eyes that seemed to sparkle from an inner radiance. At five feet nine, Linda was an inch taller than she was, and their weights appeared to be about the same — at least her own normal size before she'd lost many pounds during her bedrest.

As Jason examined Cass and took her vital signs, Linda recorded the information on a chart, asked several questions about the man's instructions, and observed the easy rapport between physician and patient. It was obvious to Linda that the two people had respect and affection for each other, though one behaved professionally and the other politely in her presence.

After his examination, Jason smiled and said, "You're already doing better, Cass. I have a golf game this afternoon, so I'll leave you in Linda's capable hands. I'll come by and check on you after office hours tomorrow. Either of you have any questions?" He saw both women shake their heads. He gathered his things, smiled again, and departed.

Cass looked at Linda and said, "I'll show you to your room so you can get unpacked and settled in. Inez prepared it before she left yesterday; she's my housekeeper and she's off today. I might as well warn you, if Jason hasn't done so already, but Inez can be a . . . difficult woman. She's stern faced and grouchy most of the time, but don't let her upset or offend you. She's sort of annoyed that you're replacing her."

Yes, Linda thought, Jason had told her about the annoying woman. "Don't worry, Mrs. Grantham, I'm accustomed to dealing with disgruntled people who view me as a disruption. Have no fear, I can handle Inez. Just don't you get upset if I have to be stern with her. Remember, you aren't to eat or drink anything I don't prepare and serve you; that's the only way I can control your diet. You're going to get sore and stiff from working out with me daily to get you toned and stronger, so she might think I'm pushing you too hard and try to interfere. I just hope she doesn't get angry enough to quit because a good domestic is hard to find."

"If she does, Miss Carnes, don't worry about it. I've put up with a great deal of nonsense from her for months and I was planning to replace her soon, but I'm feeling guilty about dismissing her because she's taken such good care of me since I . . . fell apart after Tom's death. But Jason says he knows of a good replacement if Inez becomes unbearable."

"You're a very kindhearted and generous woman, Mrs. Grantham. I know we're going to have fun working together."

"Please, call me Cass, if you don't mind."

"That suits me fine, Cass, and you call me Linda. . . . Well, I'll settle in while you're resting this afternoon. Right now, it's lunch time. Would you like to show me around the kitchen? Then, I'll get started on our meal. A healthy diet is important to you for regaining your strength."

In the kitchen, Cass sat at the breakfast table while Linda prepared, then served them both sandwiches, garden salads, fruit cups, and skim milk. While they ate, they chatted briefly about themselves and Cass's impending treatments.

After drinking an herbal tea blend of chamomile flower, valerian root, and other natural ingredients, Linda gave Cass a massage to stimulate weakened muscles in her body. As the nurse soothed her body and the tea and tranquilizer soothed her mind, Cass drifted off to sleep.

Linda spread a sheet over her new patient and slipped from the room to unpack her belongings. She liked the woman and understood why Jason, as a doctor and friend, was concerned about her emotional and physical health. She concurred with Jason's line of treatment, not with Hines's. She didn't like the man and couldn't understand why the older physician had medicated Cass so heavily and for so long, since Cass's anxiety and depression seemed relatively mild to her. Though he hadn't said it aloud to her, Linda sensed that Jason was as suspicious of Hines's course of action as she was. Her heart went out to the young widow and was resolved to help Cass recover fully and soon.

During a light exercise session in her home gym at five o'clock, the phone rang and Cass gave Linda permission to answer it. Cass listened to her end of the conversation.

"Grantham residence. May I help you? . . . This is Linda Carnes, Mrs. Grantham's nurse. . . . No, Doctor Hines didn't assign me to her; Doctor Jason Burkman, her personal physician, did. . . . Doctor Burkman took over her case yesterday and I started today. . . . Yes, she's here and I'll see if she can speak with you."

Linda turned to Cass and said, "It's Peter Grantham. He wants to talk to you. Are you up to speaking on the phone?"

Cass took a deep breath, dreading Peter's reaction to the change. "That's fine, Linda, thank you," she said, taking the receiver. "Hello, Peter. How is the business trip going?"

"That nurse said you're seeing Doctor Burkman. Why?"

"Considering my alarming condition and his heavy hand with drugs, I wanted a second opinion."

"If you didn't like or trust Doctor Hines, why didn't you tell me?"

"He's all right, but I've seen Doctor Burkman several times since I moved to Sea Island, so I consider him to be my physician. Is there a problem?"

"No, the only thing that matters is getting you well. If he makes you feel more comfortable, by all means use him. But if you'd told me about him earlier, I would have phoned him instead of Hines."

Cass was relieved that Peter's tone of voice was pleasant and tinged with concern. "I wasn't in a state of mind for thinking clearly," she reminded him.

"Of course not. Well, are you feeling any better?"

"Yes, I am. Doctor Hines lowered my medication yesterday before I changed to Doctor Burkman, and then Doctor Burkman lowered it even more, so this is the clearest my head's been since I started treatment. The rest and medication have helped me a lot. Thanks for getting me started."

Peter couldn't contain his sudden barrage of questions. "Who's the nurse and why was she needed? What's she supposed to do for you? Why couldn't Inez continue to take care of you?"

He hardly listened as she explained, his thoughts running in a different direction. With Cass returning to her normal self and sooner than planned, he was relieved he had her home phone line switched back to her house from his residence and had the mail delivery changed from the temporary post office box he had rented back to her house before his departure. He couldn't ever let her discover what he had done to her with Hines's help, and with Inez's unknowing assistance. He didn't like Jason Burkman being in the picture, but that could play nicely to his advantage if he pretended his only concern was her health. Besides, he could get rid of the man any time he desired with a few well-chosen words spoken into Cass's ear. *That's it, my greedy stepmother, get real close to him; then, if you require a little relapse, exposing*

Jason's motive to you should certainly do that trick. Peter decided he'd phone Inez for a full report on this matter as soon as he hung up. "Besides having a clear head, Cass, how are you doing?"

"Better; the other symptoms are gone, and I feel calmer, rested."

"That's excellent news, so Hines did help you. Right?"

"Yes, and I hope he doesn't get upset because I changed to my own doctor. How are things going out there?" she tried to change the subject.

"Excellent, but we'll discuss our family business after I return home on Wednesday. While I'm on the road, I might as well check out all of the companies. . . . If you're feeling up to talking or having visitors, we got some calls and mail while you were . . . under the weather. They're on my bedroom dresser, so you can ask Inez to fetch them for you tomorrow; she has a key to my place. I didn't mention them before I left because you were too out of it to see or speak with any of Dad's friends or anybody else. People at the companies have been asking about you. I told them you're taking a holiday as we agreed. I didn't know when you'd be feeling up to it, so my secretary finished the thank-you notes for Dad's funeral flowers and donations. I hope you don't mind."

"Thank you, Peter, that was kind of you. Why don't we go over the correspondence after you return home? And perhaps we could have dinner with some of the people who showed concern."

"That sounds good, let's plan on doing it as soon as you feel like going out for the evening. I have a late meeting now, so I'd better get going. You take care of yourself, Cass, and obey your doctor's orders."

"I will, and thanks again, Peter. Good-bye."

At seven, Cass shared a pleasant dinner with Linda, then the two women sat in the den and watched television and chatted. Cass enjoyed Linda's company. She was glad Jason had chosen the affable and interesting woman to be her nurse. If things continued, before Linda Carnes finished her assignment, they would be good friends; and she needed a friend badly.

That night, following her medication and another cup of herbal tea — a blend including passion flower, catnip, scullcap, and hops flower — Cass slept peacefully and dreamed only of Jason Burkman.

When Inez Doughtery returned to work on Monday morning, Cass noticed how quiet and polite the woman was, she also noticed how the housekeeper tried to observe her and Linda on the sly. Cass assumed that Inez felt her job was in jeopardy and was trying to behave herself. The black-haired woman went about her chores with eagerness and skill and kept asking if there was anything she or Linda needed. But Cass saw Inez glaring at Linda and clenching her teeth when the housekeeper didn't know she was watching. *When I get back to myself, woman, I'm afraid you're gone.*

When Inez asked again after lunch if Cass needed anything, Cass said, "Yes, I do. Peter said there was a box of mail and messages on his bedroom dresser and you would fetch them for me."

Later, Cass sat propped in her bed with the box in her lap. First, she went through the messages, some written by Peter's secretary, which meant they had come to his office at the seafood company, and others written by Peter, which meant they had come to either his phone or hers. Several were from Jason, so it was obvious Peter had not intended to keep her ignorant of his calls. There were a few letters without envelopes from men Tom had known, more like brief notes to express condolences to her and Peter. She glanced at the names on the most recent sympathy cards, recognizing some as acquaintances and business contacts. Regardless of whether or not those people knew or liked her, Cass reasoned, at least they had manners.

She came to several cards that touched her heart, brought tears to her eyes, and told her she had not been forgotten as she'd believed in her emotionally disturbed state. There was one from her ex-in-laws who had focused on Brad's second family instead of her following his re-marriage and the birth of their grandchildren, children Bradley Stillman had denied her. Another card was signed by a group of employees at Smooth Rider in Augusta where she had worked for years, where she had met the deceitful Tom, the golf cart company he had purchased, and perhaps she now partly owned. Another card had a special message written by Kristy Stillman Franklin who had read about Tom's death in the Augusta newspaper. Cass assumed that Peter or one of Smooth Rider's managers had notified the newspaper and supplied the information on Tom.

Cass put aside the box, leaned back into the pillows, and closed her eyes to reminisce. Kristy had been her best friend for years before she married Tom and carelessly discarded her ex-sister-in-law because of Tom's insistence she have nothing to do with Brad's family. She had sneaked a few calls to Kristy during the first five months of their marriage; then a busy schedule, an argument with Tom after he discovered her action, and too much time passed swiftly until she was too embarrassed to phone Kristy and too worried about Tom's reaction to disobey him. *I was stupid and weak-willed!* Cass admonished herself. *I should have told Tom that Kristy was my best friend and I wasn't going to terminate the relationship! I was such a blind coward. I sacrificed so much to please him, to make him happy, to make our marriage work, and my thanks were countless sordid betrayals!*

Cass hoped and prayed that Kristy would understand and forgive her. Cass suddenly realized that since Kristy and her parents knew about Tom's death, so did Brad. She was glad her first husband hadn't sent a card or phoned her; he was out of her life and that's the way she wanted it!

Cass also realized she was getting agitated by those potent feelings and grim thoughts, and she cautioned herself to calm down just as Linda entered the room. "Time to take your vital signs, Cass," the pretty nurse told her, "before we go exercise. I'm sure your lunch is settled by now."

"I'm ready when you are," *more than ready for a distraction.*

Linda took her pulse and blood pressure twice each, then looked at Cass. "What's wrong? One's too fast and the other is slightly elevated. And your cheeks are flushed and your muscles are taut. What brought this on?"

Cass hoped her half-lies would be convincing as she answered. "I was looking through sympathy cards and letters that arrived while I was . . . incapacitated, and thinking about Tom and old friends I haven't seen for years. I can hardly believe how much my life has changed in the last month. Soon, I'll have to make plans about my future; and I have to admit, that's a little scary."

"It's only normal to be intimidated and frightened of the unknown, and normal to have contradictory emotions," Linda assured her. "One can't help but be angry at a loved one who died from . . . a preventable accident." Linda knew from news reports that Thomas Grantham had been speeding and not wearing a seat belt. "I'll fix you a cup of herbal tea to calm you. It isn't time for your next pill and I'd rather not give you an extra one unless you really need it."

"Tea and exercise and a soothing shower will do the trick," Cass told her, then watched Linda record her symptoms and readings for Jason. She hoped the brief episode wouldn't cause him to increase her medication, as she needed clear wits to deal with her problems.

While Linda was downstairs preparing the tea, Cass phoned Kristy in Augusta, but, according to her answering machine, she was out of town. After the beep tone sounded, Cass left a brief message and her phone number.

As Cass sipped the calming beverage Linda brought her, she planned the letter she would write to Kristy that afternoon so it would be waiting when her friend returned home. A letter, she reasoned, was the best way to contact Kristy after so long, as she could explain her feelings and actions and it would give Kristy time to think things over before responding.

On her way to the spacious and well-equipped gym situated in one corner of the sprawling house, Cass halted for a few minutes to ask the housekeeper to clarify a point that troubled her. "Inez, why didn't you tell me that Doctor Burkman stopped by to see me weeks ago?"

Inez's words tumbled forth in rapid-fire succession. "I knew you were upset about those other nosy people and I didn't realize you knew him that well and wanted to see him. You were asleep that day and I was busy with chores and I forgot about him with all that was going on. You had me so worried about you, ma'am."

Cass was skeptical of the woman's explanation, though the woman's tone and expression didn't indicate she was being dishonest. "Have those two detectives come around during my illness?"

"No, ma'am, I haven't seen or heard from them."

"Have they spoken with Peter again?"

"I don't know, ma'am; he didn't tell me. And I haven't seen anything on TV or in the newspaper about it."

"Are people still driving by the house?" Cass continued her questioning.

"Very few, ma'am, and nobody bothers me when I'm out."

"That's good news. Maybe things can get back to normal soon."

"I hope so, ma'am; you don't deserve being treated badly."

"Thank you, Inez. I'll be in the gym with Linda doing exercise. When you finish your chores, you can leave." Cass halted her departure, turned, and said, "Oh, yes, I'm grateful for all you've done for me and I hope Linda's presence isn't too much extra work and disruption for you."

"She's no trouble, ma'am. She's nice and she's helping you a lot."

As they worked out in the gym, Linda asked, "Is it all right to invite Jason to eat with us when he comes over after work? He must get tired of dining alone, and he's good distraction for you."

"That's fine with me. He's interesting and entertaining. And it will be a nice way to thank him for his concern and care."

As Cass showered and got ready for dinner and their handsome guest, she thought how excited she was about seeing Jason. She was glad she didn't detect any romantic interest in Linda for him, nor any in him for the nurse.

As she put on a light touch of makeup and a subtle hint of perfume, Cass decided there was a very important and private errand she needed to get out of her way and off of her mind tomorrow.

Chapter Seven

Jason wondered whose idea the invitation was. He hoped it was Cass's, who looked good enough to devour in a blue pants outfit, her shiny brown hair caressing her shoulders as he longed to do. Her color appeared normal tonight on a flawless face with a dark-ivory complexion, and her mood serene. He yearned to trail his fingers over her high cheekbones, to gaze for ages into those expressive chocolate eyes, and to hold her in his arms. She had a magical way of chasing away his loneliness. It was a treat just to spend a brief time with her and a delight to converse with her. It would be ecstasy to lie in bed with her and — "This is a pleasant surprise, ladies," he said as he quelled his provocative thoughts and took a seat at the glass-topped table to Cass's left. "Otherwise, I'd be going home to a cold sandwich, chips, and cola and a dive into a pile of medical journals afterward."

"You work too hard, so you can use a break," Linda remarked.

Cass wondered if Jason was eyeing her in more than a professional manner. Her emotions were bruised and seeking appeasement, and her imagination was running wild. Maybe after Tom and Brad's betrayals, she needed to feel wanted. If only Jason didn't look so appealing, she wouldn't be so affected by him. He had removed his coat and tie, rolled up his sleeves to a few inches below his elbows, and unfastened the top two buttons of his shirt, giving her a partial view of a virile chest and strong forearms. His physique was excellent; his smile, easy and engaging; his blond hair, finger inviting. His blue eyes seemed to sparkle from an inner vitality and even his laughter was sexy. To cool the heat assailing her body, she said, "Linda's right. Relax and enjoy yourself because this is a social occasion among friends. I'm sure we can all use a break tonight."

"I know the customer is always supposed to be right and, in this case, I'm certain the patient is, so I'll take her advice," Jason remarked with a grin, causing Cass to send forth a radiant smile that fanned the flames of passion's fire which already was ignited within him. He ordered himself to cool his blaze of hunger for her or he could expose his improper feelings. "It looks and smells delicious. Thanks, Linda," he said as the nurse put a filled plate before him and set a basket of rolls nearby.

"Just let me know if you two want seconds. I'm keeping everything covered on the stove. For some stubborn reason, broccoli and rice refuse to behave themselves by staying warm on the table, and gravy likes to blanket itself with a yucky film to hold its heat."

Jason and Cass exchanged smiles at Linda's amusing descriptions.

The nurse observed how they looked at each other; then how both almost shyly glanced away as if they didn't want to be caught. *So,* she mused, *I wasn't wrong; they are attracted to each other, and they'd make such a perfect couple. After all he's suffered in the past, Jason deserves a good woman like Cassandra. As for you, Cass, methinks you didn't have a happy marriage, my new friend, or you would be grieving more over your husband's death and you'd show no interest in your virile physician this soon after your loss. It will be most interesting to watch a romance blossom between you two. Perhaps I can help this little bud come to fruition.*

Cass eyed the golden-brown baked chicken sprinkled with assorted herbs, fluffy white rice with gravy made from the chicken drippings and canned cream of chicken soup, steamed broccoli with butter, and spiced apple rings on her plate. "Linda's a wonderful cook, Jason," she half-jested, "and I suspect she's trying to fatten me up."

"Well, you have lost weight since I last saw you at the club," Jason observed before taking a bite of chicken, "so take advantage of it. I have to say, Cass, you look and sound better every time I see you."

"That's because I'm receiving such excellent care from you two. I just may get spoiled with all of this superb attention and service."

Jason chuckled. "Well, it never hurts to be

spoiled and pampered once in a while. Isn't that right, Linda?"

"Absolutely, and Cass deserves it. She's one of the best patients I've ever had. We're becoming good friends and having fun."

Cass laughed and joked, "Even when she works me hard in the gym. Mercy, I must be terribly out of shape because she has to massage me after every session so I can move again."

Jason couldn't help but envision Cass lying naked on a bed while *he* massaged and stroked her from head to feet, both soothing and arousing her body. As he collected a forkful of rice and gravy, he told her, "Exercise and proper diet will help keep that blood pressure down so we won't have to depend on extra medication to do the trick."

Cass knew he was referring to what he had read earlier on her chart about her tension this afternoon. He, like Linda, had believed her deceitful excuse. Though she felt guilty about lying to them, some things were too personal and humiliating to reveal. She was certain her thoughts and emotions would be vastly different tonight if she didn't know the truth about Tom and it didn't ravage her soul. "That suits me better than using drugs."

"They serve their purpose when needed, but they shouldn't be abused. In my physician's opinion, it's better to let the patient and nature do most of the healing work."

Jason was elated by Cass's physical and emotional improvements. He was delighted he had taken the risk to reach her and to bring her back from a dazed state which he still found dubious. There was no way he could prove it, but he believed her original condition was caused — probably by drugs secreted into her food and/or drink — by someone whose wicked streak he knew too well. He suspected there was a devious reason why Peter Grantham had needed to keep Cass's mind clouded for a while, a reason that most likely had to do with money and inheritances and that had Peter worried and angered and desperate. Jason had known Cass for less than a year, but he didn't think her recent erratic behavior was normal for her, even in the midst of a tragic ordeal. She was so good and trusting that it probably hadn't entered her mind she was being duped and harmed. No matter what he had to do, Jason vowed, he was going to make sure she wasn't tricked again. He turned his attention to the two women. "I'm glad to see you're getting along so well; I was certain you would."

"It's wonderful having someone nice around me every day," Cass admitted. "A house can get awfully big and quiet and lonely by oneself."

"I know what you mean," Jason concurred. "Especially with children grown and gone."

"I wouldn't know about that since I've never had any. Tell me about yours," Cass coaxed as she tried to suppress the anguish and disappointment she carried with her at being childless. But it wasn't too late to have a family, she told herself, if she could find a special man who was agreeable to starting one at their ages.

Jason noticed the momentary sad look in Cass's eyes before she concealed it. He couldn't help but wonder if not having children was a medical problem for her or Tom, or a personal decision made with her husband because of his age or a reluctance to share her. He wouldn't mind having another child, especially with Cass; in fact, the idea was most appealing to him. "I have fraternal twins," he revealed. "A boy and a girl, twenty-three. I married and had children while I was young. I lost my wife to breast cancer four years ago. My daughter lives in Savannah with her husband and her two-year-old boys, identical twins named Larry and Harry. Traci's husband owns and runs a construction company there; he does residential and small job commercial building. My son is studying at the medical college of Georgia in Augusta; Stacey wants to become a surgeon and practice in Atlanta. Considering his high grades, dedication, and determination, I'm confident he'll succeed."

Cass knew he had spoken of his first wife, a woman to whom he had been married for nineteen happy years according to Linda. He had wed his second wife less than a year after his beloved's death and had divorced after only two years of marriage, thirteen months ago. Linda hadn't revealed the reason for the break-up if she knew it. Cass reasoned that Jason could have remarried too hastily out of loneliness and a need to fit into a "couple's world." Possibly his second wife had wearied over competing with a ghost, or his two children could have caused dissension. Perhaps Jason Burkman wasn't the perfect man she presumed him to be. Considering her track record selecting husbands, maybe she wasn't a good judge of character where men were concerned. Being twice wed and both having marriages that terminated in death and divorce gave her and Jason something in common, though a sad and negative matching thread in their lives. "Does Stacey have a girlfriend or fiancée?"

Jason pierced a broccoli flower with his fork. "Not yet; he claims he's too busy studying and working to have time for a serious romance."

"Ah, one of the woes of becoming and being a doctor," Linda quipped. "So little time and energy for taking care of matters of the heart."

Jason nodded and asked Cass, "Do you have any family back home?"

"No, unfortunately. I was a late and only child, and my parents have been dead for years. What about you, Jason, any other family?"

"No siblings, but my parents are alive. They live in Richmond where my father owns and runs a medical supply company. My mother's hoping he'll retire this year so they can travel while they're still healthy."

"Is Richmond your hometown?" Cass asked.

"No, I'm from a little dot on the map that's close to the Virginia capital. You said you're also from a small town, right?"

"Yes, a tiny rural one called Neece; it's near Athens; that's where I moved to and worked for a while after high school graduation; then, later to Augusta." Cass stopped her narrative to eat for a few minutes because she didn't want to tell them she had relocated to Augusta because she had married her high school sweetheart and he was going to college there. Brad had assumed it would be easier to get through a small college rather than the University of Georgia in Athens. She had worked her fanny off to support them, as Brad had failed three courses and had to improve two grades in his major, so he had required an extra year to finish. That sorry excuse for a husband had shown his love, devotion, and gratitude by cheating on her!

"Did your parents move to Augusta with you?" Linda asked, trying to help Jason get better acquainted with Cass. She couldn't do the same for her new friend because she herself knew the answers to the same questions she was asking Cass. Any forays she made into that territory would tell Jason she was playing cupid and that could make him nervous, so it was up to Cass to glean any facts she wanted from him.

"No, my parents stayed on their farm until . . . I lost them five years ago." She hurried on with the first thing that came to mind to prevent a wave of sadness from attacking her. "I attended college in Augusta. I started at twenty-three and it took me five and a half years to finish. The first two years, I went full-time on a grant, but that was a struggle when funds were reduced. The rest of the time, I took night classes and worked during the day as a secretary at a company that makes golf carts. I stayed there after graduation because they promoted me to administrative assistant."

"Augusta, Georgia, is mighty big on golf," Jason remarked to keep her talking and him learning more about her past.

"Yes, it is; the Masters Golf Tournament is held there every April."

"It's next week. Stacey asked me if I was coming up to attend, but my schedule is too busy at this time. His, too, for a visit. Augusta has several golf cart makers, doesn't it?"

"Yes: E-Z-GO, Club Car, and Smooth Rider. I was working for Smooth Rider when Tom purchased the company three and a half years ago; that's where we met, then married a year later. What about your family, Linda?" she asked to change the subject. She intentionally had mentioned Tom before one of them inquired about him, which would be normal.

"I'm from Jacksonville," Linda related. "I still have parents and two married sisters with children living there. I worked in the southeastern Georgia Regional Hospital in Brunswick before I signed on with a home health-care agency to do private-duty assignments. I fell in love with this area and the pay is excellent, so I decided to stay here. Well, now that we're finished eating, why don't we play some gin rummy after I clear the table and load the dishwasher? I have a deck of cards with me upstairs. A lot of my older patients loved the game, so they got me addicted to it."

Cass laughed at her expression. "Suits me. What about you, Jason?"

"Suits me, too, but I'm sorely out of practice with cards."

"Don't worry," Linda teased, "we'll only play for funzies."

Cass and Jason insisted on helping Linda with the clean-up chores before she left the kitchen to fetch the cards from her guest room.

While the nurse was gone, Jason said, "You look lovely tonight, Cass, and I'm really enjoying myself. I play golf regularly and play a little tennis with friends, but I don't get out much like this. Having a social life is difficult at times, especially for a single person and somebody my age."

"You make yourself sound ancient. How old *are* you?"

"Forty-two."

"That's young, Jason. So, how else do you spend your leisure time?"

"On occasion, I go boating, fishing, crabbing, or shrimping; the fresh air would do you good if you want to come along. You already know I enjoy the local ballet, orchestra, and symphony. Any of those would be nice diversions for you. This area also has more than its share of excellent restaurants. What about joining me for some of those outings? As you said earlier, we can both use occasional breaks."

"All of them sound tempting, Jason, and I could sorely use distractions, but it wouldn't look proper for me to go socializing with a man so soon after Tom's death. I would appreciate it if you ask me again later," she added for encouragement and to soften her refusal.

Jason lowered his voice to a whisper to ask, "Who's to know and judge you, if we go only to places mostly frequented by tourists?"

"Peter and Inez would know and probably disapprove."

Before Jason could ask why that mattered to her, Linda returned and he dropped the subject. At least Cass hadn't turned him down flat.

Jason, Cass, and Linda sat at the breakfast table to play gin rummy for the next two hours and to talk about many local, national, and world topics. Each relaxed in the genial and comfortable atmosphere.

As time passed in a sluggish yet swift pace, Cass lost many hands because her attention was distracted by Jason's arresting looks, easy laughter, and interesting conversation. She found herself just wanting to sit there and stare at him and savor his delicious company. It was a constant struggle not to yield to those temptations. She didn't want him to think she was coming on to him so soon after her husband's demise. She cautioned herself over and over to behave as a lady, one he would find respectable yet desirable. If only he would stop capturing her gaze each time she looked at him as he played his hand, perhaps she could resist his pull. Then again, perhaps she was misreading his interest in her.

Jason was fighting a similar battle, though he believed he managed to conceal it. He felt charged with energy and elation. He wished Cassandra Grantham wasn't so tantalizing and irresistible. He needed to concentrate and behave himself, but she made both difficult. Only in his dreams had she been available and responsive; now she was free for him to pursue and she seemed to like him more than as a physician. He yearned to win her heart, but it was too soon to seek it and waiting was blissful torment.

Linda was almost bubbling inside with excitement and suspense as she watched the two of them try to ignore each other and fail to do so. She could almost feel the romantic sparks passing between them and the sexual tension building within them. She suppressed her grins of pleasure and any verbal encouragement, but an eagerness to help them find their way to each other flowed through her.

At ten-thirty when he could endure the bittersweet strain no longer, Jason said, "I have to go, ladies; I have early office hours."

"Would you like to join us again tomorrow night?" The words shot from Cass's mouth and dazed brain before she could stop herself.

Jason smiled in pleasure. "If it wouldn't be any trouble, yes."

Cass looked at the nurse and said, "Linda, since you're the cook, you decide. Of course, I could help; I'm not a stranger in the kitchen, though Jason treated me after an accident there shortly after I moved to Sea Island. I still have the burn scar on my foot from that hot grease."

"I think it's a wonderful idea. We'll see you about six o'clock."

"Thanks, Linda. Is there anything I can bring?"

"No, Cass and I will throw something tempting together. She has a well-stocked pantry, freezer, and refrigerator."

On Tuesday morning, Cass asked Linda to drive her into Brunswick for an appointment with a gynecologist. She had chosen the doctor at random and when she called yesterday was fortunate that the office had a cancelation the next day. She felt terrible about lying to Linda about going for a routine check-up, but she couldn't relate the truth about her health fears. Nor could she go any longer without discovering if Tom had passed a disease to her.

The female gynecologist examined her and found nothing unusual, which assuaged some of Cass's fears. The physician had her nurse draw several vials of blood for the tests that Cass requested following an embarrassing explanation of the reason for wanting them done. The doctor told the rosy-cheeked widow that she could phone for the results on Friday.

Afterward, Linda drove a noticeably quiet Cass down Newcastle Street in the small pre-Revolutionary town with its mixture of Victorian and Old South flavor, the largest small town, Linda said, on the National Registry Historic Districts of Georgia and birthplace of the famous Brunswick Stew over one hundred years ago. Its revitalization was still in progress, but the area was a thriving seaport — "Shrimp Capital of the World" — with wide streets and numerous squares, many of them featuring enormous live oaks.

Linda parked in front of the Royal Cafe, situated among stores and shops with quaint facades on mostly one- or two-story buildings in various colors. Clean sidewalks were dotted here and there with palms and old-fashioned lamp lights and poles with American flags. The large redbrick Ritz Theater, the old Grand Opera House when it was constructed in 1898 and where she had met Jason Burkman, was down the street.

Inside the small cafe with its white-clothed

tables and salmon-colored walls with white woodwork, Cass and Linda were seated at the front windows where they had a nice view of Main Street, which was bustling during the lunch hour. They enjoyed their lunch of curried chicken salad with pecans, celery, and onions, piled in a pineapple boat and garnished with fresh fruit.

As Cass sipped from a "bottomless glass" of 7-UP and glanced around the restaurant, she realized that no one seemed to stare at her and perhaps didn't recognize her from past news reports. She hoped the investigation of Tom's accident would be finalized soon. She worried that a continued probe into their lives might result in the exposure of Tom's philandering ways and a scandal would assail her. If only that dread and the one about the blood tests she took earlier could be resolved this week, she could get on with her life now that she was feeling better.

As the two women talked about their childhoods, school years, families, and work experiences, Linda avoided any mention of Tom or Cass's future plans so she wouldn't become upset and spoil their outing.

En route home, they drove along the lengthy Torras Causeway and several bridges connecting all but one of the Golden Isles to the mainland. They crossed the intercoastal waterway with a sweeping marsh view to their right and left, a vast one that extended for miles. Wading birds — ibis, egret, and heron — searched for their meals among the strong stalks in shallow water and gulls and blackbirds were abundant and often loud with their shrill calls. Marinas were filled with boats of various sizes, some with tall masts. On occasion, shrimp boats plying their trades and large vessels heading toward other ports or into Brunswick's natural deepwater harbor were visible.

In the distance to their front and rear, the landscape was green with oaks, pines, palms, swamp holly, and other vegetation. Spanish moss draped limbs of many of those trees and bushes like lacy shawls. Spring was apparent everywhere they looked. Bees, butterflies, deerflies, and mosquitoes were sighted with frequency, as were various flowers, wild and cultivated.

After reaching the house and speaking with Inez for a while, Cass and Linda headed for the gym for Cass to do her exercises.

Later, Linda gave Cass her massage, herbal tea, and told her to rest for half an hour while listening to relaxation tapes the nurse had supplied. Cass drifted off to sleep following her exertions and medication, so Linda didn't awaken her until five o'clock to freshen up for their company.

Jason arrived on time to examine Cass and to eat dinner with them. All three were delighted with Cass's improvement, so he decreased her medication again.

At Linda's suggestion, they sat at the wrought-iron table on the patio to eat their meal: barbecue chicken with coleslaw, rolls, green beans, and iced decaffeinated tea. Beyond them, the water in Cass's near-olympic-size pool glistened in the sunlight, but their position was shaded by the tall house facing westward. Water trickled over cascading bowls in a yard fountain located among flowers and greenery and decorative rocks and with the original spew of liquid coming from a dolphin's mouth. Three stone statues of Greek goddesses had been placed in several areas by an imaginative landscaper, with floral beds and white rocks surrounding them. A cabana equipped with a wet bar, mini kitchen, bathroom, and sitting area was on the left side of the pool to prevent it from blocking the ocean's view from the bottom floor of her home. To the right of the pool was the guest house where Peter lived, a luxurious residence sitting atop a double garage and totally separated by a walkway from the sprawling multi-storied mainhouse. The six-thousand-square-foot residence on a large corner lot overlooking the Atlantic Ocean was decorated for lavish entertaining, though they hadn't had overnight guests or a party since moving there early last October.

As Cass took in the beauty of her surroundings and thought about her life with Tom in this location, she was tempted to conclude Tom had wanted her secluded there so he could come and go and do as he pleased elsewhere. Before moving to Sea Island, their life "on the road" for two years had been filled with social engagements and constant activity. Afterward, Tom had made it known he wanted their home to be a place where "they" could have peace and quiet and be away from those distractions and demands, a place where they could concentrate only on each other, where they could rest and relax. She should have been suspicious when he refused to get to know other people living nearby and didn't want her fraternizing either during his absences or becoming involved in any community charities or organizations.

In a way, this house had become a golden prison for her, as mostly she had obeyed his requests. She hadn't done so the night she met Jason Burkman; she had sneaked to the Ritz Theater to view a play while both Tom and Peter were out of town. She hadn't mentioned her outing to Tom and was relieved Jason hadn't made a slip during brief encounters with him at the country club when she and Tom enjoyed a rare night out of the house. It was so nice having Jason and Linda there and to have Peter and Inez gone. She —

"I called earlier today, but no one answered the phone."

Cass gathered her strayed attention to respond to Jason after his remark interrupted her

167

line of thought, "Inez must have been outside or cleaning Peter's place and didn't hear the phone ring. Linda and I went into Brunswick; I had a gynecologist appointment and we stayed in town to have lunch. We had a marvelous time. She drove me around and told me some interesting things about this area."

As Cass related them to him, Jason wondered what had preoccupied her so deeply moments earlier and why she appeared to almost chatter as if trying to conceal its troublesome effect on her. He didn't pry, but closely observed her for clues while she spoke and ate, yet found none. Despite her physical and emotional improvements, he sensed she still had heavy burdens on her shoulders and wished she would allow him to lighten them.

Later, to help settle their meals, they took a walk on the beach. A lengthy distance from their position they saw several pairs of strollers, all heading in the other direction, guests at the Cloister Resort.

The evening was warm and pleasant, the sand soft and white, except for where it darkened from being wet every few minutes at ebbtide. A setting sun reflected its colorful glow on the water whose gentle waves sent forth soothing sounds and white-fringed edges. Sea oats with their ribbonlike leaves and spikelet heads, rock sandwort, and eelgrass swayed in the constant breeze. Sandburs and saw palmettos also dotted the low dunes and were avoided for their prickly tips and spines. A few gulls stayed within hearing range with their raucous cries. They watched sandpipers seemingly play tag with the outgoing tide, as did diminutive mole crabs who captured plankton with their feathery antennae on incoming waves before burrowing themselves into the sand afterward to await the next roll.

As he strolled between the women, Jason remarked, "At least the sand gnats aren't bad tonight; they prefer calmer and warmer days, but those tiny buck-toothed no-see-ums will be pestering us soon, especially on the golf course. So will those love bugs that get on everything in sight."

"Sand gnats haven't bothered me since I moved here," Cass responded, "but I recall their vicious bites from past visits. They seem to love getting into one's hair and gnawing on the scalp with razor teeth."

"I've played golf when they were so bad, I smacked my head so many times and so hard that I got a headache and it was sore for days. Give me mosquitoes any time; at least repellent discourages their attacks. Not those little no-see-ums; they act like it's an aphrodisiac and they go crazy."

Cass and Linda laughed as Jason reflexively scratched his head as if it itched just from talking about the irritating insects.

Linda pointed out several dolphins as they swam southward as if chasing two young men

169

who were windsurfing. "They're such beautiful and graceful creatures. I love to watch them. They'll even come up to you when you're swimming and try to play with you. After their fins scared the daylights out of you thinking they might be sharks," she added, and laughed.

Cass laughed, too, but said, "I've never cared for deep water, so I doubt I'll ever have that experience. I prefer not going more than ankle deep or staying with pools. I love being at the ocean, but I hate for crabs and fish to nibble on my toes and legs or have a jellyfish sting me."

Jason thought, *I'd love to nibble on your toes and legs and other parts, but I'd never sting you.* "Those terns fascinate me with their speed and skill. Those birds are great fishermen. Look at that one dive straight into the water, grab a fish, and take off somewhere to devour it."

Cass watched several terns plunge into the blue surface where large fish had driven smaller ones upward, snag their prey, and vanish from sight in the cobalt sky. She saw pelicans lined up overhead as they flew to where they would roost for the night.

"Did you know that the infamous pirate Blackbeard frequented these islands long ago? It's rumored some of his stolen booty is still buried on them, and those tales lure many treasure hunters to seach for it. Perhaps we should don our boots and cutlasses and try to locate one of his chests."

Cass's gaze met Jason's as he lowered his

voice; the level and tone seemed as if he was trying to fill her with intrigue and suspense. His amusing expression caused her to smile and her body to warm and tingle. "Why not? We could all get rich and famous if we recovered one, if the government allowed us to keep it and sell it," she quipped in return, then turned to Linda and more serious matters. "How much longer will you be working with me?" Cass asked the nurse.

"Jason said until next Tuesday. By then, you'll be fine and ready to take over your recovery program."

"That sounds good and bad; I'm going to miss you being there every day. But I'm sure other patients will need your help more."

As the nurse fingercombed her windblown blond hair, she said, "Don't worry; we'll stay in touch; I do have days off on occasion."

"If not, I'll have to fake a relapse, so you'll return," Cass jested.

"She'll be under my watchful eye for a long time, Linda," Jason said. "I'll take good care of her. There's no telling what kinds of mischief she'd get into with both of us gone. The minute our backs were turned, she'd probably be out in the ocean challenging those crabs and jellyfish."

"No way, I promise to behave myself. I'm planning to stay well."

"Excellent, Cass; that's what we want to hear, right, Linda?"

"Right, Jason. I guess we should head back now; it's getting dark."

"Peter is returning home tomorrow evening, so I suppose I need to spend some time with him going over family business," Cass told Jason during their return walk, by way of explaining why she wasn't inviting him to dinner on Wednesday.

"Just don't get upset going over such matters," he advised. "If you aren't ready to deal with them, tell him to wait until another day. I'm sure he won't mind. You've made excellent progress in a short time, Cass, so don't mess it up by subjecting yourself to unnecessary tension. Agreed?"

"I'll follow your orders, Doctor Burkman, and Linda will be there to make certain I do." *Let's just hope Peter is cooperative. He's been so nice since Tom's death, too nice, and that worries me. I keep waiting for things to revert to the way they were, or become worse. I'll know soon if or when that's going to happen.*

Chapter Eight

At six o'clock Wednesday, April third, Peter came to see Cass, ten minutes following his return home and five minutes after Inez left for the day. She guided him to the den and introduced him to her nurse. She noticed the tall and handsome man didn't appear to attempt to charm the green-eyed blond who, at twenty-seven, was a year older than he was.

As Peter shook Linda's hand, he said, "It's nice to meet you, Miss Carnes, and I want to thank you for all you've done for Cass. Even over the phone, I could tell she's better. Now I can see it with my own eyes."

Linda tried not to stare at the man with straight, thick black hair, a compelling hazel gaze, and bronzed tan. A sexy voice and brow-hooded eyes enhanced his magnificent image. He was even more good-looking up close than at a distance! She had heard rumors that Peter was a carefree playboy, but he didn't give her that impression. For certain, a warm glow was spreading through her loins! "I appreciate that, Mr. Grantham; Cass is easy to like."

"You're right; she's a strong woman who just had a rough go of it after Dad's death. How much longer will you be staying with her?"

Linda noted that he didn't ask her to call him Peter and his expression and manner remained respectful and polite, genial, unflirtatious. *So much for the rumor that you have to conquer every female you meet! Unless I just don't appeal to you.* "Until Tuesday. Then she'll be ready to take care of herself. Of course, she'll stay in Doctor Burkman's care for a while longer."

"That's good, because it's apparent his treatment has been beneficial." Peter looked at his stepmother and feigned what he knew from practice was a convincing smile. "You seem like a different woman, Cass, like your old self again. It's obvious Doctor Burkman and Miss Carnes are giving you good care; you were smart to change to him. I know from experience that Doctor Hines can be annoying at times; I think he has an ego problem and doesn't like to be questioned or overruled," he said and chuckled. "I'm not saying he isn't a good physician, because his reputation speaks for itself, but he can be a pain in the rump. Dad used him and recommended him to me, so that's why I called him when you were . . . out of sorts, shall we say? I forgot to tell you on the phone to have Doctor Burkman send your medical bills to my office so my secretary can file the insurance claims, and I'll write checks to pay for anything not covered under our family policy. I know you're relieved to be feeling better."

If Peter was annoyed with Cass for changing doctors, it wasn't detectable in his voice or expression or mood. "Yes, I am relieved. I have to admit, I was worried about me for a while."

Peter faked an empathetic air as he replied, "So was I, Cass, and Inez was, too. You just took Dad's loss too hard; he wouldn't have wanted you to suffer as you did. I don't mean for this to sound cold or harsh, but we can't feel guilty about being alive. You deserve to be happy again, and I'm sure you will be as soon as you accept that reality. What you need is to get out of this gloomy house, and have some fun; there's no crime in doing that."

"I know you're right, Peter, but it's so difficult. It's only been a month since my life changed so drastically. It never entered my mind that Tom would die so young or be . . . killed in an accident," *or betray me so horribly.* "I expected to grow old and gray with him. Besides, I don't think it would look proper for me to start gallivanting this soon. People gossip, and I don't want to make a bad impression on anyone since I'm living here."

Peter gave an exasperated sigh and half-frowned to dupe the two women. "If there's one thing I know for certain, Cass, it's that people gossip about others regardless of what they do, so you can't allow busybodies to rule your life. I get more than my share of idle chatter but I just ignore it; that's what you'll have to do. Besides, I've never seen you behave as anything less than a lady. Don't worry so much, it will get easier as time passes; you'll see. Isn't that right, Miss Carnes? I'm sure you've dealt with cases like hers before."

Linda was touched by his words to Cass. She was being drawn rapidly toward the magnetic man who seemed to be so kind, considerate, and gentle. Surely the hedonistic and self-indulgent tales about him couldn't be accurate, or they were exaggerated out of jealousy, envy, or animosity. "You're right, Mr. Grantham, but everyone must grieve in his or her own way. I think Cass's is improving daily. She's certainly giving it her best try." Linda felt as if she would liquefy into the carpet when he sent her a sunny smile and complimented her.

"You have a smart and compassionate nurse, Cass, so listen to her."

"Thank you, sir, and your advice to her is perfect. Now, if you'll excuse me, I'll prepare Cass's dinner while you two talk in private."

"Thank you, Miss Carnes, and a belated welcome to our home."

During the course of their conversation, Peter had recognized the signs of sexual attraction, so he knew he was captivating the blond with his clever pretense. By now, he concluded, she probably would give her eye teeth for a date with him. He had no doubt he could entice her into bed during the first ten minutes they were alone. Linda was appealing and even interesting and might be a good lay, but he couldn't

176

indulge himself with Cass's nurse and friend or he might antagonize his stepmother at an inconvenient time.

As she left the den, Linda hoped Cass would invite him to join them for dinner so she could study Peter closer and longer. Just in case that happened, she would prepare something special for tonight. And as soon as she had it cooking, she would sneak upstairs to freshen up a little.

Peter coaxed Cass to sit down as he reported on his trip. "All of our businesses are doing great; every one of them is operating in the black. I have to say that Dad hired some really top-notch managers to run them, so I don't intend to make any personnel changes. I also don't plan to sell off or expand any of them, but those aren't decisions I have to make any time soon. I'll keep working from my office here, but I will be taking trips to the other business locations on occasion to keep on top of matters. I'll give you an updated report each time I return."

Cass leaned back on the sofa across from his chair and tried to relax, but for some reason was uneasy. "Thanks, Peter; that's very kind and thoughtful. You said, 'our businesses'; what did you mean by that?"

"I thought you might ask," *you money-grubbing little bitch,* "so I brought along your copy of Dad's will. Now's a good time to discuss it if you're feeling up to it. Everything's clear and in order, so there's no rush. I've already met with our attorney while you were . . . ill because I had to know where things stood with the companies and I needed to familiarize myself with them and their staffs. Businesses don't stand still while a family is recovering from a tragedy. Employees and managers worry about changes that might affect their jobs, so they need reassurance from the new owner; I believe I gave it to them during my visits. As soon as you feel up to seeing Simon Johnson, he can go over the papers with you again to make sure you understand all of the legalese and disbursements. That kind of jargon can be confusing."

"I'm feeling fine, so we can discuss it now." If she was about to be cut off without a cent, Cass reasoned, the sooner she knew it, the better.

After Peter closed the door for privacy and retook his seat in a bergere leather chair, Cass listened in amazement as he revealed the provisions of Tom's will, which contained a shocking stipulation affecting her future and an astonishing dispersal schedule for her inheritance, part of a fifty-million-dollar estate that increased weekly!

Within the next ten minutes, aside from Tom's manipulative stipulation that she would forfeit a huge fortune if she remarried before ten years elapsed, Cass learned that from a combination of cash assets, several large life insurance policies, a retirement account, mutual funds in the stock market, and bonds of various types, she was to receive thirty percent of that total; Peter, forty-five percent; and certain charities and foundations selected by Tom were to receive twenty-five percent in his memory. She also was given their home, household possessions, jewelry, and her new automobile. Off the top, inheritance taxes were to be paid before those three divisions occurred so none of them had to pay that enormous amount out of one's share. She assumed the charity donations were made to help decrease those taxes and for ego purposes so Tom's name wouldn't be forgotten.

Cass didn't know why her BMW and jewelry were mentioned because she assumed those items already belonged to her as past gifts. She continued to listen as Peter related how her cash benefits and stock dividends were to be paid out in strange and lengthy increments. For the first two years, she was to receive enough to cover her living expenses based on her current lifestyle, plus five thousand dollars cash a month as "an allowance" and ten thousand cash at Christmas; for the ensuing three years, she would be given living expenses plus a ten-thousand-dollar a month "allowance" and twenty-five thousand at Christmas; five years after Tom's death, she would get fifty percent of the remaining trust fund; and ten years after his death, the balance of the account. Tom's local bank had been appointed trustee of her money until all of it was dispersed over the ten-year period. If she died during that time, everything reverted to Peter because Tom had made out a "bloodline will." If she was disabled, Peter controlled her business shares, the bank, and her remaining estate. According to the terms he had set forth, she could not alter them for ten years even with a will of her own.

Besides his forty-five percent of those assets, Peter inherited Tom's private jet: a Citation Ultra which seated eight passengers and two crew members. He also got the other four residences and their furnishings: the San Antonio ranch, LA house, Aspen chalet, and the New York apartment. He was to be given Tom's jewelry, except for his diamond-studded wedding band, which Cass was to keep, and his beloved Volante. Since the demolished convertible was beyond salvaging, he would receive the insurance settlement for it.

Tom's eight businesses had been divided into a forty-nine percent interest to Cass and a fifty-one percent controlling interest to Peter, who was to "be in full charge of running all eight": the seafood and electronics companies in Brunswick, import/export in LA, real estate in New York City, beef in San Antonio, golf cart maker in Augusta, and the restaurant and art gallery in Aspen. If Cass decided she wanted to sell her company stocks, Peter had first option to purchase them at fair-market value. But if Peter decided to sell any or all of the companies, he had the authority and power to do so,

180

then pay Cass her portion of the sales' profits, which were to be deposited into her existing trust fund account and would fall under that ten-year payout schedule he had explained to her earlier. The same was true if she sold out to Peter and for her yearly earnings from them.

Peter fingercombed his ebony hair as he halted for a while to allow Cass to absorb the abundance of information.

Cass realized it was an enormous amount of money and property, even with the long time required to collect it. But after ten years and if she was unwed, it was all hers . . . So, she mused, she could collect from the fund only as long as she remained a single widow. The moment she wed, her bequest halted and was awarded to Peter. At forty-five, she worried, wouldn't she be too old to marry and have children? Yet, if she didn't wait the time limit, she would relinquish a fortune. It was apparent to her that Tom was still controlling and manipulating her and her life from the grave!

Cass was furious. *I was a good wife, Thomas Grantham, so I deserve this bloody payoff! I earned it!* So Tom was still trying to hold on to her from his vaulted casket! A fifteen-million dollar estate, plus added yearly business and stock incomes, she reasoned, wasn't something to toss away easily.

Cass looked at Peter to question the stipulation that she would lose her inheritance if she remarried within ten years of his death, except

181

for what she already had received and spent to that point in time. Even if she sold her home, if she comprehended the restriction accurately, the money had to be reinvested in another one or deposited into her trust fund. Either way, she didn't really own the Sea Island estate outright until Tom's timetable was met! It was as if Tom had made certain with his clever legalese that if she turned to another man, she could not take her portion of his wealth with her, at least not all of it within ten years!

Cass turned to Peter in shock and said, "Tom and I never discussed money, so I didn't realize he was so wealthy. Why did he make that remarriage stipulation? Is it legal for him to control my life in that manner after he's gone?" Perhaps this was why Peter was being so nice: he didn't believe she would remain single for very long.

Peter wanted to shout: *It was his money, you bitch, so he can dole it out in any way he desired, and you're damned lucky he left you anything!* "I believe Dad divided up your payments in that manner to protect you against making unwise and costly business and personal finance decisions and from being hoodwinked. There are some clever men out there, Cass, who can dupe and defraud even a smart widow before she realizes what's happening. That's a lot of money and stock to turn over in a lump sum to a woman who isn't accustomed to handling such wealth. I'm sure Dad only wanted to make certain your inheritance is protected while you're given the time to adjust to his death and learn how to handle your estate. Don't you think I'm right?"

After she nodded, though she didn't look convinced, he continued, "As for that remarriage provision, I assume he did it to prevent a gold-digger from pursuing you for your money while you're still vulnerable. It's a fact of life that widows and widowers get lonely and often leap into another marriage too soon. There are some slick charmers out there, Cass, and you're a young and beautiful and rich woman, so you'll have to be careful in the romance department. It's probably Dad's way of forcing you to take a long and hard look at any man you'll be considering for your next husband so you won't make a mistake and lose everything if it doesn't work out."

Peter shifted his position in the chair before he added, "As for a bloodline will, I'm positive it's meant to safeguard your life. With one in force, no man will be tempted to marry and do harm to you for your estate because it would revert to me after your death, since you don't have a Grantham heir to inherit it. Spouses have been murdered for far less money than you'll be receiving. By your estate, I mean anything that came from Dad. Whatever you brought into the marriage is yours outright to do with as you please. I suppose I should ask if you are pregnant."

"What?" she asked in confusion.

"Are you pregnant with another little Grantham? If so, that changes the bloodline order to your child being your heir, not me or mine."

"No, I'm not pregnant. Your father didn't want any more children. He claimed he was too old and too busy for rearing one. He said that a man his age wouldn't have the patience and energy to deal with a crying infant or an active toddler and a worse time handling a rambunctious teenager."

"He was being foolish, Cass; he *wasn't* too old to start another family. All he had to do was hire a nanny to take care of the little bundle. You wanted to have children, didn't you?"

"Yes, and I didn't know Tom was so set against it before we married. Does the bloodline stipulation still apply after ten years?"

"I think so, but Simon can answer that question for you. If you meet someone you want to marry, Cass, and if he loves you enough, he'll wait the specified time limit. If you don't want to wait five or ten years, giving up a fortune that size would certainly prove your love for him. Besides, if you still want to have kids, it isn't too late."

"At my age, Peter, it could be risky for the child."

"You're only thirty-five, Cass, and you look much younger."

She smiled and nodded, but wanted the touchy subject dropped.

"I think you should look over the papers again to see if you have any questions for me. If I don't know the answers, I'll get them for you tomorrow, or you can make a list and ask them when you see Simon."

While Cass read everything over, Peter observed her as his mind whirled with ideas. He wasn't about to tell Cass that as a forty-nine-percent owner in the eight companies, she had a vote in their business matters. He didn't want her interfering in his affairs and decisions, and he did have the power to overrule her if she tried. Simon had promised not to divulge that fact, either, unless she specifically asked about it, and he doubted she had enough business sense to do so. All he had to do was get her married off within a few years, less than five, and she wouldn't withdraw much from that trust fund account. Perhaps Cass's desire for a child would be the key to her defeat; he was certain she wouldn't want to wait much longer before having one, surely not five or ten years. There should be plenty of men her age who wanted a baby, if only to prove they were still virile.

If he and Inez were right, Jason Burkman had more than a professional interest in his step-mother, be it a romantic or vengeful one. He hoped Jason would woo her mindless and marry her fast so she would be compelled to relinquish all claims to her inheritance, to Grantham money and belongings that should be his! *Jason, my man, if you get Cass out of my life, I don't care if you do believe you're exacting revenge on the man who slept with your wife and caused your divorce.*

Jason was only half correct in his assumptions about the past. Peter hadn't seduced Brenda Burkman sixteen months ago; the sex-hungry slut had pursued him like a voracious predator, practically dragged him off to her lair where, he admitted with a suppressed grin, she was skilled in the many arts of giving pleasure. Maybe that was how Brenda had gotten her hooks into Jason while the poor bastard was still suffering over the death of his first wife. No red-blooded man, single or married, would have turned down what she had begged him to take. For three months they had met frequently and always with great lust.

Peter was certain Brenda had arranged for Jason to discover them together in hopes of gaining her freedom and ensnaring him, but she had failed and lost both of them. Jason had been smart and clear-headed enough to prevent a nasty scandal by keeping the reason for his divorce a secret from everybody. Both men had been delighted when Brenda moved back East to seek another target.

Yep, Peter decided, it would suit him just fine if Jason snared Cass soon and she had to return what was rightfully his. But if that goal failed, he could get Jason out of the picture fast with a few clever words whispered into the bitch's ear.

Besides, he wouldn't mind screwing her silly a few times before discarding her. Despite how much he hated her, Cass was beautiful and desirable.

For a while there, Peter reflected, he had thought there might be another way of getting rid of Cassandra Redfern Stillman Grantham. She had signed a prenuptial agreement to give her only five hundred thousand dollars in the event of a divorce before five years, three million dollars up to ten years, and ten million dollars if the marriage lasted longer. But upon his father's death, Cass got thirty percent of the cash assets, their home, household possessions, jewelry, car, and forty-nine percent of the company stocks: a fifteen-million-dollar-plus gain with his death versus a divorce.

When those two detectives had questioned him about his father's possible enemies and beneficiaries, he had revealed the news about Cass's prenuptial agreement, though he had pretended it was dragged out of him. He had hoped those two creeps would become suspicious of her and cause her trouble. If he had learned sooner about the police's suspicions, he would have found a way to create evidence against her!

Peter reasoned that her discovery of his father's betrayals and a resulting divorce and loss of so much wealth could have been a strong motive in the eyes of the law for her to kill her husband. But Cass didn't know the truth about his weaknesses; his father had been clever to conceal his rapacious and diverse appetite for sex. It was too bad she hadn't opened his brief-case and found enlightening notations on his calendar and in his phone book which even her dense mind would have grasped. He had been tempted to tell her the truth just to jeopardize and torment her, especially about those homo-sexual encounters. He couldn't tell her about seeing his father and David Hines cavorting wildly in the gym while she was out Christmas shopping and he'd come into the house un-heard by the two men or Hines would retaliate by exposing their drug scheme to incapacitate Cass for a while.

Peter quelled the revulsion that almost gagged him as he recalled what he had wit-nessed on the sly that day in the gym between the naked, writhing males. Those sights and sounds were indelibly branded into his mind forever, and he despised his father for im-printing those hateful images there. After re-viewing his father's calendar and phone book and checking locked drawers in desks in his residences elsewhere, he had learned more than he had wanted to know from letters and Po-laroid shots. He had destroyed all of them, and hoped no more were in existence.

Tom's screwing around with other women didn't bother Peter, but his father's bisexual af-fairs did. He couldn't imagine how Thomas Ethan Grantham could have taken such risks

188

with his life, reputation, and wealth. Maybe his mother hadn't run off with another man as he had been told many years ago; perhaps she had discovered the dirty truth and couldn't bear it. Knowing Tom's proclivities, she had left a male child with him, who might grow up to emulate his father's behavior, and that was unforgivable! Even so, he had been sent to the best boarding schools and college available and been given everything he desired, except a mother's love. His father had educated and groomed him to step into his shoes, but it turned out the last thing he wanted was to be anything like the real Thomas Grantham! He would feel sorry for the betrayed Cass if he wasn't sure she had only married his father for his money and social status, so she had gotten what she deserved!

Cass's mind was racing as swiftly as Peter's was. She suspected Tom had included that marital stipulation to prevent her from falling in love and wedding too soon after his death; perhaps he wanted everyone to think he was so wonderful and irreplaceable and she was so grief-stricken she had to mourn him for a long time! Tom owed her for humiliating her, betraying her, and for endangering her life with his bisexual cheating. She would take his money and use it to obtain freedom from her past with him. Now that she knew what kind of man he had been, she was surprised he had left her anything. Perhaps he had loved her in a strange way.

At least, she realized, he hadn't exposed his dark side by bequeathing anything to any of his lovers! Nor had anything been left to his first wife, a woman she had been told had run off with another man.

She wasn't envious of what Peter had inherited; after all, he was Tom's only child. Nor did she have any desire to exchange this house for one of the other residences where Tom might have entertained his lovers, so she hoped Peter didn't make that suggestion. One point he hadn't elaborated on was her position in the eight companies; as the only other stockholder, surely she had some say in how they were run, and had a vote in business matters concerning them. Since Peter had controlling interests, was in charge of them, and they were profiting nicely, she wouldn't press that point any time soon and risk antagonizing him. She wouldn't even mention it to the lawyer when she met with Simon so neither man would realize she was knowledgeable in that area. They didn't have to know she had been an administrative assistant in a large company before she got married.

Cass looked up from the pages and told him, "I sent Inez over to your place for that box of messages, letters, and cards you mentioned on the phone. I have them upstairs if you want them returned."

Peter was surprised that was what she chose

to remark on after what she had read and heard today. Obviously the extent of her wealth and the demands placed upon her collecting it were too much for her feeble mind to absorb so fast. He forced out a smile and said, "Good, I'm glad you handled them. Has anyone else called or written that I need to thank?"

"Not unless a message came in on your answering machine at home. I assume you stay in touch with your office here when you're out of town, so your secretary has probably passed along any that came in there."

"You're right, and she did. I should warn you, if anybody tries to bill you for something they claim Dad owed or ordered, refer them to me; that's a scam some con men try to pull on grieving widows or other family members while they're still dazed. You might even get bills and magazines from subscriptions they'll claim he ordered before his death. I immediately canceled Dad's credit cards and had all business charge accounts changed to my name so they can't be used illegally. I also closed his bank account but left enough in it to cover any outstanding checks; we don't want a forger dipping into it. Do you need any money to tide you over until all of this is settled?"

You did it "immediately" after his death but you're just now telling me? Were there charges or checks you didn't want me to see? Perhaps some you made or wrote? Or enlightening ones about your father? "I don't think so. I have money in

191

my personal checking account and several credit cards with high limits in my name. They're still open, right?"

"Yes, but I took Dad's name off of them and added mine as the person who'll cover any overdrafts and excessive charges you make. If that happens, you can repay me later."

"Thanks, Peter. Should I take over my personal finances or let our accountant continue to pay the household bills as usual?"

"Either way, whichever you prefer; but if it were me, I'd let Harry Dredger do the work, at least until everything is settled and you've fully recovered. When you get ready to take over, meet with Harry and let him teach you how to handle your bills and records."

Cass had handled her budget for years after her divorce from Brad, but only her income and bills had been involved, not an enormous estate which could be beyond her management skills. "That's excellent advice, Peter, thanks. I don't think I have any questions at this time, but I'll let you know later if I do. Would you like to join me and Linda for dinner?" she asked, but hoped he wouldn't.

"Thanks, but I'm exhausted after my long trip and I ate a late lunch. I'm going to grab a snack, take a steam shower, and turn in early. When you see Doctor Burkman next time, thank him for me for all he's done for you. Good night, Cass, and I'm glad you're doing better. If there's anything you need, if it's only to talk, just call me at home or at the office."

"Thank you, Peter, and good night."

Cass watched him leave via the patio door rather than going through the kitchen where Linda was working. *Peter, Peter, Peter, should I trust you or not? Tragedies do have a way of bringing people closer together or healing old wounds, and your concern and advice seem sincere, and contradictory to what would benefit you most. You could have let me go off the deep end three weeks ago and legally gained control of my estate, but instead you quickly sought medical help for me! It's fortunate that you inherited fifteen percent more than I did, because a vice-versa decision or a fifty/fifty split would have angered you. Since you're the major stockholder in all eight companies, I can't really cause significant trouble to you with them. Your change of heart is so confusing! If you're being deceitful, what are your motive and intentions? And how far will you go to obtain your goals?*

But if you're truly offering me an olive branch, Cass reasoned, *I don't want to risk damaging it because we do have business connections and we're still neighbors. I just wish I wasn't so leery of you! I suppose the only thing I can do is watch and wait to see what happens, and pray it isn't bad.*

She halted her rambling thoughts and joined Linda in the kitchen. She pasted on a smile. "How is it coming? Do you need any help?"

"Just about finished. Is Mr. Grantham joining us?"

Cass noticed how Linda glanced toward the den. The nurse had clearly groomed herself, and three plates were waiting on the counter. "No, he was tired. He's already gone; he left by the patio door. I'll set the table."

Later as they ate, Linda remarked, "Mr. Grantham seems nice, and very concerned about you. To be frank, he wasn't what I was expecting."

Cass recalled how Linda had watched Peter in the den. She chose her words with care. If the nurse became interested in Peter and started dating him, it wouldn't do to say something bad that Linda could repeat to him. She laughed as if jesting and asked, "Better or worse than you anticipated?"

"Much better. Are you aware he has a reputation as a ladies' man?"

Cass saw a faint rosy flush on Linda's cheeks and sparkle in her large green eyes. *Please be careful and go slow with him, my friend, and I wish I could say that aloud, but I dare not.* "I haven't made friends here with whom I exchange confidences, so I've only overheard idle gossip and heard Tom tease him about his reputation a few times. Since Peter lived here and Tom and I resided elsewhere for the first two years after we married, I wasn't around him enough to witness anything to give me that impression. After we moved to Sea Island, he was always a gentleman when we three went out together or attended the same social occasions. I've never

194

observed him being overly flirtatious with women, and I've never seen him have an over-night guest. In fact, he's usually home before midnight even on weekends." *That much is true.*

Cass laughed and clarified, "I don't spy on him, but it's impossible not to be aware of his comings and goings since he lives in my back-yard. I do know that he's charming and capti-vating to a lot of females, and he is considered to be a valuable catch because of his looks, status, and wealth. Actually, I've seen women go after him at parties or dinners or business events with such boldness that it almost shocked me." She shrugged. "In all honesty, he doesn't appear to take unfair advantage of their weaknesses for him, but I can't say for certain if he deserves a playboy reputation."

"I suppose when such a desirable man is still single at his age, people assume there's a dark reason. Maybe he just hasn't met Miss Right."

"What about you, Linda? Have you met Mr. Right? Do you have a boyfriend here or back home? Unless that's too personal to ask."

"I don't mind, since we are friends. I thought I'd met my true love years ago, but he fell for one of my sisters when I took him home to meet my family. For a while I was bitter toward both of them, downright furious with them, but I realized he and I didn't have a commitment and they were perfectly matched. They're hap-pily married with children now. That's part of the reason why I moved here; it was painful seeing them together. But I got over him and got to love it here, so I stayed."

"I would imagine it's hard to meet eligible men in your line of work, especially since you often move in with your patients until they're well."

"Yes, it is, and most of them are married or too old for me. Even the younger women I nurse have sons too young for me, and the older ones have sons who already are taken. Of course, that doesn't stop some of the men from flirting with me behind their wives' or girl-friends' backs. Maybe I'll be like you and not marry until I'm in my thirties."

Cass felt moved by Linda's revelation and disclosed the sad details of her first marriage and the husband who had cheated on her.

"That's a shame. Men can be such asses at times."

"Yes, they can, and often, by the time we re-alize what a sorry bastard one is, we've already fallen for him."

"I know what you mean; I've had a few soured romances. Sometimes I fear I don't know how to choose the right kind of man."

Now, I know what you mean! "I only had one slightly serious relationship between my divorce from Brad and marriage to Tom, but experi-ences like those can cause us to doubt our-selves."

"Do you dread getting back into the dating game?"

"Absolutely, and it will probably be a long time before I do."

Sorry about that, Jason, Linda thought, *but she could change her mind; you could change it for her. I'll have to whisper in your ear about her bad experiences with men so you'll understand why she's gun shy about romance.*

On Thursday, while Inez cleaned the house and grocery shopped, Cass and Linda followed their established routine to return Cass to physical and emotional well-being.

Jason did not come over, but he phoned to check on Cass. While she had privacy, Linda told him about Peter discussing business and Tom's will with Cass last night but that her patient hadn't seemed to get upset and her vital signs were good afterward. She related how solicitous Peter was, and how well he and Cass seemed to get along.

When Cass was summoned to speak with Jason, she told him that Peter sent his thanks for her excellent care and speedy recovery. And she told him she was feeling stronger each day, thanks to him.

Jason wondered why Peter was not upset by or suspicious of the fact that the man whom he had helped cuckold was the physician who was treating his stepmother. He couldn't deduce why Peter had not mentioned to her that they knew each other and how; of course, Peter's doing so would expose his perfidious deed in the past. Then again, neither had he told Cass. He intended to reveal the truth to her as soon as she had time to get to know him better, because he didn't want to risk her misjudging his motive for reaching out to her.

After her talk with Jason ended, Cass realized the call had been too short and formal to suit her. Many grim tasks loomed before her, and she had missed his enjoyable visits. She dreaded calling the gynecologist tomorrow, and wondered how and what she would tell Jason if any of those tests came back abnormal or positive.

Chapter Nine

Friday afternoon while she was supposed to be resting, Cass phoned the gynecologist's office for the report on her recent blood tests. She almost cried in joy after receiving the good news that all results were negative or normal. At least Tom had spared her a sexually transmitted disease. She had one enormous worry off of her mind and burden off of her shoulders.

As soon as Linda departed next Tuesday and while Inez was gone for the night, she planned to get rid of those repulsive videos and risqué lingerie from Tom's briefcase and car. She also needed to do a thorough examination of the house and Tom's belongings to make certain there were no other revealing items secreted elsewhere. The bracelet Tom had purchased — perhaps or perhaps not for her — needed to be returned or exchanged, as it was too expensive to give to Linda as a farewell gift, and *she* certainly didn't want it after what she had learned about the man.

She was disappointed that she hadn't heard from Kristy by now, and hoped that wasn't a sign that her friend wouldn't forgive her. If Kristy didn't write or call within another week, she would make another overture. If that one also failed, she would cease trying for a while.

Inez . . . Cass didn't know what she should do about her housekeeper. The older woman had been too quiet and watchful this week. Although Inez had not been belligerent to either her or Linda, she had continued to notice the woman's offensive expressions when Inez didn't realize she was being watched. Cass wanted to be happy again; and she didn't think that was possible with Inez working for her. Yes, she was grateful for all the woman had done for her, especially recently, but that didn't mean she had to make herself miserable.

As for Jason, according to Linda, he wasn't coming by today to examine her, but was to phone for an updated report on her condition. She couldn't help but wonder why Jason hadn't been over since Tuesday, after coming to see her for the four previous days. He had seemed to enjoy himself. Perhaps he thought Peter might not approve of a housecall, since they were both single. Or perhaps he was worried about her misreading his interest in her. She hoped she hadn't scared him off by allowing her feelings to show!

Cass was in the shower when Jason phoned later that afternoon, so she didn't get to speak with him. Yet, she was delighted when Linda told her that Jason was taking them to a wonderful restaurant on St. Simons Island, tomorrow night. He told Linda to tell her that she needed to get out of the house that it was her "doctor's orders" to be ready to leave at six o'clock.

Cass decided that since Linda would be their chaperone and Peter had also advised her to get out and have fun, she would do just that! She already knew what she was going to wear: a special outfit from Gruppo Americano Studio that she had purchased last spring from Neiman Marcus. It had a white double-breasted jacket in satin-back crepe with navy buttons and piping around the pockets and lapels. A navy bustier with white trim went underneath, and its pleated pants had navy-and-white stripes in a seersucker pattern. She would complete her attire with navy Calvin Klein strappy "Sabrina" heels, matching camera bag, and pearl studs in her ears. She would shampoo her hair tomorrow and set it with large hot curlers. She would apply her makeup and perfume with subtlety so it wouldn't appear as if she were trying to impress and ensnare Dr. Jason Burkman, which could be exactly what her contradictory thoughts had in mind.

At Blanche's Courtyard on Ocean Boulevard on the next island, Jason opened the front and back doors for Cass and Linda to get out of his BMW sedan. The restaurant was seemingly nestled in a cool and shady spot with lots of greenery, and its bayou Victorian atmosphere appealed to locals and tourists.

Jason held the door for them. They were seated immediately in a raised section of booths whose benches had floral padding for comfort. Tables were decorated with striped cloths in mauve, green, blue, and gold which matched the colors on the benches. Other areas were more casual with wood tables and kitchen-style chairs in a pink-and-aqua color scheme. The decor — pictures, mirrors, art objects, some furnishings, woodwork, wallpaper — again reflected that bayou Victorian air.

Their waitress took their cocktail orders. While she left to fill them, they studied the menu and read the daily specials from a chalk board on a nearby wall. Cass decided on grilled snapper; Linda, on mahi mahi; and Jason, on steak.

"Are you sure I'm allowed to have a drink tonight?" Cass asked him.

"You deserve one to celebrate getting better; that's why I told Linda to skip your medication today. I hope you'll like that special I ordered for you."

I'm sure I would love almost anything you selected for me. "I suppose this is what could be called a day off for good behavior?"

"Absolutely, Cass. Doctors always like it when they have cooperative patients who make them look good by obeying their orders and getting well," Jason responded with a grin. "Consider tonight your reward."

"I'm sure it will be; I'm already having a wonderful time. And I have you and Linda to thank for helping me reach this point; I couldn't have done it without you two or if I had stayed under Doctor Hines's excessive treatments. I should be the one treating you two to dinner to show my gratitude."

"A verbal thanks and a bright smile are all we need. Right, Linda?" Jason asked, and the nurse smiled and nodded agreement.

"And you need for me to pay my bills on time," Cass jested.

"Don't worry about your account with me; your insurance company will cover most of the charges, and I trust you to take care of the balance at your leisure. Linda's salary goes through my office." As Cass and Linda chatted, Jason's mind added, *But I don't care if you don't pay me a cent; just being with you is all the compensation I need. I admit it, woman, I love you and want you, and the obstacle that stood in the way of me trying to win you has been removed by fate.* Then, Jason realized there could be another obstacle to hurdle. *Lord help me if Peter messes up this chance for happiness, because I don't know what I would do to him this time for screwing up my life again. He wronged me, but there's no telling what the clever bastard would do or say to exonerate himself in her eyes. He was so damned careful and devious during his affair with Brenda that he made himself look innocent but I know the sorry bastard was just as guilty as she was! I just don't know how close you two are, or whose story you would believe. But either way, I'm in an unpredictable position because it might appear as if I have an ulterior motive for helping and pursuing you. Please, Cass, trust me.*

When the "special" arrived, it was a mixture of liqueurs and fruit juices in a souvenir glass shaped like a flower pot. Across its side was printed in black letters, "I got potted at . . . Blanche's Courtyard." It also included a drawing of a Victorian lady. Cass eyed it, then looked at Jason. "If I drink all of this, I *will* be potted. You two will probably have to carry me out on a stretcher."

They laughed before Jason lifted his glass of Chivas Regal and said, "A toast, ladies: To good friends and better days ahead for all of us."

Cass tapped her "pot" to his glass and to Linda's one of white wine.

As they sipped their drinks and ate appetizers, Linda and Jason told her about the restaurant's appeal as a fun place where the band members often coaxed customers to sing along and dance in the large area near a railed-off music corner with Victorian latticework near the ceiling. Inside the semi-circle was a ragtime piano, drums, and other instruments.

"They won't start playing until later," Linda said, "but I think you'll enjoy them. I have a good time just watching other people cut up. Sometimes the guys who play here remind me of an old-timey vaudeville act."

"Sounds great," Cass responded. She looked at Jason and asked, "How are your children and grandchildren?" She saw his eyes light up with love and pride, which warmed her heart.

"They're doing fine. I talked with both of them yesterday. I'll be going up to visit them in May. I have to see those grandsons of mine at least every six weeks so they'll remember who Granddaddy is. I wish Traci and her family lived here so I could see them more often, but at least Savannah isn't too far away for frequent visits, and Atlanta won't be either after Stacey finishes medical school and goes into practice there."

"I can tell you enjoy them. I'm sure you're a wonderful father and grandfather." *I wonder if you'd want to start over from scratch . . .*

"I try to be. Having a family is a real blessing. Joan and I would have liked to have had more children, but it wasn't in the cards for her."

"Do you have pictures of them with you?" Cass asked.

"Yep. Would you like to see them?" he asked and she nodded.

As she was looking at the pictures, their meals were brought to the table, and she returned the snapshots to Jason. "Your daughter is beautiful and your son is handsome," Cass complimented. "Traci's twins are good-looking boys, too. I bet she adores them."

He chuckled before saying, "She does, but

they can be more than a handful at times. They surely keep her busy."

"I would imagine so . . . Well, doesn't this snapper look marvelous?"

"I've ordered it before and it was delicious. I don't eat that much red meat anymore, but I was in a steak mood tonight. How is your fish, Linda?"

"Divine, cooked to perfection," Linda answered before taking another bite. She wished Peter could have joined them tonight. She had seen him going to or returning from work on Thursday and Friday and when he stopped in to check on Cass this morning. Each time he had caused her heart to flutter wildly. She would be ecstatic if she could land a date with him, but there was little chance of that happening since their worlds were so far apart and he could have his choice of women. Still, he had looked at her several times and sent her smiles that enflamed her entire body, so maybe he would ask her out.

As they dined, Cass, Jason, and Linda conversed about the current dilemma of the Right Whales whose remaining three-hundred count was being dwindled by mysterious deaths, and their migration to the New England and Nova Scotia coasts for the summer. Then they chatted about the different types of businesses in the area, with the pulp company Georgia Pacific being the largest employer of residents. The next two were seafood companies, highly successful competitors of Grantham's: Rich-Sea Pack and King & Prince Seafood.

Cass was glad when they didn't linger on the last topic because she didn't want to spoil her outing with reminders of Thomas Grantham. Later, she would learn more about that subject because of her business interest.

"We also have the Federal Law Enforcement Training Center located here," Jason told her, "That's where Mary's husband teaches; she's my housekeeper, the lady I mentioned to you. FLETC provides basic training for law-enforcement personnel in all fields except for the FBI; they have their own training facility elsewhere. FLETC employs over fifteen hundred people and graduates twenty-five thousand students a year. It's a big boost to the local ecomony. So is tourism, but we're fortunate this area isn't overdeveloped and over-commercialized like so many resort locations."

"Have you heard or read about the Artrain that's coming to Brunswick during their May HarborFest?" Linda asked her.

"No, I haven't been reading many newspapers or watching much local television lately."

Linda told Cass about the Artrain that had three railroad cars altered into a gallery for displaying museum-quality works, and others fashioned into mini-studios for demonstrating the creation of all types of artwork. "The HarborFest will have many varieties of seafood to sample, arts and crafts to purchase, various kinds of music, local history and cultural lessons, and lots of other things to see and do. We should go together."

"Sounds good to me," Cass said, "and my bare social calendar has plenty of room."

"I'll get the dates for next month and call you later to arrange it. We might even persuade Jason to tag along and be our chauffeur and guard." *You would.*

For a while, as excitement coursed through her, Cass forgot she was a recent widow who should be in mourning. She coaxed, "Well, Jason, are you game to be our escort if Linda and I promise not to exhaust you?"

"Sounds good to me, too," he told Cass, then said to Linda, "Just give me the date as soon as possible so I won't schedule an out-of-town trip or put a golf game in that slot." No matter how casually he accepted to avoid appearing thrilled, Jason knew he would clear that date if it was already taken. He felt his body warm from the heat and power of Cass's radiant smile and sultry gaze. Mercy, she had captivating brown eyes; they were as rich and dark and enticing as melted milk chocolate. Her skin was as smooth as costly glass, and just as clear of flaws. She looked ravishing tonight in that navy-and-white outfit; both colors flattered her bisque skin tone. He would be in heaven if he could peel each piece off her body, caress every inch of her, and make slow and rapturous love to her.

Cass noticed that the restaurant was getting crowded and a little noisy. She saw Jason exchange smiles, nods, or waves with people who caught his eye in passing or from another table. She assumed they were a mixture of friends and patients. Perhaps, she mused, he was a regular patron of Blanche's. Perhaps he had brought some of his past dates there. At that thought, nibbles of jealousy assailed her. *I should be ashamed of myself*, Cass admonished herself, *he isn't my date, and I've just buried my husband!*

Despite that rebuke, Cass couldn't get Jason Burkman off of her mind. He was so different in looks and personality from Tom or Brad. Jason was easygoing, amusing, down-to-earth, caring; he made those around him feel comfortable and admired. He was well mannered, highly intelligent, and interesting. His suit — Armani, she guessed — fit his tall and virile build as if it were made just for him. A pale-gray shirt and patterned tie were perfect choices to complete his well-groomed image.

She noticed that his tawny hair seemed lighter and his tan was darker, as if he had been in lots of sun since Tuesday. Those two changes made his teeth look whiter and his eyes bluer. Without a doubt, she was attracted to him, and that made her a little nervous.

As Cass glanced about their surroundings,

she noticed another man. He seemed to be watching her and averting his gaze every time she looked in his direction. She could not recall ever meeting him. She tensed as she wondered if it was a television or newspaper reporter who would do a story about her painting the town red so soon after her husband's death. Perhaps it was a detective, as the investigation into Tom's accident was still in progress as far as she knew. Perhaps he was nothing more than an inquisitive person who had seen hers and Tom's pictures in the media or seen them together at some past occasion. Or perhaps it was just her imagination running wild again. No, Cass deduced, she was right, because the man's female companion became aware of his behavior and twice traced his line of vision to see who had captured his attention. Cass told herself to ignore him, or he'd wonder why he was making her so edgy.

The musicians started to perform on the ragtime piano and assorted Dixieland instruments: drums, horns, tamborine, kazoo. Patrons with birthdays and anniversaries were serenaded. Some diners clapped their hands in time with the music and sang along to tunes of long ago. Others filled the dance area and spilled over into the nearby aisles as they made merry, which blocked the stranger's view of her; and hers, of him.

After he finished eating, Jason put aside his fork and said, "I wouldn't be a good host if I didn't ask you ladies if one or both of you want to dance."

"Not me in that crowd," Linda responded in haste.

Cass smiled and said, "Put me on your card for another time, but thanks for the offer." She would love to discover what it felt like to be held in his arms and to be pressed close to his body, but she didn't think it would look proper tonight. To distract herself from his potent allure, she said, "I'm thinking about getting involved in some local activities and perhaps starting tennis again when you give the okay, Doctor."

"That sounds wonderful, Cass, but you should give yourself another week or so to get fully rested and to take care of any business matters. You don't want to leap into new things too fast and exhaust yourself."

"What about taking a course or two at Brunswick College later?" Linda suggested. "You could audit the classes of your choice. Or you could join some organizations or clubs, like the historical society. You said you wanted to learn more about this area."

"You're right, Linda, and I also need to learn my way around better. I think I'll stop in at the Chamber of Commerce and the Visitor's Center and pick up some packets of information."

Linda gave directions to both locations, then added, "There are some old cotton and rice plantations you might want to visit; maybe we can do that together one day. I've always been a history nut, and there's certainly plenty to see around here. But you shouldn't have any trouble finding your way around the city or islands because they're small and laid out well. I have a little house on St. Simons; it's the largest of the Golden Isles, but we only have a population of about thirteen thousand. I take it you're planning to stay on Sea Island and not return to Augusta or your hometown?" Linda asked for Jason's benefit.

"That's right. Except for a few friends, I don't have any other ties to either place."

That isn't exactly accurate; Jason thought, *you have the business in Augusta. Or maybe Peter inherited it. I wonder what Grantham left to you. If he was as wealthy as I've heard, you should be a very rich woman. That means too many hungry men will be chasing after you soon, and I don't mean for just your money. Lordy, the competition is going to be heavy!*

After their dessert orders were taken and their dinner plates removed, Linda asked, "Did you enjoy your career before you married and do you plan to return to it in the future?"

Cass reasoned that Linda, as a working woman, must assume that she would want or need to work and hadn't stopped to think that it was hardly necessary. "I haven't thought about it, but if I do, it won't be anytime soon. I am planning to make some changes at home that will take up a lot of my time and energy."

"You have a beautiful home, Cass. What changes are you planning?"

"I'm not sure, just things to make it look and feel different."

Linda didn't press the subject. She was aware that Cass had not removed her wedding rings yet, but perhaps Cass was worried about how that would appear to others if she took them off so soon after becoming a widow.

As they ate large slices of Key Lime pie, Jason asked, "Would you ladies like to join me for church and lunch tomorrow before my golf game? I attend First Baptist here on St. Simons. We could eat at Chelsea's on the same road."

"That sounds nice. Linda and I can meet you there. What time?"

"There's no need to take two cars. Since I live down the street from you, I have to drive by your house, so I can pick you up. It won't be any bother because I have to return home afterward to change into my golf clothes. What about ten-thirty? That will give us time to drive over, park, and get seated before the eleven o'clock service begins."

"Linda, how does that sound to you?" Cass inquired.

"Perfect, because that's where I go when I'm not on a case."

They chatted for a while longer. After the bill came and was paid, Jason escorted them to the car and drove them to Cass's home, where he dropped them off and departed.

As Cass prepared herself for bed, anticipation flowed through her. She decided she was going to start enjoying life and her new freedom. She wasn't going to bury herself with her deceitful husband, but she would be careful with her conduct so she wouldn't cause any gossip or annoy Peter.

Thanks to Jason and Linda, she felt as if she were being reborn, and she mustn't, she vowed, let anything or anyone trample her down again.

As Cass settled herself on the pew next to Linda, thinking it unwise to sit beside a distracting and well-groomed Jason, she adjusted the hems of the skirt and jacket to a pale-pink wool crepe suit from Bicci by Florine Wachter. Her fingers checked the bows sewn just above the wrists on the long sleeves of the jacket. A gold clasp connected a double strand of pale-pink pearls that rested at the hollow of her throat, and matching drop earrings dangled from her lobes. Her outfit was completed by Anne Klein scalloped pumps with sling backs and skinny heels in grosgrain and a matching handbag. She was fond of this suit and shoes because she, not Tom for a change, had selected them. Now that Tom was gone, she could part with garments and footwear he had chosen which she didn't like, and she had the money — a nice "allowance"

214

— with which to replace them.

As she glanced around before and after the service began, Cass noticed that the First Baptist Church on Ocean Boulevard was large and lovely. The congregation members smiled and nodded when she caught their eyes; the choir was talented, the music soothing and familiar; the pastor was an excellent speaker; and the atmosphere was calming. Her tension faded; her spirits were uplifted, and her past seemed a million miles away.

Afterward, they lunched at Chelsea's down the street, a restaurant that seemed nestled in an alcove of live oaks, palms, and other greenery. The building had a quaint Victorian flavor, and looked deceptively smaller from outside. Rattan chairs with turquoise seats were placed beside tables with aqua cloths over white ones, and sat atop a shiny brick floor.

They dined on Chelsea salad, chilled jumbo shrimps with remoulade and red sauce, and seafood fettuccine alfredo with shrimp, scallops, mushrooms, and scallions piled atop the pasta.

"You must eat out a lot, Jason, because you know all of the good restaurants. This place is wonderful and the food is delicious."

"Thanks, Cass. I suppose dining out frequently is one of the problems of being single. I much prefer quiet meals at home, but I'm not the world's best chef and I'm usually too tired to cook after I get off work. I surely did enjoy eating with you and Linda those two nights. It was kind of you ladies to take pity on me," he jested.

"Then we'll have to do it again some time soon," Cass responded. "Eating alone isn't any fun, nor is cooking for one person."

Jason nodded agreement. "Did you enjoy yourself this morning?"

"Yes, I haven't been to church in years and it felt good to be there again. During my youth and before I married Tom, I attended regularly, but I got out of that good habit. Tom wasn't a religious man and we stayed on the road too much during our first two years of marriage to attend one. I should be ashamed of myself for not finding a place of worship since I moved here."

"If you liked mine, Cass, I try to go almost every Sunday, so you're welcome to join me. And, as Linda told you, that's where she goes, too, when she isn't confined to a house with a patient."

"It's nice having a patient who isn't confined to bed or home," Linda added, "Cass and I have been having a wonderful time together. I almost hate for her to get better so I'll have to leave."

"Me, too," Cass concurred with a grin. "But we can still get together whenever you have time. Make sure you keep me posted on your schedule."

As the two women ate and chatted, Jason wished he were the one who would be entertaining Cass and spending time with her. Considering her improvement, he couldn't use her health as an excuse to visit her much longer. He wondered how many weeks he should wait before asking her out on a real date and, when he did, would she accept? She seemed to like him and enjoy his company, but she was so conscious of her image and obligations as a recent widow to risk doing anything that might look inappropriate. He just didn't want her to start going out where she could meet another man and become interested in him before he himself could attempt to win her. Yet, he didn't want to offend her by pursuing her too soon after her loss. He needed to discover if her marriage had been a happy one and what kind of man Thomas Grantham had been; knowing those two facts would tell him how deeply and how long she would mourn her lost husband.

Sunday evening following his round of golf, Jason received partial answers to his earlier queries when he decided to grab a bite to eat in the Putter's Club at the Sea Palms Resort before going home, as his friends already had left to join their families for dinner. As he sat in the grill area, sipped his drink, and awaited his food, a colleague noticed his presence and approached his table to speak with him.

"Hello, Jason, how are you doing?"

"Fine. How about you?" he asked the female gynecologist who practiced in Brunswick and often referred patients to him.

"No complaints. I saw you at church and lunch with a new patient of mine, Cassandra Grantham. It's terrible what happened to her, isn't it?"

"Yes, it is. Does she have any medical problems I need to be aware of? I've been treating her for mild anxiety and depression since her husband's death. I have a private nurse staying with her and taking care of her for a couple of weeks so she won't be alone."

"I know Linda Carnes, and I saw her with you two earlier. I assumed they were friends of yours. Mrs. Grantham didn't mention she's under your care or on medication. I wonder why."

Jason was glad he was sitting at a corner table and no one was close enough to overhear their talk. "Probably because she's embarrassed she went to pieces for a while."

"I can understand why. I mean, besides losing her husband, she has other worries on her mind. I'll send you a copy of her blood work, but I didn't find anything unusual. I ran a full screen and other tests."

Jason tried to mask his personal concern and to sound only professional. "What other tests?"

"She wanted a full female check-up; she was embarrassed about the situation, but she requested the full range of STDs and an AIDS test. She said she suspected her husband was having an affair when he was killed and she wanted to make certain, if it was true, she hadn't caught anything from him. I take it she didn't mention those fears or suspicions to you?"

"No, and I can understand why she wouldn't. That's a shame, because Cass is a nice lady. She didn't deserve that added problem."

"So, you two are friends; she's not just a patient?"

Jason waited until the house specialty — Cajaibbean shrimp — was placed before him and the waitress departed before he answered the rather nosy question, "Yes, we've known each other since she moved here last fall. I only met her husband on a few occasions, but that's because he traveled a great deal. I do know her stepson, Peter; he runs Grantham Seafood and Grantham Electronics in Brunswick." Jason noted the mischievous grin that creased the gynecologist's face.

"Ah, yes, Peter Grantham; I've seen him many times, even been hit on by him at least twice. He thinks he's a real charmer and irresistible to women. Well, he isn't my type and I told him so. I pity Mrs. Grantham having to deal with him; he strikes me as being real money and power hungry, and a sex fiend to boot. Perhaps father and son weren't very different, if you catch my meaning. She was plenty worried about it."

Jason didn't like the way she was acting more like a gossip than a physician, but he didn't stop her, wanting to learn more about Cass. "You said all of her tests were either negative or normal?"

"That's right; I gave her the good news when she called me on Friday. I couldn't miss her sigh of relief even over the phone. I'll send you a copy of her file for your records."

"Thanks, but don't mention that to Cass; she'll be embarrassed. Would you like to join me?" Jason felt compelled to ask the woman.

"Thanks, but I'm joining friends in the Main Course. They're probably waiting for me now and wondering where I am. Perhaps we can get together another time; I hope so. It was good to see you."

"You, too," he half-lied before she left for the main dining room.

As he ate his food with a now lagging appetite, Jason didn't know if he should be elated or saddened by the news of Tom's adultery. Without strong suspicions or proof she'd found in Tom's possessions, Cass wouldn't have requested those humiliating tests and examination. If it was a recent discovery, he reasoned, that betrayal and her health fears could have been partly responsible for her emotional crash. His heart ached over her sufferings. He didn't understand how her husband could have been unfaithful to such a wonderful woman. It was selfish on his part to hope Tom was guilty, because an adulterer would be easier to get over, wouldn't he? He wanted to be the man to teach her to love, trust, and commit again. If only his lover's skills could match his medical ones, he could help heal her wounded heart and injured soul.

While Jason was eating alone and worrying, Cass was having a rather nice time at home while Peter grilled steaks by the pool for her and Linda, who prepared baked potatoes, a garden salad, and rolls to accompany them. Cass was stretched out in a cushioned chaise while Peter and Linda stood near the grill and chatted.

She noticed that Peter was being charming and genial with the nurse, though not flirtatious, which she was certain disappointed Linda who seemed enchanted by him. Peter — dressed in casual navy slacks and a red shirt from his golf game this afternoon at the Sea Island Club — was in a jovial mood tonight, one he claimed was brought on by shooting an eagle and several birdies on six holes. He laughed and smiled often, told amusing jokes, and made certain he drew her into the conversation every few minutes. He looked sexy with that ever-present lock of ebony hair falling onto his forehead near his left temple. As with Jason, Peter's tan had deepened with his increase of outdoor sports. With his dark coloring, the shade of his fiery shirt was flattering. She had to admit, he was attractive and virile. There was an earthy, seductive sensuality about him and she understood why so many women found him irresistible. She couldn't deny that Peter Grantham was a superb catch, if his reputation wasn't true. As if he read her thoughts, that was the very topic about which he joked next.

"Did you enjoy church and lunch this morning?" Peter asked.

"Yes, I did. Linda and Jason are good company, and it was nice to get out of the house for a while. Perhaps you'd like to attend next Sunday." *If he comes, Linda, you owe me big for this favor.*

"The congregation would probably faint if I walked in. I'm afraid too many people around here put too much stock in unfounded gossip about me. They might think the world is coming to an end this week if I attended."

"No, they wouldn't," Linda refuted. "I'm a member there and I would love to have you attend. You can sit with me and Cass and I'll introduce you to everyone. They're nice people, so they'll behave themselves."

Peter told the nurse, "I'll think about it. First I have to go to New York on Wednesday morning, but I'll be back on Saturday afternoon." Peter looked at Cass. "There's a big real estate deal I have to check on and either accept or reject it. Would you like to tag along, Cass? We could catch a play, and you could go shopping while I'm busy, or laze

222

around and enjoy room service."

"Not this week, but perhaps another time. Thanks for the invitation."

"I'll keep you informed about my business trips in case you want to go along on one of them."

After eating their meals and doing the clean-up chores, Peter asked, "Anybody game for a swim? I could use the exercise."

Cass laughed and said, "Not me; it's too chilly for my blood."

"What about you, Linda?" Peter asked.

The nurse was delighted he had started using her first name. "Sounds good to me; I have a swimsuit upstairs. I'll go change."

While Linda was gone, Peter asked, "Are you sure you don't want to go to New York with me? It would be a wonderful diversion for both of us. Don't forget, Linda is leaving on Tuesday, so you'll be here alone."

"I know, and I appreciate your thoughtfulness, but it's too soon for me to enjoy a holiday like that. Another time?"

"I'll hold you to that promise. While I'm gone, if you get scared or lonely at night, just asked Inez to sleep over until I return. And I'll phone and check on you every day."

"I'll be fine, Peter, so don't worry about me, but thanks."

After Linda and Peter finished their swim

Cass joined them as they all went into her house to watch a movie he had rented at the video store.

As it began, Peter said, "I've been wanting to see this for a long time. My secretary told me it's hilarious. If you two get bored, just tell me and I'll take it over to my place and finish it there. That won't hurt my feelings."

As they watched the comedy, all three laughed, sipped their colas, and nibbled on the popcorn they had prepared.

After it finished playing and was rewinding, Peter asked, "Is there anything you want me to pick up for you tomorrow Cass?"

"Nothing I can think of. Inez keeps everything well stocked."

"What about if I bring you fresh shrimp right off the boat for supper? I can have it here by five o'clock."

Cass smiled and thought, *You'll owe me again, Linda, if this works.* "That will be fine, if you'll join us to eat it."

"I would love to, but I already have a business dinner with a new client for our electronics company. I'll take a rain check if you're issuing them."

"Consider yourself invited for another night. Thanks for buying and cooking the steaks; they were delicious. And the movie was very funny. This has been a most pleasant and relaxing evening."

"We had a wonderful time, Peter," Linda

added. "Thank you."

Peter replaced the tape in its clear container, smiled, and said, "I thoroughly enjoyed myself, ladies, and I bid you good night."

While Cass and Linda were strolling on the beach Monday morning and Inez was at the store, Kristy Stillman Franklin left a message on Cass's answering machine.

When Cass returned home and found it, she was elated, filled with relief. She wished she could speak with Kristy that very minute, but Kristy had said she was leaving town immediately because she had rented her house to a golfer who was playing in the Master's tournament this week. Many local Augustans did the same thing to earn extra money, as most rentees paid enormous amounts to have large and well-located homes at their disposal for resting and for entertaining.

Cass could hardly wait for Kristy's return home so they could talk, really talk for the first time in years. Kristy sounded just as eager as she was to renew their friendship. Since a talk was impossible today, she went shopping with Linda just to browse and have an outing, though she suspected that Linda was using that excuse to lure her out into public to get her more at ease about doing so.

They looked at clothing at several fun clothing and shoe stores at True Oaks Shopping Center and wandered through Goad's Gallery

225

at the Shops at Sea Island where Cass purchased a silk screen and a painting by the talented artist and owner. She also purchased a lovely beach scene that Linda kept admiring and presented it to her as a combination thank-you and farewell gift. After those items were placed in Linda's car, they made several purchases at G. J. Ford Bookshop.

Their last stop was at the Winn-Dixie grocery store at Retreat Village so Cass could pick up boxes to use to pack away Tom's things later this week, a task she both looked forward to and dreaded.

During their day together, Linda talked about what a good time she had last night and how attractive Peter was. Cass hoped she wasn't making a mistake by not warning her friend away from Tom's son, but Linda was an adult and could make her own decisions and form her own impressions. What's more, she couldn't risk her comments finding their way into Peter's ears if he and Linda decided to date, which she doubted would happen. All she could do was hope and pray that Linda didn't get hurt emotionally.

On Tuesday morning, Cass and Linda hugged and said their good-byes and made plans to continue their friendship with future visits.

"If you need me, Cass, call me and I'll come over if I'm not working. If I am, at least we can chat. I'm going to miss you and this cushy job."

Cass laughed at her amusing expression before she said, "I'm going to miss you, too. Call me after you get settled at home."

"I will, and you take good care of yourself."

"I promise to obey Jason's orders to the letter," Cass vowed, though she was a little surprised and disappointed that Jason hadn't come by last night or this morning, since he knew Linda was departing. He had simply spoken to Linda by phone and given her instructions to pass along to her. She hadn't seen or talked to him since Sunday after lunch, and, she realized, she missed his smile, missed his voice, missed him in entirety.

As Cass relaxed and read that afternoon in her private suite, the next call she received wasn't from Linda or Jason; it was an unexpected one from a man she had seen recently.

Chapter Ten

Inez came to where Cass was reading in the den to tell her there was a phone call for her, as the housekeeper had been instructed not to screen her calls or visitors any longer.

Cass thanked her and lifted the receiver nearby. "Hello, this is Mrs. Grantham speaking."

"Mrs. Grantham, you've been a hard lady to reach. I wanted to extend my condolences for your husband's death and to see if there's any way I can assist you if you're interested in selling your home."

"I beg your pardon? Who is this? What do you want?"

"I'm sorry, ma'am. I was so excited to finally reach you that I forgot to tell you my name. This is Samuel Tarver of Tarver Realty Company on St. Simons Island. After your tragic loss last month, I drove by your home and took several pictures, then tried to contact you to see what your plans are; widows often want to move and make a fresh start or get into a smaller place. I was told you were out of town, but one of my agents thought he saw you having dinner with friends Saturday night at

228

Blanche's Courtyard; he remembered you from pictures in the local newspaper."

Cass was relieved to discover that one of the inquisitive drivers and the man at the restaurant were nothing more than eager real estate agents wanting to drum up business. Perhaps that was also true for some of the other people whom she had believed were being nosy about her and Tom. Perhaps some had been hopeful buyers of her property. "I appreciate your interest, Mr. Tarver," Cass responded, "but I haven't made a decision in that matter, and won't be doing so for at least several months."

"Would you mind if I sent you my card and a letter of introduction so you can consider me and my company if you do decide to move? I'm sure I can get you an excellent price and quick sale. You have a lovely and valuable piece of property, and the market is in your favor at this time."

Cass was relieved and impressed that the man didn't seem pushy and persistent.

"Of course you can send that information, and I will give you the opportunity to speak with me if I decide to relocate here or elsewhere. But I'm not ready to discuss the matter at this date. I have other personal and business matters occupying my time and energies."

"I understand, ma'am, and I appreciate you taking my call today." Mr. Tarver's tone was genuinely polite.

Wednesday morning after Peter left on his private jet for New York, Cass decided to start making a few changes in herself and her home to help chase away Tom's ghostly presence. She would begin slowly to not antagonize Peter by making it appear as if she hadn't loved Tom and was eager to remove all traces of him from her existence. She wouldn't redecorate the entire house but would make alterations in needed areas, such as the upstairs suite where Tom had defiled their marriage bed.

First, she removed her wedding rings. She put them in her closet safe temporarily until she came up with the right idea for using the diamonds and gold in another piece of jewelry, if she didn't decide to sell them. She had burned the video tapes last night while she had privacy, and had placed the naughty lingerie in a paper sack and deposited it in the trash. Fortunately the garbage company picked up on Sea Island on Wednesdays so there was no chance of Inez going through the bags.

At nine o'clock, Cass showered and dressed in a khaki chambray tunic top with khaki-and-white striped sleeves and coordinating striped pants. She slid her feet into beige Nubuck slings by Bruno Magli. On her right hand, she put on an emerald-and-diamond ring; on her left, she wore a diamond-encircled five-karat Russian Alexandrite — her birthstone — which Tom had given to her when she turned thirty-five last June. She clasped a gold watch and bracelet on her wrists and inserted creamy pearl studs in her pierced ears. She applied a light covering of cosmetics, sprayed on Ciara perfume, and brushed her long hair.

She was delayed for ten minutes while speaking with Linda who had phoned to see how she was doing. After Cass revealed her plans, Linda said she wished she could join her but she was packing to head for a new assignment this afternoon.

After telling a surprised Inez she was going shopping, Cass drove to a fine furniture store in Brunswick and selected a new bed with an intricately carved walnut headboard, which would match the other furniture in her suite. The store agreed to deliver it that afternoon to Cass's delight. She went to Glynn Place Mall on the Golden Isles Parkway and purchased new bed linens and accessories at one of the four large department stores located there, all in a feminine Victorian pattern in shades of pinks, mauves, creams, and greens. She knew her choices would make her suite look different from the blacks, browns, and beiges of the English Manor design which the decorator had used and Tom had loved, but not her.

While she was at the mall, she visited several other stores and shops and made more purchases to enhance the look she had in mind. Before heading home, she splurged on a late lunch of a hamburger with all of the trimmings, french fries, and a diet 7-up.

Cass was glad Inez had left at two o'clock for a dental appointment because it prevented the woman from witnessing her actions and annoying her with questions and comments. The new bed arrived at three o'clock, and she paid the deliverymen extra to disassemble the old headboard and store it in the garage for her until she decided what to do with it. As soon as the men were gone, she carried the boxes loaded with old linens to the garage and placed them there, too.

Afterward, Cass made the bed with a new mattress pad, sheets, pillows, coverlet, and dust ruffle. She placed an assortment of decorative shams and throw pillows on it in various sizes and shapes. She stood on a ladder to hang the matching swags and ivory sheers, then added a painting over the bed of a Victorian lady sitting on a window seat and reading a book of poetry. Where she had removed souvenirs of Tom's from past holidays, including the Atlas statue he had given to her, she set other items here and there: miniature pictures of flowers, a ceramic Lenox rose, a candleholder with a pedestal-style base with tiny pale-pink and dark-mauve roses and ivy draped over it, and a hand-painted oval ring box.

When she finished, she walked around the room and paused in several places to admire the striking and soothing results. Now this bed would be hers, and no ghosts of Tom and his lovers would trouble her at night.

There was no need to redecorate her bath and dressing room, as Tom had had his own bathing and grooming area on the other side of the bedroom.

She headed down the hallway to do a few things downstairs, but halted at Tom's old office to close that door until she could redo it into a sitting room or an office for herself.

Using a laundry basket, she removed pictures and other reminders of Tom in the living room and den. Where a large picture of Cass and Tom had been sitting on a fossil stone mosaic console in the formal room, she placed the Goad silk mini-screen. She stepped back and eyed the replacement. She smiled because it was lovely; it was hers; it was perfect for that spot.

Where Tom's portrait had hung over a fireplace in the den, she suspended the new painting she had purchased this week, a serene watercolor featuring the local marsh view. She packed the portrait in the painting's box to protect it against damage until she could give it to Peter, if he wanted it.

Since it was past six-thirty, Cass took a break to eat some raw carrots, a ham sandwich, no-fat yogurt, and an apple, washing down the food with a caffeine-free cola. As she snacked, she watched the last twenty minutes of the national news and the first ten minutes of a talk show. Concentrating on the television allowed her to stop thinking about Tom and her impending chore.

After she finished and cleaned up the kitchen and breakfast room table, Cass headed upstairs to begin her next task. She decided not to box up Tom's clothes until she asked Peter if he wanted to go through them. The men were almost the same size and Tom's garments were expensive ones from top designers, so Peter might want some of them. While she had privacy, she went through every pocket of every item to make certain Tom hadn't left a revealing note or item there for his son or another person to find, but discovered nothing. Using a stepladder, she did the same with the shoe boxes and other containers on the closet shelves, then checked the drawers of the built-in chest.

Cass then went to Tom's office and sat a box on the floor. She placed his scrapbook and photo album in it to give to Peter. She examined the contents in every drawer, file folder, and on every shelf. Once more, she decided to ask Peter to go through them to see if there was anything he wanted to take for himself.

As she worked, Cass recalled the diary that she had placed in her closet safe until she was in the mood to break the lock and read it. If there was nothing scandalous written there, she would give it to Peter. But if dark secrets were exposed, she would destroy it, as it would be cruel and unnecessary to subject Peter to the same kind of torment she had endured upon learning the bitter truth.

It was almost eleven o'clock and she had accomplished a lot, so she showered and put on a shiny emerald nightgown, its satin material feeling sensuous against her bare flesh. As she lay down between the new sheets, she thought how good it felt to be in a bed that the traitorous Tom hadn't slept in. She smiled and enjoyed her new and clean surroundings. Even the smell in the room was different, fresh and invigorating. Her head was clear now that she didn't have to take medication, but she was drowsy and relaxed and calm despite her exertions and excitement.

Thursday morning, the housekeeper asked in horror, "What have you done, Mrs. Grantham? Where are Mr. Tom's pictures, his treasures, his bed, and his linens?"

Cass witnessed a look of shock on Inez's face. She continued to arrange the flowers and greenery she had gathered from outside in a lovely vase. "I made a few changes yesterday after you left to help get rid of the gloomy atmosphere in the house. Don't they look wonderful?"

"Oh, my heavens, it's awful! What is Mr. Peter going to say?"

Cass halted her task, looked at the woman, and asked, "Why would he have anything to say, Inez? This is my home, not his."

"But Mr. Tom would be terribly upset! He would —"

"Tom is dead, Inez, gone forever. I only removed things that were painful reminders of him, so —"

"But you shouldn't forget him! Not this soon, ma'am!"

It was obvious to Cass that Inez was not thinking clearly or she would remember that she was the employee and was speaking offensively to her boss! "It's been over a month since Tom's death, Inez. If I want to keep my sanity and find some happiness again, I can't mourn him day and night. I can't let this house become a memorial to him; I must put away my past with him and get on with my life. That's what Peter told me to do several times."

"But I'm sure Mr. Peter didn't mean for you to act so foolish. You even took down Mr. Tom's picture over the fireplace and others in the den."

Inez's last statement sounded as if the woman was accusing Cass of committing a crime. "Would you want your dead husband staring down at you every day after he was gone? How can I relax in the den with that constant reminder of him?" *and his blasted treacheries!*

"I would cherish my husband's memory and look at it every day."

"I guess that's where we differ, Inez, and

236

people do have different ways of grieving, recovering, and starting a new life. Don't worry, Tom's memory won't fade; several donations were made to charities and foundations in his honor."

"But you've shoved him out of his home, ma'am. That's wrong."

"This is no longer Tom's home, Inez; it's mine; you work for me now, and Peter. I have to do what I think is best for me, so I'll make any changes that are necessary for me to do so," she added in a tone of warning to silence the irritated and brazen woman. "The old bed and its linens are in the garage. If you would like to have them, they're yours." Cass noted that the woman looked as if she had slapped her in the face.

"Oh, no, ma'am, I couldn't sleep on Mr. Tom's bed!"

Nor could I, you old witch! "Then I'll donate them and Tom's clothes to a local charity or church fund to help the unfortunate. As soon as Peter goes through them to make certain he doesn't want any of them, I'll box them up and deliver them myself. Since these changes so obviously annoy and anger you, I wouldn't dream of asking you to run that errand for me." Cass hoped that pointing out how the woman's conduct appeared to her would cause Inez to grasp her unacceptable behavior and correct it. "Now, is there anything else you want to say or ask before you return to your chores?"

"No, ma'am, nothing."

Cass deduced that her ploy worked, because Inez didn't argue with her again before she left the room, but neither did the sullen housekeeper apologize for being impolite and bossy.

Cass was delighted when Jason phoned later in the evening to see how she was getting along since Linda's departure. She told him she was feeling fine and had been doing a little redecorating. She even whispered into the receiver that Inez was most displeased with her for making those changes. She also told him that Peter was away, and she missed Linda's company. "I could have used her help carrying packages while I was shopping yesterday."

"It's good to hear you've been going out and you're staying busy. I have this afternoon off, so why don't I stop by at one to check on you before my golf game?"

"That would be nice. I have appointments with our lawyer and accountant at three and four-thirty, so your timing is perfect. And would you check to see if Mary Ellis still has an opening? I'll need to make a change in housekeepers soon."

"I'll be happy to do that favor. You'll find Mary delightful to be around and she's a wonderful worker, honest, dependable, good-natured."

"Anything and anybody would improve my

current situation, but she sounds like a treasure."

At twelve-forty-five, Cass sent Inez to purchase a few items at the grocery store so the woman wouldn't be there when Jason arrived. As she showed him the changes she had made in the house, she queried him about Mary Ellis.

"She said she could come on Mondays and Thursdays if that would be sufficient for your needs," Jason revealed. "Today is the last day with her other employer because they're moving soon, so she can start next week."

"Two days a week will be perfect. I don't need a daily housekeeper; that was Tom's idea. He insisted that I not do any cleaning or cooking, or even laundry and errands. But I don't mind doing some of those things and I did them before we married. All I need is for Mary to clean the house thoroughly, and I can take care of the rest. In fact, it will give me worthwhile things to do with my time."

"That sounds like a good idea to me. And, yes, you can stop taking any medication, but continue with the exercises and relaxation techniques that Linda taught you. And make sure you eat three well-balanced meals a day."

Cass laughed and quipped, "Don't worry, Doctor, I can cook. I may be a little rusty, but I'm sure it will come back to me with practice."

Jason grinned as his blue gaze drifted over her. "You look and sound wonderful, Cass, and

I'm pleased with your progress. No, your *recovery*. In my opinion, you're totally well."

Cass made a mock half-bow and said, "Thank you, Jason, because I feel wonderful, better every day."

"What you're doing with the house and for yourself is good for you because you look radiant and relaxed. I remember when I had to pack away reminders of the past. It can be difficult, but therapeutic. New surroundings help the healing process. I resisted making those needed changes for too long after Joan died because of the children; it was their home, too, and I didn't want them to think I was discarding her memory too fast; but I moved a year later." Jason decided to drop a few facts about himself in case they made a difference to her and could hinder a future relationship. "Actually, I remarried, but it was too fast and we weren't compatible, so it didn't work out. I've been divorced for thirteen months. I bought the new house a few blocks down the street from here and completely refurnished it after the divorce. I've been happy there."

"I'm sorry to hear you had such trouble, but as you said about me, you look and sound as if you're doing great now."

"It was a mistake for both of us, but we corrected it quickly. Thank goodness we didn't have a child, so I don't have any ties to her. She's long gone and far away from Sea Island. Now, back to Mary. I'll give you her phone

240

number. She'll probably want to meet with you to check the size of your house and duties you want her to perform before she gives you a price, but she's very reasonable." Jason glanced at his watch and said, "Well, I best get going and get changed so I won't be late for our tee-off time. I do want you to come to my office in a couple of weeks and get a complete physical. Call my receptionist and make an appointment for around the twenty-fifth. But call me at home or the office if you have any problems before that date."

As Cass escorted him toward the door, she said, "I will, and thanks for everything you've done for me."

"It's easy to do things for you, Cass, because you're a special person."

Cass smiled in gratitude, but didn't respond in like kind. If he didn't leave soon, she was going to melt under that fiery blue gaze! She could hardly keep from staring at him, from touching him! He was just too enchanting and irresistible, too darned tempting! She opened the door and said, "Thanks for stopping by, Jason."

He paused in the doorway, turned, and asked, "Would you like to have dinner with me tomorrow night at the Cloister? Maybe take a scenic drive afterward? We could both use a diversion after a hard week of work."

Cass accepted before comtemplating whether or not she should, "That sounds nice. I love the

Cloister. What time?"

"I'll pick you up about six-forty-five and we'll eat at seven. Okay?"

"Perfect. I'll see you then. Good luck with your game today. Good-bye, Jason."

She watched him get into his car, start the engine, and leave. Luck was on her side today, she decided, because Jason was out of sight before Inez returned, still in a belligerent mood. With other and more important matters on her mind, Cass ignored the woman and went to freshen up for her two appointments.

Before leaving the house later, Cass not only let Inez leave early that afternoon but also gave her Friday off, which the housekeeper protested to no avail. *If luck stays with me tomorrow when I meet with Mary, you've seen your last day here.*

As she drove to the two meetings, Cass recalled that both would be brief ones because she had given the men such short notice when she'd made them yesterday. In fact, she still was surprised they had agreed to see her so soon after contacting them. She was dressed in a lovely pale-green suit by Oberon, low heels, and simple jewelry. She had worn her wedding rings out of what she considered propriety for this occasion. Her hair was clean, shiny, and wavy from hot rollers. Her makeup had been applied with a light, but flattering, touch; as had Chanel #5 perfume.

She waited only five minutes before she was shown into the lawyer's office and seated before his large burled walnut desk. She was greeted with courtesy and received an advanced apology for the impending rush. She smiled and said it was unnecessary and she appreciated him taking time from his busy schedule to see her.

Tom's lawyer got down to business immediately and went over the will with her, but there was very little to discover, as Peter had covered almost everything in their past discussion. She learned that all of the dispensations either had been handled or were still in progress. He gave her the deed to the house, now in her name, for which the loan balance had been paid off as per Tom's instructions. The trust fund had been set up at Tom's local bank and was functioning to support her. She took the file Simon Johnson handed to her containing a list of her holdings, due dates for payments of interests and earnings, and other legal papers, and was told to keep it in a safe place. He explained the re-marriage stipulation, saying she could keep anything she had collected from the trust fund to that point in time; any balance would be turned over to Peter on the day of her re-marriage. And, the bloodline will returned all Grantham monies and properties to Peter or his heirs following her demise, no matter if she rewed or the ten-year timetable had passed and she had collected the entire inheritance.

Simon also explained that although she had a forty-nine-percent interest in the eight companies, Peter was in control of running them. At that point, he asked her if she had any questions. Cass thought the man looked uneasy. She told him no, but suspected he was withholding facts in that area. Since he was Peter's lawyer and the eight companies' lawyer, she reasoned, no doubt he valued those clients and was trying to protect them from interference by a woman ignorant of business matters. As long as no problems arose and she received her earnings from them, Cass decided, she would not intrude on Peter's decisions.

The lawyer went on to explain the donations to certain charities and foundations, all in the name of Thomas Ethan Grantham: a small wing at a hospital, several college scholarships, a free clinic for the poor, funds for the arts and for conservation and ecology.

Perpetual fame and gratitude from people and organizations who don't realize what a terrible and wicked man you were! At least you did a few good things with your life and money!

Again, Simon asked her if she had any questions or comments. She shook her head and thanked him for his assistance. She left his office to meet with Tom's accountant, Harrison "Harry" Dredger, whose office was in the same business complex.

Once more she was seen within minutes after

her arrival, as if either she was an important client or the man was in a hurry to finish their talk so he could leave for the day, or perhaps be rid of her. Cass observed that his tone and expression didn't indicate tension or dislike. It was clear Harry catered to wealthy clients, since his office and clothing were in the most expensive taste.

Per Peter's instructions, the family accountant would continue to pay her household bills from her trust fund. Harry Dredger went over her monthly expenses, income holdings, taxes, trust fund, and inheritance payout schedule. April's "allowance" had been deposited into her checking account, as every ensuing payment would be on the fifth of each month. He told her he would teach her how to manage her budget if and when she wanted to handle her finances herself.

Aware of how complicated they were Cass smiled and told Harry she didn't intend to do so any time soon.

He said he would send her a monthly report on expenditures, and an annual one which would feature her assets and liabilities. He told her to feel free to phone him with any questions or changes she wanted to make.

Cass thanked him, and left with another file of papers which she would study more closely at another time. As she drove home, she realized she was a very rich woman, at least on paper and at a future date when she would fully own and control that wealth, if she didn't remarry too soon.

You were a cunning and treacherous sneak, Thomas Grantham, but I'll find a way to outwit you! I'll get your money and I'll find true love, just wait and see!

After she reached home, Cass phoned Mary Ellis, who suggested she stop by after lunch tomorrow so they could meet and talk about the job.

Within ten minutes of Mary's arrival, Cass was certain that Jason was right about the vivacious and genial thirty-two-year-old with curly auburn hair and expressive hazel eyes that brightened when she talked. As she showed Mrs. Ellis around, she learned that Mary and her husband, an instructor at the Federal Law Enforcement Training Center in Brunswick, had only one child. Their son, who had been in a coma for a year following an accident with a drunk driver, was in a local medical facility where he could be tended and observed by doctors and nurses: Jason hadn't told her that, and her heart went out to the young mother who couldn't have another child. To help pay those enormous expenses, Mary worked three jobs.

As Mary glanced around the bedroom and smiled, she said, "I work from eight-thirty to five, ma'am, unless you prefer nine to five-thirty. With a house this size to clean thor-

246

oughly in two days, I couldn't do extra things like windows and blinds and oven-cleaning and such on the regular schedule, but I can give you an extra day for those chores when one of my other bosses goes out of town and doesn't need me."

"Don't worry about that, Mary; we have a window washing service that comes several times a year to do the outsides and insides, and my two ovens are self-cleaning. I only need for you to vacuum carpets, sweep floors and porches — but no walkways or driveway because I have a gardener who takes care of those once a week when he does the yards — mop, dust, and clean the bathrooms. I'll take care of the rest between your visits. Since I live alone, most of the rooms are rarely used, except for my upstairs suite, kitchen, breakfast room, and den."

"That's fine with me, ma'am."

"Excellent. If I ever ask you to do something that you don't feel is part of your job or you don't have time for, please just tell me and it won't be a problem. Do you charge by the hour or day or what?"

"I charge eighty dollars a day for eight hours. I take twenty minutes for lunch, which I bring with me, and take two five-minute breaks."

"It isn't necessary to bring your lunch, Mary; I always have plenty of food and drinks here, and it'll save you time and energy in the mornings. As for rest periods, take them as needed and don't watch the clock."

"Thank you, ma'am. I have reference letters with me and you can speak with any of my current and past employers. I'm self-employed, so I pay my own taxes and social security out of my earnings. If that's agreeable, I can start on Monday or on Thursday. Do you have any questions for me?"

As Cass searched her mind, she assumed from the woman's next words that Mary must have thought she was being hesitant.

"If you'd like to think about it or contact my references, you can let me know over the weekend. I'll hold the opening until Monday."

Cass smiled. "I don't need to speak with anyone about you. Doctor Burkman recommends you highly, so that's good enough for me. I know this is a big house to clean and I realize doing a good job takes lots of time, so I won't expect the impossible. Either schedule you select is fine with me. If you ever need a day off for any reason, even just to rest, that's no problem. How does that sound?"

"That suits me fine, ma'am."

"Me, too, Mary, and I'm delighted I found you. I'm certain we're going to get along great. Now, do you prefer to receive a check at the end of each workday or once a week?"

"Once a week is fine with me, ma'am."

"I know that medical bills can be terribly high, Mary, so if you ever need a month's salary in advance, please feel free to request it. And if you ever want to work on a day that another employer lets you off, that's fine with me; I'm sure you can find things to do around here."

"That's very kind of you, ma'am, and it will be most helpful. If there's nothing else, I'll see you on Monday morning."

"I can't think of anything. Good-bye, Mary, and I'll be praying for your son's recovery."

"Thank you, Mrs. Grantham, and good-bye."

"What do you mean you don't need me anymore?" Inez asked as she received the shocking phone call Friday afternoon.

"I'm sorry, Inez, but the situation between us isn't working out and I'm certain you'll be happier with another employer. I'm deeply grateful for all you did for me while I was ill and you are an excellent housekeeper, but I think we agree that our personal relationship isn't a pleasant one. I just interviewed another housekeeper and hired her to come in on Mondays and Thursdays; I'll have —"

"But Mrs. Grantham, I've been with you for over two years! I've done good work! You didn't even warn me this was coming and you've hired somebody else behind my back! This isn't fair! Mr. Peter isn't going to be pleased with you for firing me like this!"

Cass was annoyed with the rude woman but she tried to remain polite. "Perhaps Peter will want you to continue working for him. You can discuss that with him after his return tomorrow or you can phone him next week. After our many disagreements in the past and particularly how you behaved toward me yesterday, I don't see why this should come as a surprise to you. As I was about to say before you interrupted me, I'll have Mr. Dredger send you your regular check for this week's salary and a second one for two-weeks' severance pay. I'll even furnish you with a reference letter."

"How can a letter from somebody who fires you be helpful?"

Cass heard the anger and hatred in the woman's voice. "I'm sorry this didn't work out, Inez, but it's for the best. I'll only put what a good housekeeper you are in the letter, nothing about our personality conflict."

"I don't need your help or pity so don't waste your time writing any letter! I wouldn't come back to work for you if you begged me on your knees!"

Cass held the receiver away from her ear and gaped at it for a moment after Inez slammed hers down on its base. "You miserable witch!" she muttered, "Good riddance. Mercy, it's going to be wonderful not having to deal with you!"

Cass stood before a full-length mirror in her bathroom and wondered if she was overdressed. She didn't want to appear as if she were trying to be glamorous and seductive, not to Jason nor to anyone who might see them out together tonight and and get the wrong impression of her. She eyed the evening suit in pale-gold lace over a darker shade of fabric in that color. It had a scoop-neck top, four ornate buttons down the front, dark-gold satin edging around the neck and down the front, sheer sleeves that halted above elbow, and scalloped hems on its skirt and top. On her feet were pale gold T-strap pumps, and her hose had a hint of gold thread in them. She wore one-karat diamond studs in her earlobes, a diamond tennis bracelet, and a gold watch with a bracelet-style band.

Her freshly shampooed hair streamed over her shoulders in waves from large hot curlers, its deep brown hue revealing golden highlights from many recent walks on the beach. Her makeup had been applied with a light hand, as had the Passion perfume, her favorite scent. Her skin was smooth and fragrant from an application of body lotion after her bath. She was ready to greet Jason when he arrived.

You're going to the Cloister, Cass, so you aren't overdressed or overgroomed, she assured herself. *Relax and have fun tonight. You deserve it. Just behave yourself around Jason. Take a deep breath and remember you're a lady.* No, remember you're a recent widow and conduct yourself as one or the locals will think badly of you.

Cass went to the front door. "Right on time, Doctor; you're just as punctual socially as you are at your office."

"Thanks, I don't like to keep people waiting; their time is just as valuable as mine is. You look absolutely stunning," he murmured as his blue gaze walked over her from shiny head to gold-clad feet. Blazes, just looking at her aroused him like crazy!

"You look very nice yourself," she said as she eyed what she was certain was an Armani suit in navy with a tiny white pinstripe. "Would you like to come inside for a minute or do we need to leave immediately?"

"We need to go soon, but I did bring you a gift I can put inside. It's heavy, so I'll carry it inside for you."

Cass followed Jason to the kitchen where he set the box on the counter. She watched him open one end and withdraw a fifteen-inch-high sculpture on a six-inch base. As she gazed at the two verdi-tinted bronze hands with fingers touching and pointing upward, she realized one was male and the other was female.

"It's called *'Cathedral'* by Rodin. This one was put out by Austin. I got it at a local art gallery today. You said you were redecorating, so I hoped this would represent a gift of our friendship."

Friendship? It's so romantic, so sensual . . . She wondered if she should accept it. Yet, how could she refuse? The important questions were, *What is Jason's motive and what does the gift truly represent?*

252

Chapter Eleven

"It's beautiful, Jason, and I love it. You're such a kind and thoughtful person. I'm lucky to have you as a friend and doctor. Thank you."

I'm the lucky one, and you're what's beautiful in this room. One day soon, I hope that our fingers will touch. "You're welcome, Cass. When I saw this piece, I immediately thought about you and had to buy it. You can decide where to place it later because we need to get going; we don't want to lose our reservation."

Cass was touched by his generous gesture. The fact that the sculpture had reminded him of her was a thrilling thought that sent tingles of pleasure over her. To prevent staring at him, surely with lust in her gaze, she smiled and said, "You're right, and I'm ready to leave." She retrieved her evening purse from the counter, glanced at the gift again, warmed in delight, and left the house with him after setting the alarm system.

They remained silent while en route, but each was thinking about the other and wondering where their relationship was going to take them. Both knew where they wanted it to go, but neither wanted to move too fast. It felt strange but wonderful to be alone with each other; yet, neither knew how to behave or what to say under these unfamiliar circumstances.

At the Cloister Resort located not far from her house, Jason parked his BMW across the street from the Spanish-style cream-colored stucco structure. The complex with its numerous matching structures, down to the red-tiled roof on all — hotel, villas, cottages, conference facility — was enormous and offered its guests a myriad of amenities and entertainments. As they crossed the street and strolled along one of the many rambling walkways toward the covered entrance, both noticed the shady and well-manicured grounds with an abundance of sprawling and moss-bearded live oaks, pollen-ladened pines, tall and short palms, and beds with blooming azaleas and assorted flowers. They passed green lampposts positioned to illuminate the lovely area at nighttime, and wooden benches for resting and socializing. At the end of the main drive beyond them, foot high scrubs spelled out *Sea Island.*

The front entrance overlooked a private marina on the Blackbank River, Rainbow and St. Simons islands, the bridge connecting them, the tidal marshland across the water, and an American flag that was flapping in the breeze. The setting was lush and peaceful, semitropical in appearance and climate.

A doorman smiled and greeted them before

they walked up several steps into a lovely lobby that featured an elegant parlor to the left with a fireplace, many cozy sitting areas, and clerestory windows. As they strolled down a long hallway, they glanced at exclusive and pricey shops on both sides. They went down a few steps to where the maitre d' greeted them, spoke with Jason, and checked his guest list. Beyond their position and along a large tiled walkway that separated carpeted eating areas was another huge fireplace. Decorative columns rose from floor to high ceilings where dimly lit chandeliers were suspended, creating a cozy ambiance.

The maitre d' guided them into the main dining room where well-dressed couples chatted and laughed in muffled voices and music from a nearby piano and violin could be heard. Other couples could dance in the adjoining area where the orchestra played, but neither had any intention of making that romantic suggestion. Along one wall were arch-shaped windows with fake outdoor scenes, complete with plants and trees and focal lights, which created relaxing and picturesque views.

The maitre d' seated Cass while Jason took his place at a table that was covered by a linen cloth in snowy white. Fresh flowers and a candle sat atop it, as did the china, crystal, and silverware that were arranged in a formal manner.

It was a place for elegant and leisurely

dining. She was glad she had worn the gold evening suit because it was perfect for this setting, and it appeared to win Jason's approval.

The waitress delivered a small tray of relishes with celery, carrots, Jicama, and olives, and a basket of freshly baked breads. She took their drink order — Chivas Regal scotch for him and a champagne cocktail for her — and handed them menus.

After they made their selections and as they nibbled on the relishes and bread and sipped their drinks, Jason told her the history of the Cloister, which Cass had learned about on previous trips but didn't halt him or reveal her knowledge because listening to him was too enjoyable.

"In 1928, Howard Coffin and William Jones carved out one of the most fabled year-round resorts on this island. Guests from around the world come here to rest and play in luxurious style. While the hotel was being built, the first guests were lodged in a three-story houseboat at the yacht club. The architect, Addison Mizner, used the Spanish design he'd made popular at Palm Beach. The grounds are some of the most beautiful and well-landscaped in the world. Things were quiet and slow until the causeway between Brunswick and St. Simons was opened in '24; then the boom came with tourists and residents. As you already know, not all of the home owners are permanent residents."

She nodded, as her nearest neighbors fit into that category, and perhaps that was one of the reasons why she knew so few people there.

"In the early days, it tried to and did attract the rich and famous who wanted privacy and an opulent setting where they could be pampered; that hasn't changed. Even Her Majesty Queen Juliana and her consort have stayed here, and presidents and movie stars and prominent citizens. The playwright Eugene O'Neill wrote *Ah, Wilderness* here. I think the reason it's stayed so popular is because of the staff; everybody who works here is friendly, gracious, and hospitable. If you want to know more, I have a copy of Harold Martin's book *This Happy Isle* I'll loan you."

"I'd love to read it; this place is fascinating." Cass didn't continue when the waitress arrived to take their orders for the six-course meal.

Afterward, the wine steward came to speak with them, and Jason chose a 1989 German Riesling Spatlese, Piesporter Goldtropfchen to complement their seafood selections for dinner.

Jason only told her a few more facts about the resort's history before the waitress returned with citrus and avocado with seagrape dressing for her and local shrimp cocktail on ice for him.

As they ate their appetizers, Jason amused Cass with "The Legend of Spanish Moss." It was the story of a Spanish villain named Gorez Goz who had a thick and long gray beard and who fell in love with a local Indian maiden and lavished her with gifts. But the girl was terrified of the man with hideous hair on his face, as her race had none. She escaped his pursuit and climbed a tree to conceal herself after she became too tired to run farther. The villain discovered her hiding place and tried to scale the gigantic live oak to capture her, but his beard became entangled on the branches and he perished there, unable to free himself, leaving behind reminders of his gray beard and thwarted love.

Jason chuckled and said, "Most tourists don't realize Spanish moss is a favorite residence for chiggers when they snag some to take home with them; the last itch they wind up scratching is one for romance."

Cass laughed and concurred, "Being from the country, I recall those nasty little pests only too well. Mother used to dot bites with turpentine that burned like fire and almost left scars."

"Ouch," Jason said with a comical grimace.

"You're right; that's why I usually didn't tell her I had sat down in the wrong place, or I wouldn't be sitting down comfortably for at least a week."

As a chuckling Jason was squirting a net-covered lemon on a shrimp, he envisioned her lying naked on a bed with him tending her irritated spots with medicine on a cotton ball. He imagined the sight and feel of her body beneath his adoring gaze and gentle touch. When

258

he felt his penis growing thick and hard, he was thankful he was seated with a tablecloth concealing his excited state, and he sought a distraction to cool the result of his flaming desire.

"Since I've been doing most of the talking so far tonight, it's your turn to take over," Jason coaxed. "Tell me about your work back in Augusta."

Finished with her appetizer and while he ate his, Cass began. "I started off as a secretary and worked my way up to the boss's administrative assistant after I received my college degree. Despite the nice title, a private office, and a good paycheck, I was little more than a glorified secretary to him. Sometimes, especially when he was out of town or buried in solving problems on the line, I got to dip my hands and wits into special projects, for which he took the credit. Needless to say, with E-Z-GO, the world's largest cart maker, and Club Car located there, we had our work cut out for us to compete with them."

After she related facts about the construction and selling of golf carts and her responsibilities at Smooth Rider years ago, she asked, "How did you get from Richmond to Sea Island and start a practice here?"

"The Cloister and Sea Island were recommended by a patient who loved to vacation here, even had a home nearby. I came down several times to relax and play golf, fell in love with the place, and moved my practice to Brunswick. I even purchased his house, and he gave me a good deal on it because he thinks I saved his life and he was retiring out West."

"I'm sure you're being modest, because I bet you did save his life. In a way, you saved mine; you rescued me from a pit I was digging for myself. Did you consider moving back to Richmond after your wife's death?"

"Not really because the kids and I were too established in Georgia."

"What about after you retire, though that's a long way off?"

"Nope, I like these long summers and short, mild winters; and I'm closer to the kids and my grandchildren here than I would be there. Besides, it's a golfer's heaven with so many excellent courses located around here. Are you thinking about moving now that your husband is gone?"

"No, I like it here, too. I don't know many people yet, but I will in time. Tom didn't care for socializing locally, so I'm still rather a stranger on the island. He liked to select my friends and activities; now, that's my job." The moment Cass exposed those private details, she wondered why she had. Perhaps it was to let him know why she had been rather reclusive. Or perhaps it was to let him know straight out she wouldn't allow any man to rule her life again.

As he gazed into her soft brown eyes, his wits

clouded for a moment and he asked a bold question. "You never had children; was that by choice? If you don't want to answer, that's fine," he added with haste.

Cass decided that as long as she spoke about certain personal details perhaps he would too; and they could learn more about each other. "Not by my choice. Tom didn't want another child. In hindsight, I should have discussed that important subject with him before we married, but I assumed that marriage naturally included having children. I love them and I miss not having any. My parents would have loved grandchildren. I might have told you they were killed in a train wreck when I was thirty. I sent them on a cross-country trip as an anniversary present, but they didn't return from it. The most comforting thoughts afterward were in knowing they had lived happy lives and they died together, instantly and without suffering. They were good people, wonderful parents; I loved them and was proud to be their daughter. The worst part was being an only and late-life child because there was no family with whom to share my grief. I was lucky I had a best friend who consoled me and helped with everything."

Jason didn't comment on her disclosures because the waitress brought their soups, shrimp bisque with sherry cream, and placed them on the china chargers before them, then refilled their water glasses. They both ate and drank for a while in silence as they listened to the musicians.

For some reason, Cass wanted him to know they had something in common besides tennis and her medical problems and to let him know she wasn't put off by his being married twice, so she said, "In case you're wondering why I waited so long to get married, I didn't; I married my high school sweetheart when I was nineteen. We divorced after five years during my sophomore year of college. We were waiting to have children until after both of us finished school and established our careers; we didn't make it that far. He's remarried now and has a family, but we don't have any contact."

Jason was relieved to hear that last sentence, and she looked as if she were being honest. He was glad she was opening up to him, but he wondered if it was out of friendship or a desire to get better acquainted for romantic reasons. "Divorce can be difficult, but it's easier when no kids are involved. It appears as if we have similar histories in some areas."

She smiled and nodded, then finished her soup. Both listened — or pretended to listen — to the musicians until salads were served.

Between bites, they talked about places they had been, skiing, golf, tennis, and current happenings in the news. A few brief mentions of their past spouses terminated those intrusions for the last time that evening. Each wanted to know the reason for the other's divorce, but didn't ask.

The wine steward refilled their crystal glasses before the waitress brought their entrees: Dover sole meuniere sauteed in lemon butter and served with parsely potatoes, snow peas, and broccoflower for Cass; Gratin of Lobster "Cardinal," flamed Maine lobster meat and mushrooms in cream, served with duchesse potatoes and asparagus spears for Jason. He was served iced tea; she, Earl Grey hot tea.

After eating a few bites, Cass said, "This is absolutely divine."

Jason smiled and concurred that his food was delicious, too.

As they ate, she noted he was at ease in the formal and expensive setting. He was well-groomed, down to clean and trimmed fingernails. His double-breasted Ralph Lauren suit was tailored to fit his broad shoulders. He had an air of virility and sensuality, and his company and conversation were enjoyable and interesting, calming but exhilarating.

Her study of him was flaming her desire for him, so she renewed their conversation to alter her line of thought. "I'm glad you told me about Mary Ellis; she's delightful. We had a nice chat yesterday and she starts to work for me on Monday. Of course," she leaned forward and whispered, "it wasn't a fun walk in the park to fire Inez after I hired Mary. She was furious and rude after I gave her the bad news. Thank you for helping me to replace Inez; she and her behavior had worn mighty thin, especially this week. And since you're my physician, the last thing I need is somebody grating on my nerves, right?"

"Absolutely and I'm glad I could be of service. If you want or need help with your redecorating, I know a wonderful lady who did mine."

"Thanks, I'll phone you if I run into any problems in that area. To be honest, I want to do as much of it as possible myself because I didn't get to assist with it the first time. The house was a surprise from Tom, and it was already finished inside and out when I saw it. When Linda gets time off between jobs, she's going shopping with me. We became friends while she was taking care of me, so that's another thing I'm grateful for."

Jason's gaze drifted over her lustrous brown hair whose long waves and soft curls were cut into several different layers, the last one ending below her shoulders. He wondered if she realized how beautiful and alluring she was. "The best way you can repay me is by keeping me company at times: go to the ballet, theater, or movies with me, maybe take that Emerald Princess cruise I told you about, and share a few dinners like this one. It gets mighty boring and lonely to go places alone or to sit home, and mighty difficult to search for diversions and compatible companions. Dating can be a real drag at our age, can't it?"

"I imagine it gets harder every year as society and dating rules change. I remember it was difficult several years ago between my divorce and remarriage."

"So, does that mean you'll be my companion when it's possible? I promise you that my parents reared a perfect southern gentleman."

Cass waited to respond until the violinist who was strolling around and serenading couples left their table for the next one. "I can promise you that my parents tried to rear a perfect lady and I do need diversions, so the answer is yes, I'll be delighted to enjoy a pleasant evening with a friend."

"Friend?" I hope that isn't all you want from me, woman! Yet, he couldn't forget what the gynecologist had told him last Sunday and he couldn't forget the hints Cass dropped unintentionally about a perhaps troubled marriage. Even if it was selfish and wrong, he almost hoped that was true, though his heart was touched by any sufferings that reality caused her. He knew from experience with Brenda that infidelity and other problems aided a faster emotional recovery from a spouse's loss. In hindsight, he shouldn't have married that deceitful stranger because he hadn't loved her enough or known her well and long enough to do so. In a period of vulnerability, anguish, and loneliness after Joan's tragic death, he'd made a terrible mistake. Not normally impulsive or foolish, he had fallen prey to those brief weak-

nesses, and to Brenda's seductive charms. He should have heeded his children's warnings, those of his conscience, and those of well-meaning friends. He somehow knew it wouldn't be the same with Cassandra Grantham, who was nothing like Brenda in looks, character, or personality. He was certain his twins would like and approve of Cass, and he was eager for them to meet.

Their dinner plates were removed and desserts, almost sinfully rich, were placed before them, and decaffeinated coffee was poured into their china cups.

"Surely this delicious fare has seven million calories," she jested to lighten the serious aura that had settled around them.

"Mine, too, but it's scrumptious. Want to sample it?" Jason asked, holding out a tempting forkful of warm blueberry crumb pie.

"Only if you taste mine," Cass leaned forward and her mouth enclosed the bite as her chocolate gaze fused with his captivating blue one. Her heart beat at a fast pace and breathing seemed difficult.

"M-m-m-m, oh, my, wonderful. Here," she offered, extending a spoonful of raspberry sour cream cheesecake with orange sauce. She watched Jason's full lips engulf the treat and almost tease it off the spoon in a sensuous manner that caused her whole body to tingle. Her susceptible senses were aware of everything about him. It was a struggle not to stare at him, not to flirt with him, not to forget where they were and who she was.

"Absolutely sinful," he said with a grin and chuckle, *and perhaps my thoughts are.* He was elated by how she was looking at him: with a potent desire she was attempting to conceal. If they weren't careful, his mind warned, everyone present could detect their mutual attraction, which could elicit unwanted and damaging gossip.

After Jason escorted Cass to her back entrance via the stone walkway, he waited while she turned off the alarm system and unlocked the door. He knew Peter was away on business, so the sorry bastard couldn't spy on or join them and spoil the short remainder of their evening.

Cass turned and smiled. "I had a lovely time tonight. The dinner was delicious and the company enjoyable. I would invite you in, but it's late and might not look appropriate to the neighbors or anyone passing by."

"I understand and agree. I had a wonderful time, too, more fun than I've had in ages. I hope we can do this again very soon." He didn't want to pressure her by asking for a specific date to get together again, and he knew Peter was returning home tomorrow. If the truth about the past was revealed, he worried, Peter Grantham was the one person who could cause enough conflict to put a wrench in their relationship. "When it's convenient for you, please give me a call, even if it's on short notice."

Cass realized he had hesitated between his flattering remark and his final request, but couldn't determine the delay's meaning. She smiled again and said, "I will, I promise. Thank you, Jason, for everything you've done for me, and that's been a great deal. Good night."

A romantic setting engulfed them. They were standing close, looking at each other. Moonlight played across their faces and danced within their eyes. The mingled sounds of her backyard fountain, the crashing waves of high tide, calls of nocturnal birds, and chirping crickets filled their ears.

"Good night, Cass, and you're welcome." Jason couldn't seem to stop himself from slowly leaning forward to kiss her.

Cass realized what he was about to do, and a myriad of feelings and thoughts rushed through her. Should she allow this intimate contact to happen so soon? If she responded, could she trust herself to control her wayward emotions and rampant desires? Could she stop her passion after tasting only one tantalizing kiss?

Chapter Twelve

Jason perceived her sudden uncertainty and tension. New anxiety was the last thing a still-vulnerable Cass needed, especially from him. He used great willpower to guide his mouth to her flushed cheek rather than to her parted lips. He made the kiss tender, light, and short. He leaned back and smiled. "Take good care of yourself, Cassandra, and I hope to hear from you very soon. Good night."

"Good night, Jason," she managed to get out before he left her side. As she listened to his retreating steps, she trembled from unfulfilled passion, disappointment, and joy. She had no doubt that was not the kind of kiss he had planned and wanted, but he had cared more for her feelings than for his own pleasure. He was such a special man with so many fascinating facets. His considerate nature increased her yearning for him, but she dared not encourage him, not this soon. How strange it was that Tom's death and her life with him seemed so long ago when less than two months had passed. Perhaps it was sinful and selfish of her to be craving another man when her husband was barely cold in the grave, but she could not help herself.

Cass locked the door and set the alarm system. She went upstairs to prepare for bed, to sleep alone by necessary choice. As she put away her clothes, she recalled with pleasure certain moments during their evening. As she washed her face and brushed her teeth, she grinned at herself in the mirror for being so downright blessed after enduring many years of misfortune with men, but playfully scolded herself for being wonderfully wicked in thought and deed. It looked as if her bad luck had changed, but at a most unpredictable time.

He's still a stranger in many ways, Cass, so don't fall in love with him too quickly and easily. So far, you haven't been able to hold a man's interest and loyalty, so don't risk another broken heart until you're absolutely certain about his intentions and character. This time, you'll chance losing far more if you're wrong about Jason. You'll be endangering a huge fortune and relinquishing your last chance at finding real love and having children.

As she climbed into bed, Cass remembered that Peter was returning tomorrow afternoon. She dreaded seeing him again, dreaded telling him about her two business appointments and about firing Inez and about seeing her doctor socially. She dreaded his reactions, though she could not allow him to rule her life as his father had done for years. She even resented the fact his nearby presence denied her of privacy.

Privacy for what, Cass, to have a torrid affair

with your handsome doctor? she asked herself. The answer came quickly. *Yes, if that's what I want to do! And if it's what Jason wants.*

Yet, she didn't want to mislead Jason by implying she would commit to him soon. She admitted she wanted to collect the huge estate she had inherited, but the money wasn't the real issue; nor was she greedy. She could go back to work to support herself, or, if it worked out between them, Jason had more than enough assets to support them. Her stimulus was retribution, just payment due for Tom's crimes against her and their marriage, and perhaps for revenge on her husband for his betrayals. Besides, he shouldn't have attached spiteful and selfish strings to it. Yet, Jason might not understand why she wanted and deserved Tom's money since she couldn't explain her motive and have Jason think some of Tom's filth had rubbed off on her. Could she sacrifice a bonanza and justice to marry him?

Marry him? Aren't I getting way ahead of myself? Again the answer came quickly. *Yes, but I need to consider all angles before I get in over my head with him and drown myself.*

Was Jason Burkman the kind of man who could be satisfied with a five- or ten-year love affair while waiting for her to collect her trust fund? Would he agree to living together out of wedlock? Could she, when that was not how she had been reared? That would mean having no children. In ten years, she would be forty five, past safe childbearing for her and the baby.

In these modern times, couples often co-habitated and had families without marrying, but that didn't appeal to her, though she didn't judge others who did so. A lengthy love affair while residing in separate homes was acceptable, but having a baby out of wedlock wasn't, and probably wouldn't be to a man like Jason. Somehow she must find a clever way to outwit Tom and his bedeviling stipulation. Perhaps a skilled lawyer was what she needed for that purpose, despite the fact Tom's lawyer had assured her the will was iron-clad.

As Cass straightened the den on Saturday morning, she noticed the red light blinking on the answering machine. She pressed the message button and heard Kristy Stillman Franklin's voice. She learned that Kristy had phoned while she was out last night and said she would call next week after she returned home, as her house had been rented this week to Master's Golf Tournament visitors and the local schools — including the one where Kristy taught third grade — were closed for spring holidays during Augusta's busiest traffic period. Kristy expressed disappointment in having missed reaching her twice and had gotten Cass's return message. Kristy related how much she had missed her and said they needed to talk soon and make plans to get together.

Cass was overjoyed by the prospect of renewing their friendship and looked forward to speaking with Kristy next week.

Cass admitted to herself that her affection and respect for Brad's family was one of the main reasons she had married him, and was the only reason she hadn't divulged the dirty truth about him to his parents, though Kristy was aware of her brother's dual — probably more — infidelities. Brad had duped her about his love and good character, and she had duped herself about the depth of her feelings for him. After dating him for so long, it had seemed natural to marry him. She recalled how Brad had taken five years to finish college because of laziness and failed courses, and how he had taken a "much needed and deserved rest" for a month after he graduated, and how he had done nothing else for three months while taking a real estate course, then waited around for his license to arrive.

It was during his "last break" before employment that she had suffered a miscarriage, unaware she was pregnant by accident. Afterward, they had returned to their original plan of not having children until she finished college, they were established in their careers or jobs, and were financially secure. She had begun college in January, before turning twenty-four in June. She had worked hard and made excellent grades, and taken care of the apartment and errands by herself in between classes and studying.

In May, Brad, like Tom, had surprised her with a house he had purchased without her knowledge, a deal he said was too good to pass up. She had tried to get him to cancel the contract. She had told him they couldn't afford it, that she feared the extra expense would force her to quit school. Yet, nothing she said had changed his mind as he argued he knew the housing and financing markets better than she did.

In June, heavy rains and flooding had attacked Augusta; and they lost everything because they didn't have flood insurance. They had moved to a small apartment, one that had bugs, bad lighting, and smelled. That was two months before she discovered Brad's adultery when she overheard a phone conversation between him and a woman.

She had been a fool to accept his claims about it being a mistake, that he loved only her, and it would never happen again. He even convinced her she was partly to blame because she was too tired and busy for him. He also placed blame on job pressures, the trauma of the flood, the stress of having to continue paying for a house that was gone, and the beatings his ego and pride had taken from his mistakes.

She had been stupid to believe and forgive him! Yet, he had pretended to be very attentive to her, going so far as to help out around the apartment and with errands to give her more time and energy to spend on him, on their relationship.

Their split came that December when she returned home early from taking her last exam, having forgotten to tell him her test schedule had been changed. She would never forget the sights and sounds that greeted her after she reached the cramped apartment and found Brad in their bed with another woman.

She hadn't kept her discovery a secret as she was compelled to do with Tom's situation. She had walked to the bedroom door and asked in a cold and sarcastic tone, "Will you please finish screwing her in a hurry, Brad, so I can get packed and get out?"

Fortunately, she had found an inexpensive but clean apartment, received a school grant, divorced the snake, and finished two more quarters to complete her sophomore year. But the grant squeezed her budget too tightly, she was compelled to get a job during the day and go to night classes for the next three and a half years until graduation at age twenty-eight. Her degree and hard work were what earned her a promotion at Smooth Rider to administrative assistant to the company's top manager.

During the ensuing years, the men she dated were mainly interested in sex or in obtaining a compliant wife to replace a divorced spouse and to take care of them. A brief romance soured; her beloved parents were killed in that train wreck; and Thomas Ethan Grantham entered her life when she was thirty-two.

She dated Tom for a year before succumbing to his persistent and romantic pursuit. He had convinced her their union would work and he would make her blissfully happy. With only her job in her life and with all of her close friends married and blessed with children, she had felt lonely and unfulfilled. She had heard her body clock ticking loudly and was tired of the dating scene. She wanted a home and family, a baby. Tom wore down her resistance with his vows of love and many golden promises. She even signed that prenuptial agreement to prove she wasn't marrying him for his money.

But life with him wasn't what she had imagined. There was no real home during the first two years or even a future prospect of children; living with him was like being on a perpetual vacation, a fast and dizzying merry-go-around. As the hectic months rushed by, the fantasy faded and the golden promises tarnished, and she was forced to accept reality, but she still gave her best efforts to make the marriage work because she believed Tom loved her, and she believed she was fortunate to be his wife and she owed him loyalty. She had been a fool for a second time!

Again, she had fallen in love with and wed a man who turned out to be a stranger and betrayer. She was glad she didn't have children, because she didn't want either of those sorry bastards to be the father of them, didn't want to have emotional ties to either one. She had turned a deaf ear to Brad's pleas to return to him. Why hadn't she been that strong with Tom? Why had she allowed him to dominate and manipulate her, to change her? But she knew why: she desperately had wanted her second marriage to succeed.

Cass pushed aside those remembrances and returned to her chores where she allowed those tasks and the radio to distract her.

Shortly before noon, Peter phoned Cass to disclose he was being delayed by business and wouldn't return home until Wednesday. "How are you doing and how are things going there?" he asked.

"Fine. I'm getting stronger and better every day, and I've had no setbacks. I don't have to visit Doctor Burkman's office until the end of the month, and he's taken me off of all medication."

"That's wonderful, Cass, and I'm proud of you, but I was confident you could do it. Just make sure you don't overdo or allow anything to stress you. Promise?"

She wondered if Peter possessed the same devious streak as his father had and if Peter also was duping her. She shrugged away the dark thought. "I promise, and thanks for your concern. I'm glad you feel that way, because I got rid of one major irritation: Inez. I fired her yesterday and I've already hired a new housekeeper to come in twice a week. That's really all the help I need."

She gave all the pertinent details about Mary Ellis and her family and revealed only that she was recommended by a "friend."

"I thought Inez was a wonderful house-keeper. Why did you fire her?"

One by one Cass listed the many annoying reasons for Inez's dismissal. "I'm sure she'll be more than happy to continue working for you," she ended. "She likes and respects you. I'm afraid Mary only had room in her schedule for one more job, so she won't be available to you. I hope my decision won't inconvenience you, but I had to get rid of Inez."

"I understand, Cass, and don't worry about me. I can keep Inez on or use a cleaning service. The important thing is to keep you calm and happy. Did you give her proper notice and severence pay?" Peter asked as he realized he needed to phone the woman immediately to make sure Inez didn't expose the secret they shared: the medication he had ordered slipped into Cass's food and drink. If necessary, he would give the woman a large parting bonus for her help and loyalty and silence. Besides, he still needed a maid at least once a week.

"Severence pay, yes, but no, I didn't give her any notice. She was too hateful when I gave her the bad news."

"That's a shame. She was always nice to me. If I had known there was a problem between

278

you two, I would have tried to resolve your differences before they got out of control."

"I doubt you could have, Peter, because I spoke to her several times about her sorry attitude and belligerence. In fact, I was totally blunt with her earlier this week; what I said went in one ear and out the other."

"When you hired Mrs. Ellis, did you get her Social Security number and alert our accountant to the change in employees? If not, I can handle it later for you."

"Mary told me she's self-employed and pays her own taxes and Social Security. I'm to give her a weekly check. But I didn't call Mr. Dredger; that never entered my mind."

"I'll phone Harry next week, so don't worry about it. We need to make sure Mrs. Ellis pays her taxes or we can get into trouble with the government."

"I'm sure Mary was being honest with me, but I understand you need to be careful; I'm sure she will, too."

"So, what else have you been doing since I left?"

"A little redecorating and dealing with Tom's possessions. It was just too painful to keep so many reminders of him around me all of the time. I have a lot of things I want you to go through before I decide their fates: his clothes, items in his office, his portrait that hung in the den, things like that. I went shopping Wednesday after you left. I purchased a new bed and redid the bedroom decor. I hope that doesn't upset you."

"Why should it, Cass? The house is yours now, and I agree you don't need to be reminded of Dad everywhere you look."

"Thank you, Peter; that makes me feel so much better. That was what provoked the final straw with Inez; she was furious with me about the changes. She said you would be too, but I told her you would understand and agree with what I had to do for my mental health."

Peter grinned as she talked, wishing he could have witnessed that old biddy jumping down Cass's throat. So, in less than two months, she was pushing his father aside and perhaps making plans for her next conquest, though he couldn't imagine her waiving her inheritance, even in the name of love. But either choice would suit him just fine. "I can certainly grasp why you kicked her out; it's none of her business what you do with your home. Anything else exciting going on?" he asked and chuckled, then tensed as she responded in an unexpected manner.

"I did see Mr. Johnson and Mr. Dredger like you suggested. The meetings were short and routine, I suppose." Cass thought she heard his breathing alter, so she thought it best to dupe him, as she suspected she was being deceived by him. "I took your advice, but it really wasn't necessary because you covered everything with me last week. I told Mr.

Dredger to continue paying the bills and handling the financial angle, unless he decides he wants me to take control of them. Is it all right if I skip meeting with the banker for a while? You've already explained the trust fund procedure to me, and I doubt I would understand all of those business technicalities. If there's a problem or question, the executor can phone one of us, right?"

"That's right, so don't subject yourself to a meeting until you feel up to it. Later, if you like, I'll go with you. I'll keep you informed in that area, and you'll receive scheduled reports from the bank."

Good, it sounded as if she had him convinced she lacked all business acumen and interest in it. She was positive that pretending to seek his advice and permission in some areas would be fortuitous to her later, would continue their truce longer. "Tom made some good contributions to wonderful causes; his donations should be most helpful to them."

"It certainly helped us. If not for those charity and foundation bequests, Uncle Sam would have taken a huge bite out of our inheritances. Dad was clever in that area. He also made sure his name wouldn't be forgotten."

Cass wondered, despite the fact Peter chuckled as if jesting, if that was bitterness she heard in his tone. If so, why? If there was any past trouble between the two men, she didn't know about it. Could it be that Peter had

281

known or recently learned about his father's dark side and detested it? She had one more bombshell to drop, then she moved the conversation onward swiftly to make it appear unimportant. "I had dinner last night at the Cloister with Doctor Burkman; it was sort of a present for getting well, and a wonderful one, since the food was delicious, the service excellent, and the music relaxing. As I told you, he doesn't have to give me a check-up for two weeks. And this is news: I heard from an old friend this week; actually she was my best friend before I married your father. Rather, I should say, we've been playing telephone tag for two weeks. I decided to take your good advice about making friends and getting out of the house occasionally; I'll just have to figure out when and where to start, but it will be soon, I promise. So, what's been happening with you?"

As Peter was listening to her initial disclosure, he wondered if she was developing a romantic interest in her physician. If she was, should he ignore it, encourage it, or squash it? He would encourage it if he thought Jason would snap her up fast and get her out of his hair, but Jason might just be toying with her for fun or revenge. If he waited too long, Jason could have more sway over her than he did now. Perhaps he should romance Cass himself. That way, he would be assured of gaining control of the entire Grantham estate, which was rightfully his by birth and hard work. That greedy stepmother of his didn't deserve anything more than she already had taken, and certainly not such a large percentage! He had no doubt he could win Cass with his charms and sexual skills. Even at nine years his senior, she was beautiful, and she had to be a hot number in bed to have captured a lusty sonofabitch like his father. If she wasn't willing to lean in his direction, he could slip some of Hines's magical powder into her food, drink, or headache capsules like he and Inez had done before. He bet himself that in less than five minutes he could have her writhing and moaning in ecstasy and begging him not to stop!

After Cass finished talking, Peter sketched over his business appointments and mentioned having dinner or lunch with several old friends or acquaintances. "In fact, I'd better get going or I'll be late for my racketball game. You take good care of yourself, Cass, and I'll see you Wednesday night. Don't worry about anything because I'll be around to help you with any problems."

His final two sentences had seemed to ring with sincere affection and concern. Again she wondered if he had changed for the better and her suspicions were wrong. "I will, Peter, and the same to you. Thanks for calling; I really enjoyed our talk. I'll see you Wednesday night."

As soon as she hung up the receiver, Cass lifted it again and phoned Jason, having committed his number to memory. Her heart raced for a few minutes when she heard his voice and she wondered if she was being forward and foolish.

When no one responded to his "Hello," he asked, "Who's there?"

"It's Cass. I —"

"Is anything wrong? Are you all right?" he interrupted to query her prior hesitation.

She laughed. "No, I'm fine. Peter just phoned to say he won't be returning until Wednesday, so I thought I would do something for you to repay you for a lovely evening last night. How about dinner at my house?"

Damn, what lousy timing! "I wish I could, Cass, but I'm having dinner with a colleague and his wife. If it weren't at their home and on such short notice, I'd invite you to accompany me. I'm playing golf with him and some other people in thirty minutes. You just caught me; I was heading out the door."

"That's all right. Perhaps another time. I know you're in a rush to get to the club, so I won't delay you. Good-bye."

"Wait, Cass! I have to come home to shower and change clothes after our game and dinner isn't until eight, so I could stop by for coffee or a drink beforehand, if that's convenient. Say about sevenish?"

"That's fine with me, if you're sure it won't intrude on your schedule."

"Nope, and I'd like to make sure you're doing okay."

"I am, Doctor Burkman, so stop worrying about me. See you around seven. 'Bye."

At ten past seven, Jason rang Cass's rear doorbell. He smiled at her after she responded, delighted to spend even thirty minutes with her. She looked ravishing in a deep mauve satin lounging pantsuit. "I hope this isn't inconveniencing you, and I'm sorry my time is so tight."

"Of course not. Please, come in." She moved aside for him to enter the mudroom, then proceed to the kitchen. As she followed him, eyeing his broad shoulders and good posture, she said, "I didn't put out any snacks because I assumed you'll be having hors d'oeuvres and dinner soon and wouldn't want to spoil your appetite. What would you like to drink?" she asked, halting at the white tiled counter.

"What are you having?"

Cass nodded toward the large clear glass with a green cactus stem. "A mischievous and delicious margarita since I'm not on medication anymore, thanks to you, so I don't have to worry about any side effects."

"That sounds cooling and refreshing after a hot day on the course and a quick shower." As he watched her measure and pour the tequila and mixer into a bottle and shake it, he said, "After I spoke with you, I phoned Sarah with hopes of being able to invite you along tonight, but I didn't ask if I could bring a guest after I found out she already had five others coming; added to her and her husband and me, that fills a table for eight." As she coated the wet rim to a matching glass with salt, which she had sprinkled on a piece of wax paper, then dropped an ice cube into it, he continued, "Besides, after I got Sarah on the phone, I decided I shouldn't make that request without asking you first; and I wasn't sure you were ready for meeting so many new people at once. I know how you women are about having notice to prepare for a night out; Traci used to take hours doing her hair and makeup and selecting her outfit."

Cass was glad he had mentioned his daughter rather than his deceased spouse or ex-wife. She smiled at him and said, "You were right, and most considerate." After she poured his mint-colored beverage, she handed the decorative glass to him and said, "Here, taste this. See if you want more of anything. The mixer is cold, so I only used one ice cube; that means the last swallow will be as good and strong as the first."

Jason sipped the margarita, licked the salt from his lips, smiled, and said, "Absolutely delicious, the best one I've ever had. Thanks. I'll have to remember that little trick about chilling the mix and being stingy with ice. Otherwise, by the time I get close to the bottom, it's as weak as water."

Cass nodded. "Would you like to sit in the den and talk until it's time for you to leave?"

"Sounds great, my feet and legs can use a break; my old back, too."

"You make forty-two sound as if it's ancient," she jested. "I hope it's not, because I'm not far behind you and I have a lot of living to do now that I'm fully recovered from my illness."

"So do I," Jason concurred, "but sometimes I feel much older than I am after a long hard day at the office, especially if I have an emergency piled atop it that keeps me up half the night."

"That's the price of being a physician, a deeply caring one."

They seated themselves in close proximity on short sofas positioned at an L angle and with a square table near the armrests where they placed their glasses on coasters. They leaned their bodies toward each other to talk with greater ease. Multi-wattage bulbs in several lamps were on low to provide sufficient light in the slowly darkening room. Soft music came from a radio in the entertainment unit, set to an easy-listening station. High tide waves were audible, though the double doors to the patio were closed. The subtle fragrance of peach blossoms clung to the air from where Cass had sprayed the room with freshener minutes before Jason's arrival.

As he entered the den earlier, Jason had noticed Tom's portrait was gone from over the fireplace, as were assorted framed pictures of him or of him and Cass which he'd seen there on previous visits. He saw the sculpture he had given to her sitting on the mantel, the bronze fingers touched ever so slightly and romantically as he longed for theirs to do.

"I don't think I could work as hard as I do if I didn't love my profession and care about my patients," Jason said. "I plan to slow down a little after I reach fifty, then retire at sixty. I've seen too many colleagues continue practicing into their late sixties or even longer. By the time they retire, they have plenty of money to spend, but often lack the health or time to enjoy it before they die. I want to leave myself plenty of years and strength to spend time with my family, and doing things I like."

"That's a smart idea." *But it doesn't sound as if you'd want to start over with a new baby to rear.* "You love golf, don't you?"

"Yep, but I wish I were a better player. Some of the guys I play with make shots the pros would envy." He sipped his drink before adding, "I also enjoy tennis, but it's harder than golf on my body as I get older. My bones just don't like to take that kind of hard pounding anymore. But chess, now that's more my speed after a hard day."

"You play chess?" she asked in some surprise.

"Yep, my dad taught me. I've played with him hundreds of times, with Stacey, too. I can hold my own with my son, but Dad, he's a champ. He could have me in check or check-mate before I got warmed up good."

"*Warmed up good . . .*" Cass felt her body heating up by the minute as she gazed into his mirthful blue eyes and handsome face, and she knew her rising temperature wasn't caused by the alcohol. "I play, too," Cass revealed, "and my father was the one who taught me, too."

"Are you also a champ?"

"I'm not as good as my father was, but I'm not bad, either."

Jason liked the way her cheeks had rosed, her brown eyes had softened. Her attention was just as glued to him as his was to her, and her voice exposed powerful emotions. He hoped he wasn't misreading those physical signs and that she was just as attracted to him as he was to her. "In that case, I challenge you to a game sometime soon. The loser will . . . Let's see . . . What should the loser have to do for the winner? Um-m-m . . ."

Cass tried not to choke on the sip she had just taken. *I must be careful, or I just might answer him honestly, whether or not I do it with words! I mustn't,* Cass warned herself, *blush, or squirm, or give a nervous laugh!* She swallowed and lowered her glass with one hand, the fingers of the other one toying with the arms of its cactus stem. *Control yourself and look unruffled.* "Cook dinner? Say a six-course meal in the Cloister style? And, of course, wash the dishes and clean up the kitchen afterward."

Jason had seen her gaze widen and her flush deepen, just as he was aware of his own arousal. *Mercy, you're one tempting and enchanting female!* "Something tells me you're better at chess than you admit, woman. That sparkle in your brown eyes says you're confident of winning. Don't tell me I've just been hustled by a chess pro."

"Why, Doctor Burkman, how could you possibly think I would do such a naughty thing to my physician and friend?" Cass realized she might sound too suggestive. She pretended not to notice her slip in proper behavior. "In fact, I'm probably very rusty because I haven't played in years, not since my father died."

A startled Cass almost sloshed her drink into her lap as a buzzer rent the sultry silence between them. She watched Jason set aside his glass and press a button on his wristwatch to turn off the beeping signal.

He took in a deep breath and exhaled. "I hate to say it, Cass, but I have to leave or I'll be late for dinner. I surely have enjoyed myself."

"So have I, Jason." *Too much.*

Jason stood, straightened his coat and tie, and looked at her. "I hope you'll be going to church with me tomorrow morning."

Cass hadn't expected the invitation and wasn't sure if she should accept. As she headed to the kitchen, she asked, "Will Linda be there?"

"I doubt it; she's working on a case on Jekyll Island this week, one of my older patients. Do you prefer not to go with me or to go alone?"

They kept walking as she said, "No, I'll ride with you, if that's okay."

Jason was happy at her decision. "It is. I'll pick you up about ten-forty."

"That's fine; I'll be ready."

At the back door, Jason stopped to admit, "I wish I could stay because I'm certain I'd have a nicer evening here with you than at a stuffy dinner party talking shop. Get a good night's rest, Cass, and I'll see you in the morning." He kissed her on the cheek. "Good night."

"Goodnight, Jason, and thanks for stopping by; it was fun."

She closed and locked the door behind him, then walked to the kitchen window to observe his departure. She returned his wave and smile when he glanced in that direction and saw her.

After he drove away, she muttered to herself, "What on earth are you doing, Cassandra? Where, in heaven's name, do you think this relationship is going?"

She headed to the den to get her margarita. "I don't have the slightest idea, but I'll probably obtain some clues or answers tomorrow."

Chapter Thirteen

At First Baptist Church services on Sunday morning, Jason introduced Cass to many people who gave her cordial welcomes and invited her to join in on other church and local activities. As he'd guessed, Linda was not there; and Cass's reaction to the nurse's absence was a mixture of delight and disappointment. She would have enjoyed seeing her friend again, but she liked having Jason to herself, if that were possible in a crowd; yet, she worried over what the congregation and pastor might think of her for being out with a man so soon after her husband's death, though no one looked at her oddly and all seemed sincere with their genial words and expressions. She made certain she behaved as a perfect lady and recent widow. She had even worn her wedding rings for appearance sake, though she hated to do so since Tom had defiled their sacred marriage vows and she detested being dishonest in a holy sanctuary. She only could hope that God understood and forgave her selfish motive.

After having lunch at Mullet Bay, Cass and Jason stopped by her house so she could change into casual clothes. He insisted she not stay home alone on such a beautiful day, and persuaded her to go to his house to walk on the beach, play chess, relax, and have dinner that evening. When she went upstairs, Jason remained in the den and glanced at a golf magazine she had purchased this week.

Cass removed her jewelry and locked it in her closet safe and didn't replace the discarded pieces with others, except for inserting gold studs in her earlobes. She put on a front-fastening bra that matched her satin-and-lace hip-hugger panties, then chose a simple but flattering ensemble by Emanuel Ungaro. She pulled a short-sleeved white tee top with a crew neck over her head, then repaired her mussed hair and freshened her makeup and perfume. She secured a reversible wrap skirt around her hips, ecru on the outside and ecru with navy stripes on the inside, slipped on navy slides, then grabbed the matching V-neck summer sweater with navy and ecru stripes in case the weather cooled down later. She tossed a few items into a fabric shoulder bag and joined Jason downstairs.

He rose as she entered the room, and smiled as he looked at her. "Perfect choice, and you look as lovely as you did earlier. You have good taste in clothes."

Cass was glad she had chosen this outfit since it was one Tom had not selected. She now felt as if he had been adorning her as nothing more than a showpiece to conceal his dark secrets and protect his reputation and image. Perhaps it was sinful of her, especially after just leaving church, but she hated him for what he had done to her. She smiled at Jason and said, "Thank you, kind sir, and so do you. Shall we go?" she hinted, wondering if she should be going to his house in her susceptible condition.

They traveled a lengthy distance down the long Sea Island Drive from her house and turned right onto a short side street to where his was located at a dead end at the beach. She noticed a circular driveway to the front door, with palms and other trees and plants in a garden section between it and the curbing. An abundance of trees and bushes on both sides of the lot concealed his house from the nearest neighbor's views. It was a two-story dwelling in a combination of Plantation and New Orleans styles with six tall columns, a first-floor porch running the entire length of the house, and another one doing the same on the second story with a white railing there for safety. He told her it had oyster shells mixed with the stucco to give it a light gray color, which matched the roof and was accentuated by white trim, including the large widow's walk atop it.

Jason parked his orient-blue BMW in a three-car garage, then guided her to the front door. "Welcome to my home, Cass," he said as they entered the enormous setting.

Jason began the tour in a foyer with a merbau

floor, a cherry console with a hand-carved mirror suspended over it, and a floral arrangement and a few other objects atop it. Hardwood stairs led to the second floor; an arch to their left into a formal living room; an arch to their right into a formal dining room. Both were furnished in the Neoclassic style and had plush carpeting. A doorway before them led to a den; and a last door to a half bath; both of which were decorated beautifully.

"Since we're at the steps, let me show you the upstairs first."

There, Cass was led into the master suite first, where nothing had been left out of place, as if he had known he was bringing her to visit. His bedroom was large and masculine with a jungle decor in browns, blacks, beiges, and greens; it even had a silk acacia tree with mauve blossoms in one corner and African artifacts on the walls and furniture tops. The suite contained an enormous walk-in closet and luxurious bathroom with separate areas for bathing, dressing, and personal functions.

The first guest room had a private bath, while the other two — one with twin beds for his grandsons — shared a bath that opened into the hall and into the third guest room. The first room had French doors that opened onto a full-length second-story rear porch, as did Jason's bedroom and the hallway. It was furnished with a Louis XV-style hand-painted headboard to the king-size bed, a matching lingerie chest, a boudoir chair in pink, and other furnishings and a variety of silk greenery.

"It's absolutely magnificent, Jason."

"Thanks. Traci claims it as hers when she comes to visit. She likes to leave the doors open so she can hear the waves day and night. Stacey uses the front bedroom when he's home."

"I imagine you miss them terribly."

"Yep, but I've gotten used to having an empty nest. At least they're close enough for frequent visits, and we talk on the phone a lot. Let's head downstairs," he suggested, aware of how close they were to a choice of several beds. He yearned to carry her to one of them and make slow and passionate love to her.

As they descended the stairs, Jason warned himself not to risk offending her and scaring her away. He wished time would move quickly and put many months between her tragic loss and when he could take a romantic move toward her. Until sufficient time passed, he had to be careful and patient, considerate and compassionate. While he waited, he would help her to get to know him better and subtly draw her closer and closer.

"This is one of my favorite rooms; I spend a lot of time in here," he told her as they entered the oblong den. "That built-in entertainment unit has a surround sound system; We'll listen to it later; it surely brings things on that big screen to life."

She had noticed the upstairs floors were carpeted in the bedrooms, and the baths were done in large Florida tiles. The stairs, hallway, and foyer featured hard woods, some areas decorated with scatter or area rugs. The kitchen and den had Tennessee crab orchard flagstone in various sizes and shapes in a muted green color. There was an eye-catching fireplace with light brick in its interior and with a raised half-moon hearth and stonework that matched the floors and traveled to the ceiling and several feet to each side. Two seven-feet-tall silk Capensia trees in brass containers had been placed in corners, their rich green leaf tops contrasting with burgundy undersides. There was a wet bar on one side with glass-paned cabinets and black Corian tile on the counter. The Chesterfield sofa and loveseat were in deeply tufted and overstuffed forest green leather and featured individually driven brass nailheads in a linear design on the front of their rolled arms and base. In another location was a leather bergere chair with a matching ottoman, a table and a lamp. The sitting area had a hand-knotted rug with a striking design in greens, beiges, burgundy, and slate blue that looked splendid atop the flagstone and beneath the furniture.

At the far end were located his home office and a playroom for the grandchildren. His office had a three-section bookcase that held mostly medical books and journals and a variety of knickknacks. Attached to one end of the unit was an executive desk in a simple but classic style, all in solid Honduran mahogany. In front of it was a comfortable-looking chair in black leather with brass studs around all edges and with wheels for easy movement for turning to work on a computer system inserted into the center bookcase. A large metal clock with roman numerals hung on one wall; a Masters Golf Tournament scene on another. Beside the desk stood a brass pharmacy lamp with an aged finish and beige shade. The customary accessories — pad, pencil/pen holder, calendar, stapler, telephone — were positioned neatly atop his work surface. A hand-stitched needlepoint rug in a Neoclassic design partially covered a shiny hardwood floor.

During her tour, Cass noted there were framed pictures of his twins and grandsons, a few photographs of the twins with their deceased mother, but none of the lovely fair-haired Joan with Jason.

The playroom next door was filled with boyish toys, games, stuffed animals and assorted action figures, and books all placed on four-feet-high wooden shelves on all walls for easy reach by little tykes. A low table with four toddler-size chairs, patterned like color crayons as were the curtains, set in the center of the room. She smiled as he told her its hardwood floor and lack of a rug were for easier cleaning when children had accidents. She concluded from his expression and tone that he dearly loved his family and that warmed her very soul. It caused her to yearn for a real home and family, for a baby, for his baby . . .

She quelled those urges as he guided her to the spacious and airy kitchen with an island in its center. A breakfast area was positioned nearby with a large span of windows that offered an ocean view. She couldn't help but imagine them having morning coffee or an evening meal there.

"I spend most of my time in my bedroom, the den, office, and hot tub out back after a long and hard day at work or a muscle-tiring day on the golf course," he explained. "Occasionally I cook, but it's not much fun doing it alone and for one person, and I'm no chef by any means. But don't worry about dinner; I do grill a mean steak and one can hardly ruin a salad, rolls, and baked potato," he added with a grin.

Cass laughed. "I'm not worried. Doc; I'm sure you can do anything you put your mind to. You got me well, didn't you?" *And you enchanted me beyond reason without even trying!*

"Yep, but I had excellent help from Linda and cooperation from you." *But if I'm capable of doing "anything," I hope it's winning you, woman.*

Cass adored the magnificent setting, felt relaxed there. She could envision herself sleeping upstairs, lounging in the den, watching him work in his office, observing their child in the playroom, and — *Stop it, Cass!* "I must say, your home is wonderful, beautiful but comfortable."

"I can't take credit for building it; the previous owner deserves that. But I had a fine decorator who met with me several times to check out my style of living and personality before she began her task. I really like what she did with the house."

"So do I."

"Of course, it's too big for one person, but I like living here and having room for the kids and my grandsons to visit; and size gives it good resale value for later when I retire, if I decide to go smaller. Samuel Tarver of Tarver Realty Company found it for me and sold my other residence. If you decide to sell later, give Sam a call; he does a fine job for his clients."

"He's already photographed my home on the sly and called me. I told him I would consider using him if I decide to sell and move. My house is big, too, so I might go smaller, but not anytime soon."

Just don't leave this area and my reach, please. "Thank goodness I have Mary to clean it for me."

"She starts for me tomorrow, but I can see she'll be well worth every dollar she charges. And I can tell you do a good job of keeping it clean and straight between her visits. A neat man impresses me."

"Thanks. I also have pool, lawn, and window-washing services. I'm not much for slaving in a yard or pool, but I want them nice and clean."

"So do I. Isn't it wonderful those services are available here?"

"Yep. One last area to see," he said and led her there.

Beyond sliding doors in the den was a screened lanai with a swimming pool in its center and a hot tub in one corner. The furniture was in white wicker with jungle-print cushions. There were matching tables beside two sofas and six chairs. Three six-foot-tall bamboo palms and four ferns in hanging baskets and several floor planters gave off a tropical air. Besides natural lighting during the day, there were recessed panels for nighttime with a dimmer switch for adjusting the level of their illumination.

"As you can tell from the silk plants, I sorely lack a green thumb."

"Then we have something else in common; so do I."

"To our left is a dressing room with a full bath for guests. That way, the kids and our friends don't have to traipse into the house wet after they've been swimming or playing in the yard and on the beach. As you can see, on our right is a Florida room with exercise equipment; with all of that glass, I have a marvelous ocean view while working out in there or relaxing in here. I added this section before I moved in. The original owner had a full-length veranda out here, but I needed this more than a fourth porch."

"You were smart; it's perfect for relaxing and entertaining."

"I don't have time to do much of either one, but perhaps I will someday."

Cass walked to the end of the lanai and gazed outside to a stone terrace with leisure furniture in a New Orleans style with floral cushions and table umbrella. Several huge urns were set here and there with live plants: ivy and shrubs, no doubt tended by the gardener. With Jason's home situated at a dead end and with a thick hedge of bushes and trees along his left and right boundary lines, some native to the island and others planted, the dense walls of greenery blocked neighbors' views of his backyard. She noticed a gazebo with white latticework and benches near the edge of his enormous lot and also a wooden gym set with climbing towers at both ends with ladders and several levels, a slide, and four swings. Beyond the grass lawn were the white sandy beach, sparkling Atlantic Ocean, and vast blue sky without a black cloud in sight. The backyard was enclosed — she assumed for safety and privacy — by a six-foot-high white wrought-iron fence that had a gate for reaching the beach.

As Jason joined her, she was thinking how this home reflected happiness, success, and even wealth. She felt both calm and elated, as if her troubles didn't exist, as if she had known

Jason for a long time, as if she belonged there, belonged with him.

"Around the side of the house is a spiral staircase to the sun deck on the roof," Jason explained. "I don't go up there often, but it has an awesome view, especially at sunrise and sunset. I'll show it to you later if you like and you aren't afraid of heights."

"I'd love to see it. You've created a marvelous place for yourself, large and elegant, yet, cozy and inviting. You have neighbors in three directions, but in this location, it seems secluded from people."

"Thanks, I enjoy it. Now, I'll go change into casual clothes and shoes so we can walk on the beach and get some exercise before we settle down to play chess. Make yourself at home."

When Jason returned, he was clad in colorful Nautica sportswear and Hush Puppies loafers without socks. He halted in the den doorway and watched Cass for a few minutes as she gazed at the ocean from a wicker chair near the back of the lanai. She had a peaceful, dreamy look on her face. She seemed tranquil, as if her recent anxiety had vanished, one he still suspected hadn't resulted from natural causes. There was no denying he was in love with her and wanted to marry her. She was perfect for him, perfect for this home, perfect for his life, perfect for his family. When he realized his loins were becoming enflamed with desire, he forced those thoughts to stop and called out, "Would you like one of my specialty drinks to take with you on our stroll? I promise you it's delicious."

Cass looked at him. "I'm game, but make mine mild, okay?"

"I'm your doctor and your good friend, so I wouldn't do or give you anything that's detrimental to your health. Trust me, woman."

Cass laughed at his amusing expression and tone. "I do; I will. Need any help?"

"Nope, just relax where you are until I return." *Maybe I can douse my blazing libido while I'm busy in here. If ever an ice cold shower was needed by any man, it's me and right now!*

After Jason joined her and handed her an insulated cup with a handle and sippy top, she took a swallow, then smiled. "Delicious as promised. What's in it?" she asked as she stood to leave with him.

Jason grinned. "Can't tell you; it's an old safely guarded family recipe. All I will say is, assorted tropical fruit juices and several liquors."

Trying to get me inebriated and vulnerable to your many charms?

They crossed his backyard, exited the gate where she slipped off her shoes, and stepped onto soft sand with grass-dotted dunes. They headed northeastward at a leisurely pace. The tide was going out and would be at its lowest in two hours, so they had plenty of strolling

304

room between the water's edge and private property of local or seasonal residents. Though it was a lovely Sunday afternoon, they were the only walkers in that area. The beach was dazzling white where dry, a pearl gray where wet. The sky was intensely blue, with occasional snow-colored billowy clouds. The ocean was a darker shade of blue with white-crested waves and frothy fringes. With spring in full force, the island's trees and plants were lush and green.

As if they knew what Jason was carrying in his hand, countless seagulls began to circle them overhead and land all around them, sending forth raucous cries in pleading. The couple halted for him to open the bag of bread crumbs and feed the birds. Pieces he tossed upward were grasped in mid-air, some devouring the bite immediately and others landing to work on a larger chunk in leisure as more gathered about it to beg for scraps.

As she sipped her drink and waited, Cass witnessed the near-frenzied activity and Jason's enjoyment of it. She liked how his cotton knit shirt boldly hinted at the broad and rippling torso beneath it. He had long, muscular legs with curly dark hair on them, despite the fact the hair on his head was as tawny as a lion's. His stomach was flat; his buttocks, taut; and his hips, slender: the build, she concluded, of an athlete or one who took splendid care of his physique.

"That's all, my greedy feathered friends," he said as he shook the bag to dump the tiny crumbs before stuffing it into his pocket to toss away later. He glanced at Cass, grinned, and suggested they leave. "Just keeping walking and ignore them and they'll leave soon to go in search of their next feeder," he advised.

A light breeze played in their hair and with Cass's wraparound skirt, frequently giving Jason a pleasant view to slightly above her knees. He saw how the sunshine caused her dark-brown locks to give off a golden glow and lustrous sheen; the same was true for her flawless complexion which reflected good health. Whenever they paused for her to pick up a certain seashell, he noticed how her toes wriggled in the sand as if in sheer delight of their freedom and that almost sensuous contact. He observed how the skirt accentuated her rounded hips and small waist and how the tee top revealed a nicely sized, taut bosom; no doubt the retention of such sleek figure was due in part, he deduced, to never having had children.

Children, Jason mused, did he want another one or two? Did she? Would that be wise to attempt at their ages, forty-two and thirty-five? What would his twins think about his starting a new family and would their opinions matter to him? What would his grandsons think about having an aunt or uncle younger than they were? There was no doubt in his mind that his parents would be elated if he remarried and be pleased to have more grandchildren. It only took moments for him to assure himself that his son and daughter would adore Cass and welcome her into their close-knit family and into their father's life. If only he could —

"Yoo hoo?" Cass said as she waved a hand before his face. "That's mighty deep thought, Doc. Are you worried about something?"

He looked at her and smiled. "Just thinking about the kids and my grandsons; they love the beach and days like this one. I'll be going up to see them in early May. Since Stacey's in Augusta where you lived and worked, if you'd like to come along, that would be a nice outing for you."

"I might go, if you don't mind. I'd like to see Kristy again soon. For the past few weeks, we've been leaving messages for each other. She was my best friend for years, but we drifted apart after I married and moved away. We sort of had a problem that came between us: she didn't like Tom and tried to talk me out of marrying him, and he didn't like her because he sensed her ill-feelings and she's my ex-sister-in-law."

He wondered if she now wished she had taken her friend's advice, if what she knew or suspected about her deceased husband was true. He was inclined to believe terrible things about Thomas Grantham since his son was such an awful person. "It's bad when you get caught in the middle of a conflict between people you love. That's happened to me. Sometimes it turns out we were right and sometimes, they were. All we can do is learn from any mistakes, let them make us stronger and wiser and try not to repeat them."

"You're an understanding and compassionate man, Doc."

"Thanks, and those same traits apply to you. Perhaps we get along so well because we're so much alike in many ways."

"That seems to be an accurate assessment of our rapport." When Cass saw several couples walking in their direction, people who might know Jason and stop them to talk, she suggested, "Why don't we turn around and head back? We need to conserve enough energy for our chess game."

Jason was agreeable, "You're right; I'll need plenty of stamina and wits if I'm going to meet your challenge."

Cass laughed and quipped, "You challenged me, remember?"

"Ah, but you accepted it without hesitation and with confidence. I have a feeling I've met my match." *I know I have, Cassandra Grantham.*

I surely hope you have, Jason, because I feel so drawn to you.

As they strolled toward his home, they chatted about other things and finished their drinks. Each assumed the other didn't want to talk about past spouses, as neither had followed up on earlier mentions or hints of them. When their cups were empty, Jason carried them.

Cass paused here and there to pick up pretty augers, whelks, slippers, cockles, and one perfect angel wing. She held her shells in one hand and used the other to collect treasures which she planned to place in a small decorative jar as souvenirs of this wonderful day with him.

Just before they reached his gate, Cass shrieked "Ouch!" and hopped about on her left foot. "Sandspur," she explained as she winced, putting down only her toes to keep from driving the spines deeper into her heel.

Jason knelt, dropped the cups, and said, "Hold on to my shoulder and lift your foot." As she obeyed and he clasped her ankle, he warned, "It's going to smart when I pull it out." He grasped the spur and removed it, noting her flinch and the prickles on his fingers. "I'm sure a spine is still in there, so I'll take a look at it after we get inside and I'll tend it for you."

"Thanks. That's what I get for going barefooted, but I couldn't resist."

Jason closed and locked the gate behind them, collected Cass's shoes, and had her hold on to his arm as she hobbled to the lanai. "Sit here while I fetch my medical bag and a magnifier. Trust me, woman, I've done this plenty of times for Stacey and Traci and my grandsons."

As she watched him disappear into the house,

her mind quipped, *He wants me to trust him, but do I dare when so much is at stake? Do I stand a chance of having a happy future with you? Will you break my heart?* She cautioned herself to travel a slow and easy road where he was concerned, but could she when he tempted her at every turn and stop along the way?

Jason brought out his medical bag, magnifier, and items from his medicine chest. He left again to fetch a large plastic bowl of water, liquid soap, and a cloth. When he returned and set them aside, he propped her right leg on an ottoman with her foot extended over its edge. He sat on the floor to wash and dry her foot. Afterward, he examined the injured area with the magnifying glass. "Yep, there's the little troublemaker. You're lucky, woman, the tip is protruding slightly so I can get a grip on it. Relax, Cass, I'm going to numb it a little with Xylocaine ointment so it won't hurt."

With a cotton ball, he dabbed the reddening spot with anesthetic balm. "Now, we'll wait a few minutes to let that work before I start poking on it. How about a Coke or some water?"

"Water would be good. Thanks."

"I'll be back in a flash."

Cass glanced at her leg and foot, glad she had shaved and lotioned one and polished the toenails of the other after removing dead skin from her heels and soles with a pumice stone last night. Her skirt had parted slightly, but not enough to be suggestive, so she didn't lean forward to conceal her knees. It was sheer rapture to have him touching her, being so close to her, being so attentive and almost pampering her, which was something she was unaccustomed to with Tom. Thomas Ethan Grantham needed to be catered to. But Jason, he was so different from that, so kind and considerate and thoughtful. Unless he was putting on a good front to dupe her, which she doubted.

After Jason fetched her water and a Coke for himself, he sat on the floor and checked her foot again. "Can you feel that?"

"Yes and no. I feel you touching my toe, but it doesn't hurt."

"Good, I'll get started." He took out a small pair of forceps, grasped the spine, and removed it. He checked its tip to make certain it hadn't broken off under the skin, and it hadn't. He applied an antiseptic solution, smiled at her, and said, "Finished. Shouldn't give you any problem later. Of course, it may be a tiny bit sore and sensitive for a day or two; that's normal. To be so small, those spines can hurt like the devil."

Cass nodded agreement, then held up the angel wings from the beach and said, "I would give these to you, Doc, if I could figure out a way to pin them on your back. You certainly deserve them. Thanks."

"You can show your appreciation by not

311

being too hard on me in our chess game," he joked with a grin, absently stroking her bare foot as he did so.

Cass laughed and teased, "Are you asking me to lose on purpose?"

"Moi?" he asked, tapping his chest and chuckling. "Would I do something wicked like that?"

Cass sent him a playfully skeptical look and teased, "You might be a little deceitful or mischievous under certain circumstances, such as when you don't want to have a bruised ego, but never intentionally dishonest."

Having stood while she was speaking, he made a half-bow and said, "I appreciate your confidence and faith in me. You rest a minute after your trying ordeal while I put these things away and set up the chess table and board. Which color do you want: black or white?"

"Black, because a white knight should always wear his code of honor."

Jason grinned and asked, "Do you have any idea how much fun you are? It's a pleasure to spend time with you."

Cass hoped her cheeks weren't a rosy color, but they felt mighty warm. *My, oh, my, Jason Burkman, are you too good to be for real?* "Thanks for the compliment, and I enjoy your company, too."

"Great. I'll return for you soon." *I need a little distance and time to get myself under control.*

Twenty-five minutes into their game, each had made many moves and countermoves, sacrificing or losing by accident certain pieces, and taking a few from the opponent. The folding chess table with squares painted atop it was small, so there wasn't much distance between them as they leaned forward to watch each other's plays and to plan strategies. Beneath it, their knees often touched, his bared by his shorts and hers by parted panels of her skirt. Their gazes often locked for a minute or two. They sipped on another tropical drink, but only half the size of the first one; its fruity fragrance caused them to think of an island paradise. The smell of the ocean and blooming flowers entered through the opened doors to the screened lanai which captured them from outside and passed them along. Soft music from a CD floated in the air from the surround system. Dusk was approaching, so recessed bulbs were on dim wattage to provide sufficient light. The atmosphere in the room was titillating and romantic.

Pawns, knights, rooks, bishops, and queens were used to guard their vital kings as the contest continued. Conquered pieces were placed in neat lines along the sides of the imprinted board, hers on one and his on the other, but his row was shorter by three "men."

Eventually, Jason made a playful scowl and accused, "Methinks you're trying to lure me into a trap, Cassandra. Desperate for my remaining knight and then my king, are you? Hmm, what shall I do to protect them?"

"So, it's Cassandra now, is it? Does that mean you're worried about losing your challenge?"

"What's that old saying about it not being over until the fat lady sings? In this case, until my king is captured, and I still have him."

"Not for long, I'm afraid," she murmured as she took her next turn. Her mirthful gaze met his and she said, "Check."

Jason studied the setup and tried to think of a way to thwart her sly ploy, but realized he couldn't move to defend his king. He looked at Cass and jested, "Well, Fat Lady, you can sing now."

"Checkmate," she said, unable to suppress a grin of pleasure. "I win, so that means you owe me . . . What was the bet, dinner and slave labor."

"Does tonight count as payment?"

"Nope, because we made these plans before the game."

"All right, I'll pay my debt next weekend, same time and same place."

"Suits me; my calendar is blank on that date."

"Since tonight doesn't count, you can help me in the kitchen. I'll marinate the steaks while you get the potatoes ready to bake. We'll set the table and do the salad and rolls while we're waiting to start the grill."

Cass liked the idea of working together. "Let's go; I'm game."

"The last time you said that I made a foolish wager with you."

"Relax, Doc, it was an innocent statement this time. Besides, I can't imagine you ever acting by foolhardy."

I could act impulsive over you, woman, if I'm not careful. "Oh, I've been impetuous a few times in my life."

"So have I. Hasn't everyone?"

"Yep, human nature, I suppose. Let's get cooking."

As they worked in the kitchen, they laughed and talked easily. They seemed totally relaxed with each other yet the sexual tension was mutual . . . and increasing. While fetching items or passing them along, their hands, bodies, and gazes often touched.

As Cass turned to tell him the potatoes were scrubbed and wrapped in foil and ready for the oven, he turned to take them from her. Instead, their eyes met for a long, meaning-filled moment and they found themselves in each other's arms, kissing hungrily as their eager hands caressed and stroked the places they'd ached to touch.

As Jason spread kisses over her face and neck, he murmured in a husky tone, "I want you so badly, Cass. You've been driving me crazy since the first time we met."

Cass knew her response and reaction would determine what he did next, what they did soon. Could she, should she, surrender to him, to her own desires; was she ready to trust him with her heart? Once she did, there would be no turning back.

Chapter Fourteen

Cass's unspoken answer came from the depths of her heart and soul where there existed an intense need to be held, kissed, comforted, cherished, and made to feel whole and clean again. And yes, she would admit to herself later, she also yielded to pure lust for Jason Burkman.

Jason took her heated response as permission and encouragement and he pulled her even closer. Supreme anticipation surged through him as his fantasy edged toward reality. He wanted to make her his, now and forever. With skill and eagerness, he set out to obtain his precious goal.

Locked in each other's embrace, Cass and Jason almost danced their way to the den sofa in time to the romantic song playing on the music system there.

As they were starting to recline on the sofa and were parted slightly for a moment, Jason whipped off his shirt and tossed it to the floor, then kissed her again. His elated spirits soared; his happy heart sang; his loins pulsed from a bittersweet ache. After a short time, his fingers pushed up her tee top, unfastened her front-closure bra, and freed her breasts from confinement. As one hand stroked her cheek and hair, the other caressed her bosom, and he took intense pleasure in feeling her nipples grow to taut peaks. He kissed a path down her throat to lick and suckle upon both breasts.

As he tantalized her senses, Cass's hands roved his strong back and journeyed through his thick tawny hair. It felt wild and wonderful when he teethed her nipples and swirled them with his hot tongue. She shifted slightly to help him when he parted her skirt panels and was wriggling off her lace-and-satin panties. She moaned and writhed when his fingers touched her bare, wet flesh. As the emotions she had kept constrained and guarded after Brad's betrayal, during her dating years after her divorce, and even during her marriage to Tom — as if she had known deep inside it wasn't true love — broke free and surged forth in a deluge of fiery passion, she gasped in sheer rapture.

Even if what she was doing was wrong and her wits were crystal clear, she couldn't have prevented herself from responding, from sating her hungers, from assuaging the longing within her. She never stopped to consider what Jason would think about her for her unbridled behavior.

Jason shucked off his shorts, grateful for the compliant elastic waist and the attached briefs which made underwear unnecessary. He inhaled and groaned in delight when Cass's hand enclosed his erection and fondled it, though her movements were a little restricted by their positions and a lack of sufficient space on the couch.

Together they titillated each other until both were murmuring their need aloud, Cass parted her thighs wider as Jason's hips sank between them and he slid into her welcoming body.

What began as hot, fast, uncontrollable, and urgent sex became slow, tender, deliberate, and gentle lovemaking, a bonding of souls, a sharing of needs, an entwining of hearts, and a revelation of mutual attraction and deep affection. It stayed that way for timeless moments, then it waxed ardent and swift again. They shifted positions so Cass straddled his lap and his penetration was deeper and snugger.

Jason unbuttoned and removed her skirt and peeled the tee top over her head as she lifted her arms, leaving them both completely naked. As she rode him, his mouth, tongue, and teeth worked on her breasts and his hands clasped her hips to help control his thrusts as he undulated his own.

With her eyes closed and while absorbing every sensation, Cass rested her rosy cheek atop his head as her questing fingers traveled his face, ears, throat, and shoulders as if mentally mapping those features. As she rocked to and fro or moved up and down, she felt every movement flash like splendid lightning through her, building a sweet tension she savored and stoked. She rode him faster, taking all of him inside her. When her climax came, it was potent and long and almost breath-stealing. She moaned in the throes of ecstasy and urged, "Don't stop, Jason. Oh . . . Oh . . . Heavens above, you're marvelous, and I need this so much."

"Take it all, Cass, my beautiful angel."

"You're driving me wild, Jason."

His heart pounded in love and joy; his mind soared in pride at being able to give her such enormous satisfaction. "Mercy, woman, this is so good I can hardly control myself. I've wanted you for so long."

"Come now, Jason; take me; take me. Don't wait any longer."

Not until Cass untensed and sighed dreamily — despite her permission and encouragement — did Jason roll them to lie flat on the sofa with him atop her and driving ardently into her until he also achieved a potent and rapturous release. He could hardly breathe from his exertions, but he kept kissing her anyway and groaning deep within his throat as he did so and until after every spasm ceased. Not wanting to put his full weight upon her or break their connection, he wiggled them to their sides and kept her nestled in his embrace as he kissed her forehead and hair.

Cass relished the feel of his naked body pressed against hers, and she listened to his breathing as it sought to return to a normal rate, as did hers. She was fulfilled and aglow, almost euphoric from the experience. Sex had never been this spontaneous, this splendid, this intoxicating, this powerful with either Brad or Tom.

Then reality returned: Cass could hardly believe what she had done six weeks after her husband's death. Yet, strangely, she wasn't sorry she had surrendered, unless it gave Jason a bad impression of her. It certainly didn't appear to have done so. A woman could tell a lot about a man by the way he made love to her, by what he said and did during and after sex, and by how he treated her in the ensuing days and weeks and months. Now that she had made love to Jason Burkman, she felt as if she should have guessed something was wrong in the past when Brad and Tom had made love *at* her more than *to* her. Perhaps this sensual episode would help her determine if a promising relationship was in store for them in the future or if his interest in her was merely sexual; surely it was best for her to make that discovery before she fell hopelessly and madly in love with him and learned too late he, too, was a cunning and selfish stranger. She took a deep breath.

Jason heard her heavy sigh and felt her body tense. "Cass? Are you upset or angry with me because of what happened between us? Did I spoil our friendship?"

She shook her head and admitted, "No, Jason, I'm only a little embarrassed. I don't know what came over me and I wish it hadn't happened this soon, but I enjoyed it." She saw him smile and exhale, as if with great relief and joy.

Her answer and expression calmed his agitation, and her words gave him renewed hope. "I sort of lost my head, too, but it was wonderful. I guess we both were in great need of some TLC. I care deeply for you and I want us to keep seeing each other. I realize it is too soon for you to think about starting a new relationship, and I didn't invite you over here to seduce you. I wouldn't do anything to intentionally hurt you, Cass, I swear it. If you're willing to give me a chance, we'll go slow and easy; I promise."

"I have great respect and deep affection for you, Jason, and I do enjoy spending time with you, but this is too soon to begin dating, despite what just happened between us; and don't worry, it was a mutual decision. We can continue to see each other, but for the time being, let's just work on strengthening our friendship."

"That sounds good to me, Cass, because you're very special to me."

She smiled and quipped, "In that case, you won't mind if I use your shower before I get dressed and we start working on dinner again. We did get sidetracked." Cass felt new heat blaze within her as he smiled, kissed her forehead, and spoke in a husky voice.

"Take your choice; all of them are clean and stocked."

"Thanks. I'll use the one near the pool and return soon." Cass got off the sofa, retrieved her clothes and purse, and left the den.

Jason's appreciative gaze roamed her nude backside as she departed in a graceful walk. After she closed the bathroom door, he rolled off the couch, snatched up his clothes, and took the flight of stairs two steps at a time in a state of euphoria. He knew his interest in Cass was more than a physical one; it also was emotional and spiritual. As he took a quick shower and groomed himself, he hoped and prayed she wouldn't panic and flee before he rejoined her.

Jason returned to the den before Cass did and, with haste, used a wet cloth to wipe off signs of their lovemaking session from the leather sofa. He hurried into the laundry room near the kitchen and draped the cloth over the washing machine, removing any intimate evidence that could embarrass her. He went to the terrace and lit the gas grill, relieved when he heard sounds in the bathroom as he passed through the lanai. He unwrapped the foiled potatoes and placed them in the microwave, since the oven would cook them too slowly. He enclosed the rolls in paper towel for heating them later, then went to work chopping the salad.

Cass walked into the room and gave Jason a reassuring smile when he looked over at her, to which he responded in like kind. After his gaze returned to his task, she glanced around the kitchen. "My goodness, either you've been rushing like crazy or I've been terribly sluggish."

"I figured you must be starving by now. You want a Coke or 7-UP?"

"What would you like? I'll fix them."

"I like Coke with my steak, especially since I can't prepare tea worth a darn and I hate that instant stuff. I warned you I'm no chef."

"I'll have to teach you how to make tea one day."

"Thanks, I'd appreciate the lesson." *Any lesson from you.*

After Cass had the beverages ready, she arranged the dishes, utensils, and napkins Jason had put out earlier, as placemats already were on the table. She added the condiments, then suggested, "Why don't I finish the salad while you grill the steaks? I bet you're hungry by now, and I'm eager to taste your specialty." *Your other specialty, since I've already sampled the best treat you have to offer, and I look forward to seconds, and thirds and fourths and fifths.*

"Is that what I told you?"

"No, but I assume it is since that's the main course. Doesn't everyone cook his or her best meal for company?" she jested as she nudged him aside with her hip and took his place at the island.

"You're a clever and perceptive woman, Cassandra Grantham. What are you going to make as my rain check for last night?"

"That's a surprise, so you'll just have to wait

324

and see. Don't forget, you owe me another meal for winning our chess game."

"I won't forget; I promise. When you finish the salad, come outside and talk to me while I grill the steaks. How do you like yours cooked?"

"Medium-rare, pink, but no blood, and I'll join you shortly." Cass watched him get the meat-laden tray from the refrigerator and tongs from a drawer, smile at her, and leave the room. She was glad the feeling between them was relaxed, and both were ignoring their romantic interlude. Yet, as she chopped the remaining vegetables, she couldn't stop thinking about the delicious ecstasy she had experienced and savored in his arms, and she already yearned for another taste of it. *Heaven, help me, Doc, but you could make a sex fiend out of me in two seconds flat!*

She joined him outside and watched him for a while in silence.

"Cass, there's something I have to tell you," Jason murmured, though he didn't want to spoil the tender moment. "I'm sorry I acted so impulsively and didn't put on a condom. No woman has ever affected me like you just did. I hope there won't be a problem from not using protection."

Cass was touched by his concern and delighted by her effect on him. With her gaze averted from his, she said, "I'm still on birth control pills, Jason, so there shouldn't be a complication. I was so accustomed to taking one every day and my mind's been consumed by so many other thoughts that I didn't think about no longer needing them."

After he turned the steaks and glanced at her, she added, "If you're worried about . . . medical problems, I had those tests done during my recent gynecological exam, and all of the results were negative."

"I'm a safe partner, too." He looked at his watch to check the cooking schedule, then queried, "May I ask why you had a second series of tests done with your gynecologist? Was there a particular reason why you thought it necessary to repeat them?"

Cass looked at him in confusion. "What do you mean? I only had one series done."

"Does that mean you didn't know Doctor Hines included all of the STDs and an AIDS test in his bloodwork while he was treating you?" He watched her gaze widen in astonishment and she nodded. "I saw them listed when he sent me a copy of your records." Jason didn't explain that he had requested them to see what Hines had charted about her medication and diagnosis, both of which factors he was still suspicious. Yet, he had no proof of mistreatment or drug overdosage upon which to base accusations against Hines. "I knew we were both infection free, but I should have considered birth control. I behaved like an irresponsible teenager. I'm sorry, and I'm glad you remained on the Pill."

Cass nodded appreciation of his apology and sensitivity, then, curious and puzzled, asked Jason, "I vaguely remember Doctor Hines taking blood samples, but I was pretty much out of it at that point, so I don't know why he ordered those kinds of tests. Is that normal?"

"Sometimes, particularly when a physician wants to rule out all possibilities for an illness or certain symptoms." Jason reasoned that they weren't necessary in her case, but didn't reveal that to her at this time because he didn't want her questioning Hines and putting the man on alert. If something sinister had occurred, he didn't want to risk endangering Cass again by panicking Hines and/or Peter. "Is it routine for your gynecologist to include them in a complete examination?"

"I don't know; that was my first visit with her, but it wasn't true for my old gynecologist; at least, I don't think so. I requested them on the second because Tom was traveling a great deal by himself during his last six months and it seemed he almost sneaked that model into town on his final trip, so I was concerned about his fidelity. I've already gotten the results and they were all negative, so I embarrassed myself for nothing."

"Not if it eased your fears and worries. It's best to deal with any doubts promptly. I did the same thing after my divorce from Brenda. Concerns like those could have been partly to blame for your anxieties and depression after his death, and I hate to say it but a negative result doesn't mean you were wrong about him, just that he was careful."

Cass recalled the panic and revulsion she had experienced after her vivid discovery of Tom's betrayals, so Jason was partly accurate in his assumption. Yet, she couldn't bring herself to confirm it to him. She realized how lucky she was that she hadn't caught anything from Tom, since the video had shown her that he hadn't always been careful during sex.

As they ate at Jason's breakfast table, using the casual rather than a formal setting, they chatted about upcoming local events which had been featured in the newspaper and on television. They agreed to attend a May performance at the Ritz Theater in Brunswick where they had met. Jason told her about the HarborFest they would be going to next month with Linda. He mentioned a trolley tour of Saint Simons Island and invited her to go fishing and/or shrimping with him one day. He repeated his past invitation to take a dinner/gambling cruise on the *Emerald Princess*. They planned the May trips to Augusta and Savannah for him to visit with his children and grandsons and her visit with Kristy and the "old gang" at work.

As she chewed a bite of steak, Cass knew she wasn't sure if she would go to Smooth Rider. Since it would be as the past owner's widow and the current part-owner, she would be deluged with questions about Tom or her partial business interest in the company. If she didn't want to see Kristy so badly, she wouldn't go to Augusta and risk running into Brad. Every time she did, she either had to listen to his incessant whining and pleading to reconcile in resentful silence or wind up being provoked to discourage him with insults and reminders of his past betrayals.

While sipping her drink, Cass thought about the many invitations Jason was extending to her tonight, as if he wanted to book her calendar completely with dates with him before she could fill it with other social or business obligations. "This is delicious, Chef Burkman, as expected," she commented.

"Ah, so, earned me a promotion, did it? Excellent, because I always aim to please my best friends and favorite patients. But I can take only half the credit; the other half belongs to the steer. Without a good piece of meat, even the best cook in the world couldn't make it taste like this."

Jason grasped that his words had sounded sexually suggestive; her flush and lowered gaze told him her thoughts had raced in the same direction his had. Yet, her glow was one of desire and arousal, not modesty or embarrassment. Knowing she wanted him again increased the pulsing and heat in his crotch. Since tomorrow was April fifteenth, the tax deadline, he leapt on that subject as a cooling diversion. "If you haven't taken care of your business matters and you need any legal assistance in that area, I can help you find a good lawyer; I know most of the local ones. Wills, finances, and taxes involved in a large estate with many diverse interests can be confusing and frustrating, especially if you aren't knowledgeable in those areas and accustomed to dealing with them. I remember it was difficult for me after Joan died; I had to hire a lawyer to handle her affairs and appease Uncle Sam."

He took a calming breath. "If the deceased was wealthy and prominent like your husband, distant relatives, charities, friends, business partners, and even strangers can crawl out of the woodwork to assail you with pleas for money or possessions. And I don't know how you and Peter get along, but families often have bitter disputes over inheritances. I wouldn't want anybody to take advantage of you, Cass, so let me know if you need help or advice from me or from a lawyer."

"Thank you, Jason, that's very kind and considerate; and Peter gave me this same talk and warnings. Tom's will has already been probated by the Grantham lawyer: Simon Johnson. We also have a financial manager and accountant who pays our bills and handles our taxes. Tom had four residences elsewhere, so Harrison Dredger took care of the expenses and payments for all of them; he's continuing to do the same for me until I get my bearings. As for my inheritance, it's protected by a trust fund at the bank, and Peter takes care of my shares in Tom's eight businesses; he owns their controlling interests, and he was left the other four residences around the country and Tom's private jet. I don't think I need a separate lawyer or accountant because Peter is being kind and cooperative about everything."

So, her money is tied up in a trust fund; I wonder for how long and what its stipulations are and if there are any loopholes Peter can use to get his hands on it. . . . "He hasn't contested the will or any of the bequests, terms, or provisions?"

"No, none of them. Why?"

Jason shrugged as he tried to sound casual with his queries, but was determined to protect her from that scum. "It's just that you and his father weren't married for very long and considering how some people will try to con or take advantage of grieving widows, nothing would surprise me."

"But Peter got a fifty-one-percent controlling interest in all companies, forty-five percent of the liquid assets and other funds, Tom's jet, four expensive residences and their furnishings, and lots of other possessions. Charities and foundations preselected by Tom received twenty-five-percent of the liquid assets. I was given the balances. Since he inherited a larger portion, why would he fight me for my lesser share? Besides, it was Tom's money and belongings, so he could disperse them in any way

331

he desired. In addition, inheritance taxes were paid by the estate before the three divisions were made; so, since his tax bill would have been higher than mine if done otherwise, in a way, I helped him pay his, right?"

As Jason nodded, he tallied her shares: forty-nine percent and thirty-five percent, the house and its contents, and other items; all tax-free. *But that still means Peter only gets twelve percent more, which isn't much for a greedy and devious man like that bastard is.* "If Thomas Grantham was as wealthy as I imagine, your share is a hefty one to result from a short marriage. Some children might resent that and go to court to recover what they feel is rightfully theirs by birth."

"I'm sure you're right in some cases, but Peter couldn't be any nicer to me than he's been since Tom's death. He's been keeping me informed in all areas, and Mr. Johnson and Mr. Dredger told me the same things he had when I met with them last week."

"Both men worked for your husband and now for Peter, correct?"

"Yes, so what's your point?"

"It might be wise if you have your own lawyer and accountant, Cass. Since Johnson and Dredger work for Peter and he's a bigger client of both, wouldn't they side with him if a conflict arose between you two? I'm not saying one will come up, but it could when millions of dollars are at stake. I know you don't want to think the worst of him, but neither do you want to get caught off-guard and unprepared if trouble arises."

Cass blurted out, "Peter would be furious and hurt if I acted as if I don't trust him or as if I'm trying to snag a larger share than I deserve."

"Are you afraid of him?" He saw her stare at him oddly.

"No, why? Should I be?"

"It's just that you looked and sounded as if you were." *If you aren't wary of him, you should be; he's a snake in the grass, a poisonous one.*

Whether or not she believed her words, she felt she had to say, "I didn't mean to give you that impression. I only meant that things have been going so well between us that I don't want to do or say anything that Peter might misconstrue and could cause trouble. As business partners, family, and friends, we need to stay close to work together for both of our sakes, and for the employees who depend on us for their jobs."

"I understand, Cass, and you're smart and considerate to do so. I'm sorry if I upset you by sticking my nose where it doesn't belong. Forgive me? Please. My only concern, as your doctor and friend, is in protecting you from all harm. I don't want you to get stressed out again over anything or anyone and have to go back on medication."

"I know, Jason, and I'm grateful. Except for

you, Peter, and Linda, I'm alone here on Sea Island, so I depend on my few friends for comfort and advice. But if I encounter any future crisis with my estate, I will call you for assistance with hiring a separate attorney."

"If a difficulty arises, please deal with it however necessary before you get anxious and depressed and exhausted. If you do that favor for me to safeguard your health, I won't intrude again; I promise. Now, how about a piece of low-fat, no-sugar-added apple pie and a cup of decaf coffee?"

Cass was glad he dropped the upsetting subject. "Sounds scrumptious, Doc. Do you have any cheese slices?"

Jason grinned after he swallowed the remainder of his drink. "Don't tell me you also put cheese instead of ice cream globs on yours?"

"Absolutely, since childhood; that's how my mother served it."

"The more I get to know you, Cass, the more I realize how much we have in common. Apple pie with melted cheese coming up."

"Right." *Just like sex, which would be my dessert of choice.*

Jason walked Cass to her back door and waited until the alarm system was switched off and she was poised in the opening before he said, "I had a wonderful time today. I'll call you tomorrow."

"Good night, Jason, and I also enjoyed myself. Thanks for everything."

"You're more than welcome, and we'll do it again very soon." Jason gave her a light kiss on the lips, exchanged smiles with her, and left.

While turning off the downstairs lights, Cass checked her answering machine when she saw the red light blinking. Linda had phoned that afternoon and evening, but, after glancing at the clock, she realized it was too late to return the call tonight, since the phone could disturb her elderly patient.

As Cass prepared herself for bed, she remembered Jason's hint — or slip — about Brenda. She wondered if it meant his ex-wife had been unfaithful to him and her adultery had provoked their divorce and his need for STD blood tests. If so, that would give them something else in common. She warmed when she recalled Jason's words: "No woman has ever affected me like you just did," and "If you're willing to give me a chance . . ."

Cass stopped brushing her hair and stared at her reflection in the mirror as she pondered if "no woman" included his two past wives. Perhaps he had meant what he said, or maybe it was only pillow talk, or maybe it was a natural reaction during a golden afterglow to such a splendid lovemaking.

"A chance" for what, Doc? To win me lock, stock, and barrel? Why did you mention my wealth tonight? And why were you concerned about Peter

trying to steal it? Do you have an ulterior motive for trying to plant seeds of doubt about him and for delving into my money yourself? Or am I reading your intentions wrong? Letting my imagination run wild? That must be it; you're only concerned about me like you said.

Cass got a cup of water and took her birth control pill. Just in case she lost her wits again, she warned, she had better not forget to take them daily! *When and if I get pregnant, I want to be married. A baby . . . Jason's baby . . . Our baby . . . How glorious and fulfilling that would be.*

On Monday at eight o'clock, her new housekeeper arrived to begin her new job. Cass went over her instructions, showed Mary Ellis where everything was located, and took down the woman's Social Security number and tax information for Harrison Dredger.

While Mary was busy downstairs, Cass phoned David Hines to solve the mystery nagging at her. When the receptionist told her he was busy and asked to take a message or to let her speak with one of the nurses, Cass insisted on talking with Hines.

"What is it, Mrs. Grantham?" Hines sounded annoyed. "I was told Burkman is treating you now."

Cass used a pleasant tone to say, "He is, Doctor Hines, because he was my physician before Peter called you in after I became so ill. If I had been thinking clearly that day, I would have told Peter to call Dr. Burkman because he's familiar with my medical history. I'm sorry if you were offended by the switch; it wasn't intentional and I should have called you sooner to explain." *Did he just sigh with relief?*

"That's fine, Mrs. Grantham, and I appreciate the clarification and apology. Thanks for calling. Good —"

"Wait a minute, sir! I want to ask you a question."

"What . . . 'question'?"

He sounds a little nervous and hesitant. That's odd. "Why did you order those STDs and that AIDS tests for me? Is that routine?"

"Routine? Ah, yes, I remember; I ordered a full screen to be done so I wouldn't overlook any possible cause for your condition: they're included in a full screen. Don't worry, all of your bloodwork was normal."

"I know; Doctor Burkman told me. I was just embarrassed that he might think there was a particular reason for running them."

"Don't worry about that; Burkman knows they're routine for a full screen" — *thank God* — "so he won't think anything peculiar about it. I would have discussed your tests and treatment with you after you improved, but I wasn't given the time and opportunity. How are you progressing? You should be off of all medication by now and back to your old self again. Are you?"

"Yes, I am, and thank you for asking."

"How is" — *that sonofabitch* — "Peter doing these days?"

Cass was surprised when Hines seemed to drift into chitchat. "He's fine, too."

"That's good to hear. He was worried about you and your collapse."

"Peter's a good friend and a kind person."

"Yes, he is. Well, was there anything else? I have patients waiting and they get antsy if I delay them too long from the golf course or office."

"No, that was all. Thank you for taking time to speak with me."

"You're welcome. Good-bye, Mrs. Grantham. Take care of yourself," *if you want to stay alive and healthy! Maybe I should tell Peter your curiosity is aroused. Hellfire, we had to run those tests with Tom screwing you, too!*

"I will, sir. Good-bye."

After she hung up, Cass stared at the phone as she wondered if Hines had lied to her. If so, why? Did the man think either she or Tom was an adulterer or they were both swingers? Or did Hines know about or suspect Tom's dark secret? Had he told Peter which tests he was running, the reason for them, and their results? And was she really afraid of Peter as Jason had asked? Had Tom been murdered? If so, by whom and why? Surely Peter wasn't to blame! Both men made her skin crawl in a curious manner and caused alarm bells to go off inside her head. Or maybe it was only her imagination running wild again or her anxieties returning.

Please, God, she prayed silently, *help me get through these next few weeks without falling apart again. Take away any groundless doubts and fears. And give me the courage, strength, and intelligence to unearth and handle any real ones. And please, don't let me fall in love with another unworthy stranger.*

When Cass walked to the mailbox after lunch, she found a letter there from Kristy, who had written to her after being unable to reach her by phone last Friday. In an elated state, Cass returned to the house, eager for four o'clock to arrive so she could phone Kristy. Over and over she planned what she would say to her best friend, her anticipation increasing by the hour.

Chapter Fifteen

At four-thirty, Kristy Franklin squealed into the phone, "Cassie! Heavens, it's good to finally hear your voice. I've been so worried about you and I've tried to reach you so many times. I always got that blasted answering machine or your housekeeper and you were either out of town or out of the house. Don't you ever stay home, girl? I'm so sorry about what happened to Tom. There were several articles on him in the newspaper and reports on TV. How are you holding up?"

Cass couldn't help but grin as she realized Kristy hadn't changed from her bubbly self. The thirty-four-year-old woman was as vivacious as ever. "I'm doing fine. It was rough for a while, but it gets better every day. I've missed you and I'm sorry we lost touch for so long."

"So am I, best friend, and I've missed you something fierce. The old town isn't the same without you here. You don't have to worry about me being angry with you because it was mostly my fault Tom didn't like me and didn't want us staying in touch. I should have kept my trap shut about him. I just wanted you to be happy and not make a terrible mistake. It's obvious you were right and I was wrong about him. Am I forgiven?"

If only you knew how right you were about that swine I married, but I can't tell you, not yet anyway, if ever. It wasn't because she thought Kristy would gloat or say, I told you so; the dark truth was just too private and humiliating. "There's nothing to forgive, Kristy, except for me allowing our friendship to go astray. It just got so complicated and painful being caught between you two, and we moved around so much and kept such a hectic schedule."

"I know, but I'm still sorry I hurt you. Will you be moving back to Augusta? Maybe we can be neighbors. We'd have a wonderful time, especially in the summer when I'm out of school. We can do all sorts of things. We can —"

"Whoa, wait a minute! I'm staying here; I'm firmly entrenched on Sea Island; this is where I live and plan to stay."

"But all of your old friends are here. I'm here, for heaven's sake! It's because of Brad, isn't it? Every time I think about how he screwed things up for you two, I could strangle him with my bare hands. He and his third wife are separated and probably heading for divorce court soon. God have mercy on his poor children. I hardly see him anymore because every time I do, I want to kick his ass, scream at him to shape up, and — Oops, sorry, diarrhea of the mouth syndrome like always." Kristy laughed before she continued, "The last thing you want to talk about is my son-of-a-gun brother. Lordy, Cassie, I wish it could have been different. You're the best thing that ever happened to Brad and he botched up badly, but he's paying for it."

As Cass changed the subject when Kristy took a breath, she could envision her friend rolling her eyes and shaking her head in disgust. "How are your mom and dad and the kids and Jerry? I bet Billy and Debbie are growing like weeds. How's third grade? Where are you teaching this year?" Cass knew from experience that all she had to do was ask a few pertinent questions and Kristy would take off with exuberance on one of her famous rolls. She listened as her friend talked about her eleven-year-old son and eight-year-old daughter, her husband who was a successful real estate agent, her parents whom Cass had known since eighth grade, and her teaching job which she was good at and loved. But during Kristy's enthusiastic delivery, she uncontrollably ventured back to a taboo subject.

"Mom and Dad are so angry with Brad and disappointed in him. They're so worried about their grandchildren, especially Randy. Brad rarely sees his firstborn from his second marriage and his ex-wife is always dragging him into court for delinquent child-support payments. Martha Anne gets so furious with him that she sometimes refuses to let Randy visit Mom and Dad so they'll put pressure on Brad for her; she'd better wake up and realize that ploy won't work and only Randy and my parents suffer because of it. I don't see how Brad affords his two families now and certainly not a third one, especially with the bad real estate market these days. Thank God, he doesn't work for the same agency that Jerry does or he'd be driving my husband nuts. Damn, I'm doing it again! Sorry. It's just that we always talked about anything and everything, so it seems natural to pour out my thoughts and feelings to you. It's strange, Cassie, but it doesn't seem like nearly three years have passed since you left town. It's like we're taking up right where we left off. Isn't it wonderful that women are more forgiving when their friends make mistakes, like I did? When can we get together to talk face-to-face?"

"As a matter of fact, in a few weeks. I'm coming up on May fourth with a friend. He's driving to Augusta to visit his son at the medical college."

"He? How good of a . . . 'friend' is he?"

"Kristy Franklin, behave yourself! I'm a recent widow, remember?"

The woman quipped, "Yeah, yeah, but who is he?"

"Jason Burkman is a close friend and he's also my physician."

"So, . . . how old is he? Is he married? Is he a hunk?"

Cass laughed and playfully accused, "You

haven't changed at all, girl. He's forty-two, widowed, and divorced — in that order — and he's gorgeous."

"Wow! Do I get to meet him if I promise to keep my big mouth shut and my opinions to myself?"

"Of course you'll meet him when he drops me off at your house, but we're only friends, so don't be disappointed or try to play match-maker. Better check your calendar to be sure that date is available. I know how busy you get with the children's activities during spring-time."

"If it's filled, I'll cancel anything scribbled in that slot, or Jerry can take over for me. Now, tell me about you and what you've been doing."

Cass glossed over the last thirty-one months in an attempt to play down the luxurious life-style her marriage had afforded her. It wasn't because Kristy would be envious or jealous; it was to avoid having to talk about her deceitful husband in any kind of detail.

"Are you really doing okay, Cassie? The news reports said the police were investigating the cause of the accident as if it were suspicious."

Cass told her about "Mutt & Jeff" and their hunger to make a big case out of a tragic acci-dent so they could win attention.

"I bet you were scared when they questioned you."

"I was a little intimidated at first, but they wore thin on me pretty fast and I gave back as good as I received. Tom's son and our lawyer say the matter will be cleared up and the file closed soon." Before Kristy could ask more questions about Tom, she said, "I hate to end our talk, but I have a new housekeeper and this is her first day, so I need to check on her."

"Good, that other one was a snot every time I spoke with her! I'll call you again soon and I'm eager to see you, and to meet your Jason."

"I'll hang up before that naughty syndrome returns. 'Bye, Kristy. It was wonderful talking to you at last. See you soon."

Jason called Cass around four o'clock. Since he was in a rush between patients, they didn't talk long, and neither even hinted at their romantic interlude yesterday. He wanted to make sure she was doing all right, and to tell her he could see her tomorrow night for a short visit, because he had a medical dinner meeting tonight and it usually ran late.

Before she hung up, she invited him to eat a light meal with her when he came over. He accepted the invitation without hesitation.

At five o'clock when it was time for Mary to leave, Cass told her what a splendid job she had done that day.

"Look around and see if I missed anything or didn't do something the way you like it; then tell me about it Thursday morning."

"Everything looks wonderful, Mary, and I'm

glad I found you. Now, scoot along home and join your husband. See you Thursday."

"Good-bye, Mrs. Grantham, I mean, Cass, and thanks."

Later that evening, Cass returned Linda's call from yesterday. During their short conversation, Linda told her about her new job that would terminate next Wednesday and suggested they get together for a day of fun on Thursday before she started a new assignment on Friday. Cass said that was wonderful and she looked forward to their visit and outing. When Linda asked her how Peter was doing, Cass responded that he was fine and would return home from a business trip on Wednesday.

After finishing their talk, Cass decided she should not interfere with any possible relationship between them, as Linda was an adult and it wasn't her place to intrude on her friend's personal life. Even so, Cass resolved she wouldn't say or do anything to encourage a romance between them, as she was certain Linda would get hurt; she couldn't imagine Peter having a serious interest in any woman who wasn't wealthy and a member of his social status.

Tuesday morning Cass answered the phone to hear Detective Adam Beals — "Mutt" — on the other end. He made an appointment with her for one o'clock and told her, "I have good news for you, Mrs. Grantham."

After lunch, Cass opened the front door to let in Adam Beals and his partner, Carl Killian — "Jeff." Now that her wits were clear, she realized why she had tagged them with those nicknames: one was short, stocky, flush-faced, beady hazel eyes, and auburn hair; the other was a tall and thin brunette; and both men — almost sloppily dressed — were in their thirties. As she guided them into the living room and asked if they wanted a cola or coffee, she almost blushed in recall at how she had behaved toward them the last time, but she didn't draw attention to it by apologizing. "What can I do for you gentlemen today? You said you have good news for me?" Beals was the one to respond, and not how she expected.

"Your stepson is mighty protective of you, isn't he? After our last talk, his lawyer contacted our captain and told him we couldn't bother you anymore unless it was necessary and he was present. Said you were ill and under a doctor's care. You seem fine now, right?"

"I'm much better, thank you; and I didn't think it was necessary for Mr. Johnson to be present today." She sensed the man was stalling, so she pressed, "What is your good news?"

"We finished the background checks, except for Mr. Grantham's ex-wife; we couldn't locate her; heard she's living in Europe or someplace. You wouldn't happen to know where we can reach her, would you?"

"No, but you can ask Peter when he returns tomorrow. As far as I know, neither Tom nor Peter have had any contact with her for years. Why do you need to speak with her?"

"Just checking out any and all possibilities. We talked with his friends, associates, and employees, but nobody gave us anything useful. I've already told your stepson the air-bag removal was illegal, but nobody will 'fess up to taking it out. His mechanic knew it was missing a long time ago and warned Mr. Grantham about it. You and your stepson told me neither of you knew about it being missing, right?"

"If I had known, I would have insisted it be replaced, and I'm sure Peter would have done the same thing," Cass affirmed. "I do recall Tom telling me about some of the negative aspects of air bags, such as the fact some people had been injured badly when their bags opened. Perhaps those fears were why Tom wanted his removed, but he didn't tell me he had done so. In my opinion, the man who removed it is partly responsible for his death."

"You're right, but that person's identity remains a mystery. I suppose a rich person can find somebody willing to do just about anything for him or her for the right price, don't you think? Getting to the brake failure, the car was so badly mangled, we can't tell what really happened and we still don't know what caused him to wreck. We do know he either never tried to stop or couldn't, because there weren't any skid marks on the highway, and he was traveling at a high rate of speed. The line that carries the brake fluid either ruptured during or was severed before the crash. The strange thing is, there weren't any signs of fluid on the ground under the vehicle, which would have been the case if the crash caused it. Without fluid in the brake line, there was no way he could slow down or stop before the crash. The mechanic said he hadn't worked on the car for over two weeks prior to the incident and the brakes were working fine then, but he didn't see anybody messing with it while your husband was out of town."

"As I told you before, Tom didn't allow anyone to drive or touch his car except his mechanic. As for somebody tampering with it during his absence, I don't see how that's possible since it was kept in a tall fence with a barbed-wire top and a ferocious guard dog on duty. As for all of that mechanical stuff about brakes and fluid, I don't know anything about cars in that area; I depend on my dealership to keep mine serviced and repaired when needed. Tom did like to drive fast, but I've never known him to be reckless or careless or to drive while drinking. Whenever we partied, in or out of town, he always hired a chauffeur and limo. If I understand you correctly, it's rare but not impossible for brakes to fail in that manner and cause an accident?" she asked, using the word *accident,* which Beals seemed determined to avoid.

"That's about the size of it. Since we can't prove foul play, the boss says we have to halt the investigation because it's taking too much time and money and we ain't doing nothing but butting our heads against a brick wall. We're going to file his folder, but we ain't marking the case closed just yet. I guess you know by now, your insurance company won't make a settlement until we rule it an accident; they don't pay off in murder cases. From what I understand, yours will be a big settlement since he had a double-indemnity clause for accidental death."

Cass knew about the insurance hold-up from Peter and their lawyer. She corrected the smug Beals by saying, "Non-payment applies only if Tom was killed by a beneficiary, which he wasn't. Is there a time limit for you holding open a case without evidence to support your suspicions?" She noticed Beals' annoyance at her for seeming to call his clever hand.

"You could say there is. I know you want this matter resolved fast, so if you think of anything, call us. Either your husband had a tragic accident or somebody's gonna get away with cold-blooded, premeditated murder, unless a clue is dropped in our laps soon."

"If Tom was murdered, which I don't believe

he was, I hope you find and punish the person who's responsible."

"I hope so, too, because I don't like loose ends, and this case strikes me as having at least one or two. A man without enemies, odd, very odd."

"As I told you before," Cass began in an attempt to emphasize his stubbornness and redundance in certain areas, "if Tom had any enemies, I don't know about them."

"Why did he bring Miss Lowery to town with him?"

"I don't know; you'll have to ask her or Peter, but I think it had to do with a new advertising campaign for the seafood company. She's a model."

"We know, but we can't reach her; she's out of the country for the next month on an . . . assignment, I believe her agency called it. I did want to ask her a few more questions to clear up some hazy areas that clouded up after we let her leave town before those clues popped up. You can't think of anybody who hated him for any reason? I mean, for any reason?"

Cass didn't know why Beals stressed those last two words, and hoped they hadn't learned about Tom's dark secrets. Perhaps it was wrong of her to withhold that information, but she was positive it had nothing to do with his death, and revealing it would open a horrible scandal that would taint her image as well as his. She had suffered more than enough because of Tom's wicked actions, so she kept silent. Besides, if it was pertinent, hound-dog Beals would track it down and attack it!

She remained poised on the exterior as she looked Beals in the eye and said, "No, sir, no one. Of course, I traveled very little with Tom after we moved here early last October; if he made someone that angry since then, he didn't tell me about it. That isn't unusual since I had nothing to do with his business matters, just as I assume your wife isn't informed of your work. Since you have explanations for the two points you originally thought were suspicious, exactly what is it that keeps nagging at you?"

"I just find it mighty strange — unbelievable, you could say — that a rich, powerful, and handsome man like Mr. Grantham didn't have any enemies; at least, that's what everybody's been telling me since day one."

Cass focused an odd look on him. "Are you saying that if Tom was poor, ugly, and un-important, no one would have a motive to kill him?"

"Not exactly. But everybody has an enemy or two, right?"

"I have no way of knowing that answer, and I certainly hope I don't have any. I suppose there might be a few people who disliked Tom, per-haps even intensely, but not enough to kill him."

"How did you and your husband get along?"

Cass eyed him as she mentally charged that

his phone call about delivering "good news" had been a ruse to disarm her and get her alone with the hope she would drop that "clue" he wanted so desperately so he could keep the case open. "We got along fine. Why?"

"I'm sure you're a very wealthy woman now, right?"

She realized the man rarely answered her questions and instead posed another one to her. She wondered if he had access to a copy of Tom's will and her prenuptial agreement. "I'm very comfortable, thank you. Tom was a smart businessman, so he made certain I would be taken care of."

"Did you know about the terms of his will before his death?"

Cass's tone was edged with light sarcasm as she responded, "Would it be normal for a husband to withhold such important facts from his wife? Would you do that?"

"I'm just a hardworking common man, Mrs. Grantham. I don't even have a will; don't have enough to leave behind to justify paying a lawyer to write me up one."

"Everybody should have a will, sir, especially a husband and bread winner. . . . May I ask, do you resent us because we are wealthy?" Beals looked surprised by her bold question, but composed himself with haste.

"Why should I?"

"I don't know, and you shouldn't, but your manner and attitude imply that to me at times.

353

Do you keep pressing this case, even though you've been told by your superior to close it, because so much money is at stake and solving a murder mystery could make big news for you? Is that why you keep hoping it will turn out to be — What did you call it? — 'foul play'?" She saw Beals scowl at her, but Killian remained stone-faced and silent.

"Just doing my job, Mrs. Grantham, and going on my gut feelings. If you've got nothing to hide, you've got no reason to be nervous or worried, and you've got no reason not to co-operate fully with us, right?"

Cass frowned at him. "That's precisely what I meant, Detective Beals; you added that last sentence to make a point I dislike. I have to dis-appoint you, because I was not involved in any form or fashion in my husband's death; that is what you're asking in what you mistakenly think is a clever roundabout way. Please feel free to keep digging for answers to resolve your doubts, but I insist you stop subjecting me to your insinuations. I find them improper, impo-lite, and cruel; and I'm certain Mr. Johnson and your chief would feel the same way. If you don't believe what I've told you, I'm certain there's nothing more I can say or do to change your mind."

"I do have one last question," the detective shot out. "Why did your husband put in that crazy stipulation about your remarriage? That's a new one on me."

Two disturbing questions shot through her mind like bolts of lightning: *Does the offensive man think I have a secret lover and Tom knew about him and that's why he added that "crazy" provision? Does he think we killed Tom or had Tom slain for his money and my freedom?* Cass related the explanations about the trust fund and remarriage restriction which Peter had told her about almost two weeks ago. She hoped he believed them because she didn't. Afterward, she added, "Besides, if I remarry in the future, I won't need Tom's money for support, and it should revert to Peter as his only child. Tom's son has more of a right to the Grantham estate than my next husband would, if I wed again."

"You're seeing Doctor Jason Burkman now; isn't that right?"

Cass stared at him, but concealed her sudden tension. "Are you spying on me?"

"Just checking out all the angles. That stipulation was odd, and you surely inherited more from his death and will than you'd have gotten with a divorce and that prenuptial you signed. Isn't that right?"

Cass straightened in her chair and glared at him. "I don't like your insinuation, sir, and it's groundless. Jason Burkman is my physician and he's a close friend. He's been treating me recently for . . . a health problem. He's also been trying to get me out of the house to help me deal with my grief. Is that a problem for you?"

"I thought David Hines was your doctor.

He's the one who told our captain you weren't in any condition to be questioned. Was I wrong?"

Cass explained why she had switched her medical care to Jason Burkman. "I've had dinner alone with Dr. Burkman one time since Tom's death, so what do you mean by, am I seeing him now?" If he called her bluff about it being twice, at the Cloister and his home, she would pretend she had forgotten one time in her provoked agitation.

"Why would you think I was suggesting something . . . lewd?"

"If that weren't true, sir, you wouldn't have mentioned him in the way you did. I see no reason for you to outright lie to me and then insult my intelligence by claiming I misunderstood you. It's as obvious to me as the nose on your face that you tricked your way into my home by using the ploy of delivering . . . 'good news' as you called it on the phone, when all you intended to do was interrogate me in private without my lawyer being present. I have been more than patient with your cunning tactics and have cooperated with your absurd investigation. If you disagree, take me to your station and let's speak with your superior. Otherwise, this meeting is over, and I'll escort you to the door." She stood and headed for the foyer with the two men trailing her and Killian apologizing for upsetting her. She opened the door and stepped aside with a stern expression on her face.

"That's all, Mrs. Grantham, for now," Beals said.

Cass frowned at him. "You told me the case is being filed away, so if you need to question me again or report any further . . . 'good news', contact me through my lawyer and we'll meet you in his office or in your superior's. Since you say I misunderstand your meanings and intentions, I'm certain Mr. Johnson will be delighted and able to explain them to me." It was apparent to her that Beals was as angry as she was at that point, and he must feel as if she had thwarted his challenge, which didn't sit well.

"As you wish, Mrs. Grantham. Good-bye."

Cass was repulsed by Beals's behavior and his response. She closed and locked the door and watched the men from a window, but made sure she was out of sight. She saw them stand by an old car for a while and talk before they got in and drove away.

Beals's stubborn persistence worried her and could be intrusive on her life. After what happened between her and Jason on Sunday, she warned herself to be careful around him and when she was out with him. If "Mutt & Jeff" were going to cause her more aggravation and trouble, she didn't want an innocent Jason drawn into the predicament. Nor did she want Beals's digging to unearth and expose Tom's sordid past and find herself at the center of a sleazy exposé.

Cass walked to the den, sat down, and phoned Simon Johnson. She told the lawyer about the incident in accurate detail. She was relieved when he promised to handle the matter for her.

Cass wished she hadn't asked Jason over for dinner tonight and risk embroiling him in her humiliating predicament. But she hadn't known it was still looming over her when she extended the invitation. As she prepared their meal, she fretted over the dilemma until she was edgy.

When Jason arrived, she let him in and guided him to the kitchen as she said, "Dinner's almost ready. Sit down and relax while I finish it."

Jason removed his jacket and tie and placed them over a chair, then unfastened a few shirt buttons. He saw that the table was set and the condiments were out, so he took his by-now familiar place. During her polite greeting and when she delivered things to the table, he noticed she avoided meeting his gaze, was oddly quiet and subdued, and yet appeared tense. He wondered why and dreaded the reason. He hoped and prayed she hadn't asked him over to tell him they couldn't see each other again.

Cass served the boiled shrimp, steamed broccoli, potato salad, and rolls before she took a seat opposite him. "The empty plate is for the shells, and I made iced tea for you. Am I missing anything you need?"

"Thanks, and nothing. This looks delicious." *The only thing missing is your sunny smile, Cass. What's bothering you, my love?*

As he helped himself from the bowls and platters, she asked, "You said you like shrimp, right?"

He smiled and nodded. "I love it just about any way it's prepared."

Jason peeled and ate a few before he paused — just to get a conversation going and break the silence — to ask, "How did it go with Mary?"

Cass knew she had answered that query yesterday, so she deduced his motive for asking it again. "You were right; she's absolutely wonderful. I can't thank you enough or tell you how pleasant it was having her here instead of Inez. How did your day go and your dinner meeting last night?" *You do the talking while I calm down.*

"Both were fine, but I missed seeing you. I really enjoy your company, Cass, and care a lot about you. I haven't had so much fun or been this relaxed in ages. I have you to thank for accomplishing both tasks."

"I'm the one who should be thanking you, Jason, for bringing me back to life in so many ways. I'm sorry if I seem a little tense and distracted tonight, but I had a meeting this afternoon that was most unpleasant."

Jason lowered his tea glass. "With your

lawyer or accountant? Did you ask them about the things we discussed Sunday night?"

Cass wondered why that was his first thought. "No, I haven't seen them or spoken with Mr. Dredger today. I did phone Mr. Johnson, but it wasn't about that subject." As she sipped her drink while deciding how and what to tell him, Jason asked another unusual question.

"Did Peter come home early and say something to upset you?"

"No, it wasn't Peter, and he's still away until tomorrow. Those two detectives came to see me again. Actually, they tricked their way inside to get me alone to interrogate me about Tom and his accident. After I almost kicked them out, I reported them to Mr. Johnson and he's going to handle the matter and force them to stop harassing me as if I were a criminal. They even asked me about you, about us." She saw she had his full attention. She related the incident, then said, "I don't know exactly what Beals has discovered or was implying about us, but I don't like his sorry attitude or conduct. He's one of the most devious and insensitive people I've ever met. I swear to you, Jason, I had nothing to do with Tom's death, nothing."

"You don't have to swear that to me, Cass; I know you didn't because I know you. You're a good and honest person, a very special person. If your husband was murdered, it's their job to find his killer, but they have no right or reason to harass or accuse you. A prenuptial agreement isn't uncommon in a remarriage for a wealthy person. And you aren't Tom's sole beneficiary; Peter inherited more than you did. Are they investigating him, too?"

Cass deliberately had omitted the enlightening fact that had sparked Beals's suspicion about them: the remarriage stipulation. At this early point in their relationship, she didn't want Jason to know about that intrusive angle. She didn't want to explain her feelings and motives, and she certainly couldn't reveal the dirty truth about Tom. She wanted to make sure her wealth didn't hold any sway over her appeal to Jason. She also didn't want him to think he didn't stand a chance with her because of what it would cost her: millions of dollars. Nor did she want him to suspect that Tom had a reason for distrusting her and that was why he included that bizarre term. "I suppose so, but they didn't tell me. I know they've questioned him before, but he didn't seem upset or worried afterward."

"You don't think he had anything to do with the accident, do you?"

"No, absolutely not. I don't know everything about Tom's and Peter's relationship, but Peter didn't hate his father and surely couldn't have killed him or had it done. As I told the police, if Tom had any dangerous enemies, I don't know about them. I just want the case closed so I can forget about this tragedy and get on with my life."

Jason reached across the table, grasped her hand, and gave it a gentle squeeze. He sent her a reassuring smile as he murmured, "Relax, Cass, I won't let anything or anyone harm you. If Johnson doesn't settle this matter for you soon, I'll hire a lawyer who can do the job."

She pulled her hand from his grasp and said, "You can't do that, Jason. If you get involved, that might look odd to Mutt & Jeff. I don't want your reputation getting tarnished."

"Don't worry about me, Cass; I'll be fine. The most important thing is protecting you. But who are Mutt & Jeff?"

Cass couldn't help but laugh before she explained about the cartoon characters and how she had labeled Beals and Killian with their names.

Jason chuckled in amusement. "Well, at least you haven't lost your sense of humor."

"Thinking of them in those roles keeps me from allowing them to intimidate me. But I have to admit, they made me nervous and wary today. If they're watching me, I have to be careful of everything I say and do so it can't be misconstrued. Beals would like nothing better than to make a name for himself and take sadistic pleasure out of accusing me of my husband's murder."

"I won't let that happen, Cass, I promise."

"Maybe I'm overreacting to their visit and

crude personalities, but I know my imagination isn't running wild and crazy; Beals was too clear for that to be true. He thinks he's so clever, but he's despicable and mean. Now, let's drop this subject so we can relax and enjoy our meal. Tell me about your meeting last night; that should distract us."

Later, they sat together on the sofa, watched television, talked, and kissed a few times. Yet, they were cautious not to arouse their passions, each wondering if Beals was parked outside and observing the house.

At ten o'clock, Jason said with reluctance, "I best get going. I'll call you tomorrow to make certain you're okay. If you don't settle down and can't get to sleep tonight, take one of those tranquilizers you have left over."

"Thanks, but I'll be fine." *You're the only medicine I need. I'd love to let you calm me down and lull me to sleep, but that's too risky.*

She walked him to the front door, and said, "I'll talk with you tomorrow. Thanks for giving me a shoulder to lean on tonight, and I'll be in a better mood the next time I see you. I had a good time."

"So did I, but I won't steal a good-night kiss in case Beals is around. Sleep well, Cass, and my shoulder is available any time you need it."

Wednesday evening, Peter phoned from his

apartment to let Cass know he had returned home. "As soon as I grab a quick shower, I'd like to come over and talk, if you don't have other plans."

"I don't, and that's fine with me. Have you eaten or do you want me to prepare you something? It's no trouble."

"I've already eaten, but thanks. I could use some bourbon and Coke, Wild Turkey if you have any, when I get there."

"I'll have it setting out on the kitchen counter."

"See you in about thirty minutes."

"See you soon, Peter," she replied, having no idea of the shock in store for her during their impending conversation.

Chapter Sixteen

After Peter arrived and was preparing his drink at the kitchen counter, Cass studied him on the sly as she poured herself a diet cola. Peter was dressed in a casual outfit: a mint-green knit shirt with matching pants, a medium-hued brown belt, and the same tone of brown loafers without socks. Curly black hair peeked from the opening at his collar where he had left all three buttons unfastened and the shirt's edges flapped aside.

It was obvious why so many women found Peter Wesley Grantham irresistible. He was traffic-stopping handsome. He emitted a sensuous, earthy, animal magnetism and radiated self-assurance, managing to avoid an arrogant or cocky impression. Without a doubt, she concluded, Peter was six feet of enticing masculinity. Considering his wealth and prominence, he was one of — if not the — most sought-after bachelors in the area and probably beyond it.

Peter was cognizant of her stealthy study. Maybe, he reasoned in spiteful pleasure, she was getting aroused after being a widow for almost two months. He was aware of his enthralling effect on women and — when it suited his purposes or needs — used it to the hilt to ensnare them. Yet, in these times when so many nasty bugs were running loose and particularly that lethal one, a man had to be extra careful. He knew Cass would be a safe partner for him, because he had ordered Hines — in light of their knowledge of his father's secret lifestyle — to run certain blood tests on her to rule out an STD or AIDS. As he replaced the top on the bourbon, he glanced at her and asked, "So, how have you been doing? How do you feel? You certainly look fantastic and well."

So much had happened to her during his absence that Cass wondered if Peter sensed the changes in her. She smiled and picked up her glass. "I'm doing fine, thanks. Why don't we sit in the den to talk?"

"Suits me, because those no-see-ums are roaming outside. I'd rather relax in the house instead of beating and clawing my scalp to death fighting them off on the terrace." As he followed her into the other room, Peter's gaze drifted over the brunette from head to feet. Cass was wearing a white jewel-neck sleeveless top with pearlized buttons down the front and slit pockets near her small waist. It traveled to below her firm buttocks, partially covering black georgette pants with quarter-size white dots. She wore black sandals, and her toenails were painted dark mauve, the same as her fingernails. She had pearl studs in her pierced ears. As she moved, he detected the teasing scent of her perfume. She was beautiful and sexy, especially for a woman her age. Yet, he didn't consider his thoughts and feelings incestuous because she wasn't his mother, wasn't any blood kin to him. And he wasn't betraying his father since the bastard was dead, cold and buried. If he told her the repulsive truth about her husband, would she sleep with him out of revenge?

Cass sat in the overstuffed chair, not wanting to be to close to him on either the sofa or loveseat. She held on to her glass to have something to occupy her trembly hands and to drink from as a stall tactic if she needed to think about a question before responding to it. To appear deceptively calm and poised, she rested her feet and legs on the ottoman and propped her elbows on the armrests. She smiled. "How did your business trip go? Did you enjoy yourself and get a lot accomplished?"

Peter lazed back against the sofa and, crossed his legs. "It couldn't have gone better, Cass; the deal's signed, sealed, and delivered, earning us a nice profit. But I didn't plan on being away for a week, even had to pick up a few extra clothes to tide me over. I suppose I should train somebody to take over for me here to be prepared for when I'm delayed out of town again."

"Is there anything I can do to help out in that area?"

"Thanks, but no. It has to be somebody who's already familiar with the business or things could get screwed up badly in only a day or two. It's not the type of job you or anybody else could train for in a short time because it includes knowing all about shrimp and shrimping, and other seafoods. I have a man in mind to promote to that position. As for the electronics firm, we have an excellent office manager over there: Pat Marlowe."

"Do you need me to fill in or take over anywhere else in the company?"

"No, but thanks again for the offer. All positions are filled with good workers. Besides, it could be distracting for employees to have you there. You wouldn't be the boss's wife, but you're still his widow and the new boss's stepmother. That would make staff members and workers uneasy, make them feel as if they're being watched for me. Understand?"

So much, she scoffed, for getting involved with companies she partly owned and as Peter had hinted she could do a few weeks ago! *Let it pass unchallenged for now.* "Of course, I understand, and I'm sure you're right. But if an emergency arises and you need my help, I'm willing to pitch in for as long as I'm needed. As it stands, I certainly have plenty of free time."

"Thanks, Cass, I really appreciate that. I'll tell my secretary to keep you in mind when she can't find a temp or can't reach me. Now, there are a couple of things I should tell you about today." He sipped his drink before relating, "I put all of the other residences and their furnishings up for sale on Monday. Since I won't be using them, it's foolish to let them stand empty and cost me money for maintenance and taxes." His plan was to prevent her from wanting to vacation in or move to any of them when he needed to keep her close for other reasons. "I'm also putting Smooth Rider on the market next week. I don't have any interest in owning or running a golf cart company and the competition there is fierce. It looks as if one of those other two companies is interested in merging it with theirs, so our employees' jobs won't be jeopardized." That action was being taken to prevent her from wanting to move out of his reach by returning to Augusta. "I'll keep you informed of Smooth Rider's sale, and you should have a fat check from it to deposit in your account very soon. Now, tell me about the trouble between you and Inez and about your new housekeeper. She came to work on Monday, right?"

Cass was surprised by his quick discard of the other four properties and one company, but his explanations were logical, and he had the power to make those decisions. "Yes, and I got the information from Mary that you requested about her Social Security and taxes; I've already phoned it in to Mr. Dredger," she began, then responded to his other query.

"Since Inez worked for us for nearly three years, that's a shame, but it sounds as if she provoked the trouble and deserved to be fired. She never gave me problems, but that's probably because I wasn't around her much and I'm a man." *She's doing fine, sitting on her ass and earning her regular salary from me until she finds another job.* "You certainly don't need or have to put up with such aggravation and tension. I'm hiring a cleaning service next week to do my place, so don't worry about inconveniencing me. How did you find Mary Ellis? You said a friend recommended her?"

Cass worked hard to look and sound casual as she answered, "Yes, Doctor Burkman."

"You were fortunate," he said and smiled, though he didn't like the fact that Jason was the person supplying and surrounding her with *his* staff and friends too often these days.

"When I spoke with Simon this morning, he told me you've been harassed by those two detectives again. What did they want this time?"

Cass revealed the episode in detail. She didn't exclude their question about Jason, since they might ask Peter about that relationship and he might wonder why she had kept that fact a secret. Besides, she had told him on the phone about their dinner at the Cloister, but she didn't mention being with Jason at his home on Sunday and hoped it wasn't exposed.

"Perhaps you should be careful about being alone with any man for a while; it sounds as if they might be watching you and could misinterpret such a friendship. It shouldn't be for much longer, Cass, because Simon said he's going to squash this matter for good very soon.

Those two creeps don't have any reason to suspect us of wrongdoing and I don't believe my father was murdered. You have them pegged right, and we're going to halt their foolishness fast. As soon as we do, we'll settle with the life-insurance company."

"I'm glad, Peter, because it's nerve-wracking. Why do they want to speak with your mother and Miss Lowery?"

"With Miss Lowery, I suppose because she was with him shortly before the accident and they want to know how he was behaving and if he said anything about having trouble with somebody. It's a waste of time because he wouldn't have discussed anything personal with a mere model. As for my mother, she's been long gone for a long time and I don't know her address. But if she hated my father and wanted him dead for any reason, she wouldn't have waited until now to do him in, right?"

"I suppose so. Tom didn't talk about her. I don't even know her name; Tom said it was too far in the past to matter to either of us."

Peter decided to win Cass's sympathies and draw her closer to him by tugging on her emotions. He took a deep breath, stared at his shoe, and murmured, "Allegedly she ran off with another man. She hasn't written or called me since she left, so I have no idea why she felt it necessary to abandon us without a trace or second thought; the note she left behind for me certainly didn't give me any answers. For a long time I kept thinking she'd come back or contact at least me, but she didn't. My paternal grandparents died a long time ago and Mother's parents are in a fancy nursing home up North. Their minds and health are so deteriorated that they don't know who or where they are, who she is, or who I am. They have perpetual trust funds taking care of their expenses, so they'll have the best care possible until their deaths; then the funds revert to me as their only grandson and because my father was the one who provided them." He summoned a fake tone and expression of anguish to dupe Cass. "I stopped going to see them and phoning them years ago because it didn't help them any and it upset me every time I saw them like that."

Cass was surprised to learn that fact about Tom, reminding her he had had some good traits. Unless, she reasoned, those trust funds had been his first wife's idea and part of their divorce agreement. She was touched by the sufferings of the young man before her and assumed those ordeals had helped to mold him into the contradictory person he was. "I'm sorry, Peter; that must have hurt you deeply."

"Yep, but time is the healer it's proclaimed to be; you'll see." He looked at her and feigned a wry smile. "I practice that old adage about changing the things you can and accepting the ones you can't. To do otherwise would drive one nuts."

"That's excellent advice, and I'll take it to heart. I have been staying busy as you suggested." To change the topic to one less hurtful, she told him about redecorating the bedroom.

"I bet it looks wonderful; I'll go up and see it before I leave if that's all right." She nodded. "Send the bills for those items to the bank, Cass; they shouldn't come out of your monthly allowance. They weren't really personal purchases; they were home improvements; that's covered under your living expenses and reasonable needs. If you have any problem convincing the banker to pay those charges, I'll talk to him and straighten him out."

"Thanks. I put the old bed and linens in the garage. If you don't want them, I'll give them to a local charity."

"I don't need them, so donate them wherever you wish."

"As you see," she said, motioning to the mantel, "I took down Tom's portrait and the pictures of him and us; they were painful reminders of him every day. Would you like to have the portrait, his scrapbook, and photo album? It seems more appropriate for you to have them instead of me."

"I think it would be nice to have the portrait hanging in one of the businesses; I'll decide which one gets it later. As for the scrapbook and album, I'll pack them away for my future family. Thanks."

So far, so good, he's taking everything well. "Do

you want to go through your father's clothes before I box them up and donate them to a charity? He has some expensive, good-looking things."

"I'll take a peek at them this weekend when we aren't busy. There might be something among them I'd like to keep and use. Dad did have good taste, and he never looked at a price tag," Peter added with a grin.

"Do you want anything from his office: furniture, papers, books?"

"Yes, I do need to make certain there's nothing important in his desk and files. I'll store the furniture until I can use it later. That reminds me: I returned the bracelet he bought you. The jeweler said it was too long since its purchase to give a refund, but he allowed me to exchange it for a necklace that I think you'll like. If not, and don't worry about hurting my feelings, I'll put it in my safe and pay you for it. I'll bring it over tomorrow so you can see it and decide. I assume he purchased it for your birthday in June. He was probably holding on to it for months; he always was one to be prepared in advance for everything."

Or he bought that little trinket for one of his lovers. "Thanks for taking care of that matter for me. I would always feel as if it were a parting gift, and it would make me sad to wear it."

"Glad I could help. As I said, I'll bring it over tomorrow or Friday, and I'll go through the clothes and office over the weekend. Just let me know later what's a convenient day and time."

Cass nodded before she told him about the real estate agent's call, then asked him if he was planning to stay in the guest house.

"Are you thinking about selling this house and want me to move?"

Don't let him see you're lying about the last part. "No, but I thought you might want to distance yourself from sad reminders of your father."

"That isn't necessary; I've accepted his death. But if you decide you want to sell out or you just want privacy, let me know and I'll find something else."

"I'm not planning on moving, not unless the house seems too large for me or too much of a reminder of my life here with Tom. What I plan to do is a little more redecorating; I need something to occupy my time."

"I agree, Cass, but don't rush yourself into anything; just take it easy for a little while longer. You don't want to over stress yourself again. You're looking and sounding marvelous, so please stay that way. I have an idea: why don't we go out to dinner and a movie Friday night?"

Go on a date with you? "How would that look to others?"

"What do you mean?" he asked, uncrossing his leg.

"For us to be seen together having fun. People, especially those two detectives, might misunderstand the situation and our relationship." For some reason, the idea of going out with him socially unsettled her. There was something about Peter tonight that both enticed and repelled her.

"I wasn't referring to avoiding me earlier; we're family, Cass."

"Yes, but you're unattached; it could look as if we're . . . on a date. You know how some people gossip, so we have to think of appearances."

You didn't think of them when you gallivanted with Jason! Why, Cass, I do believe you're blushing. Maybe getting aroused? Are you afraid of falling prey to me or to your own desires? Or trying to shove me aside to get to Jason? If you get too close with him, he could put bad ideas into your head. That wouldn't please me at all.

Peter chuckled and teased, "Are you afraid I'll make a move on you because of my ridiculous reputation? If it would calm you down, I could promise you, it's a bunch of bull." *I could promise you, but I won't, and I'd be lying through my pearly whites. Yep, I'm getting to her; look at that blush deepen and those lashes lower.* "Just because I'm almost twenty-seven, still a bachelor, and have dated lots of women, that doesn't mean I'm a bad person. I just haven't found the right woman for myself. Besides, why would it look any different to others being seen with me than with your doctor?"

Stop looking at me with that sexy gaze and using

that sexy tone of voice! "You and I practically live together."

"Not exactly."

"Well, people might think we do."

"Are you saying they'll suspect us of . . . hanky-panky?"

Cass watched him grin and listened to his hearty chuckles. "It isn't funny, Peter, and some people do have dirty minds."

"I doubt anybody would think we're out on a date just because we're having dinner together in public. *We are* family and business partners."

"You're right. You know what? It seems so strange to be talking with you about such things, to be sitting together calmly and enjoying ourselves."

"Yes, it does, but it's nice to be relaxed around each other and to be friends for a change, isn't it?" He watched her nod. "You're an intelligent, attractive, interesting person, Cass, and I enjoy spending time with you. I didn't realize you were such a good and honest person, and so much fun. I just wish we hadn't waited so long to settle our misunderstanding. It was mostly my fault; I admit I didn't give you a chance. I honestly thought you married my father for his money, but I know now that wasn't true. After Dad died and we got closer, I had the time and opportunity to get to know you, and I like and respect what I see. I guess my suspicions come from all the tricks women have used on him and on me just to meet us

377

and try to land us. When you get ready to date or marry again, don't worry about me being angry or resentful. You're a beautiful and desirable woman, so I don't expect you to hang around the house and pine for Dad. He's gone, but you're still alive."

Cass wondered if it was only her imagination running wild, or if Peter was flirting with her in a subtle manner. Did she harbor repressed desire for him? Or had her tryst with Jason awakened her passions to where they could attach themselves to any man? Or was she, like so many women, susceptible to Peter's numerous charms? Or was he cleverly trying to test the depth of her feelings for his father? To prevent him from worrying about her turning to another man in the near future, she said, "This is too soon for me to think about dating or remarriage, Peter."

"Perhaps, but one never knows when one will meet the right person. Don't allow that stipulation in Dad's will to control your life. We'll figure out some way to get around it so you can get what you deserve. Hardly a legal paper exists that doesn't have some tiny loophole to exploit."

What appeared to be a sincere expression and tone did nothing to help her understand Peter's intent. "It isn't the money or will that concerns me, Peter; it's doing what's proper and fair."

"Then you have nothing to worry about, be-

cause that's what you will do; I'm certain of it."
As Peter downed the remainder of his drink, he
concluded it was a bad idea to allow anything
to happen between her and Jason. It would be
better to marry her off to somebody else in the
near future and to get Jason Burkman out of
the picture fast. He held the empty glass and
rolled it back and forth between his hands, wet-
ting them with the moisture on its outside. He
took a deep breath and exhaled. "When you do
start dating, Cass, be very careful of whom you
select."

She sensed there was a particular meaning
behind his softly worded warning, so she asked
in reluctance, "What do you mean?"

"I just don't want you being used and getting
hurt. We've become close friends and I care
deeply for you. I want you to be happy."

"Thanks for your concern and advice, and
I'll be cautious."

Peter stared at the floor as he murmured,
"Cass . . ."

Her tension mounted as she eyed him. "Yes,
Peter, what *is* it?" Was he about to confess romantic feelings for her? If so, what should
she —

He flopped back against the sofa and locked
his gaze with hers. "How well do you know
Jason Burkman?"

Cass stared at him. Did he know about last
Sunday or was he just digging for information?
"Why do you ask?"

"Please, just tell me how well you know him. It's important."

Cass revealed details of her affiliation with Jason being careful to omit even a hint of her romantic feelings toward the man. "We've gotten to know each other more during the last few weeks," she concluded. "Why?"

Peter sent forth another heavy sigh. "I've tried to keep my mouth shut, but now I must tell you I don't trust him. It just seems a little too coincidental that of all the women in this area, he would zero in on you. Unless I'm wrong, he wants to be more than a friend and your physician."

"In light of what you said to me earlier, why does that bother you?"

"If it were any man but him, it wouldn't."

"Do you have a grudge against Jason?"

"Not exactly. He's the one who has a grudge against me, so going after you strikes me as being suspicious."

"What makes you think he's going after me? And I take it you and Jason know each other well?"

"Yep, very well, too well; yet, not at all. This might not be any of my business, Cass, and I could be wrong about him and I hope I am, but I would feel responsible if he hurt you out of a desire for revenge."

"Jason doesn't have any reason to be vindictive toward me."

"Not toward you, toward me. I don't want

him to seek vengeance on me by hurting you, and it would hurt me if he harmed you."

"I don't understand, Peter. Please explain what you mean."

"He hasn't told you about the trouble between us long ago?"

"No, he hasn't told me or even mentioned knowing you."

"Well, he knows me and he hates me, would probably like nothing more than to see me dead and buried. I'm the reason for his divorce, Cass, but it was an honest mistake on my part."

"You and his wife were . . . lovers?"

"For about three months, over a year ago, I'm sorry to say. I didn't know the Burkmans. I met Brenda on the beach, corny as that sounds. We had fun together, talked for hours, and had dinner afterward. I found out later her husband was out of town at a medical convention that week. I didn't know she was married, Cass, I swear it. She used her maiden name and had an apartment in north Brunswick. When we couldn't see each other, she claimed she was traveling for her job, even used the name of an out-of-state business so I wouldn't catch on to her lies. She said she did some of her work at home; she even had a computer and clothes and everything there to back up her story. There was no reason to suspect I was being duped."

Peter knew that if Cass checked out that part of his story, she would learn it was true. "I phoned and saw her at the apartment, and thought she lived there when she wasn't traveling. How she got away with leading a double life still amazes me. Within two months, she started talking marriage, but I told her I wasn't ready to settle down. She was exciting and enjoyable, but I didn't know her that well, and I suspected my money and social status were too alluring to her. Looking back, I should have known there was a reason why we almost always ate and . . . saw each other at her place. She would say she was too tired to go out and she wanted me all to herself. When we did go out for the day or evening, it was always somewhere away from this area; I realized later it was so we wouldn't be seen together by the wrong person."

Peter frowned. "One day she took me to a big house she said belonged to friends of hers, that she was watching it for them while they were out of town. While we were in the Jaccuzi and having drinks and playing around, Jason came home and caught us together. I'm positive she planned for that to happen, hoping when he kicked her out, I would take her in. I didn't; I was furious with her, never saw her again. It was her house, Cass. Can you believe any woman would be so reckless and cruel? Of course, Jason didn't believe me when I tried to explain how she tricked me; he's hated me ever since. That's why I was so shocked and worried when you changed from Hines to him. I didn't even know you knew him. All I'm saying is be careful around him. Promise?"

"I don't know what to say, Peter; this is such a shock."

"If he's willing to forget and forgive, so am I. I'll even apologize to him again for the hundredth time if that will do any good. I won't stand in your way if he means something special to you; I just want to be sure he doesn't have a hidden agenda." *If he's sincere, let him have you. If not, I will, or you'll be dumped on somebody else because that money and those shares are coming home to me!*

"One thing Jason did do, Cass, was keep the truth a secret to prevent a scandal, so nobody knows about me and Brenda. If I had been named co-respondent in his divorce case, I would have fought that charge; I would have hired a lawyer and private detective to prove I was duped just like him. I suppose he wanted to protect his reputation, so he didn't force my hand in that area. Maybe he decided I was telling the truth. What I can't understand is why he would befriend my stepmother of all women."

Stay calm, Cass. "Maybe he didn't know we were family."

"That's unlikely, Cass; everybody knows who the Granthams are. He knew you were Thomas Grantham's wife and he knew I was his son."

"Perhaps he does believe you're innocent, Peter, and he's put all of that behind him. He's always been nice, respectful, and kind to me." *He even sneaked into this house to save me when he thought I was in jeopardy! Or was he only trying to get to me, to ensnare me, to —*

"Cass, I'm sorry if I upset you. I had to wait until you were stronger and your head was clear before I told you. I swear to you that my only motive in revealing the truth is to prevent you from being taken in by him if he's up to no good. Please don't think the worst of me for what I did."

"You said you didn't know she was married, Peter, and I believe you," she told him, and — oddly — she did, this time.

Peter smiled. "Thank you, Cass, that means a lot to me, more than you can imagine. Maybe I should meet with him and have a serious talk, see if he drops any clues about his intentions toward you."

"I would prefer it if you didn't do that, Peter. I don't have a doctor's appointment with him until the twenty-ninth and I only see him as a friend on occasion. It could just bring the past to life again for naught. I promise to be on guard with him, and I won't let him take advantage of me to spite you. If he's up to no good as you said, he'll do or say something to expose himself. I do like him and since I don't have many friends here, I'd hate to lose one over a problem that might not exist."

"Maybe I was just overreacting and he's really only interested in you as a friend and patient. Since you're such a special person, that wouldn't be strange at all."

Cass jested to dupe him, "Besides, if you approach him about 'his intentions' toward me, that could look and sound as if you're trying to protect my honor and checking to see if he's serious about me. It's much too soon to push him into a corner about any feelings or plans he might or might not have for me. And, unless I decide to date him later, there's no need to test him, right?"

Peter chuckled and nodded. "I guess I was sounding a little overly protective and old-fashioned. Boy, that's a new role for me. I won't rebuke it because it could be good practice for when I have children one day, especially if I have any daughters." As he set his glass on a coaster, he said, "In a way, you're lucky you don't have many friends and acquaintances here; if you did, they'd be trying to fix you up with every single male they know. Then you'd have to worry about hurting their feelings when dates don't pan out. Lordy, I've met women with some really bad problems who want nothing more than a rich and powerful man to solve them. I admit it does get lonely and I do get envious of friends who are settled down, happy, and have families. But when I marry, I want it to be for life, none of this two and three marriages. I want to be the man rearing my children, not have a stepfather or two taking my place. It's a shame you and Dad didn't have at least one baby; you'd make a great mother, and I wouldn't mind not being an only child anymore. Do you want children, Cass?"

"Doesn't every woman?" she responded, warmed by the tender tone of his voice and gentleness in his gaze when he spoke about children. He was showing her touching and appealing facets of him she had never seen before tonight. It amazed her how he had changed since his father's death, and perhaps no longer being in Tom's overwhelming and dark shadow had accomplished that feat.

Peter grasped the yearning in her for a child and a growing fondness and respect for him, so he presumed his clever ruse to win her over was working perfectly. "It isn't too late; any unattached man would be lucky to get you. He . . ."

"Why did you stop and frown? I was enjoying the compliments."

"I just realized I probably sound selfish and devious to you considering that ridiculous stipulation in Dad's will. No matter what I told you two weeks ago about why I thought he added it, Cass, I don't know why he did and it was wrong of him to do so." He scowled again. "In fact, it makes me angry and disappointed. He had no reason to try to control your life after he was gone; I bet he did it out of jealousy and selfishness. He just couldn't stand the thought of you falling in love and marrying again, so he wanted to make it hard for you to do so. Don't worry, he won't get away with his little ploy.

There's nothing in the will that says we can't right his wrong, create our own little loophole to foil him."

"What are you talking about, Peter?"

"Well, since the money reverts to me if you marry, there's nothing to stop me from giving you a large wedding gift from it, is there?" He saw her chocolate gaze widen in astonishment, then narrow in curiosity and suspicion. "Of course, I couldn't come up with fifteen million plus in cash, but I could get my hands on three to five million; that's better than losing it all if you decide to marry again within five to ten years, right?"

Be wary of him and this line of talk, Cass. "You don't have to do that, Peter, but it's kind of you to make the offer. I didn't marry Tom for his wealth, and I won't allow the inheritance to control any future decisions I make. If I should marry again, the Grantham money rightfully belongs to you."

"But you deserve something from his estate, Cass, and I would insist on making a generous settlement with you. Don't say another word of protest; the matter is closed, but I will honor my word. Now, let me take a quick peek at your redecorating magic before I head home. It's been a long day and I need a good night's sleep."

As Cass prepared herself for bed, she recalled Peter's smile and praise about the decorating

387

changes in the master bedroom. He had kissed her on the cheek before leaving the house, gazed into her eyes for a minute, smiled, and walked away with jaunty steps.

Peter Grantham, the instant I think I can't trust you, you do something to prove I can. The instant I'm sure I can, you give me the impression I should watch you like a hawk. Why are you confusing me this way? What was the real motive behind your revelation about Jason? If you thought we were getting sweet on each other, why wouldn't that please you since it would profit you greatly if I married again?

And you, Jason Burkman, why didn't you tell me you know Peter and detest him? Are you up to spiteful mischief as Peter speculated? Is that why you've been trying to create doubts about him, to turn me against him? Is that why you were so interested in my inheritance? Do you hope to get revenge by snagging me and swiping a huge chunk of Grantham money from Peter? Is that your intent to punish him for stealing your wife?

You had to know Peter would tell me eventually, so why wouldn't you want me to hear your side first? Were you hoping to so enchant me before I made that discovery so I would believe you and not reject you?

Until my head clears and I decide if you're trustworthy, I can't see you again. Oh, Jason, why did you have to make yourself a stranger to me after I fell in love with you?

Jason was phoning her tomorrow, possibly

stopping by while en route to his Thursday afternoon golf game. Before either one occurred, Cass had to decide how she was going to respond.

Chapter Seventeen

While Mary was working upstairs and Cass was in the laundry room washing the bed linens on Thursday after lunch, Cass heard the rear doorbell ring. She hurried to the kitchen window, peered outside, and saw Jason's blue BMW parked in the driveway behind her housekeeper's old Ford. She walked through the mudroom, donning a pair of sunglasses which were laying on a shelf there. Opening the door, she told him, "Mary's here cleaning today, so let's walk by the pool to chat."

As he stepped aside and she moved past him, Jason realized she hadn't smiled or given him a warm or even polite greeting. He wondered what had happened now, aware that Peter had returned last night. He followed her until she halted near the cabana, wishing he could see her eyes, could read the clues revealed in those brown depths.

"I was going to call you tonight after you returned home," she informed him, "but it's good that you dropped by so I wouldn't have to do this over the phone."

The serious note in her quavering voice and hints in her words filled him with dread. "Do what, Cass? Is something wrong?"

"Yes and no. I can't see you for a while, Jason, not until I get my head clear. I'm sorry if I gave you the wrong impression of me or if I led you on. I don't know what came over me and let me behave like that. It's just too soon for me to get involved in a romantic relationship. I'm very fond of you and I enjoy your company, but it's wrong for me at this time."

"But I promised I wouldn't put any pressure on you, Cass. We agreed to take it slow and easy, to work on strengthening our friendship first. I thought that was what we were doing."

"I know, but things have a way of getting out of hand when we're alone. You're a very desirable man, Jason, and I am attracted to you. That's the problem: I can't handle those feelings and actions so soon after . . ."

Cass looked down and took a deep breath. "Either you have to give me time to deal with my emotions or we have to end whatever is between us here and now." She did not want to question him about Peter because she could not bear it if he lied to her at this point.

"Is it anything I said or did to you? Have I overstepped your bounds?"

Cass was grateful for the way he worded his queries because it enabled her to look him in the eye and answer truthfully, "No, Jason, it isn't. I just need time and distance to sort out some things. Don't you remember how you felt after Joan died? And when you started seeing someone again?"

He nodded, but asked in a strained voice, "But you will see me again later, won't you? Please."

Cass smiled. "I'll see you in a couple of weeks; I promise."

"I think you already know how I feel about you, so I won't say anything to make this harder on you. I'm going to miss you. Can I call every so often to see how you're doing? I *am* your doctor and friend."

"No, Jason, please don't. That would only confuse me even more. What happened be-tween us came too fast. Right now, I should be getting myself and my life back together, but the situation between us is making me nervous and depressed again. By seeing you, I feel as if I'm doing something wrong. I know," she said to halt his protest, "I didn't say it *was* wrong, but I can't help how I feel, how I was reared by my parents and the Church. I have to make certain I'm over Tom before I get involved with you. I don't want to reach out to you because I'm lonely and vulnerable." *Or to spite Tom for his betrayal and that stupid clause!*

"I understand, Cass, and I'm sorry if I rushed you into anything that's causing you anguish. I'll do as you say, but it will be hard on me. I don't want to risk losing you, woman. I'm sorry," he said when she winced. "I'll leave, but call me when you're ready to talk or see me again. I'll abide by any rules you set for us; I swear."

"I will, Jason. Thank you, because I really need your cooperation, patience, and understanding."

"You'll have them, Cass, just don't forget about me."

"I won't." *As if I could!*

There was so much Jason wanted to say to her, but it was risky to do so. "See you later," he murmured, unable to say the unsettling *good-bye.*

"See you later, Jason," she responded for the same reason.

As he was walking away, he halted and turned. "Will you be keeping your appointment with me next Monday?"

"I'll be there, Doc, so don't worry."

His anxiety calmed a little with the smile she gave him. "You will take good care of yourself?"

"I promise. You, too."

"If you need anything, anything, Cass, please call me."

"I will."

"See you soon," he said and smiled.

"See you soon." She watched him vanish from sight around the corner of her house. *I hope and pray I know what I'm doing, because I might have just pushed away the best thing that's ever happened to me.*

Bradley Stillman came to her door on Friday afternoon. She had expected to find "Mutt &

Jeff" standing there, but her ex-husband was just as bad.

"Hello, Cassie. I had to —"

She glowered at him as she interrupted, "What are you doing here? How did you find me? What do you want?"

"I read about your husband's accident in the Augusta newspaper. I've been wanting to call you or come see you to make sure you're all right. I figured it was best to wait a while for you to calm down."

She almost spat out her frigid reply between clenched teeth, "I'm doing fine, or I was until you arrived. You aren't welcome here, and I don't want or need your condolences. Leave and don't return."

He grasped the edge of the door to prevent her from closing it. "Wait, Cassie love! Please, let me come in and talk. I'll behave myself, honest."

The use of that past endearment sent fury racing through her. How had she ever loved and slept with this despicable creature? "We said everything we ever need to say to each other years ago."

"Give me a chance to make it up to you, Cassie. I'm sorry I hurt you. I made a terrible mistake. I —"

She glared at the dark-haired man with light-blue eyes. "You made *plenty* of terrible mistakes. I don't want to see you, Brad, not now or ever."

"I still love you, Cassie; I've never stopped loving you. I've tried to get over you, but I can't. I need you, Cassie. I —"

"You loved me so much you screwed other women in our bed? You risked bringing home horrible diseases to me so you could have some fun? You're a sorry excuse for a man and an ever sorrier excuse for a husband."

"Please, Cassie, give me a second chance. I swear I'll cha—"

She felt anger spread throughout her entire body. "Second chance, Brad? I gave you a second chance and all you did with it was betray me again. I've tried to make it crystal clear to you numerous times: I detest you; I have no respect for you; it's over!"

"At least give me a loan, Cassie; I need it badly and you're rich now."

Though it shouldn't have, that plea took her by surprise. "Money? Is that why you really came here? To beg from me? From *me*, you louse?"

"I'll get down on my knees if I have to, Cassie; I'm really strapped. My life has turned upside down since we separated."

"*Divorced*, Brad, divorced because of adultery, remember?"

"How could I forget? It cost me the only woman I love."

"Love? You don't know the meaning of that word! You're selfish and no good, Bradley Stillman, no good!"

"I don't know what I'll do, Cassie, if you don't bail me out. I'm in deep water and barely holding my head above the surface. I'll —"

"Then, you'd better look for another bucket because I won't furnish you with one."

"Damn it, Cassie, you owe me! You were my wife! You —"

"*I owe you?* Pray tell for what? For all of the anguish and humiliation you put me through? For imperiling my health and life? Get real, Brad! You're lucky I walked away from you without suing your pants off! I didn't ask for or take anything from you, remember? All I walked away with were my personal possessions, and I worked and supported myself afterward."

"But you snagged yourself a filthy rich man; I read all about him. He's dead now, so you've got plenty of money. What harm could it do to give me a small loan? I'll pay you back when I get on my feet."

"I said no, Brad."

"Why not? Damn it, Cassie, stop being so vindictive! I told you I was sorry about what I did to you."

"What's going on here, Cass? Is this man giving you a problem?"

Cass jumped, startled by the voice from behind her. She looked at him and said, "I didn't hear you come in, Peter."

"I'm sorry I scared you. What's the problem?"

"There isn't one. Brad was just leaving."

"Cassie, please help me. I promise I won't ever come back if —"

Peter warned, "If you don't leave now, I'll report you to the police and file charges against you for harassment."

"Who the hell are you? This ain't none of your business!"

"I'm Peter Grantham, Cass's stepson, and I'm making it my business."

"Stepson?" Brad muttered, looking from one to the other. "I see, you've already replaced the old man with his son, right?"

"You filthy-minded bastard! Get off of my property!"

"Go inside, Cass, and I'll handle this offensive matter."

Cass looked at Peter, smiled sweetly to vex Brad, and said, "Thanks." Without even glancing at her ex-husband, she vanished from his sight.

As Peter stepped before him, Brad realized from the expression on the man's face that he wasn't one to be challenged. "I only wanted to talk to her."

"You did; and now you're finished. Don't bother her again, Stillman, or I can give you more trouble in a week's time than you would want to face in a hundred years. You're out of her life for keeps, so stay out. If you don't, I have ways of painfully and permanently dealing with scum like you. Understand?"

Brad was intimidated by Peter's firm stance, wealth and power, and rapidly surfacing fury. "I understand, Grantham. I'm going." He turned and left, the tastes of defeat and cowardice bitter in his mouth and mind.

When Peter joined her in the kitchen where she was preparing margaritas, Cass smiled and thanked him. "I thought we could use a drink after that nasty scene. I'm sorry you had to be dragged into my past problems."

"I should be the one to apologize for just letting myself in like that, but I was coming around the side of the house when I heard the commotion. I won't enter your home again without your permission. I only kept my set of keys in case of an emergency," he said, but didn't offer to return them. "He's gone now and I doubt he'll return. Men like him think they can run over vulnerable women and get away with it. I won't let him bother you, I promise."

She was impressed by how Peter had sent Brad scurrying off with his tail between his legs. She could not help but get wicked pleasure out of seeing Brad put down by the strong and virile man nearby. "I appreciate your most timely arrival, Peter, and I guess I owe you an explanation."

Be careful of how you look at me, woman, his elated mind warned her, *or I'll be carrying you up those stairs in a flash.* "Not unless you want to give one."

She passed him his glass as she began the painful story of her marriage to Brad Stillman. "I don't know what I ever saw in him," she ended with a sigh. "I guess I was just young, and naive."

"Don't beat up on yourself for being a nice person. We all make mistakes. Lordy, you already know about my whopper with Brenda Burkman. Why don't we make a toast to putting the dark past behind us and to having bright futures?"

"Sounds wonderful to me."

Peter lifted his glass and said, "Dark and bitter pasts be gone forever; sunny and sweet futures come to us quickly and eternally."

Cass tapped her glass to his, smiling as she did so, and took a drink.

"I was coming over to bring you this," he said as he picked up a black velvet box from the counter where he had placed it earlier. He opened it and held it out for her to view. "It's a Brazilian amethyst. I'm told these gems bring good health, good luck, and happiness; things you deserve."

"It's beautiful, Peter, exquisite and feminine," she remarked as she eyed the purple stone in the size and shape of a dime, encircled by cut diamonds and suspended on an eighteen-inch gold chain. "Surely that cost much more than the bracelet did."

"Not much, and I covered the difference as a friendship gift; that way, it won't seem as if it's from Dad. Let's see how it fits and if you like it. If not, don't hesitate to tell me."

"Of course I like it; it's one of the most beautiful pieces I've seen."

She turned around and lifted her long hair as Peter fastened the catch, all too aware of his fingers brushing against her flesh. When she faced him, he used his forefinger to tug her scoop-necked T-shirt down a smidgen into a *V* to make the setting visible to his inspection. He held her shirt in place using the soft and warm pad of his fingertip to keep from sticking her with his well-manicured nail. She looked down, but couldn't get a good view of it, and his contact felt strange. "I need to use the bathroom mirror; I'll be back in a minute."

She went into the half-bath nearby, flipped on the light switch, held down her shirt as he had done, and stared at the necklace.

Peter came to laze against the doorjamb. "Looks perfect on you. That vivid shade of purple suits your coloring. What do you think? I'll take it off your hands and pay you for it if you don't like it."

"I don't like it, Peter, I absolutely love it. Thanks," she said, and gave him a quick and impulsive hug of gratitude. Suddenly, the bathroom felt awfully small with him blocking — almost filling — its doorway. She was all too aware of his presence, scent, and allure.

Peter sensed her uneasiness, and delighted in his effect on her. Yet, he felt it was unwise to take advantage of her weakness for him. Perhaps later, he told himself, savoring the cat-and-mouse game too much to terminate it too soon. He straightened and turned to head back into the kitchen as he said, "I was also coming over to bring you good news; actually, fantastic news: the accident investigation has been closed, permanently, and Dad's life-insurance claim is being processed as we speak." At the counter, he retrieved his drink. "Why don't we go out and celebrate? We could throw on some casual clothes and ride over to the Crab Trap to grab a bite to eat."

"That sounds like a great idea." *Get him out of this private location fast!* "Why don't we have our drinks while we're changing clothes? If we hurry, we won't have to stand in line forever. You know how crowded it can get on a Friday night."

He gave a lock of her hair a gentle tug and grinned. "Smart woman. I'll meet you at your back door in . . . say twenty minutes?"

The Crab Trap on the next island had a rustic and casual ambiance. Its facade, with a long fenced-in porch, reminded Cass of the Old West, except for the white rowboat sitting atop its roof. A covered side porch with rough-hewn posts and exposed ceiling beams and with high-backed wooden benches and matching tables allowed for pleasant outdoor dining. Inside, the decor featured anything to do with water. It was a favorite eating spot for tourists, but the height of the season hadn't gotten into full swing yet. The restaurant was famous for its variety and generous portions of fresh seafood prepared in any way the customer requested.

Peter grinned and chuckled before he suggested in a playful tone, "Let's get down and dirty and order the messiest dishes they have. We can pig out for a change and have another margarita to wash it all down. How's that for a celebratory diversion?"

"Perfect. You order, and I'll prepare my tummy for the barrage."

They were seated near the back on the left side, given menus, and their drink order was taken. It was only a few minutes before the waitress returned with the pale-green drinks in salt-lipped glasses and garnished with limes. Peter told her their dinner selections, and she left to fill their orders.

While they sipped the tangy beverages and waited for their meals to arrive, Peter said, "We should hitch a ride on one of our company shrimp boats soon so you can see that work in action. They catch all sorts of things besides shrimp: shells, starfish, sand dollars, crabs, fish, and sometimes even a small shark. We sell those items to souvenir shops and artists who make crafts out of them. Our captains take special care to protect the dolphins and Right Whales that frequent these waters. Another

402

thing you may enjoy and find enlightening is a company tour, watching how seafood is processed, packaged, and shipped to our customers."

"I would like that very much, Peter, thanks."

"Good, we'll make a date to do them real soon. I'll also give you a tour of the electronics firm, but I'll warn you now, it's a little boring. Still, it might be wise for you to learn a few things about our companies. I'll request a report on each one of them for you to study. Afterward, we can discuss them, and I'll go over the annual reports with you at the end of the year. Currently, they're all making money for us. Smooth Rider is the only one I'm dumping. We just don't have the cart supply contracts the others do; their names are bigger and they've been in business longer, and they put out fine products. I'm afraid if I hold on to it too long, it'll lose its sale value and wind up in the red. I think Dad kept it more for sentimental reasons than because it was profitable. Do you have any objections to unloading it?"

"No, none, but thanks for asking. I would like to know something about our companies because I don't want to appear ignorant if somebody asks me about them. But I think you're doing a fine job operating them, and I'm certainly not knowledgeable enough to give any opinions about them."

"Thanks for the vote of confidence and faith in me, and we'll have to get you knowledgeable.

You're welcome to tag along with me on any of my future business trips if you want to tour the other companies."

After the waitress brought their she-crab soups, Cass said, "That will be good to do in late summer or early fall; first, I think we should give the employees time to settle down following all the changes. We don't want them to think we're doing an inspection and evaluation for sale purposes."

Peter nodded and said, "You're right, and I didn't think of that angle. As I said, Cass, you're an intelligent and kind-hearted person."

She smiled her appreciation and sipped soup to prevent having to respond. The truth was, she didn't want to travel alone with him at this unpredictable time when he was getting too close to her too fast. But, the main reason she didn't want to go gallivanting with Peter in the near future was she needed to be at home to make a decision about continuing her relationship with Jason.

Peter looked at her and said, "I almost forgot to tell you; I invited Pat and Dana Marlowe to have dinner with us tomorrow night at the St. Simons Island Club. Pat is the manager of our electronics firm. I thought it would give you a chance to meet people, get to know one of our staff members, and give you practice socializing without Dad. They just had their first child, a son, about six weeks ago, and this will be the first time Dana's gotten out of the house since the baby was born. I sent them flowers and a gift certificate and signed both of our names to the cards; so if they thank you for them, that's what they're talking about."

"That was very kind and thoughtful of you, Peter, and I would be delighted to go along."

"I picked the Island Club over the Cloister or one of the other clubs because it's less formal and I figured they would feel more comfortable in that setting." He glanced beyond her and grinned. "Well, here it comes, so get ready for the onslaught."

They were served battered fries, hush puppies, coleslaw, and corn on the cob, along with a combination of boiled and fried shrimp, deviled crab, and a large platter of crab legs. The waitress put down an ample supply of napkins and ice water.

The moment she left their table after smiling and telling them to enjoy their food, Cass took a deep breath, laughed, and said, "Wow! If we consume all of this, we will be puffed out like fat pigs."

"For one night, we can forget about fat content and salt and cholesterol levels, right?"

"Why not? We deserve to splurge on occasion."

"That's my Cass talking. Dig in. Oink, oink," he jested.

Amidst laughter, she peeled boiled shrimp and tossed the shells into the hole in the table where a trash can caught them. After eating for a few minutes, she murmured, "I love these battered fries, and the hush puppies are delicious; everything is delicious."

"To steal a quote: 'It doesn't get much better than this', right?"

"Right." As she tried to nibble daintily on the ear of corn, its juices dribbled down her chin. Before she could put down the cob and grab a napkin, Peter rose slightly in his chair, leaned over, and dabbed it for her.

He grinned. "Messy like I warned, but well worth it."

"Thanks. I don't have to look like a pig because I'm eating like one."

"Don't worry, I'll let you know if anything dares to mar that lovely and clean face. You do the same for me."

Cass scooped out several forkfuls of deviled crab, holding each in her mouth for a few moments to relish their flavor before swallowing them. She sipped alternately from the ice water and the margarita, resolved not to allow the second drink to go to her head.

They remained silent and busy for a while until Cass remarked, "I would love to have these batter and coleslaw recipes. I wonder how much they would charge me for them."

"They're probably closely guarded secrets and no amount of money would bribe them away from their cooks and owners. Contrary to popular belief, Cass, everything does not have a price."

"Such as?" she probed before biting into a fried shrimp.

"Let's see . . ." he murmured.

Cass was amused by the comical expression he put on his handsome face as he reasoned on her query and cracked crab legs. She felt relaxed with him this evening, was having fun, a lot of fun.

He finally replied, "A good man's honor, his reputation, his soul, his wife and kids, and things like that."

"Are you a good man, Peter?" she teased.

"I hope so; I try to be, despite having a naughty reputation. People who don't know me, really know me, judge me by what they think is true or from their own prejudices. Tell me the truth, Cass, do I really give off a terrible and one-sided impression?"

Whoa, boy, don't put me on that hot seat! Yet, she answered, "Not to me. In fact, I find you to be a very complex and multi-faceted person with a lot of excellent traits and qualities. However . . ."

"Whoops, here it comes," he jested when she paused.

"However, you have a tendency to conceal or play them down. It's as if you think showing them will make you appear weak."

He pretended to consider her words, and came up with what he was certain was a clever and touching reply. "You're right. A man is reared and trained to control and hide his emotions, to be strong at all times, to be the shoulder to lean on, not need to lean on one himself. I'll have to work on being more caring and considerate."

"You are caring and considerate. What you did for the Marlowes and for me prove that to be true. You're more open and relaxed around friends, but seem to be on guard and wary around others."

"So, I'm suspicious by nature and habit, huh?"

"Considering who you are, I suppose that's necessary."

"So, how does one find and walk that middle ground?"

"I don't know, Peter; I'm still trying to locate it myself."

"Then, perhaps we'll find it together. You want more crab legs?"

"No, thanks, I'm stuffed. You can order more; we have time."

At home, Peter walked Cass to the door, kissed her cheek, and said good night. "I'll call you in the morning to see what's a good time to look at those things you mentioned. And don't forget, dinner with the Marlowes at six-thirty."

"I'll be ready. You can come over any time after nine in the morning."

"Okay, I'll see you then. Good night, Cass; I had a wonderful time."

"Me, too. Good night."

She locked the door, set the alarm system, turned off the lights, and went upstairs. Though it was only a little past ten o'clock, she got into a nightgown and climbed into bed. She pressed a remote control button and turned on the television to lull her to sleep. She had a long and busy day tomorrow, good impressions to make.

Jason sat in his BMW on Sea Island Drive with Cass's house in view but not his car from her windows if she looked outside. It was cloaked by the dark shadows created by huge live oaks whose giant limbs almost canopied the street in certain spots, including the one he had chosen to use.

Earlier, he had been driving down Ocean Boulevard while taking a colleague home whose disabled vehicle was towed from their joint parking lot when he sighted Cass and Peter getting out of his Porsche Carrera at the Crab Trap. After dropping off his friend in the north beach area of the large island, he had — like a lovesick fool — waited in the parking lot of a shopping strip on Fredericka Road, knowing they had to pass by it to reach the Sea Island Causeway.

It had been unmerciful hours before they did so, just before he called a halt to his impulsive vigil, thinking they might have taken the long route or gone elsewhere after supper. As he sat there, his rebellious mind had envisioned them huddled over a wooden table, eating, laughing, chatting, and having a good time, while he was miserable, jealous, and lonely. After they passed, he had trailed them at a safe distance and taken this observation position. He had watched the lights go out downstairs and go on upstairs not long after Peter pulled into his driveway.

Now, Cass's bedroom light was out, and he couldn't help but wonder if — hope and pray — she was alone there. He had vowed to give her the time and space she said she needed; but could he keep that promise when Peter was so close to her every day and night? Could he when he knew Peter was so evil, so lecherous, so deceitful?

Chapter Eighteen

Jason rebuked himself for stooping to such deceitful measures. He loved Cass and must have faith in her. If he went to her tonight, he not only would be breaking his promise to give her space but would be implying distrust of her. That action would be detrimental to their future relationship. *Go home and get to bed,* he told himself and obeyed that difficult order after staring at her bedroom window for a minute.

Saturday morning, Peter walked to Cass's house to go through his father's things. It didn't take him long to make his decisions and, with her help, to box up those items and carry them to his garage apartment. After thanking her and reminding her of their plans for that evening, he left to play golf.

Cass spent the rest of her morning and most of the afternoon folding and packing the remainder of Tom's belongings. Soon, she would make this house all hers by changing the carpets, drapes, and many of its furnishings. In particular, she wanted Tom's lingering presence to be removed from the den, gym, his office, and the kitchen. Since he had rarely used the living, dining, and guest rooms, there was no need to redo them. But it would be time-consuming and expensive to tackle that project if she decided to relocate elsewhere on the island or on the next one.

At seven o'clock, Cassandra and Peter Grantham and the Marlowes entered the dining room of the St. Simons Island Club which featured a low-country setting and tranquil atmosphere. They were seated at a square table beside a partition which had lush plants decorating the waist-high barrier and balloon valances at its top. Beyond it was a row of tall paned windows that provided a lovely view of the club's magnificent grounds, complete with a spectacular covered bridge on the entry drive, countless pines, sprawling live oaks, and a well-manicured golf course. The armed wooden chairs were beautifully carved and had soft, thick cushions for comfort. At the far end of the room was a large fireplace. The men were attired in suits and the women, in Sunday dresses.

As the room filled with other guests and as they ate their appetizers — Escargot Bourguignoe for Peter, assorted fruits for Cass and Dana, and smoked trout for Pat — they talked about the couple's six-week-old son.

Dana was obviously delighted to be out of the house for the first time since Steven's birth. Even so, the first-time mother glanced at her watch numerous times as if checking to see what her baby was doing at that minute.

As their soup was being served, Cass looked at pictures of Steven. That fierce yearning for a child of her own engulfed her again. What good, Cass fretted, was a lot of money if one was miserable and denied such a joy?

Following their Caesar salads and continued genial conversation, their entrees arrived: sauteed Atlantic swordfish steak for everyone except Dana, who chose the grilled breast of duck.

During the meal, Pat told Cass details about the electronics firm and offered to give her a guided tour any time she wanted to see it. They talked about local and national news, and about their families and backgrounds. Peter was praised for his work at the company, but Tom was mentioned rarely for which Cass was grateful. Even so, every fifteen minutes or so, the topic returned to Steven and children.

On the sly, Peter watched Cass's reactions to that particular subject. He applauded himself for his successful ruse tonight, as it was evident Cass was gnawing at the bit to have a child, for which she would need a husband. He was elated by the many chances he was given to flatter her, to make her smile, to keep her relaxed, especially with a certain person witnessing their fun and rapport.

As Cass was returning to their table after

going to the ladies' room with Dana, Cass noticed Jason dining in the far corner near the enormous fireplace with an older couple and who she assumed was their adult son. No doubt Jason had sighted her and might be wondering what she was doing out on the town. She was glad she had been sitting with her back to him and hadn't known he was present, or she couldn't have enjoyed herself as she had. Now that she knew Jason was there, she was relieved the pleasant meal was over and they were preparing to depart. She made certain she didn't even glance in his direction as they made their way from the room, with Peter's arm on her waist.

The four stood in the reception area for a while as the Marlowes thanked them and told them what a wonderful time they had tonight.

"So did I," Cass concurred, "and it was a pleasure to meet you two. Maybe we can do this again in the near future."

Dana said, "That would be wonderful. Oh, yes, there's something I almost forgot to tell you; I guess because we kept getting sidetracked talking about Steven. We have a company cookout on the first Saturday of every June at our house. We want you to come this year. If you take the company tour with Pat soon, the cookout will give you a chance to get better acquainted with the employees and to meet their families. We have games and swimming for the children, and the company provides the food and drinks. If you like, you can bring a friend, and Peter can bring a date."

"We'll be there, Dana, but I'll escort Cass," Peter responded. "It'll be more relaxing if I don't have to entertain a strange young lady all afternoon, and it'll give me more of an opportunity to mingle with my staff and their families. Does that suit you, Cass?"

"I'll write it on my calendar the moment I get home tonight. Thanks for including me."

Outside, after once again exchanging enthusiastic words about the evening, they bid each other good night and walked to their cars, parked in opposite directions.

As Cass settled herself in the leather sports seat of Peter's Porsche Carrera 4s, she gave a peaceful sigh and said, "I'm glad you arranged that dinner; I like the Marlowes; they're a nice couple."

As Peter fastened his seat belt, he added, "And Pat's a super manager for our firm. Things wouldn't run as smoothly and profitably as they do without him. I gave him a raise; I figured he deserved it and needs it with a new baby in the house. That's a cute little tyke they have, isn't he?"

"He looked absolutely precious in those pictures. He has such a head full of dark hair, and those huge brown eyes are darling."

Peter turned on the ignition switch, put the car in gear, and drove along the paved drive and across the covered bridge as he continued,

"It's got to make one's heart pound with love and pride to gaze into your own baby's face and to hold it in your arms. People kid about single women hearing their body clocks ticking at certain ages, but mine seems to tick more loudly every few months. Lordy, it would be nice to find the right woman, settle down, and have a family."

At the entrance, he turned right onto King's Way to head toward the Sea Island Causeway and home. "It's strange how one trots along thinking he's happy and carefree and lucky to be a bachelor; then, blam, he runs into a brick wall and wakes up to realize he's alone and real life is passing him by fast, too fast."

"Have you ever dated any woman you considered marrying?" Cass asked.

"Oh, I was tempted by a couple of them, until I got to know them better. I was even engaged once, when I was nineteen."

"What happened? If that topic isn't painful or too personal."

"It isn't, not any more. I almost got to the marriage altar with the first one. But when she started making all of these grandiose plans about how and where we were going to live, I figured I'd better find out which she loved and wanted more: me or my family's money. I told her I was going to work for my father after college graduation, but I'd have to start at the bottom of the company and work my way up the ladder just like everybody else employed by him, and support myself. I told her we would have to live on a tight budget for a while, and maybe she'd even have to work until we got ourselves financially secure. Needless to say, she bolted on me within two weeks. The second time was when the woman I was dating at twenty-two got pregnant by accident and had an abortion on the sly, even though I told her we would get married and have the baby. She told me afterward she didn't want to be tied down to a kid at her age, but she still wanted to marry me; said we could have kids later, but I didn't believe her. I guess those two experiences and a few others are what made me so leery of women's motives. Sometimes good looks, money, and prestige are more of a curse than a blessing. Just think, Cass, I could have a four-year-old son tagging after me today. We could be. . . ." Peter's sigh was deep and filled with hurt. "Damn! I lied, Cass; it does still anger and pain me even after all these years. Sometimes I find myself wondering how he would look and what we would be doing. She got rid of him without a second thought just like my mother abandoned me."

She heard anguish in his voice and read torment in his expression. His hands gripped the steering wheel so tightly his knuckles blanched white and his arms were stiff. Her heart went out to him for those sufferings, as she was too familiar with those feelings.

"I'm sorry, Cass; that slipped out. I guess

maybe I had too much to drink or I'm tired. Ignore what I said, please."

Cass knew he hadn't drunk too much wine because he had appointed himself their "designated driver." Despite his smile and chuckles, he appeared ashamed of his slip. "Don't be sorry or embarrassed you have those feelings; you're only human, Peter."

"Well, they go against my motto of accepting what I can't change. We can get ourselves into some real pickles at times, can't we?"

"Yes, we can; I've certainly been in a few: Brad, for one." *Tom for another; and now, with you and Jason.*

"You think we'll ever find anybody that's perfect for us?"

"I hope so, Peter, or we're in for long and lonely lives."

"I hope not, Cass, because we deserve better." *You're a naive and gullible woman, Cass! How can you believe such bullshit? Don't you know real men don't talk like that? No wonder you get yourself into so much trouble with men! You don't know anything about them. You just let them lead you around by your pretty nose and cunt. Yep, my sexy and stupid stepmother, you're just about ripe for plucking by a new man.*

Peter was so caught up in his devious and lewd thoughts that he failed to realize the change in his feigned somber expression and mood, but Cass witnessed the smug grin that curled his mouth up at one corner and the dev-

418

ilish gleam that filled his hazel eyes. The alteration was alarming to her. She had no doubt that Peter still disliked and distrusted her and was deceiving her. What remained to be discovered was his motive.

When they reached her door at home, Cass faked a sunny smile, told him good night, and thanked him for a lovely evening. She almost cringed when he kissed her cheek before he departed. *You may have won a few battles, Peter, but you haven't won the war, and you won't; I swear it. You may think I'm blind and dense, but I'm not; you'll see very soon.*

On Sunday morning, Cass didn't go to church. Though she wanted to be there, she thought it unwise to see Jason with an audience present. When they next talked, she decided, it must be in private.

That opportunity came sooner than Cass expected when Jason came over that afternoon while Peter was playing golf again. She was standing at the kitchen window when he wheeled his vehicle into her driveway. No doubt he was breaking his word about leaving her alone temporarily because he saw her out last night with Peter. Now that she had a different view of Tom's son and the police investigation was over, it was time to learn if Jason Burkman could be trusted. She opened the front door as he approached the porch.

He looked at her and said, "I know I promised to wait until you called, but I had to see you, Cass. I have to know the answer to one question: Did Peter tell you about our past problem? Is that why you stopped seeing me?"

"That's two questions, but the answer to the first one is yes, he did. The answer to the last one is yes and no. Perhaps we should have a serious talk. You have a right to tell me your side of the story. Please, come in. Have a seat in the den and I'll join you in a minute with some colas."

Jason walked to the fireplace and gazed at the painting above the mantel. He was nervous and worried, despite the fact she was willing to give him the opportunity to explain. All he could do was tell the truth and hope she believed him. When he heard her enter the room, he headed for the sofa and she, for the loveseat nearby.

Cass focused her gaze and attention on him and listened to his version, which was similar to Peter's account in most areas.

"I'm sure Peter must have proclaimed his innocence to you, like he did to me. I can't prove he lied either time, but it sounded fishy to me. I don't see how Brenda could have secreted enough money from a household account to rent an apartment, and afford all the expenses that go with it; I think somebody had to be paying for at least half of those costs. Since she was having an affair with Peter, I had to assume he was footing the bill for their love nest. I was skeptical that he wasn't suspicious of her crazy schedule. I also can't believe he never saw our pictures on the society page since we were featured in that section on several occasions at charity functions. Since we lived and socialized in the same area, how could he not see us out together at least once or twice?" Jason shrugged. "Maybe he was telling the truth about Brenda using him, but I think there were too many holes in his story for me to believe him. What did he tell you?"

Cass was honest with him. She watched his gaze widen as she told the whole story.

Jason stared into her brown eyes and vowed, "Even if he's as guilty as sin, Cass, I would never use you to spite him. If you knew me better, you'd know I'm not that kind of person. Besides, if I was only out for revenge, I would have come after you sooner. I could have tricked you into divorcing Tom, then rejected you and created a terrible scandal for them. You would have hated and blamed Peter for provoking me to revenge."

Jason took a deep breath and an even deeper plunge into murky emotional waters as he confessed, "I started falling in love with you the first time we met and those feelings have gotten stronger as time passed. I need to have you in my life, Cass, but more so, I want you there. If I do or say anything to turn you against me, it will be the biggest and most painful mistake I've ever made. All I'm asking for is a chance to prove myself to you. Am I praying and wishing for too much? I know this is probably not the right time to be pressuring you, but I don't want to give myself false hopes."

"What I said by the pool the other day is still true, Jason; it is too soon for me to be dating seriously. But I do have deep and strong feelings for you. I enjoy being with you. I look forward to seeing you or even to speaking with you on the phone. I do want to date you. I do want to get to know you better. I would like for us to have a relationship one day. Where it might lead, I don't know. It's just that I've been through so much in the last few months that I have to make sure I'm ready to turn to another man. I don't want to hurt you and I don't want to get hurt."

"I would never hurt you, Cass, not intentionally."

"That's what my first husband said, and what Tom said. They both lied to me and deceived me. I can't fall in love with another stranger and end up with another broken heart. Besides, there are things you don't know about me and my marriage to Tom and about my current position in certain matters. I can't divulge those things to you, and you wouldn't understand certain decisions I have to make without knowing my reasons."

"There's nothing we can't work out together, Cass. Let me help you."

"Perhaps I'll tell you everything one day, but

not today or any time soon. Now that I know about Brenda, I understand why you were giving me subtle warnings about Peter and why you were so concerned about my ill health. I must tell you, at those times, I found your attempts to cast doubts on him strange, and after I learned about the trouble between you two, I viewed them as being suspicious. That's no longer true. I know now Peter can't be trusted. It's nothing he's said or done overtly, it's just a feeling I have. He and I never got along until after Tom died; now, he's trying to act like my best friend."

"Since you've told me that much, Cass, I'll reveal another worry I have: I think Peter and Hines were responsible for your strange condition."

"So do I." She saw him look surprised. "I think Peter needed me doped up so he could discover the will's contents and carry out other business matters without my interference. I can't say anything because I have no proof. Rest assured I know he's up to mischief — or was — and that I'm being alert. For those reasons I can't explain at this time, I have to pretend to believe him and be friends with him. I appreciate all you've done for me, but this is something I have to handle on my own."

"Do you think he had anything to do with his father's accident?"

"No, but I think he will go to great lengths to get the entire estate, short of murdering me. So if you see us together and we appear to be having fun, understand it will be nothing more than a pretense, each of us trying to dupe the other for different reasons."

"You don't know how happy and relieved that makes me, Cass. I was afraid he would turn you against me and might harm you."

"The only thing that could turn me against you is if you're lying about your feelings for me. I won't be fooled in that department again."

"I swear to you, Cass, I love you and want to marry you, that's all."

"I have strong feelings for you, too, Jason, but I have to be honest and tell you that marriage isn't in the picture for us for a long time."

"I can wait, Cass, as long as I know my hopes aren't in vain."

"If you're trustworthy and sincere, they aren't." *Because I have a plan to outwit Tom and Peter. With it, I'll get you and the money.*

Jason gazed into her eyes and vowed, "I'm both of those things, Cass, believe me."

She smiled and urged, "Then, be patient while I resolve one final matter."

"You have my word of honor; I won't break it again."

"I believe you. Now, if you resist the urge to phone me or visit me this week, I'll come over to your house Friday night for dinner."

"You will?"

"Yes, but you have to leave now before Peter returns home and finds you here. I don't want to antagonize him."

"Consider me gone, but as a happy man this time."

They exchanged smiles, and kissed. The kiss was long, deep, and filled with emotion; and it ignited their desires.

When they felt their passions rising, they parted as if on cue and grinned knowingly at each other.

"I best hightail it while I can keep my new promise because you're mighty tempting. I'll see you Friday night at my house about six."

"I'll phone you I'm on the way so you can open the garage for me; that way I can hide my car from everyone's view, especially Peter's."

"I do love an exciting adventure."

"So do I when I'm on the winning side. Now, scat, Doc."

"I love you, Cassandra Grantham. Good-bye until Friday."

She caressed his cheek, smiled, and echoed, "Until Friday."

After he was gone, Cass thought, *You went with your head the other two times and did what you thought was best for you; this time, go with your heart and your feelings and see where they lead you.*

Linda called her later that afternoon and they made plans to go to a local beauty spa and have lunch on Thursday. Cass didn't tell her about Jason or Peter or Brad; she would wait until they saw each other to mention those subjects, if she decided to do so. Perhaps Linda would be willing to be her alibi for her planned mischief Friday night.

Mary came on Monday, and they did their separate chores; then Cass ran an errand that took longer than she had expected.

When she returned home at seven-ten, Peter joined her at the car and helped her unload the sacks. "I was wondering where you were and I was getting worried about you. It'll be getting dark soon."

Cass pasted on a bright smile and said, "As you can see, I went to Winn-Dixie. I've been there since Mary left at five. I must be bored out of my skull because it was fun. I walked up and down every aisle and probably looked at every item on the shelves. I haven't gone grocery shopping in ages; Tom insisted that Inez always do it. I must have bought enough to last me for months. With her gone, I'll get to plan my own menus and I'll have to bone up on my cooking skills." *That's it, Cass, make him think you're simple-minded and easily appeased, totally gullible, and oblivious to business and his deceits.*

As she unpacked the bags and put away her purchases, Peter asked, "Would you like to grab a bite to eat at Mullet Bay? Afterward, we can go for a swim or take a walk on the beach to settle our tummies."

Cass glanced at him and forced out another phony smile. "I'm tired tonight, Peter. But we can do those things on another evening, if you don't mind. Besides, I've already eaten," she lied to get rid of him.

"You did have a busy day. I'm glad to see you so well, and getting out a little, even if it's only to run errands."

"I have you to partly thank for my improvement. If you hadn't called Doctor Hines when you did, I may have had a nervous breakdown. I don't know what got into me or came over me to cause me to act so crazy. It was weird and scary, almost like I was inebriated or on drugs." She gave a fake nervous laugh. *Don't let him suspect you're watching him for slips.* She used a serious expression and tone to add, "I hope it didn't give you a bad impression of me, and I regret other people saw me like that. I'm going to take good care of myself because I never want to go through that dark maze again."

"You won't, Cass, because you're completely recovered, and you're a smart and strong woman. You just got caught up in a terrible ordeal with Dad's death, the police investigation, and nosy people. I'm sure everybody realized you were suffering from grief and exhaustion. As for me, it helped me understand how much you loved and missed my father."

"I suppose you're right. But it showed me a side of myself I didn't like." After placing the folded paper sacks in the pantry, she stretched and yawned to deceive him. "Well, that's all of the groceries put away. I think I'll take a long bubble bath, curl up with a book and cup of hot herbal tea, and relax."

"In that case, I'll get moving."

"Bye, Peter, and thanks for helping with the groceries."

After he left, she leaned against the kitchen counter and frowned. If she wasn't mistaken or grasping for straws, Peter had looked strange for a moment when she mentioned drugs and her erratic behavior. The fact Jason — a physician — also suspected she had been tricked with them convinced her she was wise to be wary of Peter and Doctor Hines, and even Inez. She also believed that Peter had requested those unusual blood tests, either from knowing about his father's sexual antics or from distrusting her. Hines certainly was nervous when she questioned him about them. And, Johnson and Dredger had seemed tense and alert when she saw them, as if they were concealing something from her. Jason had been right and kind to caution her about those men.

On Tuesday and Wednesday, Cass went shopping for a new wardrobe, and took those items selected by Tom to a secondhand store in Brunswick and sold them. She decided not to do any more redecorating of the house in case she decided to move soon.

Cass ate with Peter on Wednesday night at Bennie's Red Barn on St. Simons Island. Afterward, she let him take her to Ziggy Mahoney's which was adjacent to the restaurant. Reluctant to spend private time with him at home, she lingered there with him for hours and listened to the male duo perform old hits from the 1940's up to the sixties. She especially liked Keenan's voice and delivery style; he sang several of her country western and rock and roll favorites upon request and even visited their table during a rest break to chat for a while.

She shagged with Peter twice and allowed him to think he had her fooled, but she was relieved they didn't slow dance together. Actually, she was having a good time at Ziggy Mahoney's, partly because she was meeting Peter's concealed challenge head-on, and partly because she enjoyed the music.

As Peter lazed back in his chair, sipped his drink, and tuned out the music, he made mental plans for his business trip tomorrow. There were a few problems he had to straighten out with the Los Angeles export/import company, problems if left unresolved could get him in to deep trouble with the law.

On Thursday morning after Mary arrived to clean the house, Cass and Linda left to go shopping, have lunch, and spend the next few hours at a beauty spa getting groomed and pampered.

For a while, they chatted about Linda's job on Jekyll Island that began tomorrow and her just-completed one, talked about how Cass was feeling and what she had been doing with the house and herself, and planned future outings.

"How are Jason and Peter doing?" Linda asked.

Cass lowered her fork. "Funny you should mention them in the same sentence. Did you know about the past trouble between them?"

Linda leaned forward and asked, "What trouble?"

Cass surmised from the nurse's reaction that Linda was uninformed in that area. "Do you know why Jason and Brenda got divorced?"

"No, but, knowing Jason, I assumed it was her fault."

"How about it was hers and *Peter's?* Adultery," Cass clarified, then watched the blond gape at her in astonishment. "That's right, they were lovers for three months, over a year ago."

"Are you sure? Who told you?"

"Peter and Jason. This conversation must stay strictly between us."

"It will, Cass; you can trust me."

"I believe so; that's why I'm telling you this, and for another reason which I'll explain in a minute. Since you know Jason so well, you can give me advice about him." Cass related what the two men had told her.

430

"That's so incredible and shocking, I don't know what to say. Heavens, how Jason must have suffered from what they did to him. I never liked Brenda and didn't believe she was good enough for him. The little bitch snared him while he was vulnerable and still grieving over Joan's loss."

Cass took a calming breath, then asked her friend, "Do you think Jason still grieves over Joan?"

"Not anymore. I mean, I think he's over her loss, but I guess he still has feelings for her. They were married for a long time and have children, so that would be natural. I didn't know her; she was gone before I met Jason, but I've heard she was a good woman. Why the frown?"

"This part is probably none of my business, Linda, but I care about you and feel I have to warn you about Peter." Cass saw that her friend looked confused by the sudden change in topics. "I don't trust him, but I have to pretend to be friends with him for personal and business reasons, at least for a while longer. I think the gossip about him is true; in fact, I think he's worse than his colorful reputation paints him to be. He's cunning and skilled at fooling people; he even tricked me for a while. I know you're attracted to him, but I don't want you getting hurt by him."

"I'm sure you're right, Cass, and I appreciate your concern and caution. I guess I knew it all

431

along, but I sort of got dazed for a while."

"It gets worse, Linda: I think he was slipping drugs into my food and drinks; I believe that's why I almost went off the deep end. Jason agrees."

"So do I, your reaction just wasn't natural. What are you going to do about it?"

"There's nothing I can do without proof, and Peter isn't one to make a mistake of leaving anything lying around for me to find and use. I'll just have to accept that part, ignore it, and make sure it doesn't happen again. Actually, I don't think it will; I think he just needed me looped for a short period while he checked out Tom's will and businesses."

"I don't know Doctor Hines well, but I've heard rumors about him, and I don't like him. He gives me the creeps, and I'm positive he was overdosing you on medication. But as you said, without evidence, your hands are tied. You certainly can't make accusations against either one without it."

"I know, but at least Jason is taking care of me now. That's the other thing I need to discuss with you. I . . . we . . . How do I put this?"

Linda grinned. "You two are attracted to each other and want to start dating?"

"Is it that obvious?" Cass worried aloud.

"Only to me because I was around you two so much and I got to know you so well. Don't believe what Peter told you about him. Jason is a good and honorable man, Cass; you can trust him. I truly believe he's falling in love with you, and I think you two are perfect for each other."

"But our timing is lousy. I mean, I've only been a widow for two months. I didn't intend for this to happen, and surely not so soon."

"Love doesn't read a calendar or clock, Cass. It's rare to find the perfect man, so don't risk losing him because of misplaced fears."

"That's what my heart says, but my head warns me about gossip."

"No matter what you say or do, Cass, people are going to gossip about something. Just be discreet and you'll be fine."

"I suppose it's obvious to you my marriage to Tom was a mistake. I was trying to make the best of it. I shouldn't have allowed Tom to dazzle me and convince me to marry him. I was alone and lonely, I wanted children and a home. I married for all the wrong reasons."

"I know what you mean; I've almost settled for men who weren't right for me on several occasions. I probably would have if those men hadn't changed their minds and walked out on me. Lordy, Cass, I'm twenty-seven and I've never been married and see no good prospects in sight!"

"It's better to not be married or be divorced, perhaps with children, from some sorry bastard who tricked and betrayed you. Would you believe Brad came to see me last Friday?" Cass related her ex-husband's visit and motive and how Peter supposedly rescued her. "At least I can be grateful to Peter for that favor. He so terrified Brad that he'll never bother me again."

"That's good news."

"Oh, yes, I received other good news this week: the police have halted their investigation into Tom's death and ruled it an accident."

"That's wonderful! No more stress from those angles."

"Now, all I have to deal with are Peter and Jason." *And Tom's will.* "Have you ever met Jason's children?"

"Yes, and they're wonderful. You'll like them and they'll adore you. In fact, I wouldn't mind snagging Stacey for myself, even if he is a few years younger than I am. He's terrific like his father; and a real hunk."

"Maybe you can snare him; Jason said he isn't involved with anyone."

"That would be a smidgen difficult since we live so far apart."

"Well, he does come to visit his father, doesn't he?"

"Yes, but I'm rarely around when he does."

"Well, we'll have to make certain you *are* around in the future."

"Any help you can supply in that area will be appreciated."

"Do you think Jason would want another child since his are grown?"

"He's an excellent father and loves kids, so I think so."

"I know I do. First, I need to see how Jason feels about having more children. I've certainly learned how important it is to discuss something like that early in a relationship. Do you know anything about him I should be warned about?"

"No, he's as close to being perfect as a man can get, in my opinion."

"Maybe that's what scares me a little, or a lot: I'm afraid to trust my judgment of him because I've been so wrong about my past choices."

"This time, trust your feelings and intuition, Cass; he's a jewel."

"Well, we'd better pay our bill and get moving to the beauty spa or we'll be late for our appointment."

What she was about to do that night would be anything but fun for Cass, yet she hoped the unpleasant task would give her needed clues about Tom and possibly about Peter. She sat on her bed with pillows propped behind her back, her knees raised, and Tom's diary resting against her thighs. She had used a screwdriver to break its lock and not felt the least bit guilty for invading his privacy.

She perused many entries over a year's time period. Tom's recordings about his wicked actions were almost all short and choppy, often crude, and featured a scoring system of one-to-ten and listed the types of "skills" his secret lovers possessed. She flipped from page to page, repulsed and shocked by what she read, but felt she had to learn the truth about the dark stranger who'd been her husband for over two years. Most of the entries for June through September seemed to correspond with the episodes she'd seen on the videotape. Then she got a few surprises.

October 5: Marlee: 9, Did first drugs today. Great sex. Didn't like loss of control. Never again.

"So, even you have your limits. That's a shock."

November 6: Going home. Must be crazy to risk losing Cass. Love her and need her more than anybody in my life. Can't help myself. Forbidden sex is like a potent and addicting drug.

"You had a strange way of proving you loved and needed me, you bastard! Am I supposed to feel sorry for you because you were an uncontrollable sex addict? Well, I don't and never will."

November 7: my sweet Cass, always an 11+.

"How nice," she scoffed in a sarcastic tone. "I rated over a ten."

December 19: Took huge chance today with Dave in my gym. Next time, I'll let him do me in his office. Maybe that sexy male nurse of his will join us for a threesome. Dave says he's great.

"Dave? Are you possibly talking about David Hines? You two did those wicked things here in our home? You used those benches for . . . Oh, my heavens, and I've been lying on them while exercising! I'll have to scrub and sanitize them tomorrow."

January 13: Dave wants another shot at me. Said no. Too risky; he's too promiscuous. What a fucking shame!

"And that filthy doctor touched me and treated me!"

February 9: Must give up other life and fight weakness for it. If lost Cass, would kill me. Mine forever, even after death. Would die if she ever cheated on me, but she never would. She's the only person who loves me for myself, but she would never understand my weaknesses.

"For once, Thomas Grantham, you're absolutely right!"

February 18: Marlee: 7 today. I just wasn't into it and distracted.

February 21: I know Cass wants a child and she deserves one. Maybe it's a good idea and timing is right this summer. Must get treatment if necessary to change, but must stop taking chances. Need to get closer to Peter; he's becoming too much like me.

"I'm glad I don't have your child, you sorry bastard!"

March 3: Doing Gretchen for last time this weekend. Love and need Cass more than these pleasures. No more risks. Get rid of tapes and journal. Burn all names, addresses, and phone numbers. Never again.

"So, you were on your last sordid fling, were you?" Cass muttered in disgust. "Perhaps fate was kind to me by taking you away before you had the chance to dupe me further and before we could have a child."

Cass closed the book and stared at its black leather cover and broken lock. How strange it was, she thought, that Thomas Ethan Grantham had kept a diary like a teenage girl, and how risky it was of him to make such detrimental recordings for someone to find. Had Tom been mentally ill, so sick in mind that he truly wasn't responsible for his actions? Had he been crying out for help?

Who were you, Thomas Grantham? Cass agonized. *What were you? What would Peter pay to make certain this diary is burned? Could I use it to force him to make a settlement with me to get what I deserve, to let me outwit Tom? I wonder how much Peter is like you. If he's ignorant of your evil, this discovery could hurt him deeply, though he probably doesn't deserve my help and compassion. How badly do I want at least part of my inheritance? Enough to do anything necessary to obtain it? Enough to risk enraging Peter to perhaps a dangerous degree? I'd better think about those questions seriously, because I'll have to act on their answers soon.*

Friday evening and fortuitously before Peter came home from work, Cass left her house at a little before six o'clock to drive to Jason's. She wondered what was in store for them tonight.

Chapter Nineteen

Cass settled herself on a thick multi-striped coverlet that Jason had spread inside the widow's walk railing atop his home. As he poured two glasses of wine, she reflected on how they had prepared supper together in his spacious but cozy kitchen and had cleaned up afterward as a team. Broiled swordfish steaks, baked potatoes, rolls, and a garden salad had never tasted better; nor had she ever found routine chores to be more stimulating. They had taken a stroll on the beach, daring to hold hands in their solitude on the sand, then climbed the exterior spiral steps to enjoy the view and each other's company. The sun had set and nighttime engulfed them, but a full moon and countless stars gave soft light. A cooling breeze with intermingled floral and ocean scents wafted over them. They were positioned to the rear of his house where the gentle slope of its roof, many tall trees, and the one-storied adjacent dwellings prevented them from being visible to inquisitive eyes and minds.

As Cass took the glass of blush wine from Jason, she smiled and said, "Thanks. This is wonderful, Jason, so tranquil and lovely. I think I could sleep up here."

"Yep, a perfect night for stargazing. And romancing," he added.

Cass saw his eyes brighten. He appeared to be trying to look and sound calm, but she perceived his suspense and anticipation. Those same feelings assailed her. So did the annoying question of should she relent to her rampant desires. She had been the one to make the restrictive rules for their relationship, but she yearned to break them. Over the rim of an upturned glass, she watched him lick his lips after he sipped some wine, shift his position to be closer to her, and let his adoring gaze roam her face. She knew she was weakening, and suddenly she didn't care, couldn't retreat. "Careful, Doc."

Jason asked, "Why? I'm in no danger of falling." He watched her tease manicured nails over his forearm and was enthralled by her magnetic allure. He yearned to undress her and make love to her.

Cass lifted her right hand and toyed with a windblown lock of tawny hair. "I meant, be careful of how you look at me or I might seduce you. Besides, I thought you already had fallen, fallen for me."

"I have; I took a hard and fast tumble the first time I met you. I'm more than willing to become putty in your lovely hands." He captured the empty one and kissed each fingertip, then its palm several times.

Cass warmed and quivered in desire. "If

anyone on this roof is a lump of susceptible putty, Doc, it's me. You got me here, didn't you?"

"I'm glad you came and I'm overjoyed you trust me. I love you, Cass."

Please convince me that's true and you aren't a perilous stranger. Just above a whisper, she said, "But you hardly know me, Jason."

"I know you well enough to know I love you and want you." He noticed she was breathing more quickly now, and her cheeks were flushed. Her eyes glowed with what looked like passion as she held his gaze. It was a struggle not to yank her into his arms and kiss her, but he wanted her to make the first move tonight to make certain he didn't overstep his bounds.

Cass wanted Jason Burkman with every fiber of her being. Right or wrong, wise or foolish, she must have him again tonight, here and now. She set aside her glass and slipped a leg over his hips to sit across his lap. She clasped his handsome face between her hands, gazed into his blue eyes, and said, "I want you and need you." She kissed him with boldness and fierce longing.

Jason's arms banded her back and he returned the kiss with fervor. He realized she craved him as much as he craved her. She was giving him permission to pursue her. He pulled her more tightly against him as his lips feasted on her mouth, face, ears, and throat. As she erotically rubbed her body against his, his trembling fingers unfastened her blouse, peeled it off, and cast it aside. He did the same with her bra, then nestled his face between her breast, his tongue teasing the sweet skin there before wandering to taste each taut, waiting nipple. His hands caressed her sleek bare back and delighted in the warmth and silkiness of her skin.

Cass leaned back her head and sighed with pleasure as her fingers roamed his broad shoulders. She moaned and writhed in his lap, aware of the hardness straining against his shorts. Ever since her arrival, or perhaps before she left home, a gigantic ache for him had been building within her and she had to assuage it or surely go mad. She grasped the hem of his shirt and pulled it over his head. As she fumbled with the drawstring at his waist, wanting to feel her flesh in contact with his, he halted his actions to assist her.

Cass slid from his lap to remove her skirt, half-slip, and panties and toss them into an increasing pile of clothes. She worked fast; she didn't want either of them to cool down a single degree and she could hardly wait to be embraced by his arms again.

Jason stripped off his shorts and briefs in an eager rush, glad he had taken off his dock shoes and socks earlier. He lay atop her, but didn't enter her, wanting to prolong their foreplay and regain some control.

Moonlight danced over their naked and

writing bodies as the ocean's waves crashed on the nearby beach at hightide. Gusts of wind blew across their enflamed flesh, but failed to cool them or even be noticed.

He fondled and kissed her in an almost mindless frenzy, his control strained. At one point, he leaned back, looked down at her, and said, "You can't possibly know how beautiful and tempting you are or how much pleasure you give me."

"Oh, Jason; you make me feel so good, and you drive me wild. We probably shouldn't be doing this, but I can't help myself."

"Neither can I, Cass. I would beg for mercy, woman, but I don't want to receive any."

"Me, neither." She parted her thighs to coax him to unite their bodies, and he did.

Jason sank deep into the core of her need and Cass gasped with pleasure. Sweet ecstasy coiled steadily within her as she eagerly moved with him as he drove her ever closer to the brink of ecstasy.

"Tell me when you're ready, my love," he murmured against her ear.

"Now, Jason, now."

"Love me, Cass, take all you want."

They came together in a blissful and stunning climax that left them clinging tightly to each other.

Cass felt like purring in satisfaction. Never had sex been so powerful and soul-thrilling. She wondered if each time with Jason would be better than the time before. It hardly seemed possible!

Jason stayed ensheathed within her as he relished their closeness. The love, satisfaction, and serenity that encompassed him was wonderful and overwhelming. While controlling his weight atop her, he gazed into her limpid brown eyes and ravishing face, leaned forward and kissed her tenderly.

The kiss was so filled with strong emotion that Cass almost cried in happiness. For the first time in her life, she felt as if she had experienced genuine lovemaking and had given of herself completely. At last, she had found the perfect man to share her life and claim her love. She hugged him tightly.

Jason eased himself out of her body, hating to break the intimate contact, and lay beside her. Relaxed in the golden aftermath of the exhilarating experience, he cuddled her in his embrace and took a deep breath. "This isn't pillow talk, Cass: that was the most wonderful lovemaking I've ever had. I don't know what it is about you, but you do things to me no other woman ever has. I want you around me all of the time. Just your smile or laugh or voice warm me. I love you with all my heart, all of it, Cass. I want to marry you."

Cass had been about to reveal she felt the same way, until his last sentence reminded her of the obstacle between them. She rolled to her side, propped herself up by an elbow, looked

444

down at him, and said, "There's something important I have to tell you."

When she looked over his head and hesitated, Jason feared the worst. "What is it?" he asked.

Cass felt his body tense, heard the strain in his voice, and saw his look of concern. "It's about Tom's will and my inheritance. I don't. . . ." As she paused to select her wording, Jason interrupted her.

"I swear to you I'm not interested in you for your money, Cass. I have plenty of it and a profitable practice. If you want a prenuptial agreement, that's fine with me. I don't care whether you come to me with a nickel to your name, just as long as you do come to me."

Cass hugged him and gave him a brief kiss in gratitude before she related the truth of her situation, numbers and all. "Tom was very cunning with his will; if I marry again within five years, I forfeit everything left in my estate, which would be the major portion of it. And until those five years pass, I get only living expenses, a monthly allowance, and a Christmas bonus. It almost sounds as if I'm an employee instead of his widow. It makes me angry, disappointed, and embarrassed to be treated that way. He dangled a huge golden carrot over my head, but he attached a lengthy and strong and unbreakable chain to it. It's not that I'm greedy, Jason, and I didn't marry him for his money and even signed a prenuptial agreement to prove it; but I deserve and want my inheritance, at least part of it. I'd have to wait ten years to get the other half, and I'm not willing to make that sacrifice. But if I walk away now, all I can take with me are my personal possessions and a few thousand dollars in my checking account; I can't even keep my home and its furnishings."

After Jason sat up and tossed his shirt over his groin, Cass donned her long-tailed blouse to conceal her nudity for the serious conversation.

Jason chose his response with care. "You told me last week what your percentages were and I knew Grantham was a rich man, but I didn't realize how much wealth was involved. Are his stipulations legal?"

"According to what Simon Johnson told me, legal and binding; that bloodline provision stays in force for life. He said there's no way I can break or change the terms. I started to see another lawyer as you suggested, but I decided Mr. Johnson wouldn't lie to me about something I could easily disprove, then cause trouble for him. Since he's such a prestigious and skilled attorney, I'm sure he knows his business and there's no loophole."

"What happens to the money if you decide to remarry?"

Cass revealed the one omitted point, "It reverts to his son or heirs."

"Peter gets it?" He saw her nod. "All of it? Everything?"

"That's right, and it's the reason he tried to dupe me about your motive for wanting me. I had to question why he would destroy a budding relationship with you when it would profit him to toss me into your lap."

"I can't imagine, unless he's romantically interested in you. Is he?"

"Not that I know of; in fact, I'm sure he still dislikes and distrusts me. If he wants me, the only reason is to get his hands on the money. Don't worry, I have no interest in him in that area. I think he drugged me because I had to be mentally and physically incapacitated for him to get to the will and companies' books before I saw them. I suspect Hines helped him either for money or to protect some secret Peter knows about him."

An estate that size was nothing to sneeze off lightly, Jason reasoned, that choice had to be hers. If he coerced her into making one in his favor, it could cause resentment later. But was collecting it worth costing them five or ten years of marital bliss? Was he willing to settle for a lengthy love affair if that was her decision? He had to discover her stand on the matter. "I realize that over fifteen million dollars plus added future income is a lot of money, and I know the value of real estate here, so are you telling me you can't marry me for at least five years?"

"I honestly don't know. Our relationship happened so fast that my head hasn't cleared yet, and we're still getting to know each other. I don't want to leap into another marriage until I'm certain it's the right thing for me to do. The same caution should apply to you. We have to make sure there's more than a physical attraction between us. It's a lot of money, Jason, and I deserve it for what he did to me."

"What do you mean by deserving it for what he did to you?"

Cass drew a deep breath before revealing to Jason the truth — though partial — of Tom's sexual dalliances.

"After Tom was killed in that accident, I discovered he had been cheating on me with countless lovers. He used me and betrayed me and he endangered my life by taking risks that could have given me AIDS. If those detectives or the media had gotten wind of his secrets, I would have been humiliated by a scandal. He manipulated and dominated me for years, and he's still trying to do that from his grave. Damn him!" Cass was positive Jason assumed she was referring to female lovers and she couldn't force herself to tell him otherwise.

He put his arm around her, drew her closer, and urged, "Relax, love, everything will be all right."

"I shouldn't have married him, Jason; it was a huge and stupid mistake. I realized too late I didn't love him enough to be his wife, but I tried my best to make it work. I just wanted to have a real home and a family, to be happy and fulfilled. Tom wasn't the man to give me those things, and no amount of money makes up for them being denied."

"I understand. I did the same thing: I married Brenda for all the wrong reasons, the same ones you mentioned, and paid dearly for doing so. We're only human, my love. But now, we've found each other. We can be happy, Cass; we can have a family together. You don't need Tom's money, but I understand why you want to collect it. I'll even admit I'm tempted to encourage you to do so just to keep Peter from having it and to repay Tom for misusing you badly, but I have to let the past go to be happy and free."

Cass leaned away to gaze deep into Jason's eyes as she said, "I love you and want you, Jason, but I can't give you an answer until I resolve this matter for myself. I won't come to you with ghosts haunting me; that isn't fair. And as I said earlier, we have to get to know each other better before either of us should make a serious commitment."

Jason beamed at her confession. "You don't know how happy it makes me to hear you say you love me. The last thing you need is more pressure and stress, especially from me. I'll give you time to work out that problem. But that doesn't mean we can't be seeing each other, right?"

"Right, but we still have to be discreet. We do have to protect our reputations since we're residents and you practice here. There is one more thing to tell you," she ventured with a grin.

"Your expression tells me it's going to be good."

"I might have a way of tricking Peter into making a settlement with me very soon," Cass revealed. "If so, all we'll have to wait is a proper mourning period."

After Cass told him what she had in mind, Jason said, "But his offer might be canceled if he learns I'm the man wooing you."

"I don't think so, because he stands to gain a lot by settling with me ASAP. I'm sure Peter would be thrilled to get me and you out of his picture within the next month."

"Would you be satisfied with his offer?"

"Yes, I'd get you and justice, so I'd be perfectly content."

Jason grasped the hands that cupped his face, covered them with kisses, and said, "So would I, Cass, so would I." As they sank to the thick coverlet with their mouths fused and their passions rising anew, before his wits were scattered by her, he thought of a way he could ensure Peter's cooperation with Cass if a particular person — perhaps two — could be won over to his side or he wasn't immune to using blackmail.

Saturday morning, instead of being on the golf course as planned, Jason stood on Inez's front porch. When the stern-faced woman responded to his knock, she scowled at him and asked what he wanted. "I need to speak with you in private, Miss Doughtery. It's important." He watched her squinty gaze walk over him in near contempt.

"What do we have to talk about? You're Mrs. Grantham's friend."

Jason ignored her hateful tone and expression. He smiled and said, "Something that could be valuable to you: fifty thousand dollars." He saw the dark-haired woman's matching gaze widen, then narrow. "You'll be taking a big loss at easy money if you don't hear me out. May I come in to explain?"

"Only for a minute. I wasn't expecting company and I'm busy."

Jason followed her into a small living room with furnishings that were sparse and cheap. It was obvious the ex-housekeeper didn't spend her good earnings on improving her surroundings. However, the place was clean and neat. He sat on a lumpy and well-worn sofa and said, "I need information about how and why Peter and probably David Hines were drugging Cassandra Grantham and I'm willing to pay you for your assistance." He witnessed Inez's brief look of panic before she scowled again. *You're on the right track, but convincing her to betray them isn't going to be quick or simple.*

"I don't know what you're talking about. Is that what that crazy woman told you? You know she's sick in the head."

Jason controlled his anger and feigned a pleasant and polite air. *Try to throw a scare into her but don't antagonize her.* "No, Miss Doughtery, she isn't. Her symptoms and behavior were brought on by being slipped drugs, illegal drugs; and I believe it was done with your help, perhaps without your awareness of what you were doing."

"You're as loony as that snooty woman!"

"I'm a physician, Miss Doughtery, so I know the signs and I know Mrs. Grantham's history and personality. I promise you I won't tell the police about your involvement, whether it was accidental or intentional, but if you refuse to cooperate with me, you could be charged as being an accomplice. All I want to do is protect Cass from Peter's threat to her, one you know exists. Before I can do that, I have to know what he was doing to her."

"He was helping her. He got her a doctor when she went nuts."

"He provoked her near breakdown with illegal drugs, then David Hines kept her drugged and overdosed for weeks. Since you were the one administering those drugs to her, you are a part of that crime." Jason saw her pale for a moment at the use of that last word. *She's guilty, so terrify her if you must.* "If you'll help me protect her from future harm, I'll pay you fifty thousand dollars in cash and forget you were involved."

Inez stared at him. She reasoned it would be

his word against hers, Peter's, and Doctor Hines's, and he couldn't prove anything. If he was willing to pay so much to uncover that information, she deliberated, what would Peter be willing to pay to keep it hidden? "You may as well leave, Doctor Burkman, because I don't know nothing about your silly ideas."

Jason had almost seen the mental wheels turning in the woman's head. "I suppose you need to think this over, so take a week or two to decide and call me with your answer. I should warn you, Miss Doughtery, Peter Grantham isn't a man to challenge; he's cold-hearted and ruthless. If you tell him or Hines about our talk this morning, you'll lose from both sides. At least by taking mine, you'll earn a lot of money and stay out of trouble. If you take his, I can't imagine what will happen to you. Good-bye."

That afternoon, Peter Wesley Grantham stood inside Inez's door and gaped at her as he snarled, "How dare you summon me like a lacky and try to blackmail me, you old bitch! You can tell Cass or the police anything you want. Who would believe you without proof? I'm willing to bet Cass will testify you detested her and are being vindictive because she fired you. If anybody even suspects drugs, they'll think you were the one giving them to her out of hatred and spite and jealousy. You'd better think hard and long about who you'll be going up against; Hines and I will eat you alive in or out of court. You'll have to be punished for this challenge: I'm not paying you another cent, so get off your ass and get yourself a job! And don't call me again, Inez, or you'll be sorry, very sorry."

Inez glowered at Peter as he stalked from her house, slammed her door, and sped off in his expensive sports car. *You're the one who'll be sorry, you bastard!* She hissed. *A hundred thousand is a drop in the bucket to you, and you owe me plenty for the risks I took. I'm not going to jail for you and you can't treat me like this. You forget how much I know about your little doings and you don't know what I have in my dresser. I can fix you good and be gone from here.* Yet, she warned herself not to be hasty or impulsive, and praised herself for not telling Peter about Jason's suspicions and visit.

At six o'clock, Cass glanced out the den window and saw Peter swimming back and forth in the large pool. She noticed an empty glass on a nearby table and assumed he had been drinking since his return home. She couldn't imagine what had him so agitated, but she was positive it had nothing to do with a bad golf game.

In the kitchen, she prepared herself a glass of wine in an insulated mug and went to speak with him, to put her clever ruse into motion. She took a seat in a chaise and crossed her legs at the ankles. As she watched him, she sipped the tasty beverage and plotted her strategy again.

When Peter glanced up in mid-stroke and saw her, he paused and waved and swam toward her. He heaved himself from the water, grabbed his towel, and claimed the chair to her right. As he dried his face and fingercombed his ebony hair, he said, "I missed you last night. Where did you go? I was worried about you."

"I went to supper and the movies with Linda. We had a great time."

"You two went out alone on a Friday night?"

"Linda's between boyfriends and I'm in mourning, so yes, we did. What did you do last night? Did you have a hot and heavy date?"

"Nope, I stayed home and watched TV alone. I was hoping we could eat together and talk, but I couldn't find you."

"I'm sorry if you were worried about me. You'll have to remember I'm a big girl and I can take care of myself."

"You're too trusting and sweet, Cass, and I don't want anybody taking advantage of you. Including me," he added, and tossed the towel aside.

Take his cue, Cass. "What do you mean?"

"This is a crazy place and time to have this kind of conversation, but something's been gnawing at me for a long time." He looked at the ocean.

"What has, Peter? Is there a problem? Are you annoyed with me?"

455

He looked at her. "No way, Cass, but there is a problem."

"What kind of problem, Peter?"

"Something you might not want to hear about, now or ever."

"Am I going to have to drag an explanation out of you?" she jested.

Peter reached for his glass, found it empty, and set it down again. He looked at his feet. "I'm in love with you, Cassandra Grantham, and it's eating me alive to think of you turning to another man. I was giving you time to get over Dad's death before I said anything about my feelings, but I can't with Jason trying to worm his way into your life."

Those words were shocking and unexpected to her, though she knew they were lies. "Peter, I —"

"Wait, Cass, and let me finish, please," he urged as he turned to face her. "I've been working up the courage to do this for over an hour, so let me continue before I lose it. I've been in love with you since I first met you. Damn, what a day that was! I met the first woman who completely stole my heart and she was about to marry my father. It's been a fierce struggle to resist you. That's why I tried to make you hate me, so I wouldn't yield to your temptation. If you had leaned in my direction even slightly, I would have come after you; I couldn't have helped myself or stopped myself. Dad didn't deserve you; he was evil and deceitful."

She was about to stop his ruse, but his impending words halted her.

"I found awful stuff in his wall safes at the other residences. He was cheating on you big time, Cass, and I detest him for it. I destroyed the evidence so nobody could find it. I wasn't going to tell you and hurt you, but I thought you should know so you won't keep grieving over him when he doesn't deserve it. Did you suspect or know the wicked truth about him?"

Play along, girl, and learn all you can, and set him up for your ploy. "Not until after he was dead. While I was going through his belongings, I found filthy pictures and revealing notes. I destroyed them immediately. I didn't think you knew the truth, so I didn't want to hurt you by exposing him. I still find it hard to believe Tom was so evil and he took such risks with our lives, considering the sexual diseases running rampant these days. I'm lucky he didn't pass one along to me."

"I realize Dad put you through hell with his manipulative and lewd ways." He laid his hand on her forearm and stroked it with his fingertips. "Let me make it up to you. We can marry and have children. We can have a home and family and be happy, Cass. I love you and need you."

She gazed at him for a minute, delighted when her eyes misted — from dirt carried on the wind! "I'm sorry, Peter, but I don't feel the same way about you. I'm very fond of you, but I don't love you, and I can't marry someone I don't love. Please understand and forgive me."

He took a deep breath, moved his hand away, and said, "There's nothing to forgive, Cass, unless it's me for putting you on the spot like this. Just forget what I said, okay?"

"No, Peter, I won't. It's flattering and appreciated. You're a sexy and handsome man, but you deserve to have a woman who loves you like crazy. I know you'll find the right one some day."

"So what are you going to do with yourself?"

Thank you, thank you, thank you, her mind shrieked in delight, as he gave her the opening she needed. She also noticed how fast he dropped the phony romance angle; if he was sincere, he would be begging her to change her mind. "I'm thinking about making serious changes in my life."

"What kind of changes?"

"I may move to St. Simons Island to get away from the bad memories here. I was thinking about opening a boutique to support myself. I just want and need to break all ties to Tom and start a new life. The problem is, he fixed it so I can't, unless a bank will loan me money to finance my business based on my trust fund and stocks. Do you think that will be possible since Tom tied them up with so many stipulations for so long?"

"I thought for a minute there you were

considering marriage."

"If I marry again, I'll lose my inheritance, and I need at least part of it to make a fresh start. Since you know the truth about Tom, you must realize I deserve payment for his many betrayals. I suppose I'll have to wait until I withdraw enough funds to carry out my plan."

"You don't have to wait, Cass, if you're willing to settle for five million cash and this house; it'll bring in another one to two million. Would that allow you to carry out your dream?"

"Yes, Peter, but what about the will's restrictions? It says it reverts to you if I remarry, and I don't intend to do so in the near future."

"What about Jason Burkman?"

She sent him an odd look. "What about him?"

"I thought you liked him and wanted to date him."

"I do like him and he's good company, but he's only a friend and my doctor. After what I went through with Brad and Tom, I'll be slow to wed again. I want to regain my independence and self-confidence. I don't want to be dependent upon any man, or be fooled by another one. I couldn't date Jason until I convinced myself he's trustworthy. Besides, despite what Tom did to me, nobody knows about it, so I have to observe a proper mourning period or I'll make a terrible impression on people."

"I think that's wise. As to the will, Cass, I

know a way we can get around Dad's stipulation. If you sign over everything to me, I can give you the money and house; I'll even pay the gift taxes on them. Simon can draw up the papers; we can meet in his office to go over them and sign them; then you can get on with your plans."

"Is that legal? I mean, revert it to you without me marrying?"

"Yep; that's one loophole Dad didn't think about and cover. Would you be satisfied with that amount and the house?"

"Of course, and you're welcome to the rest. What about you, Peter? Where will you relocate? How will you get that much cash?"

"I may sell the businesses except for the one in LA. The house there hasn't sold yet, so I could move into it. One company is plenty for me to run, and I like California. Maybe it's best if we both break free of the past. Just give me two weeks to get the money together and papers ready. Okay?"

She nodded. "I hope I haven't hurt you today, Peter. If it could be different between us, I would ... I'm sorry."

"I have a feeling we're both going to be fine, Cass, so don't worry."

"Thank you, Peter, for everything you've done for me."

"At least we'll part as good friends; that's worth something, right?"

"Yes, it is. I'm glad we had the chance to get

to know each other." *You'll learn what I mean after we settle up, you snake in the grass!*

"So am I, Cass. Now, let's change the subject to happy talk. What are your plans for tomorrow?"

"I'm going to Linda's church in the morning and spending the afternoon with her tomorrow. I would invite you to come along, but she might think I'm trying to initiate a romance between you two, and that wouldn't be wise."

"You're right. Well, have a good time."

"I will," she responded, knowing it was Jason she would be seeing.

Chapter Twenty

On Sunday morning, Cass and Jason arrived at church in separate vehicles; she preceded him by a few minutes. After he entered, he pretended to sight her and, following a casual greeting, asked if he could sit with her. She smiled and moved over on the pew. They chatted in whispers as if they were nothing more than old friends. When the service began, they shared a hymnal, then listened to the pastor's sermon.

Afterward, he spoke with friends and she, with new acquaintances. They got into their cars and drove to Jason's home where they concealed hers in his garage, changed into casual clothes, and went to a close-by marina.

Aboard his thirty-five-foot cabin cruiser, *J's Prescription*, they ate a picnic lunch which he had purchased along the way before heading down the Frederica River, through the St. Simons Sound, and into the Atlantic Ocean.

Jason chose a slow speed that would prevent a rough ride, heading his boat northeastward into the incoming wind. They traveled for a while without talking, only enjoying being together. Cass sat beside him and exchanged smiles with him every few minutes. A moderate breeze played through their hair, but they were shielded from the harsh rays of sun by a fiberglass canopy. They saw other recreational crafts and a few ships in the distance, but none came close to their position, as Jason intended.

"This is wonderful, Cass," he finally said. "A placid sea, a clear day, a warm sun, a pleasant breeze, refreshments below in the galley, and the woman I love beside me."

"It's perfect, Jason. I wonder how long we can continue to use Linda as our alibi for these little trysts before we're exposed."

"She's a good friend to us for providing one when needed. I'll have to thank her, and I'd like to see her find a special man to love and marry."

Cass didn't mention Linda's attraction to his son, but thought it would be amusing if her friend and nurse became her daughter-in-law. She also decided not to mention her talk with Peter yesterday until later, as she didn't want talk about Tom or his son to intrude on and spoil their serene afternoon together.

They were about five miles out to sea with the lush coastline and towering lighthouse on St. Simons Island still visible to the naked eye when Jason cut off the engine to allow them to drift while they relaxed and talked. As an experienced and knowledgeable sportsman, he knew the gentle wind and tide would very slowly push them back toward the shore in a few hours.

"Ahoy, mate, how about we head below for a refreshing drink?"

"Sounds good to me, Captain," she said and followed his lead.

"Watch your head on that hatch; she has a low beam."

In the mini-kitchen area, her gaze scanned the cabinets' contents. "This is a well-stocked galley, Captain. Do you entertain here often?"

Jason chuckled and glanced at her as he opened a bottle of wine. "Not the kind of entertaining you mean. I purchased this sleek beauty after my divorce. The only people who've been aboard are friends of mine, mostly fishermen. If you're interested in becoming my only crew member, I'll sign you up today."

"Where's the dotted line?" she quipped and laughed.

"Right here," he said, motioning to his lips.

She kissed him and jested, "Seaman Grantham reporting for duty."

"Duty, eh? In that case, I'll have to come up with a list of them."

"Just don't include scrubbing the deck; that would ruin my nails."

"Don't worry, mate, that's not how I want to use your time, energy, and talents. I'm sure I can put them to much better use with other chores. This wine isn't chilled, so I'll have to toss in a couple of ice cubes."

464

"That's fine with me."

He handed her a glass of Far Niente, a California white Chardonnay bottled in '93 in the Napa Valley. He tapped his glass to hers and toasted, "To our first voyage together and to the best mate a man could find."

Cass smiled again and said, "To the best captain in the world."

Instead of confining themselves in the eating booth, they stood in the middle of a rather spacious cabin. The windows were open on both sides, so a nice air current flowed through the area. The spring weather was balmy; the location was quiet except for the sounds of mild waves lapping against the hull, the cries of various sea birds, and ice clicking against their glasses as they drank. Their surroundings were romantic, secluded, and tranquil.

"This is a cozy cruiser, Jason. Do you ever spend the night aboard?"

"I haven't yet, but it would be fun with you. We could anchor near one of the smaller islands, perhaps Little St. Simons or Egg Island. We could cook in the galley or on the shore, swim, fish, and do whatever comes up," he said with a grin as he drifted his fingers over one of her shoulders, as both were bare in a strapless sundress. He leaned forward and trailed kisses from one shoulder joint to her collarbone.

As his mouth headed up her neck, Cass glanced past him to the bunk. Though the craft's swaying was mild, she replied, "With the way the boat is rocking, wouldn't we roll off that narrow bed and crash to the floor?"

Jason nibbled at her earlobe and murmured, "I don't know; I guess that's something we'll have to find out."

Cass quivered with desire and teased, "Ah, yes, you're the man who likes sharing adventures and solving mysteries."

He fused his blue gaze with her brown one. "That's me all right."

After he kissed her long and deep, he said, "I want to make love to you, Cass; I have since the moment I saw you this morning. How about we test your theory over there?" he suggested, nodding toward the bunk.

Consumed with suspense and anticipation, she told him, "I'm ready and willing. But what happens if we drift ashore while the captain's busy?"

"We won't; I know these waters. We'd be back on deck long before we could reach the shoreline."

"What if a friend spies *J's Prescription* and comes to visit?"

"Nobody will board this craft without permission, and we'll hear them coming. I'll even lock us in for privacy. Unless this makes you nervous."

"No, but keep your ears open anyway."

He stroked her cheek. "I can't make that promise, because when I'm with you, I go blind and deaf and lose my wits completely."

"I know what you mean, Doc; I seem to suffer from those same symptoms when I'm with you. Perhaps I need a skilled physician to examine me and give me proper treatment for them."

"I'm the perfect man for that job. These are registered healers."

Cass glanced at his hands as he held them up and yearned to have them touching her all over her body. "Are you finished with your drink?"

"Yep. I have another and better thirst to slake, one for you."

She took his glass and set both in the galley sink. As she did so, she noticed he locked the hatch. Then he met her near the inviting bunk.

Jason pulled Cass into his arms and kissed her. He relished the taste of her unrestrained response. She was the most exciting and alluring woman he had ever known. He couldn't seem to get enough of her in and out of bed. He adored the soft and warm feel of her skin. He loved her flavor and scent. His heart felt so full of emotion that he wondered if it could burst with joy. She was perfect for him.

Cass looped her arms around his neck and guided her fingers into his sun-lightened mane to draw his head closer. She loved his kisses. His strong and gentle hands stroked her arms and back, making her aware of every inch of her yearning body. Her tongue played with his at the same time his hands tugged down her elastic-topped dress, then cupped her breasts and kneaded her nipples. Heat and tingles raced over her flesh.

Jason separated his mouth from hers, bent down and took turns swirling his tongue around her taut nipples and sucking them into his mouth. He pleasured her in that manner for a few breathless minutes before his lips traveled slowly down her rib cage and navel, and across her flat stomach. As he advanced toward his target, his fingers eased her dress and panties lower and lower until Cass stepped out of the two items. He slid the garments beneath his knees to cushion them against the hard deck. He spread kisses over her hipbones and abdomen before his hands nudged her legs apart. He kissed and nibbled a path along her smooth inner thighs before his fingers invaded her thatch of brown hair and his questing mouth found its goal. He grasped her buttocks and pressed her body forward. His tongue flicked and swirled around her nub of delight. His lips suckled upon it, then he teethed it gently, aware of her growing arousal.

Cass trembled and moaned in ecstasy. She thrilled to the magic of his deft tongue and talented hands. She sighed in bliss as the peak hardened and pulsed under his masterful touch. There was a quickening in her stomach and a sweet tension building in her loins. "I'm going to melt into the floor," she murmured. "My knees are weak and my legs feel like jelly."

"Lie down, my love," he suggested, his hands

clasping her waist to draw her down to the bunk.

Cass obeyed his husky command and reclined on the soft surface. When he parted her thighs wider, she felt no shame, modesty, or inhibitions with this man she loved. He pleasured her in wild abandonment before his finger slipped within her; she moaned and thrashed as the sensations drove her wild. Soon, she could control herself no longer and was washed away in the powerful waves of passion. She writhed and cried out her rapture as she drew every drop of splendor from that new experience with him. "Surely I've died and gone to heaven."

Jason peeled off his garments in a hurry and joined her as he refuted, "Not yet, my ravishing mate, but I'll give it another try." He pulled her into his embrace where he kissed and fondled her to arouse her again.

Cass captured sleek strands of his tawny hair and twirled them around her fingers. She responded to his slow, seductive kisses and caresses. Within minutes, there was not a spot on her that did not burn or quiver with pleasure. She was nestled in his strong embrace as his hands wandered over her, then as his deft lips fastened to a breast and tantalized its nipple to pointed eagerness, she gasped in passionate longing. She wanted, needed, and loved this man with her heart and soul. She was amazed he could enflame her to such a high degree so soon after satisfying her.

Jason had reached a near feverish level himself. She was caressing his shoulders, arms, and back with light but stimulating gestures. He ached to bury himself inside of her, but he didn't want to rush. He wanted this to be the most gratifying and memorable lovemaking session she had ever known, as it was for him. His fingers stroked the shiny and thick waves of her brown hair as he brushed kisses over her face and throat. He loved feeling her naked flesh in contact with his.

Searing heat stormed Cass's body. She had to feel Jason inside her. She couldn't wait a moment longer. When Jason moved atop her, she wrapped her arms around his back and pulled him closer to entice him to enter her. Their lips tantalized and their tongues teased as he slid the tip of his erection into her, paused a moment to draw a deep and needed breath for renewed restraint, then thrust further past her delicate folds until it seemed he'd reached her very core.

Cass trailed her fingers over the flexible muscles of his back near his waist. She felt those in his lithe buttocks repeatedly contract with each passionate thrust. She clung to him, almost ravishing his mouth as she refused to allow him to withdraw for any length of time.

Jason wished their lovemaking could go on forever but he felt his restraint begin to slip at Cass's enthusiastic responses. When he felt her stiffen and heard her gasp for air, he knew she was in the early throes of sweet release. He let himself join her in a burst of supreme pleasure.

As they each came back to earth, they cuddled quietly, enjoying the aftermath of their loving.

Finally, Jason looked over at her and grinned. "I want to thank you for never showing me any mercy, woman. It gets better every time."

"You're right, as impossible as that seems. I love you, Jason."

"I love you, Cass. I thank God we met last October, or we might not be together today. We could both still be alone and miserable if you hadn't come to that play."

"I really believe in destiny and fate; and we were destined for each other. In a strange way, we shouldn't curse our mistakes because they got us to meet. If I hadn't married Tom, I wouldn't be living on Sea Island; and if you hadn't married and divorced Brenda, you wouldn't have been single and alone that night at the Ritz Theater."

Jason pondered her words, then said, "You're right. It's as if we were being led through a dark maze to find each other at the sunny end."

"Oh, Jason, it feels wonderful to be happy again." *To feel whole and clean again.* She sighed peacefully and stroked his bare chest.

"I can hardly wait until you agree to marry me, woman. Maybe that will be sooner than you think with Inez's help."

Cass propped up and asked, "What do you mean by that?"

Jason told her about his talk with her ex-housekeeper yesterday.

As he made his shocking revelation, Cass bolted up on the bed. "Surely you didn't! Please tell me you're teasing."

"What's wrong, love? Maybe she's the ace we need up our sleeve to force Peter to settle with you so we won't have to wait so long to marry."

"It could ruin everything, Jason. I made a deal with Peter last night for a pay-off." She related their conversation to him. "If Inez tells him about our suspicions, he could renege on it. Then we're right back where we started, either losing a fortune or waiting for Tom's timetable to be met."

"She won't tell him, Cass; she's afraid of him, and I think she was tempted by my offer. I honestly expect her to call me and accept it."

"You don't know Inez like I do; she fears nothing and no one. And you're forgetting how much she detests me; she'd like nothing better than to spite me. I wouldn't put it past her to try to blackmail Peter for more than you offered her now that she realizes how valuable his secrets are."

"I'm sorry, love. I never dreamed you and Peter would make a bargain this quickly. I thought I was being helpful. I hoped it would

472

be a nice surprise, but I can see I shouldn't have interfered."

"It's a done deed, so don't worry about it. If any repercussions arise, we'll find a way to deal with them. Who knows? Your little ploy may work in our favor if you truly put the fear of God, or rather the law, into her. Even if she tells Peter, that doesn't alter the fact he wants me out of his picture. I can always pretend I didn't know about your suspicions and intention and I believe he's innocent of any wrongdoing. Besides, the moment after we settled, I was going to tell him I knew what he did to me."

Jason sat up and caressed her cheek. "Then you aren't mad at me?"

She smiled. "Of course not. You were only trying to help me."

"For selfish reasons. I want you free of Peter and Tom and the past."

"I know, and so do I. Everything will work out soon; you'll see. After it does, we will 'begin' a romance."

"I have an idea about how we can explain us getting close so fast."

Cass noted his broad grin and sparkling eyes. "What is it?"

"My receptionist is going on leave next week to have surgery Friday; she'll be out for a month or two. How would you like to fill in for her? By working together, we'll have a good excuse for becoming close friends; then we can start dating openly. That'll also give you a chance to meet people, many of them my close friends, and get you out of that house during the day. I promise I'll be an easy and good-paying boss. All you'll have to do is greet patients, answer the phone, and make appointments."

"You're a sly man, Jason Burkman. It's perfect. Who could possibly fault a lonely widow for falling for her charismatic boss?"

"Or fault a lonely physician for succumbing to the many charms and great beauty of his temporary receptionist. Excellent idea I had. We'll discuss it tomorrow during your check-up with me."

"Is it going to be a complete examination?" she asked with a grin.

"As complete as I dare make it in my office. So, Peter made a play for you, did he? Perhaps I should go over and beat the daylights out of him."

"You know you have no reason to be jealous. And we both know he wasn't serious. I think I'll accept your job offer so I can keep my eye on you and all of those pretty nurses."

"I promise you, Cass, you're the only woman who catches my eye."

"And you're the only man who catches mine."

On Monday while Mary Ellis was cleaning her house, Cass kept her appointment with

Jason, who examined her in a professional manner with one of his three nurses present. After she was fully clad and they were left alone in one of the many rooms to discuss her health following her checkup, they stole several kisses and embraces.

While she was at his office, Cass met his receptionist who would begin training her on Thursday. She liked Jason's staff and knew she was going to enjoy the job.

Late Tuesday afternoon, Jason received a surprising call from Inez Doughtery, who requested a meeting with the doctor after he finished with his patients. As she had told him to bring his offer with him in cash, it was not hard to deduce the reason for her request.

He phoned his bank and gave instructions to have a cashier's check for fifty thousand dollars ready for him to pick up at five o'clock and to deduct it from his savings account.

Afterward, Jason leaned back in his chair and smiled. *You're going to pay through the nose for what you did to Cass and me, you sorry bastard, and you'll be delighted to do so. So will Hines if Inez has the proof she claims to have against you two.*

Jason got up to return to work. He needed to hurry so he could get to his bank between patients. It was only a few miles away, so that errand wouldn't take long. He could hardly wait until six-thirty to meet with Inez and discover the truth — actually, buy it.

You'll be free of that sonofabitch soon, my love; we both will.

At ten after seven that evening, Peter spoke with Cass in her den. "Our deal is in progress, if you haven't changed your mind."

"Of course I haven't. Why should I when you're being so generous and kind to help me make a new start without having to wait for years?"

"It's the least I can do for you, Cass. The papers should be ready for you to sign within a week, two at most. Simon is preparing them now. He wants to make sure he covers all of his bases so the law can't find any loopholes. As I told you, I'll be paying the gift taxes on the settlement I make with you. You'll get a cashier's check for five million dollars and clear title to this house and its furnishings. Is there anything I've forgotten to include that you feel you're entitled to?"

Cass pretended to think for a minute, then shook her head.

"You do understand you'll be relinquishing your claim to everything you've inherited: the entire trust fund and all of your company stocks?" He waited for her to nod. "You also understand you won't receive any future dividends of any kind or any profits from eventual company sales?" He paused again for her to nod comprehension. "Do you have any ques-

476

tions or reservations about this deal between us?"

"No, it sounds clear and simple to me."

"Good, but Simon will go over the terms again in his office before we sign our agreement. If you have a problem with it, let me know now."

"The settlement you offered sounds fair to me, Peter. I just want this matter taken care of as soon as possible so I can get on with my life. Are you sure you can come up with that much cash by next week?" *Please don't take longer so I can tell you what I really think of you, you treacherous snake!*

Peter lazed against the sofa and grinned. "Yep, because I have buyers lined up for Smooth Rider, Texas-G Beef, the ranch, Big G Real Estate, and the restaurant and art gallery in Aspen. Those contracts are being drawn up as we speak. As soon as those deals are settled, I'm putting the electronics and seafood companies on the market. I've decided to keep the import/export company and house in LA; I'll be going there tomorrow to get things set up for my relocation, but I'll return home Saturday. So, when you decide to sell out here, I won't be living in your backyard."

And I won't miss you for an instant! "My goodness, Peter, you work fast when your mind is made up."

"There's no need to hesitate, and this move will be good for me. So will dumping Smooth

Rider. Club Car just received an award as the Exporter of the Year with forty-six million dollars in foreign sales; that's stiff competition for golf carts. Besides, my import/export company will involve plenty of international travel; that sounds exciting and satisfying, just the challenge and diversion I need." *Yep, I gotta get my ass out there and make sure the authorities don't catch on to what I'm importing and exporting for big bucks.*

"You're lucky our companies are in such good shape and you found buyers so quickly." *So am I.*

"Yep, that was the winning stroke. You do understand, even if we didn't have a deal, you couldn't profit from those sales for five to ten years because the money would go into that trust fund to be doled out slowly?"

"I know, and I don't resent you for getting it. The majority of the estate is rightfully yours. Just be on alert for female piranhas who'll come swimming after a super rich, sexy, and handsome bachelor."

Peter chuckled. "Thanks for the compliments, and I'll be sure to be careful. I would offer you more money, Cass, but our settlement has to come out of my pocket, not the companies' holdings; that wouldn't be legal. Besides, Uncle Sam is going to take a huge bite out of those gains."

"Perhaps Harrison Dredger can find tax loopholes for you. Isn't that what an expensive accountant is supposed to do for his clients?" she jested, trying to dupe Peter with her playful mood.

"Why, Cassandra Grantham, I do believe you have a wicked streak."

"At certain times in our lives, don't we all have one?"

"I suppose so, or the human sharks would eat us alive."

Cass leaned forward, sent him a mischievous grin, and asked, "What's the worst — or should I say, cleverest? — trick you've pulled?"

"Hmm, let me think for a minute. . . ." Peter glanced at his watch, leapt from his seat, and said, "Damn, I'm almost late for dinner with friends! You'll have to excuse my rush, Cass, but I gotta run."

"Coward! That's a sneaky way to avoid answering," she teased him. She wished he would leave fast so she could relax her guard.

As his hazel gaze swept over her and a curious desire for her plagued him, he wondered if it had been a mistake not to pursue her for himself.

Cass followed him to the back door. "Good night, Peter, and have a nice time tonight with your friends."

"Thanks, Cass. I'm flying out early, so I won't see you again until this weekend. Take care of yourself while I'm gone."

"I will, and have a safe and successful trip. 'Bye." She almost cringed when he gave her a light kiss on the lips before departing. Despite her loathing, she smiled and waved to him when he glanced back at the wrought-iron gate and did the same to her.

Wednesday morning in Brunswick, Jason sat at his office desk and sipped a cup of coffee after he planned his talk with David Hines that evening. He had phoned David after seeing Inez and insisted they meet to discuss what he had learned, dropping clear hints to the nervous man about the topic in store for them. While he waited for his first patient to be prepared for an examination, he picked up the morning paper which he didn't have time to read at home and received a jolting shock.

On Sea Island, Cassandra Redfern Grantham was staring at the same news article, her gaze wide and her lips parted in astonishment.

Chapter Twenty-One

Jason buzzed his nurse and told her he had to make an important call and he would join his patient as soon as he completed it. He phoned Cass and asked if she'd seen this morning's paper.

"I'm reading it now. My heavens, Jason, I can't believe he did it. This is horrible; his family must be terribly upset."

"Yes, I'm sure they are. I'll be over as soon as I finish work so we can discuss this matter. We don't want to say anything over the phone in case somebody we know is bugging yours; I wouldn't put it past him. Just stay calm and I'll see you about six."

"I will, and I'll cook supper for us, something quick and simple. By the way, Peter's out of town until the weekend. He flew out early this morning, so I doubt he knows about this tragedy."

After embracing and kissing Cass, Jason said, "Let's sit in the den and go over this before we have supper; we don't want our stomachs tied up in knots while we're eating."

They went into the other room and sat side

481

by side on the sofa before Jason started the conversation. "I was supposed to be seeing Hines right now. I phoned him early last night and arranged a meeting. I —"

"Why were you going to meet with him?"

"To talk about what he and Peter did to you. I —"

"I thought we agreed on Sunday that you wouldn't take any further action on your suspicions until I settled with Peter."

"After I saw Inez again, I had to make sure —"

"You spoke with her again? When? Why? I'm surprised and dismayed by your actions, Jason."

Jason held her hand and urged in a tender tone, "Give me time to explain, and you'll understand and agree. Inez called me at my office yesterday afternoon and wanted to see me after work, with the money." As Cass stared at him, he said, "That's right; she accepted my deal. You were right about her trying to get more money out of Peter than I was offering her, but her little scheme backfired. Fortunately for us, he provoked her to the point of revenge." Jason related what Inez had told him about her talk with Peter.

"You mean she just came right out and admitted trying to blackmail him and told you everything about their misdeeds?"

"Yep, and even gave me proof she was being honest. By now, she's probably cashed that check and vanished forever to protect herself from Peter and the law. I hated to let her get off the hook scot-free, but I had no choice since we were after bigger fish to fry."

"I'm curious as to what 'proof' she gave you."

"Inez had two of those mystery pills I told you about and one of those doctored aspirin capsules. At first, she thought she was only giving you medicine prescribed by Hines when she sneaked it into your food or drink. Peter convinced her you needed medicine but wouldn't take it willingly. Later, she suspected the truth but kept helping Peter because of the big salary increase he gave her, and because she was certain you would fire her as soon as you were well and your head cleared. Hines supplied the drug samples Peter used before he took over your treatment and kept you in a daze. Before Hines removed those extra drugs, Inez took one of each, and she kept one of the aspirin capsules Peter had prepared and was giving to you — or you were taking — without knowing they were tainted. That explains what happened to you, Cass, just as I suspected."

Jason reminded her of how he had stolen two of the pills but lost them before he could analyze them. "Without them, my hands were tied. I couldn't make accusations against Peter and Hines without proof. And I hated to worry you with charges I couldn't prove. That's why I insisted on becoming your doctor and why I brought Linda in to help me protect you. I knew there was no way they could continue to sneak drugs into your system without your symptoms alerting me to a problem; they realized it, too, and stopped doing so."

"I hate to think what would have happened to me if not for you, Jason. Thank you for caring about me so much. I love you."

He gave her a quick hug and kiss. "I love you, too, woman, and I had to protect my interests." He hurried on with their talk before they could become distracted by rising desires. "Inez also told me that Peter had your mail forwarded to a post office box in his name for a while so he would get all of the correspondence first. He had your phone line switched to his place so all calls would either go to him or to his answering machine; that way he could screen them. Later, he had the mail and phone line changed back to your address before your head cleared and you caught on to him. That's why nobody could reach you, Cass; he had you cut off from the world and thinking no one cared about you, when a lot of people did care."

Cass smiled inwardly, relieved to make that discovery.

"I wanted to see Hines to tell him I'd be watching him like a hawk to make sure he didn't do something like this to another innocent patient—"

"I'm sure you wanted to bring him up on charges," Cass interrupted gently, "but were reluctant to do so because that would have involved me in a scandal. Even so, Jason, we both know we couldn't have allowed Hines to go unexposed and risk him doing that to somebody else in the future."

"I was torn between doing what was right and protecting you, Cass, but Hines took that difficult decision out of our hands. The same dilemma applies to pressing charges against Peter, even with the evidence we've gathered. Other than taking his precious money, I don't know how we can punish him since we don't want to go to the police with the truth. Peter has powerful contacts and lots of money for mounting a strong defense. With Inez and Hines gone, we have no witnesses to corroborate our accusations, so it would be our word against his. Considering our romantic relationship, I don't know how much weight ours would carry. I have no doubt he would drag us through the courts and hell with a lengthy trial, and countless appeals if he lost. The media would have a field day with the story."

"And I'm sure Mutt & Jeff would like nothing better than getting another chance to dig into my private life and to harass me; I don't want the truth about Tom and our marital troubles to be exposed. I'm sorry Doctor Hines felt he had to take his life, but at least he can't harm any more patients."

"I got a special delivery letter from Hines today. He wrote and mailed it before he took his life late last night. The timing was such that the news of his suicide was included with this morning's article which was originally intended to reveal only his closet homosexuality. He said the news was already leaking out by yesterday and patients were canceling on him right and left and he was receiving vulgar calls from people who wouldn't identify themselves. He knew what was coming today because the reporter doing the exposé called him for a rebuttal, which he refused to give. He said he couldn't endure being raked over the media's hot coals."

"I suppose he panicked," Cass deduced, "because he could have relocated after the news hit."

"Yes, but his family and friends would know about his dark secret, and he couldn't bear the thought of their scorn and rejection. He knew what I wanted with him, and he suspected Peter was the source of the news leak — though I doubt that's true — so he gave me the facts about what Peter did to you out of revenge and hatred toward him. That would have been a marvelous piece of evidence, except he typed the letter and didn't sign it, so we might not be able to prove he wrote it or that was the paper inside the special delivery envelope."

Jason released her hand, took a swallow of cola, then explained, "Hines helped Peter because of blackmail; he knew about Hines's secret life and threatened to expose it. Of course, when we confront Peter, we don't have to tell him the letter wasn't handwritten or signed. We finally know the truth, my love, but the only way we can use the evidence I gathered from Hines and Inez is to force Peter to settle with you so we can get married sooner."

"He already has, Jason. I mean, our deal is settled and the papers are being drawn up by Simon Johnson." She related her talk with Peter last night.

"Will you be satisfied with the amount he's offered after all he's done to you?" he asked.

"I just want this obstacle removed. I wouldn't dare be so foolish as to try to blackmail him for more. Besides, I would feel like a criminal if I tried to pull a stunt like that. After everything is settled, I'll let Peter know I'm not dense or a naive fool. I also believe that people like him eventually get what they deserve; somewhere along the line, he'll make a mistake and he'll be called upon to pay for it. I won't dirty my hands by trying to be his jury, judge, and executioner; I'll leave those jobs up to fate."

"I'm glad you aren't a vindictive person, Cass; that speaks highly of you."

She snuggled into his arms and hugged him. "The same is true for you, Jason, or you would have found a way to spite Peter long ago."

"Hatred and revenge take a lot of energy and animosity, my love, and I don't want my life and thoughts filled and controlled by ugly emotions."

"Neither do I. As the saying goes: 'Let's take the money and run'."

"You're so wonderful and tempting, woman, that the only place I want to run is upstairs with you, unless it's straight to the marriage altar."

"We'll act on your first suggestion after supper, Doc, because I'm starved. I confess I skipped lunch, but don't scold me. As for your second suggestion, we should have that matter taken care of by Christmas."

Following an erotic shower where they lathered each other from neck to feet, Cass and Jason almost leapt into her new bed and upon her new linens to continue what they had started in the bathroom.

Jason's arms slipped with gentle purpose around Cass. He nestled his cheek against her dark hair and relished the feel of her naked body against his. They cuddled, caressed, and kissed each other, treasuring every moment of their loving.

Just as he was about to enter her, Jason leaned back his head and gazed into Cass's glowing eyes, so full of love and desire for him, and trust in him.

"I love you, Cass, and I'm the luckiest man in the world to have you."

Cass smiled and said, "And I'm the luckiest woman in the world to have you." She pressed kisses to his nose, cheeks, and chin as he rolled them over to place her atop him. His strong hands grasped her hips and he partially lifted her so he could join their bodies. She gazed into his yearning blue eyes and handsome face before he rested his head on her chest as he held her in place and slid inside her. She clung to him and rode him wildly.

Jason could barely retain his control. As Cass rocked upon his lap, he suckled at her breasts, his muscles rippling as he strove onward and upward in his thrilling quest to sate them both. When the moment approached, he held her close. After her release came and her tension subsided, he ceased his thrusts and surrendered to his own climax.

Afterward, they kissed and embraced tenderly, gazing into each other's eyes and murmuring vows of love, satisfaction, and commitment.

On Thursday morning after giving Mary Ellis instructions to lock up the house upon her departure at five o'clock, Cass drove to Jason's office to begin a five-day training period by his receptionist.

Upon arrival at the large and lovely office in Brunswick, Cass was reintroduced to the three nurses, receptionist, and bookkeeper/secretary: a staff of five friendly and efficient ladies whose ages ranged from mid-thirties to early fifties, all married with children.

Cass listened, observed, and took notes as

the genial woman gave her instructions which she would practice next Monday through Wednesday. The position entailed greeting patients, dealing with salesmen, answering the multi-line phone, making appointments, and writing reminder cards or phoning patients about their impending visits.

Since Jason's practice was full, he only accepted new patients upon referral from the hospital or from other physicians as a professional courtesy.

She was told that besides working with patients, the two younger nurses pulled and filed daily charts. The older one also held the position of office manager, which included handling medical supplies, making sure specimens and samples got to the proper outside laboratories for tests, making sure those results were returned and recorded on patients' charts, dealing with any problem, and unlocking and locking file cabinets upon entry and departure to protect patient confidentiality. The secretary/bookkeeper took care of incoming and outgoing mail, typed letters, filled out insurance and Medicare claims, recorded payments, made bank deposits, did the staff payroll, and ordered supplies required for her responsibilities.

Their workday began at eight-thirty with preparations to open the office at nine o'clock. They closed for an hour at twelve-thirty so everyone could eat at the same time, with an answering service taking over. Four days of the week, the women brought their lunches and ate them while relaxing and chatting in the break room. On Fridays, they splurged on a meal at a different restaurant each week. Though today was Thursday, they were treating Cass to lunch at the Royal Cafe in town. They finished their day between five-thirty and six o'clock so everyone could have quality time with their families, which was one of the many reasons why Jason was so well liked and respected and why the women were longtime employees of his.

After they reached her house that evening and she was unlocking the door, Cass grinned and said, "Considering how many unattached female patients you have, it's smart of you to keep a nurse around when you have to work late with one of them. I've heard that some women will go to any lengths to ensnare a handsome and virile man like you are."

"Thanks for the compliment, and I'm always careful in that area. I've never had a problem in the past, and I don't want one to crop up in the future. It's just that some people are sue-crazy these days, trying to make money any way they can. Rest assured, I would be innocent of any charges filed against me for improper behavior with a female patient. Excluding you, of course," he added. "I'm absolutely guilty of pursuing you."

"Rest assured," she began, paused playfully,

and laughed, "I would never bring charges against you for openly doing what I was doing covertly."

As they entered the kitchen, Jason sniffed the air and asked, "What's that delicious smell? Did Mary sneak and prepare supper for us?"

"No, I did. I put pork chops in the crockpot this morning. I tossed a whole lot of spices and such into the pot and let it simmer for six to eight hours. It makes them tender and scrumptious. With Inez doing the meal planning, shopping, and cooking in the past, I had forgotten what a good cook I am. Mother was the best and she taught me her secrets before I left home."

"This is a wonderful surprise. Watch out, woman, or you'll spoil me and I'll have you slaving in the kitchen every night."

"As long as you're slaving beside me and we take an occasional break, I won't mind."

Jason nuzzled her neck as he murmured, "I promise to give you plenty of breaks before, during, and after kitchen duty."

Though she also quivered with rising desire, she teased, "You have a one-track mind, Jason Burkman; I was referring to a break from kitchen duty."

Amidst chuckles and nibbles on her neck and earlobe, he admitted, "I know, but a man can try, can't he?"

With her palms flattened against his chest, she leaned back and fused their gazes. "In the last seven days, we've made love three times, four counting tonight, if you have any energy left after a hard day at work."

"Rest assured," he began, paused as she had, and chuckled. "I'll never be too tired or distracted for you, my love. Soon, Peter will be gone for good and we'll have total privacy to do as we please, when we please."

"That sounds fantastic, doesn't it?"

"Without a doubt," he said, then embraced and kissed her.

After their lips parted, Cass suggested, "Why don't we eat now so our stomachs can settle while we clean up the kitchen. Let's get moving in here. Why don't you take off your coat and tie and roll up your sleeves and set the table with those dishes over there. I already have broccoli, carrots, and cauliflower cut up in a Baggie in the refrigerator, so all I have to do is toss them into the microwave steamer. While the veggies are being zapped, I'll run upstairs and get out of my 'business' clothes. I'll heat the rolls and prepare our drinks after I return. I even made you iced tea."

As Jason watched her leave the kitchen, he smiled to himself as he thought about how fortunate and blessed he was to have met and won Cass as his future wife. Everything, he presumed in an elated and confident state, was coming together nicely for them. Only Peter, he worried, could find a way to mess up things for them. They seemed to have enough facts and evidence to tie him over a nail-riddled barrel if necessary; but Peter Grantham, Jason knew, could be devious, unpredictable, and perhaps dangerous when challenged.

After Cass returned and meal preparations were completed, they sat down to eat and chat as if they already were a married couple. They talked about her day at the office, and she told him how much she enjoyed it and liked his staff. They spoke about Jason's imminent trip to Augusta on Saturday to visit with Stacey. They decided he would go alone and relate news about the woman he was dating, as it seemed unwise to spring their serious relationship on his son. They also didn't want to upset the apple cart with Peter at this fragile stage in her negotiations with him, since he was returning that day and might not react well to her outing with Jason and his family after she had told him they were only casual friends.

After the meal was over and the kitchen cleaned, Cass and Jason went to her bedroom to enjoy almost two hours of glorious lovemaking before he left for home, as they both needed a good night's sleep.

Friday morning before Kristy left for school and Cass for the office, Cass phoned her old friend. She told a disappointed but understanding Kristy all that had transpired in her life since their last conversation and the reason for the delay in their visit to Augusta. As quickly as possible, Cass told Kristy about Brad's recent visit. Her old friend and ex-sister-in law was dismayed by her brother's actions. Since both had to get to work soon, they couldn't talk long, but both promised that they would speak again and longer in a few days.

Afterward, Cass enjoyed herself at the office and lunch with Jason's staff. Then, she finished the day having supper and splendid lovemaking with him.

On Saturday, May fourth, while Jason was in Augusta with his son, the disgraced physician Doctor David Henry Hines was buried after a small and gloomy funeral service in Brunswick.

At home, Cass talked with Linda Carnes on the phone and learned the nurse had finished her current assignment on Jekyll Island today and would be home later that night. After Linda said she would see her and Jason at church tomorrow before she had to wash clothes and repack them to head to the small and nearby town of Waverly for a lengthy stay with an elderly bedridden patient, Cass invited her to have lunch with them after church. During their conversation, Cass related the same news to Linda she had told to Kristy yesterday.

Linda was delighted to learn Cass was doing so well and was working for Jason and romancing him on the sly.

Cass told her where Jason was and why she hadn't gone along. "Who knows? After I worm my way into Stacey's life and affections, maybe I can help you do the same."

"That would suit me just fine, Cass, and the sooner the better. I'm not getting any younger."

"Neither am I. It seems as if our maternal clocks are ticking loudly. At least you don't have the drawback of being a recent widow, though I'm doing the best I can with the hand fate dealt to me." Cass laughed and jested, "Oh, my, doesn't that sound poetic and dramatic? Speaking of dramas, did you hear the news about David Hines?"

"Yes, and despite the fact I didn't like him, I feel sorry for his family; I even feel sorry for him. People surely can make some terrible mistakes."

"Yes, they can, and none of us are immune to that disease."

They talked about Dr. Hines and other topics for a while before they hung up, both looking forward to their visit tomorrow.

Peter arrived home later that afternoon and came to see Cass within minutes after he drove into the garage beneath the guest house.

Cass greeted him with a smile and cheerful hello, but she dreaded spending any time with him. Before he could tell her about his trip, she revealed the sad news about Dr. Hines.

Peter stared at her, shocked speechless at

first, then forced to struggle not to yell his delight at having that threat removed, just as Inez's was. After deliberating the matter, he had phoned the ex-housekeeper to offer her a settlement to keep silent and leave the state, but discovered the woman had already moved, which he considered good riddance. He deduced he had frightened her so badly during their last talk that she took off for places unknown. With Inez and Hines gone, he was sure he was sitting pretty. "That's a shame, Cass, but I guess David's better off where he is, considering the scandal which would have engulfed and destroyed him. So, what have you been up to while I was gone?"

Dropped that subject fast, didn't you? But I saw how it affected you: astonishment, then relief. "I got a job; I'm a working woman now." She noted that she surprised him again.

"A job?"

She saw him look even more surprised for a few moments after she told him all the details before he could conceal his reaction. "It's perfect for furthering my plans, Peter. I'm meeting nice people who might become prospective clientele at the business I've pretty much decided to start. It's getting me accustomed to dealing with the public and taking me out of this somber house for a while. At last, I'm doing something constructive and enjoyable with my time and energy. As I told you, it's only for one or two months. Then I'm selling this place, moving to St. Simons, and opening my boutique."

"That sounds wonderful, Cass, and I'm happy for you. I suppose Jason is thrilled to have you around him almost every day? Have you changed your mind about trusting him and dating him?" *Maybe I'm giving up five million dollars and this valuable property too fast and too easy.*

Careful, Cass, he's baiting you with a clever hook. "He's thrilled to have a good replacement for his receptionist, but I don't think it would look right to date my boss and certainly not this soon after Tom's death. We seem to be getting along all right; he's acting as friendly as can be, but totally professionally. In fact, he doesn't mention you or the past at all; nor does he flirt with me. We also see each other at church, but that's it. Speaking of church, I'm meeting Linda there in the morning and afterward we're having lunch and going boating with friends of hers."

"You two have become close friends, haven't you?"

"Yes, she's a likable person, and we're very compatible."

"That's good to hear. Well, I'm exhausted, so I'll see you Monday night. By then I should have some good news for you."

"I can hardly wait, Peter."

As she watched him walk away, she realized he hadn't given her a report on his trip to Los

Angeles. *Please, please, don't change your mind about moving there, and don't you dare challenge me over my just due!*

On Sunday, Cass and Jason met Linda at church and they sat together during the service. Afterward, they had lunch before Linda had to go home to prepare to leave for her new job.

Cass and Jason went to his house to spend a quiet afternoon relaxing and talking. After he told her about his visit with Stacey in Augusta yesterday, he suggested they go for a swim in his lanai pool.

"You didn't tell me to bring a swimsuit."

"I can solve that problem: Traci keeps several in her room, so borrow one of them. You two look to be about the same size."

Cass followed him upstairs and selected one of his daughter's suits, a tad reluctant to wear the item without Traci's permission. She walked into his bedroom and asked, "How's this one?"

"It should look wonderful on you, woman, because everything you wear does. You can change in the bathroom if you like."

"Why? You've seen and touched every inch of me," she quipped, feeling relaxed and safe in his presence.

After Jason and Cass shucked their clothes and shoes, he hung his on a valet stand to put away later, and she laid hers on a chair. She returned to the bed where she had tossed the turquoise swimsuit and collected it.

Jason looked at her shapely body and said, "Actually, your birthday suit is the most flattering one you could choose."

"Is that right, Doc?" she teased, noting how he stood with his blue trunks in his hand ready to don them. Instead, he tossed them aside.

"It's fun to glide through the pool with nothing touching your skin but silky water," he said in a husky tone as his palms massaged her nipples.

Cass let her adoring gaze rove him from tawny head to bare feet. Her fingertips lightly and lovingly brushed over his tanned face with its expression of fervent longing for her. She inhaled his manly scent and stroked the raised muscles on his chest and arms. She moved her hands over his shoulders. "Sounds wonderful, Doc."

"Careful, you enchanting siren, or we won't make it to the pool."

As her fingers began to travel down his torso, she smiled and purred, "Oh, I think we'll make it there, but after a short delay in our schedule. Now that you've lured me up here and got me naked, Doc, what are you going to do about it," she teased as her hand captured and stroked his erection.

Chapter Twenty-Two

"Well, my lovely patient, if you'll lie down, I'll give you a thorough examination."

"I certainly won't refuse the offer of a free check-up by the world's best physician," she murmured as she fell upon his bed.

Jason joined her and let his hands, lips, and tongue roam freely across her body, enjoying her eager responses. Her long, thick hair was spread around her head and shoulders like a brown halo and his fingers toyed in those lustrous locks. He savored the silky texture of her bare skin, creamy throat, and taut breasts. His playful tongue darted around her nipples. Then he tasted her lips in a series of tender and slow kisses that grew increasingly ardent as his hands roamed her flesh. He felt her tremble and he knew this bond between them was meant to be.

She clasped his handsome face between her hands and tried to convey all her emotions in a deep and loving kiss. Then she leaned back her head when his lips left hers to roam her throat and trail kisses over the pulse point there, which was throbbing from the excitement racing through her veins.

Jason was exhilarated by the way her body responded to his every caress. As his lips moved down to tantalize her breasts, he let one hand trail down the soft flesh of her abdomen until he reached the core of her desire.

Cass opened herself completely to his actions. She wanted. She needed. Aching to join with him completely, she begged him to enter her.

She grasped his arm and steered him atop her. She urged him to penetrate her with forceful, brisk, deep thrusts.

Jason moved over her and, with one swift thrust, made her his once more. Cass made a welcoming sound deep in her throat and pulled him even closer. This was what she'd been yearning for — this moment of joining, of loving.

Afterward, after all the heated passion and sweet satisfaction, they lay nestled together, knowing they had found and shared the perfect harmony of which they had always dreamed.

After they swam naked for an hour, Jason suggested they relax their tensed muscles in the hot tub nearby. After they left the pool, they drank some refreshing juice before he turned on the jets and they stepped into the bubbling water that reached their collarbones and swirled around their bodies. They sat side by side with her wet head leaning backward and resting on his outspread arm near his shoulder joint. The dancing liquid felt silky and sensuous on bare flesh; and, despite their nudity, neither felt modest nor restrained.

They closed their eyes, mellowing in the serene and cozy ambiance of the lanai, with its silk plants and white wicker furniture.

Cass took a deep breath and exhaled as she gave a dreamy sigh. "This is sheer heaven. I'm so relaxed and calm I just might melt away. You couldn't give me a better prescription, Doc."

After Jason dropped several kisses on her drying hair and temple, he said, "Well, I did promise to take good care of my favorite patient."

Cass shifted her head and gazed at him. "And you've more than kept it. How shall I ever repay you for all you've done for me?"

Jason's instant reply came from his heart, "By marrying me as soon as possible and promising we'll spend the rest of our lives together."

"You couldn't have made an easier and more appealing request."

He grinned and asked, "Is that a clever way of saying yes? Wait a minute before you answer and let me make this official. Cassandra Redfern Grantham, will you marry me in the near future?"

Cass shifted her position so she could give him a kiss after she told him without a single reservation, "Yes, yes, yes."

And then, as the heated water swirled around them, they made slow, tender, gentle love. To Cass it seemed that every caress, every kiss was a promise made between them . . . to be happy together, to be good to each other, to build a future full of joy and passion that would stand the test of time.

In the golden aftermath of their lovemaking, they lay snuggled on their sides on the hard bench and soft towels, her fingers stroking his still-damp chest, and his drifting up and down her back.

"I love you, Cass," he murmured against her forehead.

"I love you, Jason," she responded.

A few minutes later, he said, "Can I ask you a serious question?"

She looked up into his blue gaze. "Of course, anything."

"I think we should settle one matter before we get married so there won't be any misunderstandings or false hopes. How do you feel about having a child?"

"Do you want another one or are you satisfied with the two you have?" Cass held her breath waiting for his answer.

"I love my son and daughter and grandsons, and some people might think we're too old to have a baby, but I'd like for us to try. Do you agree?"

With joy-misted eyes, Cass smiled, nodded,

and hugged him. "I do care about your children's feelings. What do you think those will be?"

"I can guarantee they'll love and respect and accept you, Cass. I know I'm biased, but they're good children. They were glad Brenda and I didn't have a family because they knew she wasn't right for me, though they never gave me a hard time about her. Brenda didn't want kids, because they would have intruded on her secret life. As for Joan, she was a good woman, good wife, and good mother. I loved her, but not in the same way I love you. With you, it's as if we're soul mates."

"I feel the same way about you. In all honesty, Jason, I've never loved, wanted, or needed any man the way I do you."

"I'm a lucky and blessed man."

"And I'm a lucky and blessed woman."

"You probably heard that it's sometimes difficult being married to a doctor; but in my case, it won't be bad since I have so few emergencies during the night and on weekends. I suppose that's the advantage of being a general practitioner."

"I had noticed it's rare for your beeper to go off."

"After I retire in a few years, that won't ever happen. You'll be stuck with me all night and for most of the day. Tell me, do you have any desire to work outside our home after we're married?"

"Our home . . . doesn't that have a lovely sound?"

"Yep, it surely does. So, what are your feelings on that subject?"

"I would like to do occasional volunteer work with certain charities and be involved in certain organizations; that would make me feel more useful, help me meet people, and keep my mind and body in shape. I also wouldn't mind filling in at your office if or when you need help; I really like your staff. But for the most part, I plan to be very busy with my husband and our child and home."

"That plan sounds perfect to me. Speaking of homes, where do you want to live? One of our places, or sell both and move to a new house?"

"I don't want to stay where I am. In fact, I'd like to sell it as soon as I have clear title to it; then, find a smaller place, perhaps a condo, on St. Simons Island. If I rent instead of buying, it will make moving easier in a few months. I love this house and would like to live here. It's big enough for us and the baby; and it's convenient for your work."

"It suits me perfectly because all of the memories I've made here are good ones. In fact, you're the only woman I've entertained here." Jason glanced outside and said, "It's getting late, so we should dress and eat. We both have a busy day tomorrow. Now, up, woman of my heart, time to clad these bodies and feed our tummies before I send you home before dark."

As they gathered their things and went inside to dress, Cass was dreading going back to the house she had shared with Tom and possibly running into Peter and facing his questions to her about her day out with Linda and her friends. She felt too happy to have to go on guard and carry off a strenuous pretense. She would be ecstatic when Peter Grantham was no longer a part of her life and thoughts.

On Monday, Cass went to Jason's office to practice what she had learned from his receptionist last week; Mary Ellis cleaned her house from eight to five; Linda Carnes left for her assignment in Waverly; and a five thousand dollar "allowance" check was deposited into Cass's bank account.

After work, Cass received a call — thankfully not a visit — from Peter telling her the settlement meeting was scheduled for two o'clock tomorrow at Simon Johnson's office. Before hanging up the phone, Peter asked if she had any reservations, questions, or changes; and she told him she didn't.

Cass called Jason to give him the good news in a subtle manner in case her phone was bugged, and to request time off from work.

Jason grinned in relief and said, "Of course, you can take a few hours off, Mrs. Grantham, to get your business settled."

"Thank you, Doctor Burkman. I would talk longer, but I can't. I'll see you in the morning."

The following afternoon, Cass — dressed in a peach-colored suit and looking poised — sat before Simon Johnson's huge oak desk with Peter seated in a nearby chair as the lawyer explained the deal and papers to her. He mostly reiterated what Peter had told her recently, adding only a few unknown facts and details about their agreement.

"As soon as you sign these papers relinquishing any and all claims to your trust fund, company stocks, and other financial holdings, I'll give you a cashier's check for five million dollars and a clear title to your property and its contents. As Peter told you, he's paid the gift taxes, and I have a paper stating they come to you free and clear of that obligation. As you recall, the property's mortgage was paid off at Tom's death and the deed was given to you as part of your inheritance. However, its sale or full release to you was tied up by one of Tom's stipulations: if a sale occurred before you honored Tom's timetable, the money was to be deposited into the trust fund or reinvested in another home, which would also fall under that same stipulation. We had it appraised last week for its fair market value, and Peter deposited that amount into the trust fund in your name as if it were a real estate sale to you to prevent legal problems over its release at this date. I have a signed affidavit from the trust fund executor at the bank attesting to the fact that it's been released to you. Of course, when and if you sell the property, you will have taxes due on any gain you make, which will come out of your sale profit and be your sole responsibility to pay."

"I understand, sir." Cass wondered how and when the appraisal had been done without her knowledge and presumed Peter had provided the man with a key to her home. Since the deed was done and she didn't want any trouble, she ignored it.

"According to the terms of Tom's will, Peter can't withdraw the trust fund until you marry, but this paper states you're forfeiting your claim to it. He'll receive the monthly checks and yearly bonus from it for the next four years, one-half of the balance in five years, and the remainder of it at the end of ten years; or all of it upon your remarriage. He'll also have full ownership and control of the company stocks and other holdings. You will not receive dividends or any sales profits in the future. Is that clear?"

Cass nodded and said, "I understand, sir."

"Once you sign these papers and I turn over this check and deed, you walk away from the Grantham estate forever. Is that clear?"

Cass nodded again and said, "I understand, sir."

"I hate to be redundant, Mrs. Grantham, but I want to make certain you fully grasp what you're doing. I want to make certain you have no reservations, hesitations, or questions. That's one reason I'm videotaping this meeting. Being of sound mind and body, you willingly — without any type of coercion or doubts — agree to this settlement; is that correct?"

"Yes, sir; that is correct."

"For our video recording, please state your full legal name and your understanding of what Peter and I explained to you during this meeting. It's typed on that paper which I just handed to you. Do you concur with it?"

Cass perused the page and nodded, then held it before her and read, "I, Cassandra Redfern Grantham, being of sound mind and body, and without coercion or doubts, willingly and with full knowledge of the terms of this agreement, am reverting everything which Thomas Ethan Grantham bequeathed to me upon his death to Peter Wesley Grantham, in exchange for Peter gifting me with five million dollars cash, clear title to my current home and its contents, and with their taxes paid in full. Peter can do anything he desires with my previous portion of the Grantham estate, which I neither want nor have any claim against from this day forth. Since the trust fund has a remarried-release stipulation, I will inform Peter immediately if or when I remarry so he may collect it as agreed today."

Simon smiled and said, "That's fine, Mrs. Grantham; thank you for your cooperation. Now, all you have to do is place your legal signature and today's date on the lines where you see red X's, and we can finalize this matter quickly and easily. Unless you have a question?"

"None, sir. I'm ready to sign."

"Before we continue with the final phase, I want to give both of you a last chance to back out of this deal or to ask for more time to consider its ramifications. Especially you, Mrs. Grantham, since you'll be relinquishing all claims to an estate currently valued at over fifteen million dollars and increasing monthly. Do either of you want to renege on this settlement or consider it for a while longer? Mrs. Grantham?"

Cass looked him in the eye and shook her head.

Simon asked, "Peter, what about you?"

"I'm ready to close the deal right now."

As Simon Johnson buzzed his secretary and asked her to join them, Cass and Peter glanced at each other and each feigned a happy smile.

After she signed many pages in the presence of his secretary who acted as a witness and notary, Cass took possession of the check, affadavit from the bank, and copies of the papers she had signed minutes ago, and a few others pertaining to prepaid taxes.

"I should caution you, Mrs. Grantham: that's a cashier's check, so don't lose it, or the finder could cash it without any problem."

"Thank you, sir; I'm heading to the bank as

511

soon as I leave." *And I'm keeping alert for trouble, in case Peter tries to get his dirty hands on it!*

To her surprise and relief, Peter handed her the keys to her house and burglar alarm system. He told her he would return the ones to the guest house as soon as he moved out in the very near future. Cass thanked him as she dropped them into her purse. She knew that even if he had made a copy of the house key, he couldn't get past the alarm system, as it was illegal for anyone to copy that particular type of key. "Is there anything else, gentlemen, or are you finished with me? I should get back to work."

"That's all, Cass," Peter said. "You can leave, but I'll be here for a while longer going over other business with Simon. I'll see you again later this week."

Cass said her farewells and departed. She knew why Peter lingered behind, to discuss contracts concerning the company sales he had mentioned to her on past dates. She reasoned that for those agreements to be at this final stage, Peter must have been working on the sly to obtain them for a long time. Of course, he had the power to sell those properties without her permission or vote, but she would have profited greatly from them if not for their settlement today, which explained why he wanted it a done deal as fast as possible.

Once Cass got inside her cashmere-beige

BMW, she gave a huge sigh of relief and elation to have that strenuous meeting behind her. Before she set aside her purse, she opened it and gazed at the check with so many zeros following the number five. On impulse, she kissed it, laughed merrily, and returned it to her bag. She had told Jason this morning she was going straight to the bank to deposit it for safety reasons and to place the papers in her rental box.

As Cass secured her seat belt and started the engine, her mind scoffed, *So, you and Tom thought you had me strapped over a barrel, did you? Well, you both were wrong, and I've outwitted you two. Now, Mr. Peter Grantham, as soon as I'm convinced everything is settled and there's no loophole you can use against me, you're in for receiving a nasty piece of my mind!*
Cass could hardly wait until her meeting with Jason's attorney next Monday morning to let him go over the papers she had signed so she could make certain her deal with Peter was legal and finalized and loophole free. She wished she could see the lawyer sooner, but he was out of town until Sunday evening. Even so, the timing was perfect: Jason's office was closed on Monday for "spring cleaning" and for new carpet to be laid in the reception room, so the entire staff had the day off with pay.
Tonight, Cass planned her impending actions, she would lock her car in the garage and keep the lights out in the house to prevent

Peter from coming over for a visit. She and Jason weren't taking any unnecessary risks of having their romance exposed to him before next week, so they wouldn't see each other privately until after Peter left for Los Angeles again on Friday.

Soon, my love, we won't have to sneak around to see each other. . . .

On Wednesday, Cass received her final instructions from the office receptionist on the woman's last day for weeks, and Jason treated his staff to a nice lunch at the King & Prince Restaurant.

After she reached home, Cass took a seat in the den to call Kristy to chat. Despite the renewal of their friendship and the restoration of their past rapport, Cass knew there were some things that she could not confide to Kristy for fear of her making an inadvertent slip to Brad or her parents. Those things included the dark and bitter truth about Tom, details about Tom's restrictive will and her financial settlement with Peter yesterday, news of and the motive for her recent "mental illness," and the plans to marry Jason. Except for what Linda and the people involved in certain matters knew, she would carry those remaining secrets to her grave.

"Hi, Kristy, it's me again, your old and long-lost friend. Can you talk now, or did I catch you at a busy time?" Cass heard Kristy squeal her name and take off like a verbal jet plane at high speed.

"Cassie! It's so good to hear your voice. I'm glad you got back to me so soon. Actually your timing couldn't be better. Jerry took the kids over to his parents' house to see their new puppies. That dog is always spitting out litters faster than a bullet flies. I don't know why they don't get her fixed or keep her penned up when she's in heat because she's the horniest and most promiscuous bitch I know. Afterward they're grabbing a bite to eat at the Golden Corral and bringing me a take-out plate, so I don't have to cook supper tonight and have some free time for a change. In fact, I'm lazing in a warm bubble bath and sipping a glass of wine, Chablis to be exact, and glancing through magazines. I don't know why I order them because I never have time to pleasure read during the school year. It's a good thing you didn't get to come last Saturday because all hell broke loose that day and our visit would have been ruined. I should say, what got broken was Billy's arm." Kristy continued, omitting not one tiny detail of the incident. After many minutes, Cass heard her friend's indrawn breath before she asked, "So, what have you been doing lately and how are you feeling? And how is that doctor friend of yours?"

Cass grinned at her friend's rapid and gregarious roll, for which she was famous among her friends and social circle and at school. That trait had elicited Cass's fears about Kristy making a slip, though the kind woman would never breach a confidence on purpose. "I'm feeling wonderful and doing great," Cass revealed, "I'm back in church, making new friends, and working for Jason Burkman as his temporary receptionist."

"Why did you go back to work now that you're a rich widow?" Kristy was genuinely puzzled.

"Partly to get myself out of the house and back into the swing of things, and partly to do Jason a favor."

"So, what does that job entail?" Kristy asked, then listened as Cass explained what her responsibilities were before she jested, "I bet it's nice working for such a close friend and such a handsome and virile doctor, eh?"

Cass laughed. "Who told you he was handsome and virile?"

"You did."

"I did?"

"In more than one way. I hear how your voice softens and how you purr your words like a just-fed kitten when you talk about him. Tell me true, is romance in the air? Come clean, woman, or I'll die of suspense."

"Well, we certainly can't have you perishing over the phone. We like each other and get along well, and we've seen each other on occasion at church and with a mutual female friend.

We've had lunch and a couple of dinners. I guess you could say a romance looks promising, but first I need to put more time between Tom's death and serious dating. You know how we women have to work hard to protect our reputations and images. I've been keeping myself busy in other ways: I've done a little redecorating and gotten rid of Tom's belongings so I can get on with my life. I have a part-time, instead of full-time, housekeeper now; so I have chores and grocery shopping and cooking to do myself."

"So, you've laid Tom to rest for good?"

"Yes, I have. I even sold my company stocks to his son, so I'm no longer connected to any of those businesses, and was never involved in them. In fact, Peter is moving to Los Angeles soon and cutting my final tie to the Granthams. How are Jerry and your parents doing?"

"Jerry's doing super; the real estate market has finally picked up and he's making sales right and left. He's so relieved and excited that he almost dances around the house when he comes home at night. He hasn't changed at all since you last saw him; he hasn't even gained weight or lost any hair like so many of his friends have. My parents are doing great, but they wouldn't be if they knew about Brad's visit to you. What happened there, Cassie? You didn't have time to give me any details last week."

Cass related the facts to her, and heard

Kristy exhale in disgust.

"Even as well as I know my brother, Cassie, I find it almost incredible and totally despicable that Brad would come to your home and beg you for money. Sometimes it's as if he doesn't have a single brain cell in that head of his or an ounce of conscience. He makes me so mad I could strangle him. I can't tell you how sorry and ashamed I am that happened. I haven't told my parents; they would be humiliated to learn what he did to you."

"Please *don't* tell them, Kristy. Your parents were good to me; even after Brad and I were divorced, they came to Mom and Dad's funeral, sent flowers, and brought food over to the house. I know our split-up pained them deeply and confused them. I just didn't have the heart to tell them the reasons; it seemed wrong and cruel to exonerate myself by hurting them."

"You always were a compassionate person, Cassie, and I'm glad you haven't changed. But they know why you divorced him: I told them after you left town and married Tom. I didn't want them blaming you for Brad's mistake, and they've certainly watched him make plenty more. I wish he would just leave you alone."

"I doubt I'll ever see him again; if I do, I'll handle him. After I got over my shock and anger, I felt sorry for him. I wish he would straighten himself out. Maybe something or somebody will change him one day."

"I hope so, Cassie, I truly hope so, but I

won't hold my breath waiting for that to happen or I'll probably expire first."

They talked about other things and reminisced for a while until Kristy's husband and two children returned home and summoned her.

"It was so good talking to you, Cassie, just like old times, except we're so far apart."

"It was good talking with you again, Kristy, and we'll do it again soon."

"Don't forget, you're coming up to visit before the end of May."

"I won't. Tell Jerry, Billy, Debbie, and your parents I said hello."

"I will. 'Bye, girl, and you take excellent care of yourself."

"The same to you, Kristy. Good-bye."

The ensuing four days were busy and happy ones as Cass took Kristy's good advice. On Thursday afternoon, she and Mary did house-cleaning while Jason was in Savannah visiting with his daughter and twin grandsons and dropping hints about his budding romance with her so Traci could get used to the idea of her existence and future role in the Burkman family.

On Friday, Peter left for Los Angeles to finish preparations for his move there next week, an event Cass eagerly anticipated. After work, she and Jason visited his receptionist, who had come through her surgery without problems, in the hospital. That night, she and Jason took a cruise on the *Emerald Princess* where they had a wonderful time dining, dancing, and partaking in casino-style gambling. They spent some time on deck watching the sights on shore, and finalized that splendid day by making love in her bed.

On Saturday morning, she and Jason took a lengthy trolley tour of the historical and picturesque sites on St. Simons Island. Following a delayed lunch, they enjoyed a salt marsh nature tour on a large and comfortable pontoon where they ventured through the tidal creeks to see its plants and observe its many creatures. The weather couldn't have been nicer, nor the insects, more compassionate.

That evening, they had dinner at Chelsea's, and watched a musical performance at the Ritz Theater in Brunswick where they had met seven months ago. Later at her home, they celebrated that eventful encounter with a glass of champagne and hours of torrid lovemaking.

On Sunday, they attended church, had lunch out, relaxed at his house, savored some more glorious lovemaking, and cooked and ate supper together before she reached home only minutes before Peter's return that evening.

To her surprise and pleasure, Peter made no attempt to phone or visit her that night, as if he already had severed all of their connections.

On Monday while Peter waited for a local

moving company to arrive to pack his possessions and prepare to load and transport them to Los Angeles the next day, Cass left the house as usual as if she were going to work. Instead, she and Jason went to the bank to collect the papers in her safe-deposit box, then met with his attorney in Brunswick.

After the lawyer read the papers which had been prepared by Simon Johnson, the man told them the settlement between her and Peter was legal and finalized. That news delighted Cass and Jason, who both thanked the lawyer and departed in elated moods.

Over lunch in a quiet restaurant, Jason told Cass he would help her find a new financial adviser to assist her with investing her money. She agreed with him that it was foolish for the enormous amount to sit in a checking or regular savings account or in many bank certificates of deposit earning lower interest rates. By investing most of the cash, she would have continual income from and yearly growth in her multi-million dollar settlement.

Cass returned home alone afterward because there was one last deed she wanted to accomplish before Peter left town: a confrontation.

Chapter Twenty-Three

Cass phoned Peter and asked him to meet her on the terrace because she had something important to tell him. She didn't want to be alone with him inside her house. If he gave her any problems, she was certain the moving crew at in his place would come to her aid if she screamed for help. She didn't think that would happen, though, because Peter was too image conscious. Though he was leaving this area for good very soon, he wouldn't want to create a scene that neighbors could witness and turn into gossip. She put on sunglasses and went outside to await him.

Peter greeted her five minutes later with a broad smile, squinted his gaze against the sun's glare, and asked, "Did you get off early from work today?"

"The office is closed for spring cleaning and carpet replacement."

Peter noted that she didn't return his smile and that she appeared edgy. Her sunglasses had extra-dark lenses, so he couldn't read her gaze. "Well, what did you want to tell me before I leave tomorrow?"

Cass kept her voice low and controlled as she

responded, "After you move, Peter, I don't want to ever see or hear from you again."

Before she could continue, the astonished Peter asked, *"What?"*

"You heard me correctly. Never again. I know your show of friendship was nothing more than a clever pretense for wicked purposes. I —"

Peter interrupted in a surly tone, "So, this is 'the moment of truth,' is it? How silly and dramatic for a cheap pot to be calling an expensive kettle black! You were doing the same thing, Cass, only pretending to be friends to benefit yourself." He watched her expression tense. "Consider yourself lucky you're walking away with a fortune that rightfully belongs to me. I could have found a way to make sure you walked away with nothing."

Cass straightened her shoulders and glared at him. "No, Peter, you should consider yourself lucky — damned lucky! — that you aren't heading for prison instead of to a ritzy lifestyle in Los Angeles. I know all about your little drugging and blackmail schemes, and in case you didn't know it, both are illegal, punishable crimes." She saw him square his shoulders as he took a deep breath, and narrowed his hazel gaze after it had widened briefly — and revealingly — in surprise.

She didn't give him time to interrupt again before she said, "That's right, I know you provoked my recent condition by slipping drugs into my food and/or drink and aspirin capsules.

523

I know Inez and Dr. Hines aided your little misdeed. I know about the changes in the phone lines and mailing address so you could screen my calls and intercept my letters and cut me off from the outside world so I'd think nobody cared about me. I know you blackmailed Dr. Hines into helping you and supplying you with drugs to use on me, then had him keep me drugged senseless for weeks."

"Is that a fact, or have you gone stark raving mad?"

"All of those statements are facts, Peter; and I'm completely sane, no thanks to you and what you tried to do to me, you sorry bastard."

"You can wallow in that bed of suspicions all you like, Cass, but you can't prove such absurd bullshit to the authorities. They'll think —"

"Oh, but you're totally wrong, Peter. You see, before Dr. Hines killed himself, he sent me a special delivery letter telling me all about what he did for you and why. He wanted revenge on you for blackmailing him and because he thought — in his unbalanced mental state — that you provided the leaks to the press that were going to destroy him. I have the letter locked away in my safe-deposit box." *You actually look as if your face blanched white for a moment and sheer terror registered in your eyes!*

While she had him shocked speechless, Cass hurried on with, "As to Inez, before she left town, she exposed her part in your dirty little scheme. She even provided me with samples of those mystery pills that Hines labeled A and B, and a tainted aspirin capsule as proof of her claims. I know you met with her last week and not only refused to pay for her silence but also infuriated her with your behavior and threats. Before she left this area, she took fifty thousand dollars with her for her cooperation with me. That evidence against you is also locked away safely. If I had a mind to, I could turn all of it over to the police and press charges against you."

"Why haven't you carried out that threat?" Peter asked gruffly.

"It isn't a threat, and I have my reasons for handling it this way."

"If you have such . . . facts and evidence in your possession, why did you settle with me last week when you could have demanded more money? Is that it, you're trying to squeeze more money out of me on the sly? I'm not the man you want to threaten, or blackmail, Cass. So why the settlement and long wait to confront me?"

"First off, I don't want to create a scandal for myself by exposing you. Secondly, Dr. Hines is no longer in a position to harm other patients. Thirdly, I didn't marry Tom for his money, but I felt that he owed me for his many cruel and dangerous betrayals and because I was a good wife to him. Contrary to what you believe, Peter, I'm not a greedy, conniving, or wicked person like you are. I only wanted what I felt I deserved from Tom; you set the amount, and I agreed with it. You might find this amusing and flattering, but I actually believed you had softened toward me after his death and we were becoming real friends."

"Let me get this straight in my head: knowing the truth, you gave up that much money and holdings, and you don't intend to do anything with that so-called evidence against me?"

"That's right, Peter, because I'm not a vindictive person and I don't want my life and name dragged through the courts and over media coals. If you agree to forget I exist, I'll do the same for you. Do we have a deal?"

"What's the catch?"

"There isn't one."

Peter stared at her for a long time in utter bewilderment.

"Yes, there is another catch beside forgetting I exist."

Peter scowled. "I thought so. What is it, if not more money?"

Cass removed her glasses so he could see her eyes. "Tell me why you drugged me and we'll call it even."

He studied her again. "You're actually telling the truth, aren't you?"

"Yes, Peter, I am. So, why did you do it? I need to know."

His gaze swept over her from head to feet. "Have you got a recorder taped to that lovely body with hopes of capturing a confession?"

"No, Peter, and you and I are the only ones who know we're having this talk right now. I just want to know the truth for my own peace of mind."

"All right, Cass, I'll trust you this time. I had to keep you out of the way for a few weeks while I got to Dad's will and companies. I was afraid he had left you either everything or most of it, and I was uncertain about the companies' financial states. I needed answers before I dealt with you. I worked hard to help make those companies successful and profitable, and I'm the only Grantham left in our bloodline, so I didn't want you holding a vengeful gun to my head. I never intended to keep you drugged for long, never intended to make you an addict or mental case, and never intended to kill you even if you got it all. I would have handled the matter legally by contesting his will."

"Thank you, Peter; I thought that was your motive. Now, from this day forth, all doors are closed between us. I just didn't want you to leave without knowing you didn't have me fooled. Since I wasn't harmed by your little scheme, I'll forget about it. But I want you to know, I think it was one of the lowest things one person could do to another person, and it was totally unnecessary. Even if Tom had left everything to me, I would never have taken it all whether or not we ever became friends. In fact, I would have insisted on a one-third/two-thirds split in your favor as his son. I never tried to get Tom to leave me everything, and I had no idea what was in his will until you and Simon Johnson told me." To her astonishment, Cass saw Peter's expression soften, and he even sent her what appeared to be his first genuine smile. Even so, his ensuing words came as a shock to her, and they sounded sincere.

"I should have yielded to your potent temptation and gone after you myself instead of letting Jason snare you; that was a big mistake. What man could ask for a better woman than you, Cassandra Grantham?"

"I'm not the right woman for you; nor you, the right man for me."

"I suppose Jason Burkman is the right man for you?"

Since Peter didn't say those words in a sarcastic tone, she replied, "Perhaps. At least he's nothing like your father or my first husband."

"I never thought I'd hear myself say this, Cass, but I'm sorry."

"You've lied to me and tricked me so many times, Peter, that I don't know if that's true."

"Maybe for the first time in my life, I'm telling a woman the truth. It would have been easy to love you, but it's too late for that."

"Yes, Peter, it is. As soon as I get my life settled and I'm convinced we've parted ways forever, I promise I'll destroy those things Dr. Hines and Inez gave to me."

"Thank you, Cass, and I won't ever trouble you again; I swear it."

"Keep that promise, Peter, and I'll keep mine."

"Without knowing it at that time, I was right about one thing: my father didn't deserve a good woman like you and he was crazy to betray you. Now that I know the dirty truth about him, he probably did the same thing to my mother and that's why she left him. She was wrong and selfish to leave me behind with that bastard, but that has nothing to do with us. If I had known the truth about you and played my cards smarter, I could be a lucky man today, but I misjudged you and I folded my hand too soon."

Cass dropped that sensitive subject and went to another one that intrigued her. "Now that we've settled our business and you have nothing to lose, would you mind telling me the truth about your affair with Brenda?"

"Why?"

"So I'll know if Jason Burkman has an honest motive to hate and spite you, and to have wanted to use me for that purpose. You owe me the truth, Peter, so I won't get involved with him if he's an unworthy man."

"All right, Cass. Since she made a fool of me, it's tempting to say I knew the truth all along, but I didn't, contrary to what Jason believes. Oh, I suspected something wasn't quite right about her and her job, but I let it ride because . . . to put it bluntly, she was great in bed. I have to give Brenda credit for being smart; she even had phony pictures of her alleged family in that apartment. And that day we were caught together at her house, she had removed any signs of her and Jason living there and being married. I guess he was too furious to notice her deceitful preparations before he stormed out, and she probably put everything back in order before his return, or he would have known I told him the truth. As to the money for affording her little ruse, it didn't come from me. Oh, I did buy her things and pay for food and booze and such, but not her monthly rent and other expenses. I didn't trust her or love her or ever plan to marry her, but I was enjoying our relationship too much to rock the boat with demands for explanations. Actually, I'm grateful to Jason for halting her ruse and for sweeping the matter under the rug and preventing a scandal for both of us. I would have fought him like a tiger if he'd named me co-respondent in a divorce because I wasn't guilty. Believe it or not, Cass, but that's the truth. Jason and I were both used."

"Thank you, Peter, and I'll tell him what you said one day."

"Well, I'd better get back over there and keep that crew working so they can pull out in the morning. They're transporting my Porsche, too. I'll be flying out in my jet about ten. When I have to return to finalize the sales for the two companies here, I won't bother you. We'll make this our final good-bye, Cass. I'm sorry and I was wrong, and I hope you'll find true happiness the next time you marry; you deserve it."

I've won a major battle, and I got what I wanted, she told herself. *He'll be out of my life forever very soon, so I must be compassionate and not gloat. Everything is settled, so despite his guilt, let it end peacefully.* "Thank you, Peter, and I hope things work out for you in LA."

"I'll leave the guest-house keys in that planter over there before I take off in the morning, so don't forget to collect them tomorrow evening."

Cass nodded, then put on her sunglasses to ward off the sun's glare.

Peter looked at her for a minute, smiled in defeat, and said, "Good-bye, Cassandra Grantham; you're one terrific lady." *And I've been a complete and blind idiot to let you get away!*

"Good-bye, Peter." *And good riddance.*

Instead of watching his departure, Cass went inside her house to unwind following the tense situation. There was one thing she could always count on with Peter Grantham, he was unpredictable! She could have ranted and raved at him, but that wouldn't have accomplished anything, and it would have made her look like the bad person he had assumed she was for years. No, it was much better to have ended their stormy relationship in the sensible way she had.

You're free of all Grantham ties now, and you're a stronger and wiser person. The dark past is over and a bright future awaits you with Jason

Burkman. This time, you won't be loving and marrying a stranger, but the most wonderful man in the world. Cass closed her misty brown eyes, bid her past farewell, and said a fervent prayer of thanks for her many blessings.

At five o'clock, she almost didn't answer the knock at her back door when Peter came to see her, as she dreaded to discover the reason.

"I'm sorry to disturb you, Cass, but the moving crew is finished. Two extra packers were sent over after we talked and they got everything boxed and loaded up faster. The truck is heading to their company warehouse for safe storage tonight and it'll pull out for LA tomorrow. I'm going to a motel to spend the night; then I'm turning my Porsche over to them for loading in the morning and taking off for LA. I wanted to return the keys and give you this check; it should be sufficient to pay a janitorial service to clean up over there and to have the place repainted and to have the drapes and carpets cleaned. That way, it'll be ready for guests or to show when you put this property on the real estate market. Those expenses shouldn't come out of your pocket since I was allowed to live there rent-free for years and you've been so kind and generous to me. I also wanted to give you this as a parting and friendship gift." He handed her a small box, smiled, and said, "Good-bye, Cass. Take excellent care of yourself and be happy."

Don't cause a scene or his delay by refusing the gift; you can decide what to do with it later, whatever it is. "Good-bye, Peter."

From her kitchen window, Cass observed the simultaneous departures of Peter and the large van. She sat down in the den and phoned Jason. "The movers finished early," she told him, "so Peter's gone, out of my life and hair for good. Isn't that wonderful?"

"Yes, it is. So, how soon can you come over? I want to hear about your conversation with him. You did speak to him, didn't you?"

"Oh, yes, we had a long and revealing chat. I'll see you as soon as I freshen up and drive over, say in about twenty minutes."

"Perfect, just like you are, woman. I'll have the garage door open for you. And a glass of champagne ready for celebrating."

As they prepared and ate their meal, Cass related her meeting with Peter to him, and he listened in amazement and relief.

After she finished the detailed revelations, she asked, "Well, did I handle it all right? Or should I have given him a hard time?"

Jason grasped her hand and gave it a gentle squeeze. "You handled it with finesse and great intelligence, and as the wonderful person you are. I was sitting on pins and needles waiting to hear from you. I couldn't imagine how he was going to react, but I did expect him to get angry and call your bluff. I guess even Peter

533

Grantham has his good points. I'm glad everything is settled, Cass; now, we can get on with our lives, with our future. I want you to meet my children as soon as possible, and they're chomping at the bit to meet you. As I told you, both were excited by my news about you."

Cass had been looking through his family photo albums and asking him countless questions about his son and daughter so she could learn more about them before they were introduced, and she liked all she had learned. "I suppose you painted me as the best woman in the world?" she jested.

"Of course, because you are," he replied with a broad grin.

"I do believe you're biased, Doctor Burkman."

"Naturally, and with just cause."

As they did their chores, Jason suggested, "In early June, we can let our romance begin to heat up in public because you will have been a widow for three months. That should be all right, shouldn't it?"

"As long as we take it slow and easy and be discreet, I think so."

"Excellent decision, my love. You're a smart and generous woman."

"I thought you'd think so," she teased and hugged him from behind.

Jason warmed and his heart rate speeded up as she leaned against him and nuzzled his back with her cheek. His smoldering desires increased in intensity and heat. He draped the dish cloth over the double sink's partition, turned, drew her into his embrace, and said, "I love you, Cass."

"I love you, too, Jason."

After they kissed several times, he looked into her soft brown gaze. "Why don't we head upstairs for a while?" he asked.

"My thoughts exactly."

He placed his arm around her waist and guided her to his bedroom where they undressed and lay down together.

Jason's lips claimed Cass's in a tender kiss, and she felt herself melting inside. Her breasts felt heavy with desire and she nearly moaned when his hand moved to fondle first one, then the other, until her nipples were taut and eager for more. As if Jason sensed what she longed for, he trailed kisses down her neck and over the satiny skin of her breasts, where he teethed and tantalized her until she was breathless and writhing beneath him.

She quivered in anticipation as his hand blazed a searing path down her abdomen. It was amazing and wonderful how she never tired of his touch, but always yearned for more. He made her feel so loved, so treasured, so desirable. She trembled as he nudged her thighs apart with his hand and began to bring her a pleasure so intense she thought she might cry from the sheer sweetness of it.

Just when she thought she'd die if she

couldn't feel the fullness of him deep inside her, Jason ceased his enticing caresses and moved over her. Looking into her eyes, he entered her slowly, tenderly, teasing her by withdrawing, then moving deeper and deeper inside her until — at last — she felt every magnificent inch of him.

Cass sighed in exquisite delight, as if it had been months since they'd made love instead of just yesterday. Her hands pulled him closer. She wanted him now, all of him.

Jason could hold back no longer. And as he felt Cass surrender to the ecstasy they'd created together, he let himself join her in a rush of passion and fulfillment.

Afterward, sated and almost breathless from their exertions, they cuddled in each other's arms, sharing and savoring the closeness and serenity they had creased with each other.

"If you keep giving me blissful presents like that, I'll become the most rewarded and satisfied woman in history."

"Guess what I want Santa Claus to bring me this year."

Cass turned her head and looked at him. "Christmas is seven and a half months away, so what made you start thinking about it tonight?"

"Your mention of presents. As my gift, I want you in this bed with me as my wife on Christmas Eve. Do you think that's possible?"

"Possible, probable, but more likely a certainty," she quipped. "If that's truly what you want as your present?"

Jason stroked her cheek as he vowed, "I've never wanted or needed anything more in my life."

"Then I'll have to make certain you receive it, won't I?"

"If you do, I'll be eternally grateful, and very generous in repayment."

As Jason nibbled on her earlobe, Cass squirmed and laughed. "If you get any more generous, Doc, I'll be the one treating you for exhaustion."

After Cass was dressed and preparing to leave, she took a black velvet box from her purse along with her car keys. She handed it to Jason. "Peter gave me this before he left today," she said. "What should I do with it?"

Jason eyed the fourteen-karat gold *C*, which had about twenty-five small and sparkling gems embedded along the center of its curvature. A message on the back said: "To a real diamond." Her birthday was engraved after the words. "Whoo," he let out a rush of air between his lips. "This cost a pretty penny and wasn't a last-minute gesture."

"That was my impression, too. So, what should I do with it?"

"Why not keep it and wear it? It's beautiful, like you are, and the message couldn't be more accurate."

Cass leaned against his body and looped her

arms around his neck. "You're a diamond, too, my beloved, a priceless one."

"Then, that makes us a perfect pair."

As they kissed good night, both knew how lucky they were; and in a few months, she wouldn't be leaving again like this because she would be home, home with her husband.

Epilogue

Cass leisurely worked in the kitchen to get things ready for a special dinner and gathering of the entire Burkman family tomorrow on Mother's Day. She paused from her task to stroke her lower stomach where a baby was growing within her elated body. By this time next year, she would be the mother of a six-month-old infant who was due in late November. She smiled as she recalled teasing Jason about being so fertile, since he had gotten her pregnant in less than two months after a mid-December wedding in the First Baptist Church on St. Simons Island where they attended Sunday services regularly. Of course, her swift conception shouldn't have come as a surprise to her or Jason, since she had stopped taking birth control pills as soon as they were married and they had used every available opportunity on the land and on the sea to evoke the blessed event.

As Cass returned to the chore at hand, she thought about their lovely and romantic ceremony where family and friends had gathered to witness their marriage. She had worn an ivory lace tea-length dress, matching heels, and a single strand of pearls around her neck and studs in her earlobes. The beautician had secured sprigs of baby's breath and tiny clusters of lily of the valley in her dark hair which had been coiffed in loose curls atop her head with short tendrils dangling down her nape and at her ears. Jason had looked handsome and elegant in a black tuxedo with flowers matching hers in his lapel. They had used a traditional ceremony and biblical passages, and the pastor had performed his duty with skill. The organ music and soloist had been perfect, so had the floral decorations which she and Jason had selected for the church. The ensuing reception with ample food, drinks, and dancing had taken place at the Cloister where they had celebrated for hours, and where out-of-town guests had been treated to a weekend stay. As she hummed and worked, her mind's eye envisioned every minute of that happy and clear weather day.

Before it had taken place, she had sold her Sea Island Drive property for a hefty sum, let her financial adviser and Jason help her invest that money, and rented a large condominium apartment on St. Simons Island where she would live until she moved in with her husband last December. She had worked in Jason's office until late July, then spent the next four and a half months doing volunteer work at the hospital and in several worthy organizations, meeting and socializing with Jason's family and friends, enjoying the historical society and women's club, and planning her wedding.

She also had visited several times with Kristy, who had been her only bridesmaid. From the start, Kristy had adored Jason and his family. They still talked on the phone often and visited each other on occasion.

In January, she had learned from Kristy that Bradley Stillman was in therapy both alone and with wife number three, who had promised to give him another chance if Brad would straighten out himself; and he had vowed to do so.

Stacey had arrived on Friday evening for a weekend visit and was playing golf with his father this afternoon, before he went on an evening date with Linda Carnes. The two had mingled at the wedding, as both had been involved in it with Stacey as a groomsman and Linda, her maid of honor.

Stacey had decided to switch from surgery and a future practice in Atlanta to family medicine and a partnership with his father when he finished medical school and his internship. That union would be good for her husband and his son since Jason had to turn down new patients almost every week. With Stacey's help, Jason could increase the size of his patient list and Stacey could take over an established practice when Jason needed time off and when Jason retired. Cass knew that Stacey's decision had come before he got deeply involved with Linda, but still it added practical fuel to his new romance.

Linda was working for Jason now, as one of his three nurses had quit last October due to her husband's job transfer to South Carolina. She and Linda were still best friends and she wished Linda was joining them tomorrow, but the blond was going to Jacksonville to see her mother. No doubt Stacey and Linda would be out late in order to spend every minute possible together before their separation when Stacey returned to medical school in Augusta the next afternoon.

Jason's parents were flying in from Richmond this afternoon so Jason could spend time with his mother, a delightful woman whom Cass adored. The same was true for his father who had been Jason's best man. The four of them were going out to dinner tonight so Cass could reserve energy for the busy day tomorrow.

Traci, her husband, and their twin sons were driving in from Savannah the following morning, as they were spending an early Mother's Day with Christopher's mother today.

Cass glanced around the kitchen which was clean from Mary Ellis's labors yesterday. Mary had not filled the two-day void she had made in the housekeeper's schedule after her marriage to Jason because her son had emerged from his coma and was recovering steadily in therapy. As a gift more than a tax break, she had set up a medical fund for the boy, and Mary could not seem to express her gratitude enough to her and Jason.

As she sat down to rest and sip warm herbal tea, Cass's thoughts drifted to other people who had been parts of her life many months ago. They had not heard from Inez Doughtery again, as if her ex-housekeeper had vanished off the face of the earth. The scandal involving Dr. David Hines had quieted down rather fast following his burial; now, she heard only an occasional whisper of gossip about that tragic event.

As for Peter Wesley Grantham, he might be in big trouble. She and Jason had read newspaper accounts and seen television clips about him being under investigation for illegal business imports and exports, fraud, and income tax evasion. Cass could hardly believe that with all the money Peter had that he craved more at any cost; perhaps Peter was as much of a money addict as Tom had been a sex addict.

Yet, she felt sorry for him and presumed he had reasons for being like he was. Maybe she just had a tender heart and a forgiving and compassionate nature, because she couldn't help pitying him. At the end of their stormy relationship last year, he had been civil and a smidgen kind to her in his deeds and words, and he'd never contacted her again.

Of course, she had no way of knowing how much, if any, of what Peter had told her about himself was true. It was a shame, Cass reasoned, that someone with his many physical and material blessings was such an awful person. Perhaps he had spoken the truth to her at least once when he said those things were often more of a curse than a blessing.

After the shocking news broke, she and Jason had spoken with their attorney to make certain none of Peter's troubles could rub off on them. The lawyer had assured them that even before she remarried and Peter collected the balance of the estate which Tom had bequeathed to her, she had relinquished all claims to it and severed all ties to the Grantham holdings.

On a few occasions, she had worn the diamond initial pin Peter had given to her upon his departure from this island; and sometimes, she simply held it and gazed at it to remind herself what she had lost and gained at the hands of the two Grantham men.

As for Tom, she rarely thought about him, and when she did, she tried to tell herself he had been mentally ill and was at peace now. It was true Thomas Ethan Grantham had possessed enormous flaws, and weaknesses, but he hadn't been entirely evil, and she concurred with Jason that hardly a wicked person existed that didn't have a little good in him. Tom's goodness shone brightly in the generous donations he had made to the hospital wing, free clinic for the poor, local and national arts, college scholarships for the underprivileged, and funds for conservation and ecology. She had even used some of the money from her

Grantham settlement to set up that medical trust fund for Mary Ellis's child.

She had destroyed all of the sordid materials exposing Tom's dark side, and that was the only secret she had withheld from Jason. She felt it should remain buried in the past with Tom and revealing it wouldn't accomplish any good purpose.

Cass thought about the wrong and tragic choices she had made in the past, but she couldn't curse them because they had made her stronger and wiser and kinder, and they had propelled her toward a meeting with Jason and enabled a bright future with him.

She was no longer afraid or reluctant to trust her emotions, decisions, and herself. Three times she had fallen in love with strangers; twice she had struck out in that game; but the third time was a surefire winner.

Cass looked toward the kitchen archway as her husband and stepson entered the room, laughing and joking about their golf game at the St. Simons Island Club. Their sounds warmed her heart, her very soul. The only thing she missed in her life was for her parents to be alive and to share with them such blissful events: their only daughter's marriage to a fine man, her becoming a part of a wonderful family, and the impending birth of their first grandchild. News about her pregnancy would be revealed to the Burkmans tomorrow, and she knew each of them would be elated and excited by that revelation.

After they greeted each other and chatted for a few minutes, she asked with a smile, "Well, did we have any eagles or birdies today?"

"I had a couple of birdies, but that son of mine had an eagle on the seventeenth hole. He smashed a three wood just in front of the green and sank his wedge shot. Playing like he did, he'll never convince me he spends all of his time in class, studying, or at the hospital."

Stacey chuckled before he said, "It was just a lucky shot, Dad, and we both know it. If the wind hadn't died down at the right minute, I'd have sliced and been in that water hazard. And if you hadn't been so distracted by the company that was coming soon, you would have licked me good, as usual. Just wait until I'm out of med school and playing regularly like you are and I'll give you a run for your money."

"Careful, Jason, or he'll be sneaking your weekly allowance out of your pocket with winning bets," Cass quipped to her grinning husband.

"Don't worry, Cass, Dad'll make me earn every dime I collect."

As Stacey was talking, Jason walked to where Cass was sitting and gave her a kiss on the forehead, then another one on her lips. He smiled and caressed her cheek as his blue gaze roamed her tranquil expression.

"All right," Stacey jested, "if you two are going to get lovey-dovey on me, I'm going to take a shower and get dressed to give you privacy."

Jason teased him in return, "You don't fool me, Son; I know you're just eager to go see Linda. Since she's one of our best friends, we don't mind at all, do we, sweetheart?"

"Not in the least, Stacey, so get moving before she comes after you."

Stacey grinned, shrugged playfully, and left the room.

Jason squatted beside her chair and reached out his right hand to stroke her stomach. With a beaming smile and in a whisper, he asked, "How are we both doing today? You haven't been working too hard, have you, sweetheart? You don't have to get everything done today; Mom and Traci will help out after they get here. I will, too."

Cass placed her hand over his. "We're both doing fine, and I've just been getting a few things done in the kitchen so we'll have more time to visit tonight and tomorrow. I can hardly wait for Mom and Dad to get here soon and for Traci, Chris, and the boys to arrive tomorrow. You, I mean, *we* have such a wonderful family. I'm so lucky to be a Burkman now."

"We're the ones who are lucky you joined us. I love you, Cassandra Burkman, more every day, if that's possible."

As she stood and hugged him, she replied, "It must be possible because I feel the same way about you."

Jason gave her a long and tender kiss. Afterward, his mouth made a path across her cheek and his lips nibbled at her earlobe. His hands drifted up and down her back with gentle strokes.

Cass quivered in desire and murmured, "Careful, Doc, or you'll have me needing one of those special treatments of yours at a most inconvenient time. Mom and Dad should be arriving any minute now if they landed in Atlanta and took off on ASA for Brunswick on schedule. Shouldn't we head on over there so they won't have to wait around for us?"

"You heard what Dad told us this morning, to stay here until he phones us in case either of their flights is delayed." As he embraced her, he hinted, "We might have time for a quickie in the lanai bathroom; I hear Stacey's shower running, so he won't interrupt us before I can get you hot and bothered and —"

Cass laughed in amusement as the phone rang and Jason frowned and glanced in its direction.

He lifted the kitchen receiver and said, "Hello, Jason here." As he listened to the person on the other end, he grinned, at Cass winked, and mouthed, "Later?"

Cass smiled and nodded, because she knew there would be many glorious make-up sessions for them in the coming months and years.